# Wolf's Blood

## LAURA TAYLOR

ALSO BY LAURA TAYLOR


THE HOUSE OF SIRIUS

Book 2: Wolf's Cage
Book 3: Wolf's Choice

Book 4 coming soon

To Fabien.
For your enthusiasm, your time, your imagination, your love of these characters, your relentless questioning and the thousand other things you've done over the past year and a half. Words cannot express my gratitude.

# ACKNOWLEDGMENTS

Thank you Ellen, for getting me to look at things from a new perspective, and for being honest, even when the truth was hard to hear.

Thank you Narinder, for your impressive attention to detail and the laughs along the way.

Thank you Linda, for your amazing patience and artistic skills in creating the beautiful cover design.

# WOLVES OF THE LAKES DISTRICT DEN

| Rank | Name | Occupation when recruited | Age when recruited | Current age |
|------|------|---------------------------|--------------------|-------------|
| 1 | Baron | Gang member | 19 | 37 |
| 2 | Caroline | High school student | 17 | 34 |
| 3 | Tank | Second Lieutenant in British army | 24 | 33 |
| 4 | Caleb | Carer at animal shelter | 24 | 38 |
| 5 | Silas | Soldier in Afghanistan military | 25 | 45 |
| 6 | Heron | High school student | 13 | 60 |
| 7 | John | Runaway | Unknown. Late teens/ early twenties | Unknown. Mid twenties |
| 8 | Raniesha | Prostitute | 24 | 42 |
| 9 | Simon | Computer programmer | 22 | 37 |
| 10 | Mark | High school student | 17 | 27 |
| 11 | Alistair | Journalist | 25 | 34 |
| 12 | Kwan | High school student | 16 | 26 |
| 13 | Cohen | Homeless | 23 | 33 |
| 14 | Skip | High school student | 16 | 23 |
| 15 | Nate | Unemployed ex-con | 35 | 41 |
| 16 | Aaron | High school student | 15 | 25 |
| 17 | Eric | Plumber | 35 | 42 |
| 18 | George | Retired | 68 | 71 |
| 19 | Dee | Administration assistant | 26 | 26 |

# PART ONE – CONVERSION

## CHAPTER ONE

Dee Carman lay on the cold metal table, alternately fearing death and wishing for it. She didn't have any clear sense of time, but at a guess, she would have said it was three, maybe four days since she had been kidnapped. Snatched off the street and brought to this cold, impersonal lab and treated like these monsters' very own lab rat. She twisted her arms, tugging futilely at the restraints that kept her pinned down, locked tight around her wrists and ankles.

The metal cuffs didn't budge.

She tried hard to steady herself, to even out her breathing as she felt the rising panic again. Her heart kicked up a notch, her eyes watered as she told herself not to cry, crying wouldn't help, crying never helped.

She was alone for the moment, the masked men in lab coats having retreated after taking the latest sample of her blood, after having applied electric shocks to her body and muttered disappointed grumbles as nothing had resulted other than her pained screams.

What the hell were they aiming for, anyway? They'd taken samples of tissue, of blood, of bone, had filled the room with foul-smelling vapour, had shocked her and drowned her and, to her utter disgust and shame, had brought her to the brink of orgasm, and nothing had resulted despite her pleas, her offers to tell them whatever they wanted to know, to give them money if they'd release her, to do *anything* if it would earn her freedom. They had simply stared at her with cold, calculating eyes and moved on to the next experiment.

What the hell did they want?! None of them ever spoke to her, they asked no questions, not even how she felt after each round of tests, whether she felt anything had changed, and the complete and utter mystery behind her kidnapping was starting to drive her mad. Had they chosen her for a particular reason? Or was it a random snatch and grab, just a case of wrong place, wrong time? Did they want to harm her, or for her to help them? Were they doctors searching for a miraculous cure, or madmen, torturing her for the sheer pleasure of it?

All too soon, the door opened again, the men filing into the room as before, silent and covered from head to toe in white lab coats and surgical masks... but before the door swung closed behind them, she heard a blood-chilling sound through the gap, a strange mix of howl and scream, and she felt a new rush of fear and adrenaline.

She had to get out of here.

She glanced around at her captors and a strange sense of foreboding struck her. There was no perceptible difference in the men, but somehow she felt the atmosphere in the room change, become taut with expectation and triumph. Whatever it was they were seeking to achieve, they were close, closer now than they had ever been before.

Good God, what were they going to do to her next?

As before, there was no talking, no apparent communication between the men, but they worked as a cohesive unit. A drip stand was wheeled over, a bag of blood hooked up to the IV in her arm. Her own blood, the sample they had removed earlier? Or someone else's?

If she ever got out of here alive, she was going to have to get herself tested for every disease known to modern medicine.

The IV line was opened, but she didn't even bother protesting any more. She had begged and pleaded and offered every reward she could think of, and been met with complete disinterest at every turn. She felt a faint tingle in her arm as the fluid flowed back into her, her stomach lurching at the thought of all the infections that could be coming with it.

Dee suddenly went still, her body breaking out in sweat, and then she felt a wave of ice-cold run through her. What the hell *was* that? There was... *something* in the blood, not a disease, not a virus or bacteria, but a consciousness. Another sentient being, joining her in her body. She squirmed, gagged as her body rebelled, shuddered as the new *whatever-it-was* infiltrated her muscles, tried to make itself fit into her veins and sinews. She convulsed once, her muscles utterly disobeying her commands. The new creature moved further into her, reached her heart, made it stutter. Seeped in around her lungs, up her spine, into her mouth and nose and eyes, and suddenly she became aware of the scientists watching her intently. She tried to ask what the hell they had done to her, but all that came out of her mouth was a low growl, her tongue feeling too big, her jaw too tight, her lungs fighting for air.

There was no mistaking the look of triumph in the eyes of those who watched, though. Hiding behind surgical masks and white caps and non-descript lab coats, those eyes positively gleamed with glee. And that was when the strange new presence inside her registered that it couldn't move the limbs of this new body. It tensed, strained, struggled within her as it fought against the same cuffs that Dee herself had fought for days.

And then suddenly the presence lost interest in her body, moved further up and latched onto her mind. She had no idea what it was, its thoughts only half-formed, images and scents, rather than words, but the message it gave was clear. If she would allow it, then it would kill those who held them captive. It showed her images of blood, of broken limbs and screams of terror and the taste of blood in her mouth.

She had no idea how it planned to get free of the restraints, but the presence had absolute confidence that it could make good on an escape.

God knew what this thing was, or how many ways she would be damning herself if she gave in to it. But as she watched, the scientist nearest her reached for a large syringe, a bottle of vile green liquid. 'Pentobarbitone' was printed on the label, and Dee remembered from when she'd had her cat put down just what that drug was used for.

She was left with only two choices. Give in to this new force, agree to murder, give up a portion of her soul to a beast promising death and violence... or face her own imminent death. Because now, for all their glee at their recent success, the eyes of these men were suddenly filled with loathing, hating what they had worked so hard to create.

She glanced around the room quickly, calculating how many people were here, how many deaths she would have on her hands, how much blood her soul could bear.

And then the creature within her paused. Scanned the room. Fell still at a sudden and startling realisation.

One of these men was like her. Also infected with this *presence*. The beast within her could feel it, though it couldn't identify which man, with all the fear and glee and emotion clogging the room. It repeated the question, more specifically this time. Kill the infected man with all the others, or let this one live? Dee had no answer for the beast. She was torn between wanting to destroy the man for being an abomination, and wanting to commune with him, to understand what he was, what she was, to have someone else in the world like her.

The scientist with the syringe stepped forward, and she was out of time. 'Kill them', she told the creature, already praying for forgiveness for this terrible crime. And then, after three days of terror and pain and regret, she felt the creature surge forward into her consciousness, and blackness took over.

Dee came to groggily. Became aware of hands shaking her. "Get up! Fuck... We really don't have time for this." A firm, even voice, despite the urgency. A male voice.

The *creature* stirred, snapped her eyes open, had her up on all fours even before she'd figured out which way was up.

Blood. All over the place. The walls, the floor, the table, her clothes, her hands... oh God, it was in her mouth, too. She gagged, spat out what she could, retched, but there was nothing in her stomach to bring up. What had she done? What had the creature inside her done?

She forced her head up, glanced around the room. Bodies everywhere, the scientists, white coats now red, throats ripped out, chunks of flesh torn away, the sound of hurried footsteps retreating down the hall, and she was on her feet before she'd even thought about it, the creature eager to chase after whoever was fleeing. It wasn't panting for more blood, though, Dee realised in relief, but rather it felt a curiosity, a kinship with whoever it was that was fleeing.

So apparently the one who had shaken her awake was also the other one infected with this presence. She was surprised at how relieved she felt that she hadn't killed him.

And then her eyes opened a touch wider as she caught sight of the table. The wrist and ankle restraints were still there, locked, unchanged... She looked down at her wrists and saw no evidence of injury, beyond the red marks from days of chafing. How the hell had she...?

She looked down again and felt herself sway. So much blood... Her hand left a bloody smear on the door frame, her shoes red prints on the pristine tiles. She ripped them off, running barefoot as she sought an exit to this bizarre hell. Came to a small closet and rummaged inside. Found scrubs, ripped off her blood stained clothes and tried to wipe the blood off her hands as best she could, and then she dressed in hospital green instead. Put on someone else's shoes, one size too big, and scanned the hallway as she emerged, eyes seeking out any movement, ears straining to hear the slightest sound.

Nothing.

Ran again, up stairs, following blind instinct, a half-remembered scent, the creature in her head telling her when to turn and when to pause and bloody hell, what was that thing, crawling through her veins, tingling, tight and pulsing? A growl, inside her own head, a wave of nausea, more running, upward, south, always south, though how she knew that was the direction, she had no idea.

Then out a door, into sunlight, and her knees hit the ground with sheer relief. She was out. She was alive.

And with an extra passenger on board, heaven help her.

Dee pushed herself to her feet, frantically considering where she could go. Her apartment? No, of course not. They would know who she was, where she lived. To her family? No. That would only make them a target.

North, the *creature* demanded. Go north, to the lakes, to the open spaces and cold winters. To the wild places where they could run free.

She moved again, not knowing what else to do, ran on shaking legs until she was free of the towering warehouses and out onto the open streets of London. Cars blaring horns. People, talking, walking, stinking of sweat and money and greed. She pushed through the crowd in a daze, always heading north, feeling a half-remembered touch on her face, a non-existent breeze on her skin. What the hell was she? She should find a train station. Get a train north, out of the city.

A white van pulled up in front of her. She weaved around it. Ducked past the doors as they swung open. Dodged the hand that reached out to grab her. Darted forward to seek shelter in the crowd.

And then she felt the tight sting of a dart in her shoulder. The creature inside her roared, howled, spun around, teeth snapping, reality turning hazy as the *whatever-it-was* tried to take over, only to be sent packing by a sharp jolt of electricity. Her body shuddered, sank down onto the filthy pavement as the Taser knocked the wind right out of her. And for the second time in less than an hour, she felt the world go black.

# CHAPTER TWO

Baron stood in the centre of the small bedroom in the Lakes District manor with his arms folded, staring down at the unconscious woman lying on the bed. She'd been out cold ever since they'd tasered her, the dose of sedative in the dart knocking her out properly after they'd gotten her into the van. One of the unfortunate luxuries of modern life and big cities was that no one seemed to bat an eyelid at odd events any more, not even when a woman was snatched off the streets in broad daylight. People had just kept on walking as he'd hauled the woman's small body into the van, probably more thankful than concerned that the crazed lunatic in scrubs and covered with blood was gone, no longer their problem.

But now she was Baron's problem, and the shifter leader tried hard to ignore the cold glare that Caroline, his second in command was giving him. Second in command? Hardly, he scoffed to himself. The woman was a thorn in his side, and they butted heads at every opportunity. The problem lying on the bed would have to be dealt with, but just to piss Caroline off, he said nothing, forcing her to break the silence.

"Are you insane?"

Right on cue, and he deigned to glance over at her. She was a lean, hard sort of woman, resting her weight against the doorframe, arms folded in a mirror of his own stance, wearing her standard leather trousers, black combat boots, a tight, no-frills t-shirt, her short, black hair wild and mused. She was every bit the predator, taking no shit from anyone in the lush estate that the Lakes District Den called home, and that included him. Even though he was supposed to be the one running the show. And if anyone else had used that tone with him, they'd have gotten their arse kicked quicker than they could tuck their tail between their legs and run.

"She's a rogue," Caroline snapped, when he didn't reply. "What the fuck are you doing bringing a rogue wolf to the estate?"

Baron tilted his head to the side, felt his neck crack, stretched his wide shoulders to ease the tension in his thick muscles and sighed. "That's no rogue," he said flatly, nodding to the unconscious woman.

"What the hell are you talking about? When Mark called, he said he'd run across a rogue wolf in London, untrained and likely to kill someone. And from the state of her, she already has. So I ask again, why did you bring her here? She should be put down. Or caged, until she learns some manners."

Baron studied the unconscious woman again. She wasn't particularly tall, maybe five foot three. She was on the curvy side, pale skin, light brown hair, maybe in her late twenties. She had the look of a middle-class office worker, a meek, unremarkable member of the rat race – or she would, when she wasn't wearing scrubs and smeared with blood. And the jarring sense that something was amiss came back to him again.

A rogue wolf was a menace, a crazed beast that had no control over the animal side of themselves, and when he'd first seen the woman, weaving through the busy streets, she'd looked every bit like a convert gone mad. Some of them did, which was why newly turned wolves were watched closely, trained, sometimes caged until they learned to control themselves.

But as he'd tried to catch the woman, for the briefest moment he'd caught a glimpse of... something else. It was hard to say what. Relief? Anticipation? Gratitude, even? Twenty years of listening to his instincts had told him that this was no rogue. She was newly converted, no doubt about that, but the wolf had sprung to her defence when she'd felt that dart – a sure sign that human and beast were capable of cooperating with each other. And she hadn't tried to hurt anyone, even when there had been so many human sheep wandering past, ripe for the picking.

"She's not a rogue," Baron repeated. "And I'm well aware of the need to find out just who the hell she is, but it's going to be hard to make any progress on that until she wakes up."

Caroline stalked across the room, a throwing knife in her hand, and she jabbed him in the chest with it. Just hard enough to draw a pinprick of blood. "You could have done that in a safe house. Or down in the cages. You're putting us all at risk-"

Baron grabbed her arm and twisted, spinning the alpha female around so she was pinned against him, her back to his chest. He leaned down and breathed his words into her ear. "I run this Den," he reminded her coldly. "And unless you're petitioning for a leadership challenge, I suggest you start remembering that."

Caroline hesitated – as he expected her to – and then he let her go, without waiting for her acquiescence. Push her too hard and she was just as likely to actually go and find another male to challenge him. Tank, perhaps, or Silas. Either one had the physical strength to give him a good run for his money, and Tank could garner enough support from the Den to give it a real go. Silas would have a harder time gathering a following, but there was no point tempting fate. A healthy Den ran better when there was peace between its members. He had no desire to start a miniature war within their own walls.

"Send Silas up," he said, as Caroline glared at him. "If the so-called rogue causes any trouble, Silas will take her out, no problem."

"That's the first sensible thing you've said all day," Caroline growled, then stalked out of the room.

The woman on the bed stirred, moaned, then fell silent again. Baron settled in for a long wait. They'd used enough sedative to knock out a horse, and this newcomer was a lightweight compared to most of the residents here. But she had to wake up sooner or later. And when she did, Baron had a small mountain of questions that needed answering.

Mark paused outside the bedroom door, still debating with himself over whether he should be here.

At the time, rescuing the girl from the lab had seemed obvious, the only viable decision in a very bad situation. Leaving her there to die would have been beyond heartless – it would have made him as bad as the monsters who had been torturing her.

But now that they were back home, a whole world of unintended consequences had sprung up, and Mark was on the horns of a dilemma, trying to work out how to deal with them all.

The fact was, he should never have been in the lab in the first place. Going there, running his own private investigation without Baron's knowledge or permission was a gross violation of Den rules. That alone was enough to earn him some serious punishment. But the reason behind his being there was even worse. If anyone discovered what he'd been doing, what he'd been investigating for the last six months… fuck, they'd put him down in an instant. His research had been an act of treason, and Baron wouldn't hesitate to kill him for risking the safety of the Den in so reckless a manner.

So in the interests of staying alive, he was trying to figure out the best way to play this.

According to the story he'd given Baron, he'd come across the girl – by all appearances a rogue wolf – while he'd been out shopping. She'd been running loose and covered in blood, so he'd called in a capture squad, tracked the woman until Baron could catch up with her, and then they'd all high-tailed it north, their business in London thankfully at a close. And if anyone had taken particular notice of the van and the blood-smeared woman, then Skip was an expert at covering their tracks, able to hack any database in the world, to erase security videos, to cause police case files to get 'lost', and Alistair was a master spin doctor, managing the group's PR, fabricating media stories whenever their activities started to draw too much attention. But even so, they didn't like to make extra work when stealth and discretion would serve just as well.

But the truth was more than a short leap from that bland story. So he was eager to find out what the girl knew, whether she remembered him, could identify him, whether she intended to spill his secret. But the problem was that the very act of trying to cover his tracks could very well draw unwanted attention to himself, and he'd spent the last hour and a half debating whether to come up here and see her, or keep to himself and wait it out.

Deciding to just bite the bullet, Mark lifted his hand and knocked on the door. "What?" came the gruff reply, and he pushed it open, seeing Baron standing near the bed, Silas on the far side of the room, a knife strapped to his hip and a habitual scowl on his face. Baron's eyebrows lifted as he saw who had arrived.

"Well, well. Come to check on sleeping beauty, have you?" The smirk on his face matched the sarcastic edge to his voice, and Mark glanced at the bed, disappointed to find that the girl was still unconscious. Damn. No chance of finding out what she knew, then.

"Just wanted to see how she's doing," Mark said, feigning disinterest. "She looked the worse for wear when we picked her up." And still did, he was dismayed to realise. She was still covered with blood, still wearing green scrubs, and he felt the protective instinct he'd felt in the lab come roaring back to life. "Couldn't you at least have cleaned her up a bit?" he snapped, not liking the way she lay so still, vulnerable and helpless. She looked tiny on the big bed, her short hair spread out on the pillow like a halo, and Mark felt his gut twist as he looked at her. Okay, so much for disinterest.

Baron just looked amused. "We picked up a potential rogue who looks like she just killed someone. No, I'm not giving her a bath." Mark scowled at him, which earned him a laugh. "Oh, you like her, then? And everyone says love at first sight is just for the fairy tales. But if you're trying to get into her pants, I'd recommend at least waiting until she wakes up."

Mark swore under his breath. "I'm not trying to get into her pants. She's just…" He gestured helplessly to the bed, where she lay pale and still.

"Female?"

"Oh, for Pete's sake." The truth was, the barb hit a little too close to home. Not that he had any nefarious intentions towards the girl, would never have taken advantage of her in any way. But women shifters were few and far between, and a beautiful woman in need of rescuing? Yeah, it had tugged at his heart strings a little.

The door was suddenly flung open and Caroline marched in, glaring at

Baron. "Fucking hell, are you still here?"

"I thought this was where you wanted me," Baron said. "Babysitting the dangerous menace." He jerked his head at the woman on the bed. "Better call the riot squad. I think she just moved her thumb."

"The Council called," Caroline snapped, totally ignoring the girl. "We've got problems."

"When don't we?" Baron said dryly, and Mark groaned inwardly. It was a never ending battle with these two, neither one able to give any ground to the other, and if Baron hadn't already had a partner, Mark would have assumed the constant sniping at each other was born of nothing more than sexual tension. But then again, Baron's relationship was... complicated.

"I'm serious," Caroline snapped. "Come and see me when you've finished with your prisoner. The Noturatii are stirring up a hornet's nest again." The door slammed shut, and Baron let out a muffled curse.

He turned back to Mark, fixing him with a sardonic glare, his mood apparently having taken a rapid downturn. "Look, Romeo. She's still unconscious, so how about you take your arse back downstairs and find something useful to do. She'll wake up when she wakes up, and you can wait it out, just like everyone else."

"Fine. Whatever." Mark let himself out of the room, annoyed and frustrated. He'd used up his only real opportunity at learning anything more about the girl, and had gained exactly nothing for his efforts. Fuck, he thought, as he headed down to his workshop, deciding to finish the latest set of furniture he was building. Far from finishing the day as a hero saving a damsel in distress, this could well turn out to be one of his worst days ever.

Dee struggled against the fog in her brain, trying to figure out where reality was. She heard voices and wondered where she was. Had she fallen asleep at a friend's house? Or maybe she was at home and had left the television on. One of the voices was shrill and female, then there were others, male, one calm and placid, another deep and rumbling, and she tried to remember if she knew those voices.

And then reality came thundering down on her, images of the lab, her abduction, the pain and terror screaming back into her consciousness, the presence in her head, the blood, and she snapped her eyes open.

The room was stylishly old-world, a thick rug covering wooden floorboards, an open fireplace, beautiful paintings on the walls, and she thought maybe she was having a bizarre dream.

But then one of the lines she'd heard echoed in her mind. 'Come and see me when you've finished with your prisoner'.

Prisoner? She was their prisoner? After all she'd done to escape her last captors, she was right back where she'd started?

There were two men in the room, two large, imposing, dangerous men, and she felt a new wave of terror... followed by a most perverse kind of relief. Okay, so she was still a captive, but somewhere far different from the lab. And these men's cold glares and open intimidation were strangely preferable to the nameless, faceless scientists who had tortured her without speaking a word.

The closer man was huge, thick muscles standing out from massive biceps, wide chest, thighs like tree trunks. His arms were folded across his chest, and black hair and a short beard added to the impression of menace... until Dee got a look at the second man. He was shorter, more wiry, leaning nonchalantly against the wall, but he had the look of a man who would gut you and laugh about it as he painted pictures with your blood. Olive skin, bald head, a scar running from his left eye to his collar bone. Tattoos climbed from his wrists to his shoulders, and he held a long dagger in his left hand, silently tossing it in the air and catching it again.

Dee sat up, backing away across the bed until her hip hit the wall. "Are you going to kill me?" Presumably not, she thought, even before she had finished the question. If they were, they would have done it while she was unconscious. But she was asking more to open a dialogue, to gauge these men's reactions. To see if they would speak to her at all.

"Haven't decided yet," the larger man said. The leaner one quirked an eyebrow upwards and stroked the handle of his dagger.

Okay, not the worst start ever. They hadn't threatened torment and pain, nor tried to rape her, nor demanded ransoms or rewards in exchange for her freedom. It was a small silver lining, but given what she had endured for the last few days, any up side was a blessing.

As she sat there, trying to get her bearings, the *creature* inside her stirred. It woke up, tested her limbs subtly, still uncertain of this new body, then it seemed to scan the room, though whether it was by scent or sound or some other means, she couldn't quite tell. But the reaction of the creature to its new surroundings was startling. She felt its tight apprehension and ready aggression ease. The creature was withdrawing, *relaxing*. Why the hell would...?

But when the reason struck her, it filled her with terror.

Oh hell... these men... whatever it was that was inside her, whatever it was that she had become, they were like her. They were infected with the same strange energy, and her own beast was communing with theirs. They were killers, that much was certain.

But then, so was she now, after the massacre at the lab.

But if they didn't mean to kill her, then maybe... maybe they could explain what she was, what the presence in her body and in her mind was, and maybe tell her how she might be rid of it again? If such a thing was even possible.

Dee had never given much thought to religion, never considered what might exist beyond what could be seen and heard and touched, but… *Demon.* The word lingered in her mind, the thought that maybe she had actually been possessed terrifying her. God help her, what was she to do if that was true? Could a priest exorcise it? Could she be cured? Or was she to become a deranged killer, preying on the weak and innocent?

And then another thought struck her. "I need to call my family," she blurted out. "To tell them I'm alive-"

"No," the larger man interrupted.

"My mother will be frantic," Dee went on, heedless. "I've been missing for days."

"No."

"Please, I… Please?"

"No."

Perhaps she'd escaped from the frying pan only to land straight in the fire, then. The implacable calm of the man was daunting, and Dee fell silent, contemplating her options. She looked down at her hands, saw the dried blood on them. "What am I?"

Both men looked startled, as if she had suddenly stripped naked in front of them. "Excuse me?" The look of bewilderment on the larger man's face was almost comical.

"You're like me, aren't you? The… the thing inside you?" The man nodded, a slow, cautious gesture. "So what am I? What is this thing?"

"How did you-" the leaner man asked, but the bigger one quickly shushed him.

"How did you get… how did you acquire the… presence?" It was carefully phrased and rephrased as the question was asked, a deliberate attempt at avoiding giving away any new information.

Images of the lab flashed through her mind, the terrors and fears and implicit threats, and suddenly she was tired of being the pawn in this macabre game. "Okay, how about this," she suggested, making an effort to sound confident. "I want to know what I am. You want to know how I got this way. Maybe a little give and take is in order?" It was a bit of a shock to find herself trying to gain back some ground, to negotiate with these thugs, rather than just giving in to whatever they asked of her. Perhaps, though, it wasn't her putting on this brave front, but the beast inside her. It was alert and awake now, paying attention to details, and it seemed almost eager to lock horns with this huge man.

Her captor regarded her shrewdly. Silently. And then he suddenly smiled, looking at her with open amusement. "Fine. I'm Baron," he said. "And you are?"

"Dee."

"Dee who?"

"You first."

Baron rolled his eyes, as if talking to a particularly stupid child. "Joseph Baron."

"Dee Carman."

"Pleasure to meet you. So, you want to know what you are?"

Dee nodded.

Baron smirked. "Better hold on to your hat, then. Because this one's a doozy."

He stepped back and glanced at the other man, who nodded, palmed his dagger, stepped away from the wall and fixed his gaze on Dee. As if they expected her to do something violent. Then Baron turned back to Dee and a strange energy filled the room, like static electricity, making her hair stand on end and her skin tingle, and then the huge man in front of her blurred, shifted, *changed* into...

Dee stared at the huge black wolf that now dominated the room... and let out an ear-piercing scream.

# CHAPTER THREE

Dee sat trembling on the bed, a glass of whiskey in her hand. Whiskey? She never drank whiskey. She glanced over at Baron, back in his human form, and remembered the huge black wolf that he had turned into.

She quickly drained the glass, wincing at the taste. She was a... She was...

Baron pulled a chair up closer to the bed, turning it around to straddle it. And she imagined that beneath the scowl and the beard, he was feeling concerned about her. "Take a deep breath. Don't want you panicking again."

As if that hadn't been embarrassing enough the first time around. But a little shock was justified, she told herself, fighting to regain a small dose of her pride. She was a... "I'm a werewolf," she stated flatly. Maybe hearing it out loud would help.

"No. Not a werewolf." From his tone, it sounded like she had just insulted Baron. "A shape shifter. A wolf, and a human. Not a half-breed of either." His eyes narrowed. "But what I'm far more interested in is how you came to be... one of us."

That sounded ominous. "How does it usually happen?"

Baron hesitated, and Dee knew that whatever he said next was going to be a hedge. "In a variety of ways. But it's always voluntary. The convert knows exactly what they're getting into, and accepts it wholeheartedly. To my knowledge, being converted against your will isn't even possible. So how did you manage to have a wolf on board without even knowing what it was?"

Dee considered her answer carefully. It sounded like Baron was far from happy with her so far, and admitting to being kidnapped, admitting that she'd been turned into this *thing* quite against her will? It was like admitting that you'd snuck into an exclusive club through the back door. And that

14

was always right before the bouncers escorted you straight back out again. Which, in this case, was likely to happen at the pointy end of a knife.

But what else was she going to say? She didn't even know how it had happened.

Besides which, these men, for all their cold intimidation, were turning out to be the lesser of two evils. The scientists had tortured and experimented on her, while the men in front of her had looked after her, gotten her out of harm's way, put her on a soft bed, tried to keep her calm and comfortable.

"I was kidnapped," she said finally, hoping that honesty was, indeed, the best policy. "I don't know who they were, but they held me in a lab for days and tortured me. Tried all sorts of experiments. I'm guessing they were trying to implant the... wolf." Damn, but it was still so difficult to put that into words. But the presence was still there, alert, waiting. Watching.

"What kind of experiments?"

She explained it as best she could, fighting back terror at the memories, detailing the needles, the surgery, the electric shocks, and halfway through, Baron refilled her glass, waiting patiently while she sipped the strong liquor, waited for her hands to stop shaking, until she found the courage to continue.

"The last experiment," she said finally, staring at the bedspread, telling herself this would all be over soon. "That was the one that worked. They took a sample of my blood. Took it away, then came back later and put it back into my vein. I don't know what they did to it, but then suddenly I had this *thing* in my head offering to kill them all."

Baron was listening with rapt attention. "What exactly did it offer you? How did it communicate with you?"

"It was like a series of images in my head. Ideas. Emotions, maybe. It was very angry and showed me a picture of the scientists dead on the floor, covered in blood."

Baron regarded her suspiciously. "You don't strike me as a particularly violent sort," he observed carefully.

In contrast to Baron himself, Dee thought, who looked like he was quite capable of ripping a man limb from limb. Dee glanced down at herself – still wearing scrubs, dried blood coating her hands – what a sight she must make. But it wasn't surprising that the truth was so glaringly obvious. She had trouble even killing spiders, preferring to catch them and release them outside. "Not usually, no."

Baron continued to watch her, perplexed, curious. "So a wolf was forced to merge with you, and then it offered you an act of violence that you would normally find utterly repugnant." He shook his head. "You should be stark raving mad by now."

"Why should I be?" she objected. "I was scared, but not out of my mind. I'm not so weak willed as to faint at the sight of a little blood." Okay, so she'd quite thoroughly panicked at the sight of a man turning into the largest wolf she'd ever seen, but… She glanced down, knowing there was plenty of blood still clinging to her, and despite her words, she was a little surprised that she was still able to hold a rational conversation. Especially when said conversation involved werewolves and mad scientists and macabre agreements to kill people.

Baron raised an eyebrow at her protest. "Even in the best of conversions, if the human can't accept the wolf, then the pair of them go mad. I've seen it happen."

Dee thought back over those terrified moments, the surge of rage in her head, the cold terror as the spectre of death stared down at her. "But I did accept it," she said, almost talking to herself.

"What?"

"I did accept it," she repeated. "The offer to kill them. They were going to kill me, so I told the wolf that it could kill them."

In fitting with the inexplicable events of the day, both men suddenly relaxed, as if her admitting to being a killer bent on violent revenge made everything okay. What sort of company was she keeping here?

"Makes sense," the henchman by the door muttered, while Baron just breathed a relieved sigh.

"We'll need to talk about this more," Baron said. "But for now, I have bigger problems on my hands. So let's deal with a more urgent issue." He fixed Dee with a steely look. "You've become a shape shifter. It goes without saying that we're a rather secretive lot. Humans on the whole do not and cannot know about us. So until we figure out just what happened to you, you're going to have to stay here."

Dee nodded, having rather expected as much. And in all honesty, it was something of a relief to know she was to be kept here for a little while with more of her kind, where she could learn about what she was and how to control the wolf and what this all meant. "I'm happy to stay, but my mother and my sister… I need to tell them I'm alive. And safe. Am I safe?" she asked belatedly, then went on without waiting for an answer. "I don't have to mention the wolf thing, I know that's off limits, and you could even listen in on everything we say if you like," she added, as the frown on Baron's face grew deeper. "But they'll be worried sick, and I…" She trailed off.

"You've asked this already," Baron said softly, gentle and stern at the same time. "The answer is no."

"They could be thinking I'm dead for all I know." It came out quiet, defeated.

"Perhaps that's for the best." Baron nodded to the other man, then headed for the door. "I'll send someone up to look after you," he said, just before he closed it behind him, and then he was gone, leaving her with a much less accommodating guard, a grim smirk on his lips and a dagger balanced on the tip of his finger.

Baron let himself out of Dee's room, his mind already tracing out possibilities for the future, the myriad of plans and good intentions that could go astray. Whoever had kidnapped her most likely wanted her back. From the sounds of it, she hadn't fully bonded with the wolf yet, which meant that madness was still a very real risk. And even if she chose to stay here, to comply with the rules of the Den and the Council, Caroline could still refuse to accept her. As Alpha female, she had the absolute right to refuse new members, and if that happened, then Dee would either have to be found another Den to join, or be put down.

But aside from all that, there was the question of whether the girl even wanted to stay. Converts were usually chosen very carefully and spent several years being educated before they were converted. And they usually came with a very particular set of qualifications – they were loners, with few ties, no loose ends, minimal friends or family. Because there was one requirement of becoming a shifter that was absolute – the convert was to leave his or her old life behind. The estate became their home. The shifters became their family. There was no room for anything else.

Dee came with connections and complications galore. She'd already mentioned a family back in London. She would probably have friends. A flat, maybe. A job, most likely. A boyfriend?

Fuck, if she had a husband or children then they were in deep shit. In such cases, faking the convert's death was the cleanest, quickest way to deal with all the loose ends, but Dee hadn't chosen this for herself. And if the terms of her conversion were presented to her in such a cold, callous way, she could become a liability. She would agree to their terms, of course, because if faking her death wasn't an amicable solution, then death was still the answer, but there would be no faking involved. And after she'd agreed to live by their rules, her dissatisfaction would eat away at her, and sooner or later she would seek to escape, maybe go public, risk exposing them all, and that could lead to the extinction of their entire species.

It very nearly had done, several times throughout history, and was the reason they had the Council overseeing things now. The Italy-based control centre consisted of the wisest and most experienced shifters, and it governed all their interactions with human culture, decided the location and size of each Den, determined how many new converts could be made each year, maintained a team of elite soldiers to deal with problems that got out of hand.

One thing at a time, Baron told himself, heading down the wide stairs.

First, he had to see Caroline about whatever this latest drama with the Council was, and then they could sort out Dee's future. Assuming Caroline didn't decide to kill her on sight, once he'd explained her unconventional conversion.

Caroline was waiting in the sitting room, pacing, her every movement as sleek and graceful in human form as she was as a wolf.

"What have the Noturatii done now?" Baron asked without preamble. For all his love of needling Caroline, the safety and welfare of the Den came first, every time, and the Noturatii were their closest and biggest threat. He was in no mood to play games when they were involved.

"How's the rogue?" Caroline asked, ignoring his question, and for once, Baron wasn't in the mood to lock horns with her.

"Contained. For now. She says she was converted by force, but it seems that she reached a preliminary agreement with the wolf, regardless. So she's not insane. Yet. Silas is watching her."

Caroline seemed surprised by the explanation so easily given, her tightly defensive stance easing a little. It wasn't very often that Baron missed the opportunity to push back when she decided to push him.

"So what about this call from the Council?" Despite any grumbling that went on, every shifter had the utmost respect for the Council, any wolf more than a few years past their conversion having seen first hand how many crises their guidance and wisdom had diverted. The Council's rulings were absolute, and their requests for assistance drew immediate and violent action on their behalf.

Caroline snarled, teeth bared. "The Noturatii have started a new campaign. They're kidnapping wolves. France has reported two missing from its Den. Italy's lost one, and so has Spain. And get this – the Grey Watch sent a politely worded letter to the Council warning them to be on guard."

As with all societies, shape shifters had their detractors, and not all wolves belonged to Dens or answered to the Council. The Grey Watch were a law unto themselves, wolves who roamed the few remaining wildernesses of Europe. Thankfully, they were retreating further and further into Russia and Asia as humanity expanded to fill every corner of the globe, but England had its very own pack, in the Kielder Forest in Northumberland. It was a constant battle for the Council to decide when to leave them to themselves and when to order a cull, and as ferocious warriors with a taste for freedom, culling them never went down easy.

"Fuck me," Baron swore softly. "It's a bad day in hell when the Grey Watch gets involved." Reclusive to a fault, the Grey Watch embraced all manner of nature worship and shunned all facets of modern life, completely cutting ties with their past upon conversion. Wolves from Il Trosa – literally 'The Pack', the larger organisation to which the Dens belonged – were at least allowed to remain in human society, drove cars, some even had jobs. But members of the Grey Watch seemed to abandon all but the most primitive aspects of their humanity. And of course, there were other... complications.

But Baron had the sinking feeling that the Grey Watch was the least of their problems. "Dee – the girl upstairs – she said she was kidnapped. Held in a lab and tortured. She says the men who took her wanted to convert her into a wolf. And against all odds, it looks like they succeeded."

Caroline paced restlessly across the room again. "So you think she was taken by the Noturatii? That makes no sense. They've been on our tails for centuries, but they've always sought to preserve the ignorance of humanity as much as we have. Why the sudden change to kidnapping? It's messy. Risky. If they're taking wolves, that's one thing, but snatching humans? People notice when people go missing. They make police reports. And then sooner or later, someone always escapes, and then someone talks, and the Noturatii don't want that any more than we do. Besides, they want us all dead – hell, they've been trying to exterminate us since the middle ages. For them to be trying to create new converts makes absolutely no sense."

Baron glanced at the ceiling, imagining their newest recruit sitting upstairs, no doubt attempting to hold a fruitless conversation with Silas. "None the less, it seems the most obvious conclusion. No one but the Noturatii have the knowledge or resources to be running experiments on shifters. We need to find out more about what happened to this girl. And get Simon to up security around the manor. I don't want so much as a field mouse to cross this estate without us knowing about it."

# CHAPTER FOUR

Inside the small bedroom, Dee was feeling rather less confident than she had been earlier. Since Baron had left, the other man had stayed as her guard, but was proving himself to be far less amicable than Baron had been. He'd remained by the door, glowering at her constantly, hand never leaving the knife at his side. She'd tried asking his name, only to be told it was none of her business. She'd asked if she could wash the blood off her hands, a small, reasonable request which was met with a flat 'No,' and then she'd asked for a drink of water, to which he'd replied, "You're not going to die of thirst in the next half an hour." She'd thought of asking to see Baron again, but since he'd left in a hurry to deal with a crisis elsewhere, she had to assume that whatever his other business was, it was more important than her. And the silent, scowling man before her wasn't likely to disturb his boss because of a little whining on her part.

She went to the window and looked out. Tried to open it, but found it locked, and glanced back at her guard, to see a faint smirk on his lips. "Oh, give it a rest," she snapped at him, running short on patience now. "I wasn't going to jump out. I just want some fresh air." It was a bit of a risk antagonising him, but she had also reached the conclusion that he was under orders not to kill her – assuming she didn't do anything violent or unexpected – so a little verbal sparring was a risk she was willing to take.

Odd how a few days of captivity had changed her perspective on such things. Not even a week ago, she'd have been curled up on the floor in a quivering heap if presented with captivity at the hands of this violent thug, but now all she could think was that his surly personality was more entertaining and less threatening than a white surgical mask and silent, gloved fingers.

"You're on the third floor," the man said, sounding amused. "You could jump if you like. It would make my job a whole lot easier."

"You'd like that, wouldn't you?" He'd probably get a kick out of it, watching her body splatter on the pavers beneath them.

"I really would."

Sadistic bastard.

Suddenly the door opened, startling Dee, but the man by the door didn't even flinch. "I'm Tank," the newcomer said, and Dee's first thought was 'holy hell, yes, you are.' The man was huge, taller even than Baron, narrower at the hips but wider at the shoulders, and his tight fitting clothing showed off his physique in a more obvious way than Baron's loose sweater had. A singlet t-shirt and tight jeans were finished off with combat boots and a variety of weapons secured about his body. Blond hair in a crew cut gave him a military look, but the grin on his face counteracted what could have otherwise been a most intimidating presentation. And in his hands, he held a towel and a bundle of cloth. Clothes? Clean clothes?

"I'm Dee," Dee said unnecessarily, assuming Baron had already told him her name, but she was a little stumped for conversation starters. "Is everyone here so big?" It was a rather inane thing to say, but shock after shock today had left her off balance.

Tank and the other man both laughed, but the two sounds were startlingly different. While Tank's was a rich, genuine chuckle, the other man's was a dry, sarcastic sound.

"Size isn't everything," the nameless man said.

Tank punched him amicably in the arm. "Don't mind Silas. He's got a perpetual case of PMS. Come on. Let's get you showered and cleaned up. And I suspect you're hungry by now. "

She was, though she hadn't noticed until he'd said something. A shower was definitely the first order of business, though.

Silas rolled his eyes at Tank. "Fine. You want to babysit the chit, then tag, you're it." He was gone in an instant, ghosting silently out the door, and Dee found it quite a relief to have him gone.

Tank led her down the hall to another bedroom, this one larger, and then through into an ensuite. The manor was old, had probably stood for hundreds of years, but it had obviously been renovated along the way. The bedrooms retained a charming, old-world feel, but the bathroom was 100% modern, a large shower, ornate hand basin, a wide mirror taking up most of one wall. It was painted a delicate peach colour, and Dee wondered briefly just how many women they had in the manor. She'd heard only one so far, that dim, angry voice while she was still drugged. Everyone else she had seen had been male.

Tank dumped the clothes on the toilet seat and hung the towel on a rail. "The clothes belong to Skip – one of the female wolves. They're probably too big, but…" He glanced down pointedly at her blood-stained scrubs, and Dee hastily assured him the clothes would be fine. "I'll be waiting in the bedroom," he added. "And if you take more than fifteen minutes, I'm coming in to get you." He closed the door.

Dee glanced at the shower, longing to wash the blood off and get clean after three days of being strapped to a table... but with Baron's refusal to let her contact her mother, other plans had suddenly become a higher priority. She went straight to the window, the only other exit to the room, and slid it open, trying to be as quiet as possible. It was narrow, and it would be a tight squeeze to get through – if she could even fit – but maybe it led onto a roof. Even though she was still on the third floor, maybe she would be able to climb down, she thought desperately, maybe find a drain pipe or a balcony to use as a stepping stone. She stood on tiptoes and peered out the small gap. Maybe she would be able to...

She sighed as she saw the long, vertical drop leading straight down. Bugger. No luck there. And then she glanced in the mirror, and that did away with the last of her plans to escape. There was blood all over her face, her neck, even climbing into her hair, and she was horrified at the sight of herself. She'd been running around the streets of London like this? What must people have been thinking?

The clock was ticking, and Dee had no intention of still being naked and wet when Tank came back, so, escape plans abandoned for the moment, she quickly stripped and dived into the shower. She washed her hair and scrubbed herself all over, checking in the mirror to make sure she'd gotten every last bit of blood off.

She was pulling on the last of the clothes when a knock on the door startled her. "Time's up," Tank's deep voice filtered through the thick door. "Come out, or I'm coming in."

"I'm coming out," she called, trying to hide her apprehension. The clothes were indeed too big, but not too bad, once she'd rolled up the bottom of the jeans and wrapped a belt around her waist. She hung up the towel, wishing she had a comb to run through her wet hair, and opened the door.

Tank was standing in the doorway, arms folded, and as the door opened, his expression changed from a tense frown to a faintly relieved smirk. "They make you look even shorter than you really are," he said, running a glance over her makeshift outfit. She didn't even come up to his armpits, and so she supposed she must look rather ridiculous to him. "Come on. Let's get you some food, and then Baron will want to talk to you again."

After no more than half an hour in his workshop, Mark threw down his tools in frustration. His job, such as it was, was making hand-crafted wooden furniture – one of the many small contributions the resident shifters made towards funding the estate – and he was working on a set of chairs that were to go with a long dining table, ordered by a wealthy customer from Glasgow.

But after three attempts at getting the shape of the chair right, he had to admit he was wasting his time. And damaging some perfectly good wood in the process. Every two minutes, his thoughts returned to the girl in the bedroom, seeing her lying there, the scientists' blood on her hands and face, and after gouging a chunk out of a chair leg by mistake, he finally gave up.

Restless and irritable, he headed for the kitchen, making a sandwich even though he wasn't hungry. And then he found a newspaper and pretended to read, the words blurring on the page when all he was really concentrating on was the sound of footsteps on the stairs, waiting for Baron to show up with news, or Caroline to start screeching about newcomers invading the estate.

In the end, he gave up even that, folding the newspaper and deciding to head back upstairs. If anyone asked, he could tell them he'd been reading a book – not an uncommon pastime for him, and at least if he was in his room, he could be as restless as he liked without arousing any suspicion.

But as luck would have it, just as he was crossing the foyer to the grand staircase, he heard footsteps at the top – Tank, with his heavy boots on the wooden boards, and another sound, the light, barely there rustle of a small person in bare feet, and he felt a surge of relief and trepidation as he looked up and saw the girl standing there.

She'd showered and changed, her hair wet, her feet bare, and he couldn't help the smile on his face. "Hey," he said, heading up the stairs to meet her, but she stopped dead when she saw him, just a few steps down from the top. Tank stopped beside her, alert for any sign that she could be a danger. And for all her fragile looks and small stature, as a newly converted shifter with an untrained wolf on board, it was entirely possible she was public menace number one.

"How are you doing?" Mark asked, stopping halfway up, not wanting to startle her any more. She'd had a rather stressful day, after all, and the last thing he wanted to do was make it worse. But he needed to know she was okay, uninjured, and was surprised to find that that need was even more pressing than the need to know what she remembered about the lab.

"Fine," the girl said. "I'm sorry, should I know you?"

Oh, thank God, Mark thought to himself, the confirmation he had been looking for that she didn't immediately recognise him.

"This is Mark, one of the shifters here," Tank filled her in. "Mark, this is Dee."

Dee. Knowing her name did nothing for the inner monologue that was telling him he wasn't supposed to be taking an undue interest in her. *Subtlety* was the key here. "I was in the van when we picked you up," Mark explained, sticking to the 'official' story.

The girl recoiled slightly. "Oh. So you helped kidnap me. Good to know."

No, I *rescued* you, Mark thought blackly. But of course, it was better for both of them if she *didn't* know that. "Only with the best of intentions," he pointed out, trying to be polite.

"Right." Dee didn't sound the slightest bit convinced.

Perversely, Mark felt a wave of relief at her apparent show of attitude, small though it was. Back in the lab, he'd been more than a little concerned by her actions. She'd shifted, her arm vanishing out from beneath the scientist's needle, scant millimetres from a numbing death, to become one of the most beautiful wolves he'd ever seen. The she-wolf had leapt from the table, teeth bared, hackles raised… but instead of laying into the men as he'd expected, she had backed away and cowered in a corner, while the men reached for guns to take her out.

Which had been when he'd shifted himself, slaying the men while they were still too startled at the second wolf in their midst to think of defending themselves.

Her inaction had been worrying, the cause of it a mystery, and he'd been concerned that she'd been traumatised to breaking point, a nervous wreck of a human being, and not much better as a wolf.

But here she was, not even twenty-four hours later, telling him to mind his own business and laying blame for her situation – and it was ridiculous how he felt both delighted and offended by her mistrust.

"Okay, that'll do, Romeo," Tank interrupted, and Mark felt his face flush as the second person in only a couple of hours noticed his interest in the girl. "Dee needs some food, then she's got a meeting with the big bad wolf."

Mark sharply reminded himself that he wasn't supposed to be making a big deal out of this. "Sure," he agreed easily, forcing a smile that he hoped looked natural, and headed on up the stairs.

Dee backed away as the man – Mark – moved to pass her on the stairs. She'd been startled when he'd appeared, and not just because she'd assumed that she would be kept away from the other people here until Baron made a more firm decision about her. The man was gorgeous. Thick, dark hair cut loosely so that it hung around his eyes, rough stubble covering the most well defined jaw she'd ever seen, firm, mouth-watering muscles displayed beneath a tight black t-shirt and an almost predatory gaze that seemed to miss nothing as it took her in, from her bare feet to her borrowed clothing to the distrust in her eyes. And then he'd smiled and tried to chat to her like they were old friends.

He looked younger than the other men, maybe in his late twenties, but there was a quiet stillness to him that belied his age, shadows in his eyes that spoke of grief and suffering, and a pale yearning that was as compelling as it was heart wrenching. All in all, he looked more wild than anything. Wild and daunting.

And then she remembered that he was indeed wild, that he carried a very real, very wild animal inside himself, and she shuddered for a moment at the thought of meeting that wolf face to face.

As he approached the step Dee was standing on, she retreated until she was backed up against the banister, giving him plenty of room to pass, but the instant he came level with her, the creature in her head – the wolf, she reminded herself – sprang to the forefront, lurching her forward to get closer to him. It sniffed sharply, thrust a wave of irritation at her as it registered her thoroughly inferior sense of smell, and then Dee felt a bursting sensation all through her arms, felt her skin crackle with static electricity, and registered that the floor seemed to be rushing up to meet her.

# CHAPTER FIVE

Mark jumped back as Dee lurched towards him – perhaps he'd misread her mood, and she was more angry than he'd realised at being forced to come to the estate – but then she shifted, and he leapt away in real alarm. Being slapped by this slip of a girl was one thing, but fighting an angry wolf was a whole other story.

Even in his alarm, the wolf was as beautiful as he remembered, a lithe creature of silver and grey, white socks, black tipped ears, and he heard Tank shout for Baron and Caroline as he leapt back, up the stairs, out of reach of the animal, but she came after him, bounding up the stairs, evading Tank's attempt to grab her, and backing Mark against the wall.

"Rogue!" Tank's bellow could be heard throughout the entire manor, even as he lunged for the wolf again, and the sound of doors slamming and the thudding of heavy boots signalled that backup was on its way.

But the wolf wasn't trying to bite him, Mark registered belatedly. Her tail was up, wagging fiercely, a wolfy grin on her face as she darted around Tank again to sniff his legs, and then she simply sat down at his feet, as Tank stared on in shock, her tongue lolling out, tail thumping on the floor, and insinuated her head beneath his hand, as if asking for a pat – something no self respecting shifter would ever do!

His hand moved automatically in his shock, fingers digging into thick fur even as his heart sank. Being attacked was bad, but this could be even worse. All he could think was that his cover was blown. He'd been in the same room as the wolf, in both human and wolf form, and even though the woman didn't recognise his face, the wolf must have picked up his scent.

If Dee knew what he had done, he had no way of warning her not to spill the beans, not with Tank standing by and Baron and Caroline on their way up the stairs. The instant she shifted back, his secret would be out, and his life as he knew it would be over.

"Caroline! Do your thing." Baron had arrived, and after issuing that sharp order, he shifted, taking up a defensive stance just below the wolf on the stairs. Tank was hovering nearby, his dagger out, though he was clearly reluctant to use it. Dee wasn't actually threatening him, and killing a wolf, even a newcomer, was never an easy choice.

"Dee," Caroline snapped, racing up the stairs only a heartbeat behind Baron. "Human form. Right now."

The wolf paid no attention to the gathering crowd, just licked Mark's hand and wagged her tail again, and when Caroline saw that Dee wasn't going to cooperate, she cursed blackly, darted forward and grabbed a handful of her scruff. A pulse of electricity went out from her, spreading like a wave of lightning over Dee's back.

Mark leapt away, not wanting to be caught in the shockwave. He'd felt the brunt of Caroline's wrath before, and it was far from pleasant.

The wolf blurred before his eyes, shuddered, then Dee was back, landing on the wooden floor with a thud.

It was a rare talent that Caroline had, the ability to force another shifter to change forms, and it was one of the reasons she'd managed to rise to the position of alpha female. Especially since she and Baron didn't get along.

Dee moaned, curled in on herself, and Mark imagined she must be feeling pretty sore just then. A forced shift tended to leave you with burning muscles, stinging eyes, an ache in the chest like you'd just been kicked by a horse.

"What the fuck do you think you're doing?" Caroline was standing over the girl, arms folded, glaring down at her, and when she didn't respond, the alpha nudged her with a booted foot. "I don't give a fuck how new or special you think you are, girl, in this house you don't shift like that without warning. And certainly not when you're a fucking liability as it is. So get up and explain yourself."

Gasping for breath, Dee managed to roll over, peering blearily up at Caroline. "What? I'm sorry. I didn't…" She let out a groan, at which point Caroline reached down and grabbed a handful of her hair, hauling her to her feet.

"I said explain yourself-"

Against all good sense and his own better judgment, Mark moved almost as fast as Caroline had, grabbing her wrist in a tight hold. "Let her go."

Caroline turned to Mark, her black glare promising a slow, painful death for his interference. He glared back unflinchingly.

A moment passed, and then Caroline released her grip on Dee's hair. Mark caught her as she sagged, slipping an arm beneath her shoulder, and then braced himself for Caroline's wrath.

"How dare you-"

"You want answers, you'll get them," he snapped at her, feeling disoriented by the urge to snarl and bare his teeth. Where the hell was this aggression coming from? "But she wasn't hurting anyone, and she didn't mean any harm by it." The challenge was a foolhardy move on Mark's part – one did not simply oppose an alpha and walk away. But the rage he'd felt at seeing Dee hurt could not be contained, and he found himself more than willing to take on Caroline, if it kept Dee out of harm's way.

Out of the corner of his eye, he saw Baron shift back into human form. But he didn't dare take his eyes off Caroline. He was bigger than her, but not by much, her naturally tall frame filled out with plenty of muscle that was honed in vigorous daily workouts, and he was in for a royal arse-kicking for this display of defiance.

"If you think you can just step in and toss me aside, *boy*, you've got another thing coming-"

"No, he can't," Baron said, planting himself bodily between Caroline and Dee. "But I can." He looked Dee over, his gaze sharp and astute, and now that he wasn't focusing all his attention on Caroline, Mark realised how dreadful Dee looked. She was shaking, sagging in his grip, eyes wide and fearful. "Downstairs. Everyone," Baron ordered, then he simply stepped forward and scooped Dee into his arms. "I want to know what the hell just happened in my house."


Dee felt her face heat in embarrassment as Baron picked her up and carried her down the stairs. She had no idea what had just happened, but from the shocked looks on everyone's faces, the obvious conclusion was that she had just turned into a wolf. And given the massacre that had happened the last time she did that, she was dreading finding out what had happened this time around.

Although, maybe... She tried to mentally tune herself in to the wolf, not really sure how to do it, but the animal had communicated with her before, had shown her pictures and emotions, so maybe that might work again.

She tried to ask a question the wolf might understand, not in words, but rather calling to mind the dizzy feeling just before she had changed, and then the anger and shock all around her afterwards. Hopefully the wolf would understand the question as a simply translated *'What the hell just happened?'*

The response was immediate, and Dee was glad she was being carried, as she would have fallen over otherwise. A surge of happiness, curiosity, relief, and a strong image of Mark in her mind. What? Why would the wolf care so much about-

"Dee!"

Dee snapped her head up, so caught up in the swirl of impressions in her mind that she hadn't even noticed they had arrived in the sitting room. She was seated on a sofa, half a dozen scowls staring down at her while Baron stood over her with his arms folded. "What the hell do you think you were doing?"

Dee looked around at the grim expressions and felt a jolt when she saw Mark standing at the back of the group. A strong impression of tail-wagging in her head, and she mentally gave the wolf a shove. They were in serious trouble here, and the animal wasn't helping. "I don't know. I'm sorry. Did I just... what do you call it? I turned into a wolf, right?" Damn, that still sounded so surreal. Human beings didn't just turn into animals!

"It's called shifting," Tank said, earning a scowl from Baron.

"Of course you turned into a fucking wolf," said the woman who had attacked her on the stairs, and Dee involuntarily shrank back from her. She looked tough as nails, all black leather and weapons, and she was grateful when Baron shot the woman a glare.

"For fuck's sake, Caroline, you're not helping." He turned back to Dee. "Why did you shift?" he asked, and it was clear he was trying to be patient, no doubt feeling the weight of all the disapproval in the room.

"I didn't do it deliberately," Dee tried to explain, not wanting to cause any more trouble, but equally uncertain as to how to explain herself. "I was walking down the stairs, and then the wolf was suddenly there, clamouring to get out, and it felt like my head was going to explode, and then everything went black. I don't remember anything else until I woke up on the floor. It felt like I'd just been electrocuted." She wasn't asking for sympathy, she told herself. Just trying to explain how odd all this was for her, and even now, her legs were still trembling, her lungs aching-

"That's because Caroline zapped you," Tank said, completely ignoring the woman's – Caroline's – dirty look. And Dee took a moment to notice how odd the social dynamics in the room were. She had assumed that Baron was the leader here, and maybe that was true – he seemed to be the one trying to control things, get answers, be reasonable about it all. But Caroline clearly held some power, and Tank seemed to delight in taking subversive pot-shots at both of them. Was it simple mischief, or something more sinister? And there was also Silas, who she'd met upstairs, and, of course, Mark, standing with his arms folded, looking like someone had just asked him to clean up a pile of vomit on the carpet, but even so, her wolf perked up as she looked at him.

'*What?*' she asked the wolf, not sure if it would respond to words alone. It struck her as very odd for an animal to take such a sudden and intense interest in a human.

More tail wagging in her mind, and she managed not to roll her eyes. Not exactly a helpful response.

"Caroline has the ability to force shifters to change forms," Baron explained, not quite managing to keep the impatient edge from his voice. "So you're saying that you didn't initiate the shift, and that you don't remember anything that happened while you were a wolf?"

"That's right," Dee said, glad someone understood. But her relief was short-lived as Baron swore under his breath.

"She should be caged," Caroline announced immediately, and Dee looked to Baron for support, for some reprieve from what sounded like a horrible punishment for something that wasn't her fault. She'd spent long enough being held captive already.

But the tall, fierce man said nothing.

Oh, hell.

"I'm sorry, Dee," he said finally. "I can't let a rogue wolf run loose on the estate. You can't begin to understand how bad things could get if your wolf got loose unexpectedly. So until you learn to control it, or we figure out what the hell happened to you, you're going to have to be caged."

"No!" Dee protested immediately. "I just spent days being held captive, and being tortured, and I thought you'd rescued me, and now you just want to put me in a cage again? No! We can work something out-"

"Plenty of wolves need to be caged when they're first converted," Baron said. "There's no shame in it."

"I need to go home," Dee said, rising to her feet. "I need to see my family. And a doctor. And figure out how to get this damned creature out of my head-"

"And risk turning into a serial killer when your wolf can't be controlled?" Baron asked flatly. "What if it kills your family? Your neighbours? Innocent children? You want that on your conscience?"

Dee gaped at him. She hadn't thought of it that way. "No," she admitted quietly. "I don't want to hurt anyone."

"This isn't a punishment," Baron said, more gently now. "It's simply the safest way to keep you from harming anyone."

"The cages are more comfortable than they sound," Tank said, and Dee imagined that he was trying to be comforting. "You'll have a proper bed. A human one and a wolf one. And we'll look after you. Feed you. Bring you clean clothes."

Dee looked from one face to the next, hoping to find some support, some compassion for her situation. But none was to be found. Mark was looking at her with pity, but also a wariness that stung.

"Please…"

"It's for your own good," Caroline snapped. And with a sinking heart, Dee realised that that might well be true. Her wolf had taken over with no more effort than it took to swat a fly. She had no idea what the animal had done while it was in control, but the idea of harming her mother or her sister horrified her, and if she wasn't even conscious when it was in control, how was she ever to stop it from hurting people?

"Okay," she agreed, hating the way her voice trembled. "I'll cooperate. But…" She looked up at Baron, hopeful, scared, desperate. "You'll teach me how to control it, right? I'm not just going to be locked up for the rest of my life?"

"We'll teach you everything we can," Baron promised. "As much as it's sometimes necessary, I never like seeing a wolf caged."

That, at least, was a relief. She followed Caroline across the room on unsteady legs, Baron and Tank flanking her. Caroline activated a switch and a section of the wall swung open, revealing a dim, narrow staircase. She tried to control her shaking as she was led down a flight of stairs into what seemed to be a medieval dungeon.

Good God, what had she gotten herself into this time?

# CHAPTER SIX

Three storeys below ground, beneath one of the Noturatii's shopfronts – businesses that were set up to look legitimate but were actually used to channel funds and resources into the organisation's real purpose – Jacob Green stood in the centre of the lab, taking his time as he observed the macabre view. Body parts, blood, the scientists lying in unnatural positions with throats torn out, necks broken. The smell was horrendous, but he simply ignored it, breathed through his mouth and shot a disdainful glare at the scientists loitering in the doorway fighting not to vomit.

"And you just discovered this this morning?" he asked.

One of the scientists took a minute step forward, then retreated again when he saw he was getting blood on his shoes. "Yes, sir. Dr Andrews failed to send his usual report to headquarters last night, and he wasn't answering his phone, so we came to investigate this morning."

"You waited a whole twelve hours, and then came and started poking around yourself, instead of, I don't know, calling security?" Sarcasm was thick in his voice.

"Uh… perhaps we could have handled it better," the man admitted quietly, seeing Jacob's glare deepen.

"What's your name?" Jacob asked, not because he cared, but because he wanted to know who he was going to be yelling at later.

"Phil," the scientist said. "Philip O'Brian."

Footsteps coming down the hall got their attention and moments later, Jack Miller stepped into the doorway, one of the security guards Jacob had brought with him. Unlike the scientists, his own crew were alert, competent, not prone to making mistakes or overlooking details.

"Sir?" Miller said. "The security videos are gone. Someone broke into the server room and took the discs, as well as the hard drive out of the server. Left a fucking mess in the process."

Jacob turned back to the operating table. The metal cuffs that held the research subjects on the table were closed, locked… "What about written notes? Back ups from the computers?"

"There's a clipboard in the research room. Andrews' last entry was yesterday, 11:50 am. He says he thinks they were on the verge of a breakthrough, and there's a couple of pages of gibberish – one of the geeks could probably decipher it," Miller added, jerking his thumb at the scientists, "but he talks a lot about subject 11."

"He was working on a subject at the time of the attack?"

"That's the way it appears."

Jacob looked at the restraints again. The ones for the subject's wrists had faint red marks on the edge. Like someone had been straining against them. He tested the cuffs. Locked. "What do we know about this subject?"

A woman stepped forward from the small group of nervous, clipboard carrying intellectuals. "I had a look through Dr Andrews' notes while we were waiting for you to arrive," she volunteered, sounding a lot less nervous than the others in the group. "She was female. Late twenties. Chosen at random, no known medical difficulties, no distinctive physical features. There'd be a full profile on her somewhere, but we'd have to get tech support to hack the laptop. All the files are encrypted."

Jacob gave the woman a second look. She was young, maybe in her mid twenties, but sharp. Confident. And she looked none too bothered by the smell. "Name?"

"Melissa Hunter."

Jacob repeated the name in his head, sure he was going to need it later. She had potential, this girl.

He looked down at the body at his feet. Bent closer to examine the neck. "Tell me, Miller – these wounds don't look like ordinary knife wounds to me. What would you say could have caused them?"

Miller, like all his guards, had been chosen because of a very particular skill set. He was ex-military, a recreational hunter, and had an eye for detail. He stepped closer, taking his time to examine the raw wound. "There are multiple puncture wounds, and the flesh was ripped, rather than cut. I'm no forensic expert, but I'd say a wolf doing this would be within the realm of possibility."

Jacob turned to Melissa, completely ignoring the more senior Phil. "I want a full report on whatever notes Andrews took. In plain English. Miller, get that computer back to headquarters so someone can start decrypting it. And the rest of you, start cleaning this mess up. I want the bodies burned and the lab operational again by the end of tomorrow."

It was morning. Breakfast had just been delivered, and Dee sat alone on her bed, poking the bits of toast around the plate. It had taken her hours to get to sleep last night, and then nightmares had plagued her, dreams of labs and knives and blood disturbing her sleep again and again.

Why the hell had she let herself be locked up, Dee wondered, not for the first time. It had seemed perfectly reasonable at the time, the threat of accidentally killing more people a clever manipulation by Baron to get her to cooperate. But she shouldn't have listened. She should have run, fought, at least made an *attempt* at freedom, rather than just walking placidly into her own prison.

She'd spent the night coming up with outlandish schemes to get a message to her family, or to the police, each plan more ridiculous than the last. Her mother would be a mess. Her younger sister would be trying to hold things together, demanding that the police go and search for her, or fingerprint her entire apartment. Her father... she assumed he would have been told by now. But he lived in America, he and her mother having divorced when Dee was nineteen, and he'd married an American woman and moved away. He'd be worried, of course, but she wasn't sure he'd come all the way to England just to hear the police tell them they had no new leads.

Sometime around five this morning, her mind had finally tired of chasing ill fated escape plans and had turned itself to another puzzle – her escape from the lab. She'd let the scenes play out in her head again, remembering the wolf's insistence that it could escape, that it could kill those who threatened her, and she lingered over its realisation that another man in the room was like her. A shape shifter. A wolf.

And a gnawing curiosity now demanded to know who he was.

Her first conclusion was that it couldn't be anyone from this house. Baron had had no idea who she was or where she'd come from, and if another man in the house had rescued her, surely Baron would have heard about it.

But then again, Baron and his white van had been there, just minutes after she'd fled the lab, which seemed a rather heavy coincidence if they weren't involved. So just how many shifters were there in England?

Her thoughts were interrupted by the sound of the door opening, and she looked up, expecting to see Silas coming back again. He'd been in a foul mood when he'd delivered her breakfast, barely speaking two words to her, and she'd figured he was the resident security thug, charged with keeping her under control.

But it was a very different person who walked through the door this time. Dee sat up straighter when she saw the woman, a skinny girl who looked no taller than Dee herself, and several years younger. She approached Dee almost diffidently, clutching a worn teddy bear to her chest.

"Hey," the woman said. "How are you doing?" She noticed the tray still sitting on Dee's knees, the food barely touched. "Oh, I'm sorry. Caroline sent me down to collect your tray, but if you're still eating…"

"No, I'm done," Dee said, standing up and setting the tray back by the slot in the wall that was used to pass things in and out of the cell. "I'm not hungry."

The woman gave her a sympathetic look. "Yeah, you must be a bit turned about by all this." Then she brightened. "Well, here." She opened the slot and took out the tray, then pushed the bear through the gap. "This is Frank. He'll keep you company. I always sleep better with a bear beside me."

It was an odd gesture, and Dee immediately rethought her opinion on the girl's age. Perhaps she was younger than she looked… but she accepted the bear with a forced smile and gave him a hug before setting him on her pillow. "Thanks. That's really sweet."

The girl grinned, looking altogether pleased. "I'm Skip," she said. The name sounded vaguely familiar, and Dee realised this was the girl who had lent her the clothes. She'd expected someone larger – the clothes hung on Dee, at least 2 sizes too big, but then again, Skip's own clothes were too large. She wore a baggy, bright pink T-shirt with the word 'Princess' emblazoned in silver glitter and a pair of shorts that made her legs look like sticks. Her hair was cropped as short as a boy's, but she wore a variety of plastic chunky jewellery – a turquoise necklace of thick beads, a bracelet of large plastic 'diamonds', a bright blue ring on her thumb. The whole effect was rather disconcerting, and Dee tried to think of a polite way to comment on it.

"That's pretty jewellery," she hedged. But far from the pleased smile she was expecting, or even shy embarrassment at the compliment, Skip suddenly took on a hunted look. She glanced around the room as if looking for somewhere to escape, and fingered the necklace.

"I like it," she said defensively.

"Yeah. So do I," Dee said, not sure what she'd said wrong.

"It's mine."

"Okay." This was getting weird. Time to change the subject. "You lent me the clothes, right? Thanks."

Skip brightened right away. "Hey, no problem. Always happy to help. Baron said you got here wearing hospital clothes. But he says you weren't in a hospital, cos I was all worried you'd been hurt, but he said nope, no hospital. And then I figured you'd want some real clothes to wear, and if you stay and don't go crazy then Baron will buy you some of your own. I could go shopping for you if you like. Not, like, to a real shop, but I can buy anything online and get it delivered, and picking out some stuff for you would be real fun."

Ignoring the 'if you don't go crazy' part, Dee forced a smile. "That would be great. Thanks."

Skip picked up the tray and sashayed towards the door. "I gotta go, but Baron will be down in a bit. Hey!" She stopped suddenly, turning back towards Dee with an excited expression. "Can I see your wolf? Tank said she's beautiful and it's not often a newbie has a good looking wolf – most of them are all bedraggled and scruffy until they get the hang of shifting, but he said yours was totally sleek."

And there it was, the stark reminder that, far from a normal girl with an odd fashion sense, the woman standing in front of her was a... a wolf. A wild animal in a cute, teenage package.

"I... I can't shift," Dee said, stumbling over the words as emotions swamped her yet again. "I haven't learned how yet."

Skip pouted. "Oh. That's too bad. Well, another time, then." She bounced out of the room, managing not to spill the breakfast tray in the process, leaving Dee more confused and with more questions than ever before.

It was not quite half an hour later when the door opened again, and as promised, Baron let himself through. He came to stand at the front of the cage, giving Dee a thorough look-over. "Didn't sleep, huh?"

"Not much, no."

Baron nodded thoughtfully, and Dee imagined for a moment that he might be feeling sorry for her. "Well, let's get started, anyway," he said. "First thing you need to do to get out of this cage is learn to control your wolf."

"Um, on that note," Dee interrupted, as Baron fetched a chair from beside the wall and brought it over. "Rather than learning to control it, I'd much rather just have it removed, if I could?" Baron had said yesterday that being converted was voluntary. So, she reasoned, if she hadn't volunteered, then having the procedure reversed wasn't an unreasonable request.

Baron stared at her silently for a long moment. "To my knowledge," he said slowly, "there isn't a way to remove it."

"What? But there must be something you could at least try-"

"Our society has existed for hundreds of years. And no one has ever found a way to achieve a separation once the conversion has taken place. It's been attempted," he went on, when Dee went to protest. "Every single experiment has ultimately resulted in the death of the shifter."

Dee's heart sank. "But I can't live like this. I can't sleep. It kept me awake all night. It hates this cell, it wants to go outside, it hates the food you brought." She pointed to the bowl of chopped meat sitting on the floor in a silver dog dish. "How am I supposed to live with an animal that wants nothing to do with me?"

Baron frowned at her. "You're talking as if you and the wolf are two different people."

Dee was taken aback by that. "We are."

"No, you're not. You're one person, one mind, with two bodies. You are the wolf, Dee-"

"Then why does she know things that I know nothing about? Why does she want things that would never occur to me? How does she have so much control over me – my body, my sleep, the shifting – if she's just another part of me?"

Baron took a deep breath and let it out slowly. "Dee, you need to merge with the wolf. You need to accept it and embrace that part of yourself, or you'll go mad-"

"I do accept her!" Dee protested. "Or at least, I'm trying to. She's the one not accepting me. I offered to let her come out and eat dinner last night, but she refused. I offered to let her sleep on the dog bed, but she just snarled at me!"

Baron made a sound of disquieted confusion, and Dee felt her stomach roll. "Is that bad? Does that mean I'm going to go crazy?"

"I'm really not sure. Up until yesterday, I'd have sworn black and blue that it was impossible to force a conversion on a person, but it seems it was done to you, so maybe we should just play this by ear." That didn't sound promising.

"Okay," she agreed, because really, what else could she do?

"Are there any other questions you have before we start?"

"Um, yes, actually." There were about a thousand, but one in particular was most urgent in her mind. "How many shifters are there in England?" If there was another pack in London, maybe she could start figuring out who had rescued her from the lab.

"There are two packs," Baron said, matter-of-factly. "Us – eighteen of us here – and a group to the north-east called the Grey Watch. We don't tend to associate with them."

"Why not?"

"They don't like us, and we don't like them. They're extremely reclusive. They live in the forest and spend ninety percent of their time in wolf form. Some days I think they'd like to forget they're human at all."

Dee thought that through. "So they don't spend much time in cities, then?"

Baron snorted. "Hardly. Closest they come is dropping into the local village now and then for supplies. They'd rather shoot themselves in the leg before setting foot in a city."

If anything, the news made Dee even more confused. It didn't sound like anyone from this Grey Watch would have come to London, much less have been poking around inside a warehouse lab. But if Baron was right, then that meant that whoever had rescued her came from this house. "Are there no other lone wolves, excuse the pun? People who don't want to join either pack?"

"No. Since the late 1400s, there have only been the two of us. This estate is associated with a larger group known as Il Trosa, or 'The Pack', that spreads all the way across Europe and into Russia. The Grey Watch has their own rules, but they're just as careful to stay hidden. We're both very careful with our recruits, and dissenters are not tolerated."

Interesting. And Dee's immediate conclusion from that stark statement was that... wow... that someone from this house had broken into the lab and saved her, and that Baron didn't know about it. She resolved to keep her mouth shut – at least until she could learn more about what was going on. If her rescuer wanted secrecy, they must have a good reason, and Dee didn't want to inadvertently stab him in the back when he'd risked his life to save hers.

"Anything else?" Baron asked, and Dee meekly shook her head. "All right. Come and sit down on the floor then," he said. "Let's see if we can get your wolf to come out and play."

# CHAPTER SEVEN

Three days later, Dee was reaching the end of her patience. She was sitting cross-legged on a cushion, trying to concentrate on Baron's instructions as he sat outside her cage. "Imagine your limbs changing," he was saying, his tone low and hypnotic. "Your legs getting shorter. Your feet and hands getting smaller."

Dee concentrated, tried to imagine the shift in her own limbs, tried to reach inward to the wolf, asking her to help, but the wolf remained persistently silent, a disdainful huff the only response Dee had gotten from her all morning.

In the past three days, Baron and Caroline had spent hours with her, teaching, meditating, explaining some of the rules of the Den. Dee had tried to remain upbeat in that time, but it was getting hard to stay positive when, by all measures, she'd made absolutely no progress. Baron had even said at one point that if he hadn't seen her shift personally, he would have doubted she had a wolf at all.

In the meantime, she'd tried talking to her wolf, asking about her refusal to come out and eat or meet Baron, and been met with silence or disdain at every turn. But one question she'd asked again and again was what had happened during their shift in the lab. What did the wolf know about their rescuer? Had they met him somewhere in this house?

The replies had ranged from unhelpful to downright baffling. Emotions and scents were the language of the wolf, and she'd bombarded Dee with an onslaught of fear, respect, delight and anticipation, combined with a host of smells that made little sense to Dee. There had been the scent of blood – fairly obvious, after the massacre in the lab, then a smell that Dee could only describe as laundry detergent, then one that smelled like rain, and finally a scent that was undeniably male, sweat and soap mixed with a faint trace of cologne, but nothing that Dee could link to any particular person.

"Imagine your skin changing, fur emerging," Baron was saying, oblivious to Dee's wandering mind, and she made an effort to concentrate. But she felt no change in herself at all, no static, no tingling in her limbs, no blurring of her vision. She let out a huff.

"It's no good," she said flatly. "She won't come out while we're still locked up. She just wants to go outside and run in the forest." That had been the wolf's persistent request throughout the whole three days, images of thick trees, the impression of speed, along with an annoyance that Dee had not delivered on the wide open spaces the wolf had demanded back in London.

"Damn it, Dee, I've told you before, you *are* the wolf. If you can't embrace her wishes as your own, then we're never going to make any progress."

"Okay then," Dee said defiantly, deciding to play this game. Was it her fault if the wolf insisted on being a different person from her? "Then *I* refuse to shift until I get to go outside."

Baron looked at her with dry humour. "Let's try this again," he said in a voice that was patronisingly patient. "Close your eyes. Picture the wolf in your mind…"

Mark sat on the back patio, staring at the plaque on the memorial wall. 'Luke Adams', it read in clear, copper letters. 'Fallen in Battle. Walk with Sirius.'

The wall held dozens of plaques, each paying tribute to members of the Den who had been killed at the hands of the Noturatii. Identical walls were located at every Den across Europe, testament to the continual losses they suffered, and to the growing discontent among some factions that demanded a more strategic plan to ending this war.

Luke had died in wolf form, an honourable death for any shifter, and as his closest friend, Mark had been given the sacred duty of placing his body on the funeral pyre and performing the Chant of Sirius to guide the fallen spirit to the next world. The ritual was supposed to bring peace, but ever since the van had returned that day, Luke's body reverently laid on the back seat and covered with a towel, Mark had felt a deep, aching void in his chest that could not be relieved.

In an underground culture where contact with outsiders was strictly controlled, good friends were hard to come by. But Luke had been just that, sharing Mark's interests and his dark sense of humour, his frustration with the lack of women in the Den and long philosophical discussions on the future of Il Trosa.

His death had done more than rob Mark of a friend. It had also catalysed a lot of other frustrations that had been plaguing him for years, held at bay by Luke's droll wisdom and his ability to distract him from his blacker moods with teasing and beer.

Perhaps that was why he'd become so fixated on Dee. The first time he'd really felt something other than emptiness since that tragic day had been when he'd looked down at her, strapped to the table, and seen her determination to live, the cold steel in her eyes that refused to accept her fate, that refused to die at the hands of these madmen.

She was becoming quite the complication now, not just because she remained a loose end from his illegal explorations, but because she had become something of a permanent fixture in his thoughts. Though he hadn't been able to go down to the cages to see her himself, he'd heard news from the other shifters, from Skip, who took her meals to her, and from Heron, a shifter in her sixties, the longest running member of the estate, who had been spending time with Dee in the cage room. Rumours continued to circulate over whether she was going to go rogue, apparently unable to merge with her wolf, but she was displaying plenty of attitude, arguing with Baron, teasing Silas, and Mark found himself craving each morsel of news about her, an odd obsession that left him both frustrated and fascinated.

But Dee wasn't the only complication left over from the labs. The hard drive he'd stolen from the server was still in his bedroom, and he'd moved it three times, trying to find a better hiding place where no one would accidentally run into it. He'd thought about destroying it, but couldn't quite bring himself to do it. It contained a wealth of information on the Noturatii and their research that could prove priceless to Il Trosa. Unfortunately, handing it over to be analysed meant signing his own death warrant, as there was no reasonable or rational explanation for how he'd come to have the thing that didn't condemn him at the same time.

"Mark! Get in here!" He heard Caroline's shrill voice coming from the kitchen, and he sighed, heading inside to see what the crisis was.

"I need you to take Dee's lunch down to her." Caroline thrust a tray at him, containing a sandwich, a pear, a cup of tea and a bowl of diced meat, and Mark felt a thrill of anticipation at the chance to see Dee again... as well as a cool suspicion about Caroline's motives.

"I'm curious," Mark said, as he took the tray. "Rumour has it that Dee hasn't been able to shift since that day on the stairs. So sending me down there now wouldn't be a little experiment to see if I can draw her wolf out, would it?"

Caroline smiled at him condescendingly. "I don't know what you're talking about."

Mark was in two minds about the situation as he let himself into the basement. As eager as he was to see Dee again, after their meeting on the stairs he'd had no opportunity to talk to her about her wolf and whether she remembered him, or to warn her not to say anything, and he didn't believe Caroline for a moment that this wasn't a test to see how she reacted to him now. Though Dee hadn't said anything to Baron in the last few days, there was no guarantee this stunt wasn't going to provoke the wolf into alerting Dee to his role in the events at the lab.

"Lunchtime," he announced, seeing Baron sitting in front of the cage, Dee sitting on the floor by the bars, and he went to the slot in the wall, sliding the tray inside. Dee was looking better, he was relieved to see. The colour was back in her cheeks, after she'd looked so pale that day on the stairs, and she no longer looked tired and drained.

Unaware of his apprehension, Dee took the tray from him, offering him a brief 'thank you', and pushed a dish with a raw beef bone in it back out the slot. Despite the wolf's refusal to eat, they had continued providing food for her, hopeful that at some point in time, she could be coaxed to emerge.

No reaction from the wolf, and Mark allowed himself a moment's relief. Dee sat down on the bed and started eating her sandwich, while Mark picked up the leftover bone and headed for the door. Okay, so he'd performed the experiment for them, no result, no shift, and now that he was satisfied that Dee was doing better, he was eager to get out of the room before anything unexpected happened.

Dee watched as Mark disappeared around the corner and felt an odd stirring inside herself. There was something startling, something jarringly familiar about watching him leave, about knowing he was about to disappear out the door and up the stairs, and the wolf...

A wave of dizziness took over and Dee was grateful she was already sitting down. She collapsed sideways onto the bed, feeling like her legs were all wrong. Her arms, too, felt odd, too thin and her hands felt numb. And suddenly she wasn't able to breathe properly, her tongue too big, and what the hell was that smell? It was equal parts disgusting and enticing, and she felt nauseous at the same time as her mouth started watering.

And then she noticed Baron. He was standing in a half-crouch, a look of alarm on his face. And Mark was back, she realised with a wave of satisfaction, peering down at her with a concerned look.

She stood up, eager to tell him she was fine, but he seemed a lot taller than he'd been before. She opened her mouth to speak, but the strangest sound came out, part bark, part whine.

Dee froze. Oh hell, she couldn't be... Could she?

# CHAPTER EIGHT

Dee looked down at herself in alarm, only to have her suspicions confirmed. She no longer had hands, but paws, with grey fur and robust claws. She glanced back and saw a tail, thick and fluffy, wagging fiercely. The wolf pushed forward into the front of her mind, stood up on her hind legs and batted her paws against the bars. The movement left Dee dizzy and disoriented, and it seemed safer to retreat a little and let the wolf take control. But not too far, she protested, as the animal pushed forward harder. She wanted to stay and see what the wolf was doing. And, perhaps realising that she didn't mean to take control again just yet, the wolf acquiesced, made room for her... however possible it was to 'make room' when they were just two minds, two consciousnesses.

Baron was saying something, but she couldn't make out the words. And Mark was still there, a metre or so back from the cage, but she wanted him closer! Or perhaps the wolf wanted him closer. The clamour of thoughts in her head was chaotic, and she tried to sort out which were her own, and which belonged to the wolf. She felt something cold and hard and realised the wolf was pushing her face against the bars. Her tail wagged again, one of her paws reaching forward, but Mark was standing back, staring at her with the oddest expression on his face.

Mark had come dashing back into the room at Baron's startled shout, astonished to find Dee in wolf form, eyes locked on him, paws reaching through the bars. Bloody hell. This could get him into big trouble.

"Go to her," Baron ordered, sharp eyes fixed on him. "Let's see what happens next."

What, indeed. Against his better judgement, Mark approached the bars. The wolf whined and reached out a paw again, and Mark couldn't help

43

thinking how odd this all was. This was not the behaviour of a human in wolf form. This was the behaviour of a wolf, dignity be damned, human consciousness far removed. So perhaps Dee herself didn't remember him, but maybe, if the wolf was indeed a separate entity as she had been saying, then the animal side of her did. And he took the time to wonder if Dee was aware of what was going on. In her previous shifts, she'd claimed that she'd simply blacked out, that she had no memory of what had happened during those minutes. Was that still the case now, or would she eventually learn to retain her presence of mind while the wolf was in control?

He reached forward, catching the wolf's paw in his hand, and then leaned in further, reaching through the bars to stroke his hand through the thick fur of her neck. The wolf seemed to grin at him, teeth showing, tongue hanging out in a very convincing canine display of delight.

Dee felt a wave of embarrassment as Mark brushed his hand over her fur. The wolf was front and centre, but she could see, hear, and feel everything the wolf was feeling.

And smell, she realised, a strangely familiar scent filling her nose, of soap and sweat and the faint tingle of cologne.

And when she realised just where she'd smelled that scent before, the shock was enough to make her surge forward, thrusting the wolf out of the way and forcibly returning them to human form.

The wolf snarled at her, a short mental struggle ensuing as they clamoured for control, but this revelation was enough to give Dee the edge, strong as the wolf was.

That was the same scent that the wolf had shown her when she'd asked about the man in the lab. This time, it had been without the cloying stench of blood over the top, and there was no doubt in her mind. Mark had been in the lab. Had saved her life. She picked herself up off the floor, feeling dizzy and nauseous.

Mark and Baron were both peering down at her, Mark looking concerned, Baron looking rather more pleased. "Well, that was interesting," he drawled. He glanced sideways at Mark. "Two shifts, and both of them centred around you. Someone want to tell me what's going on here?"

"I don't know," Dee managed to say, noting Mark's grim expression. By the look on his face, he knew that she'd figured out what he had done, and was none too happy about it. But there was no way she was going to spill his secret now. He'd saved her life, and stabbing him in the back was the last thing she wanted to do. Instead, knowing Baron was waiting for information, she chose to focus on something else entirely. "I stayed conscious that time," she said, not having to fake the excitement in her voice. "I could see what the wolf was seeing. I could feel her emotions. I could smell…" She glanced at Mark. "…everything."

Not at all satisfied with her response, Baron turned his stare onto Mark. "Well?"

"I don't know," Mark said, not taking his eyes off Dee. "Maybe it's something to do with when I was tracking her in London." Damn right it was. But with Baron watching her so closely, Dee wasn't able to give him the slightest signal that she intended to keep his secret. Her silence would have to be enough. Later, though, she was going to have a serious talk with this man.

"You two wouldn't happen to have met before, would you?" Baron asked shrewdly.

Dee shook her head. "No. The first time I saw Mark was the day you brought me here." That, at least, was true, even if it had been much earlier in the day than Baron was aware of. "Why would you even ask that?"

"It wouldn't be the first time a wolf has tried to cheat the system," Baron said, not looking at all convinced by her protestations of innocence. "We have strict rules about who we convert and who we don't. But there are always situations outside the norm, wolves who meet someone, fall in love, want their friend or lover or sister to be converted, even if it's against the rules."

"I didn't *want* this," Dee protested, outraged at the accusation. "I'm locked in a cage, away from my friends, my family, my job. God knows what people will be thinking. They must be frantic with worry. And then you tell me I have to eat raw meat and let the wolf have equal time in this body, and now you think I'm trying to manipulate you? Shit, Baron, you're a real piece of work, you know that?" Dee fell silent, stunned by her own outburst and struggling to maintain her composure. This wasn't like her at all. Normally she was rational, polite, always preferring to negotiate and compromise, rather than hurl accusations and start a confrontation. But now…

She heard a low growl in the back of her mind. *So it's you who's doing this,* she accused the wolf. An impression of bared teeth, raised hackles. *Fine. You want at him, go ahead.*

She was expecting the wave of dizziness this time, retreated just far enough to let the wolf out and then hung around to watch. And was rewarded when Baron leapt back from the cage, her wolf's teeth missing his hand by scant millimetres.

"I think you pissed her off," Mark commented drily, and Dee was startled to find that she could understand him. When Baron had spoken before while she was in wolf form, the words had been nothing but noise.

And this time, instead of pushing her away, she felt the wolf tug her closer. Merging, Baron had called it, and Dee wondered if this was what he meant. She and the wolf wanted different things, certainly, but right now they were both feeling pretty damn annoyed with the man on the other side of the bars, and hell, if this was a girly bonding session, complete with an asshole of a man for them to gripe about, she was all for it. If only she was male, then she could have peed on his shoes.

"Dee?" Baron tried, then swore under his breath. "Do you even understand me? I'm sorry, okay? I know you were kidnapped, and that was a low blow. Come on. I need to talk to Dee. You want to let her back out, Faeydir-Ul?"

The wolf growled one more time, then sat down with a huff. Dee felt herself being pushed forward and was shocked at herself as she hesitated. It was a lot easier to be angry with the man in this form. But the wolf insisted that it needed her to communicate – a wolf couldn't speak human words – and so she gave Dee another shove.

Dee paid more attention to the shift this time, felt her legs lengthen, her jaw retreat, her fingers grow. And rather than lying on the mat, this time when she came back to herself she was sitting up, cross-legged, and wearing a glare that seemed far fiercer than she felt. Baron looked relieved by her reappearance. "What did you call me?" she asked, butting in before he could say anything. Somehow she had the sense that the name had been important.

"Faeydir-Ul. It means Origin-Wolf." At her confused look, he continued. "We have a rich folklore about how the first shifters came to be. Thousands of years ago, it's said that wolves and humans were just learning to work together, to hunt, long before domestic dogs were bred to serve humanity's wishes. Faeydir was a wolf prone to adventures and curiosity, and she used to sneak into the human camps at night to steal their food and listen to their stories. One day she decided she wanted to become a human, to experience life as they lived it, so she summoned all of the magic of her pack and lured a willing human away into the forest – a girl, young, maybe eighteen years old. They exchanged blood, cut their veins and let themselves pour into each other, and Faeydir cast a spell that bound the two of them together. She would be able to spend time in the human's body, while the human could spend time in hers."

"But what Faeydir hadn't realised was that her pack had tricked her." Mark stepped closer, picking up the story, and Dee got the impression that this was a popular ritual in this place, telling stories of their folklore, perhaps around a camp fire. Her wolf liked the image, wagging her tail in her mind. "Faeydir had only wanted to spend a few days as a human, but every time she crept into their camp and stole their food, she risked angering them. And the rest of the wolves knew that the humans were fierce hunters and could easily wipe out the wolves, if they chose to.

"So they warped the spell with their magic. And instead of switching their bodies, Faeydir found that she and the girl had merged into one being, sometimes a human, sometimes a wolf.

"With no body left to return to, Faeydir was unable to return to her pack. A human could not live alone in the forest, so she was forced to live amongst the humans for the rest of her life. She got her wish to be human, but paid a huge price for the privilege."

"But why would you call me that?" Dee asked Baron.

Baron smiled, an amused, but also saddened look. "Legend has it that Faeydir and her human were constantly at war with each other, never able to decide which body to be in, frightening humans with their sudden shifts and fierce behaviour." He shrugged. "It just seemed to fit."

Dee smiled despite herself. "I'm not that fierce."

"But maybe your wolf is." It was said with a hint of fondness, but also a hint of warning. "Well, this poses an interesting problem." He sighed and took his seat again. "As I've said before, for most of us, there's no clear distinction between the human and the wolf. We're conscious of being ourselves in either body. Wolves can travel further on foot. Humans can manipulate objects better with our hands. Wolves have a stronger digestive system and can handle foods that would make a human sick. Humans can climb – fences, trees, whatever. So we look at life through the lens of one united being with two bodies. But let's assume for the moment that you're right about what you've been saying, and you and your wolf are two separate entities." He fell silent, a deep frown on his face as he thought the situation through.

"We can't let a wild wolf roam free about the estate. It's one thing to have humans with wolf bodies running around. They know the rules, they can anticipate problems and make decisions based on human logic. But a real wolf, absent human direction, could make a serious mess of things. So what I need to know is are you able to communicate with her? If you tell her the rules, will she listen to you, or will she run off and do her own thing? Does she even understand that she's living in a human's body half the time?"

Talk about difficult questions. "I don't know," Dee answered honestly. "I can communicate with her, to a degree. She seems to understand some things I say to her, but I have trouble understanding her a lot of the time. She speaks in images and scents, not words, so the translation is... problematic. Maybe with practice, I'll be able to tell you more."

"Hmm." Baron's gaze narrowed a fraction, and Dee had the sudden impression that she'd just walked into a trap. "So has she said anything to you about her apparent fondness for Mark?"

Dee's eyes went automatically to Mark's, and Baron made an appreciative sound. "Ah. So she has. What did she say?"

Dee sighed, trying to look frustrated, even as her mind raced. The best lies, she remembered someone telling her, were based on truth. "She recognises him," she said flatly. "Every time I ask her about him, she gives me a strong image of her wagging her tail. And she knows his scent. But that's as much as I can understand. Like I said, I can keep trying to talk to her, and see if I can work out anything more." It was a simple stall for time, while she figured out what was really going on here, but thankfully, Baron seemed to buy the vague excuse.

"I was tracking you before the van picked you up," Mark said. "Could she have picked up my scent off the street, maybe?"

Clever man. As it stood, Dee had no idea how Baron had found her, or exactly how Mark had been involved after he'd left the lab, but he was trying to feed her information, in the guise of being 'helpful'. "I'll ask her," Dee said, then closed her eyes, feigning concentration, while mentally telling the wolf to stay calm and be quiet. Mark was in danger, she explained, at the wolf's quizzical response, which evoked the immediate reply of an image of a wolf ducking for cover. She didn't want to cause trouble, Dee understood, slightly surprised at how quickly she was picking up on the wolf's moods. "That seems likely," she said, after a moment. "She clearly recognised your scent as being that of a shifter, not a human. Maybe it's as simple as that," she suggested. "Maybe Mark was just the first shifter she discovered after we escaped. Maybe she just wants to make friends with him."

Baron didn't look convinced. But at least for the moment, he seemed willing to let the issue drop. "Well, keep practicing," he said firmly. "And if she tells you anything more, you will let me know?" It wasn't a question, and Dee nodded, hoping she looked sincere, rather than guilty.

"Now, there is something else we need to talk about," Baron said, then glanced at Mark. "Perhaps in private."

Mark nodded, not offended by the clear dismissal. "Of course."

*He's going away now*, Dee told her wolf, backing up the words with the image of Mark heading out the door. She didn't want to risk another impromptu shift just at the moment. But the wolf seemed okay with the idea. She huffed a little and did what Dee assumed was a wolf version of a pout, but that was the extent of the fuss.

Mark excused himself, and moments later, Dee heard the sound of the door closing behind him.

"People will be wondering where you are," Baron said, once it was just the two of them again. "You said you were held in the lab for three, maybe four days. Plus four days here is a week you've been gone. Skip hacked into the police database, and your family has reported you missing."

Dee nodded. Her boss would likely have raised the alarm when she didn't show up for work, and then her mother would have gone over to her flat and found her gone. There would be no sign of a struggle – the men had snatched her off a path in the park where she went jogging. No witnesses, no evidence.

"The longer we leave it, the more difficult it gets," Baron went on. "So we have to figure out what we're going to do."

Dee nodded again, feeling a weight pressing down on her. Over the last few days, both Baron and Caroline had impressed upon her how dire things could get if their unique talents were ever discovered. Historically, the shifters had walked the edge of extinction too many times. The witch hunts of the middle ages were an easy example, the God-fearing righteous terrified of a creature they believed to be of the devil. So she well understood the need for secrecy.

But that left her with no easy answers to her current situation. She couldn't just walk back into her old life – wasn't even sure she wanted to. A tiny flat in central London was no place for a wolf. But neither could she just abandon everything that had been hers. Her friends. Her job. Her belongings. They probably wouldn't even let her go back to collect her things, her hockey medal from high school, the old photo of her cat that hung on the wall above her bed, the dog-eared copy of *Watership Down* that she'd had since she was eight. She'd been planning a holiday to Spain next month with a friend, and she felt a wave of sorrow at the realisation that their trip would most likely never happen. She'd had a career planned out, two more years working as office assistant for a computer company, then the owner had said he'd pay for her to do a marketing course, better qualifications, a pay rise… Long term goals that were rapidly crumbling to dust. The silence stretched on, and Baron made no move to fill it.

Dee stared at the floor, the truth a cold weight in her chest. "I can never go home again. Can I?"

Baron was silent. Then he shook his head.

"You haven't said you're going to kill me, but I can't just wander off back to my old life, so what do I do?" She felt tears pricking at her eyes and blinked them back. "Can I stay here? Do I have to stay here? How long do I have to stay in the cage?" One tear escaped, and she felt her wolf nudge her, a small gesture of concern. "The wolf hates it in here, and… What am I supposed to do?"

Baron was rather quick with his answers, and in hindsight, Dee supposed that they must have had to deal with this sort of thing before. None the less, it was a shock to hear it all laid out so stark and bare and simple. "For the short term at least, you'll stay here. Until you learn to control your wolf, or at least get her to cooperate with you. And you'll stay caged until your shifting becomes a little more predictable. For your own safety, as well as everyone else's." That much, at least, wasn't a great surprise. "As far as your old life is concerned…" Baron hesitated, then gave her an apologetic frown. "For your family's peace of mind, as well as the safety of the Den, I think the best thing we can do is figure out how to fake your death."

# CHAPTER NINE

Dee felt her jaw drop. "Fake my death? That's a crazy idea! How is that supposed to give them peace of mind?"

"Compared to spending the rest of their lives wondering, because no one ever found your body, no murder scene, no explanation for the fact that you simply disappeared into thin air? What we can do is wrap it all up nicely, give them closure by letting them know your 'killer' is also dead, so that they don't waste years chasing some misguided form of justice."

If anything, that only added to her dismay. "So I'm going to be 'murdered', then? It couldn't be a nice old fashioned accidental death? Falling off a cliff? Crashing my car? And you seem to have all the answers prepped and ready to go, so I have to ask, how often do you do this, exactly?"

Baron gave her a wry, apologetic look. "We have a database full of ideas for how it could be done. Lists of the tools needed, synopses for what kind of scenario requires what kind of death – murder, accidental, suicide. We try to keep this sort of thing to a minimum, but when we have to do it, we don't generally have a lot of planning time."

"So what tagged me as murder victim?"

"It has to be something that can be readily identified as you, but that doesn't actually leave a body lying around. Fires and drownings are our favourites for that sort of thing, but since you've already been missing for a week, it's hard to make that kind of 'accident' pop up out of nowhere. A murder, on the other hand? Alistair handles all our PR, so once the scene's set up, he'll drop the appropriate clues to the local news stations, make sure the right people find out about the right details, and the rest takes care of itself."

Dee nodded, starting to feel a little numb at the idea. Or perhaps that was nausea. She had a flood more questions, but no idea where to start, and the desire to protest against this crazy plan, but she had no viable alternative to offer.

"What about my things? My car? My bank account? If I'm dead then my family will inherit everything and I'll have no money."

"The Den will provide everything you need. Everyone is given a monthly allowance. And some of the shifters work part time jobs to earn extra cash. One of the women works as a travel agent. One of the men writes articles for nature magazines."

Dee felt completely overwhelmed, dismayed and lost. "What if my sister has children? I don't get to see them grow up. I don't get to send them birthday cards. This sucks." That was the understatement of the year.

"Yes, you lose your family," Baron said soberly. "But you also inherit a new one. Every single member of this Den would give their life to save yours. You become part of a culture that's six hundred years old and a legacy that can be traced back nearly three thousand years. In ancient Greece, we were revered as gods, and devotees placed gifts at our feet on a daily basis. In ancient Britain, we were worshiped as forest spirits. Most of our history has been far more open and profitable than the way we're currently living. You'll have your eyes opened to the secrets of nature in a way that most people don't even believe exists. There is a heavy price to be paid, I'll give you no argument there. But the rewards are worth the cost."

Dee snorted at the grandiose description. "You make this sound like something out of 'Men in Black'."

Baron grinned, despite the severity of the situation. "It's not so far removed."

Dee tried to smile and wasn't surprised when it came out a little wobbly. "Let me think about it. After all, once I'm 'dead', there's no going back."

"All right. But we're on a time limit here. Like I said, the longer this takes, the harder it gets."


A knock on his door made Jacob look up from his laptop, and he felt his mood lift considerably as he saw Melissa standing in the doorway. Since the massacre at the lab, she had proven herself to be resourceful, intelligent and capable – just the sort of employee he liked best. Of course, they needed their share of ruthless thugs, prone to violence and maliciousness just for the sake of it, as well as a number of the fanatics who would run themselves ragged chasing the slightest, most menial task if they thought it was 'for the cause'.

But the real brains of the organisation – not the intellectual morons who ran the labs and developed the weapons – were people who could strategise, look at the bigger picture, work around obstacles. And Melissa was shaping up rather nicely in that department. The Noturatii was a rather convoluted organisation, funded by more than a dozen governments across the world, under varying guises of anything from 'Science and Research' to 'National Security' to 'Health and Medical Care'. They didn't exist on any official level, and yet politicians and spy organisations from Europe to America to Asia all had fingers in various slices of the pie.

"What have we got?" he asked, trying not to sound too eager.

Melissa didn't waste any time with small talk – another trait he liked about her. "The lab managed to decrypt the files and I've been through Andrews' notes. He had eleven test subjects, including the missing one. The other ten are dead, most of them in the lab's morgue, two of them still on the table. The first four were males. I'll email you the full report on them, but they died almost immediately when they were transfused with the shifter's blood. The females lasted longer. One in particular was interesting, Subject 8. Andrews suspected that he was successful in converting her, but she suffered a cranial haemorrhage shortly after the infusion, so his notes remain inconclusive."

"What about the original shifter captive?"

"Dead. He hung himself in his cell, probably on the same day that the massacre went down. And on that subject…" She stepped forward and handed him a flash drive. With a raised eyebrow, he inserted it into his laptop.

"Miller was right," Melissa told him as they waited for the file to load. "The security videos were stolen. But the neighbouring warehouse has an outside security camera and we asked if we could take a look – told them we'd had a break in and wanted to see if anyone came or went who shouldn't have."

Melissa came around to Jacob's side of the desk and watched over his shoulder. The video was grainy, but when the timer reached 12:13 pm, twenty-three minutes after the last entry in Dr Andrews' notes, a dark blur raced past the camera. Jacob hit pause, then backed up a few seconds, pausing the shot on the misshapen grey object.

"A wolf?" There was no disguising his excitement this time. "The subject survived? And escaped?"

Melissa cocked her head slightly, not a yes, not a no. "The tech lab has enhanced the image, and it could be a common dog, but given the circumstances, they're betting on wolf. But that's not the only thing."

She pressed play again, unfreezing the image, sped through another few minutes and then let the video play. Unmistakable this time, nearly five minutes after the wolf had dashed past the camera…

"Fuck me!" Jacob was on his feet, hands gripping the desk, bent down to peer at the video. A young woman staggered past the camera, dressed in scrubs, looking pained and confused and struggling to stay upright.

"Conclusive proof that the subject survived, I would say," Melissa said smugly. "But that leaves a rather prominent elephant in the room."

Jacob filled in the rhetorical question. "If that was the subject – converted or not, she looked a mess – then who the hell was the wolf?"

"And what was a wolf doing inside a Noturatii lab?" Melissa added.

Jacob's eyes narrowed as the weight of that revelation sank in. "We'll double security," he said after a moment. "Give everyone new access codes. Install iris scanners as well as fingerprint IDs." He looked up at Melissa, a dangerous glint in his eyes. "These wolves are getting far too clever for their own good."

Dee sat on the cot in her cage and stared at the screen of the laptop in shock. When the video finished playing, she hit replay, and watched the macabre scenes from the news channel play out all over again.

She was dead. It was official.

She glanced up at Alistair, sitting on the cot beside her, then over at Baron and Caroline, waiting outside the door of her cage. They'd brought the laptop down to show her the report – less than forty-eight hours after she'd agreed to 'die', a decision based largely on the fact that she had little other choice – and it was on every channel. A small boat had been found floating off the English coast. On the seat and the side rail were smears of blood – her own, thanks to the syringe full that Caroline had carefully extracted from her arm. In the cabin was a set of bloody clothes, the jeans pocket containing a battered driver's licence with her name on it – a perfect replica of the real thing, given that her real one had been lost somewhere in the lab where she'd been held prisoner.

And then there was the dead man found still in the boat. Greg Hinge, a serial rapist and murderer, shot with a gun that was also presumed to have disappeared overboard, along with his latest victim.

It was the perfect set up, even if she was horrified to admit it. According to the news report, she had been kidnapped and likely brutalised, but then she'd apparently fought back, taken Hinge's own gun from him and shot him. And then she had apparently left the boat - speculation was rampant about how and why she might have done so, whether intentionally or having accidentally fallen overboard, perhaps in rough seas – and been drowned as a result.

Dee fought the urge to vomit. "So this 'peace of mind' you spoke of includes me being raped?" she spat at Alistair. "This was supposed to be a story to put my family at ease, a simple shooting, maybe, a mugging gone wrong. Not a kidnapping and rape and who knows what else. And you killed a man! Because of me! That is not what I agreed to!"

"Hinge was a convicted rapist and murderer. I hardly think you need to be carrying a guilty conscience over his death," Caroline said.

"And he was on the run from the police," Dee added, continuing right on with her rant. "So you just happened to find him when the entire British police force couldn't?"

"That was more a lucky break than anything else," Alistair said. "Right place, right time. We do have connections with a number of shady characters – smugglers, thieves, money launderers – you never know when you might need to move something from one place to another. But in this case, no, it was just luck."

"But there are a dozen families out there who will be sleeping easier tonight knowing that he's dead," Baron added, earning a scowl from Dee.

"Too bad *my* family isn't one of them."

"At least they know you fought back in the end," Alistair said, sounding a touch diffident. "That was part of the plan, you know. You shot the bad guy-"

"Save it," Dee snapped, turning away from him in disgust.

With one last guilty glance at her, Alistair picked up the laptop and headed for the door. Dee flinched as it clanged shut behind him. Now she was not only caged, but any chance that someone would come looking for her was gone. She could only hope that what Baron said was true, and that she wouldn't be locked in this cage forever. Otherwise...

"Your family has announced that the funeral will be this weekend," Baron told her gently. "And hopefully now you can see why we tend to recruit loners and misfits. The sad truth is that most of us never had a family, and those of us that did were glad to be rid of them."

"Sucks to be you," Dee said bitterly. "But maybe next time around you could pay a little more attention to the effect your lies have on other people, rather than just whether they fit in with your own plans."

# CHAPTER TEN

**She was lying on the table, strapped down, the scientist looming over her. There was another shifter in the room. Should she kill it? Could she shift and attack these men? Agreement from her human. Yes! A shift! But who to kill? Who was the wolf, and who were the men? Fear, thick and cloying, anger, hate, too many scents, and the smell of disinfectant clogging her nose... she cowered in the corner, trying to find the wolf, not wanting to harm him... a man in the corner, covered in white, golden eyes fixed on her... shifted into wolf form. Leapt for the men. Tore throats out. Blood adding to the cacophony of scent. She stared at the wolf. Golden eyes. Dark fur. Grey ears. Slinking closer as he killed for her... Yes! A scent! Blood everywhere, and a snarl from the male wolf. He was magnificent, powerful, vicious as a wolf should be... but they had to go. Outside. Into the wild forests. Into the open air. The human was needed to escape. Call the human back... girl... wake up...**

Dee jolted awake, startled to find herself sitting bolt upright in bed, her wolf already awake and alert. Her eyes darted around in panic, not quite able to remember where she was, the dream vivid, the memories of the lab far too close for comfort.

The blue light above the door lit just enough of the room for her to make out the cages and the sparse furniture around her, and she sluggishly went to turn on her light. She glanced at the clock, dismayed to see it was only 5 am. But after that little trip down memory lane, sleep held no more appeal for tonight.

Taking deep breaths to steady herself, she splashed cold water on her face, then braced her arms on the sink and closed her eyes, trying to get the images of the lab out of her mind. She hadn't actually killed anyone, she realised belatedly. If the dream was, in fact, Faeydir's memories of the day,

55

then it meant, much to her relief, that she wasn't the murderer she had assumed she was.

In hindsight, the decision to let the wolf kill those men had surprised Dee. She'd always thought of herself as a pacifist, a peacemaker, and yet when she'd been trapped there, between the proverbial rock and the hard place, she'd chosen life, chosen to kill with surprisingly little hesitation.

'If someone tries to take your life, they have forfeited their own.' The statement seemed to come out of nowhere, and yet Dee could remember it being spoken to her as clearly as if it had happened yesterday. Her Grandpa had been a cop, retired by the time Dee was old enough to make sense of his occupation, but that hadn't stopped him from using his skills and knowledge to teach her and her sister how to protect themselves. With their mother's blessing, he'd spend long Saturday afternoons teaching the pair of them to fight, how to see trouble coming and avoid it, and he'd instilled in them a survival instinct that condoned violence, but only if peaceful negotiations had failed. He'd seen too many women beaten by their husbands, he used to tell them, seen too many innocent people lose their lives to thugs to let his granddaughters go through life without understanding the laws of justice and decency. They were never to throw the first punch, he'd always insisted, but then explained that if someone else attacked them first, or broke into their house, then that person had forfeited their right to safety. Grandpa had died when she was twelve, killed in a hit and run accident, but his lessons had apparently sunk in. And it was something of a surprise to look back on that violent episode in the lab and realise that she had no regrets over it. Given the chance over again, given more time to think things through and consider the consequences, Dee realised that she would have made the same decision. The men had tortured her and tried to kill her. So, by Grandpa's logic, they had forfeited their own right to life.

But her actions in the lab were pretty much the only thing she didn't regret, she acknowledged to herself painfully. The rest of her reality was rather stark. Her family and friends thought she was dead. She had a foreign creature in her head, constantly messing with her thoughts and emotions, and she was trapped in a cage for the foreseeable future, with no clear idea of what she needed to do to get out of it. Life was looking pretty grim from where she was standing.

Her breaths started to come in shaky gasps, her arms shaking, her eyes stinging, and before she knew it, the inevitable flood of tears had started, with no sign of abating in the near future.

Mark wandered into the kitchen, heading straight for the coffee pot. He was pouring himself a cup when Caroline appeared at his elbow, and he groaned inwardly as he braced himself for another ear bashing from the alpha female. He'd been in her bad books lately, and no doubt she was here to give him another earful about something or other he'd done wrong. On top of that, he'd dreamed of Luke last night, a vivid fantasy in which they'd been running through the forest, the thick scent of vegetation in his nose, playing, jumping, splashing in a river. It had seemed so real. And then he'd woken up to the cold realisation that Luke was dead and he was never going to see him again. Not the best start to the day, and a run-in with Caroline wasn't going to make it any better.

"I have a favour to ask." Caroline said, not even bothering to say good morning. "I'd like you to go down and talk to Dee."

Mark snorted. Normally, he'd be thrilled at the chance to see Dee again, but after his dream last night, and given that the request was coming from Caroline, his already foul mood simply took another plunge. "Another 'test' to see how her wolf reacts to me? Come on. We already know she's fixated on me, we're no closer to figuring out why, so how about you just let it be."

Caroline hesitated. Unusual for her. "That's not why I want you to go down there. Dee's upset. Skip took her breakfast a little while ago and said she looked like she's been crying for hours."

That sparked a wave of concern in Mark. But he was on thin ice where Dee was concerned, given what she knew about what he'd been doing in the lab, so he opted for an air of indifference. "What's that got to do with me?"

"Well… it can't be easy for her, having to give up her family, her life. And I thought… You went through something similar when you arrived here. So maybe you could talk to her. Make her see that life here has a good side."

Was she serious? But more to the point, why did she care so much? Caroline wasn't known for getting all warm and fuzzy with new recruits. So was this just another test she'd concocted? "You want me to play Agony Aunt to a woman who's had her entire life ripped out from under her and who's only ever met me twice, for a grand total of fifteen minutes?"

"Yes."

Mark sighed and set his cup down. Sometimes, talking to Caroline was like hitting his head against a brick wall. "Fine. I'll talk to her."

Heading down into the basement, he let himself into the cage room, deliberately making some noise about it. If Dee was, in fact, crying, she might like a little warning that she was about to be interrupted, and while a part of him was eager to see her, he didn't want to inadvertently embarrass her in the process.

Sure enough, when he came around the corner she was sitting on her bed, cross legged in a pair of sweatsuit bottoms and trying to discretely wipe her nose on her sleeve. Mark felt his heart lurch at the sight of her. She'd been so strong, the last few days, but the strain was clearly starting to get to her.

"Hey. How are you doing?" he asked gently.

She shrugged. "Bored. And claustrophobic. The whole 'this is for your own good' mantra is starting to wear thin."

"Yeah, I get that." He sighed, considering how to handle this. As much as he would have liked to, he wasn't in anything like a good enough mood to manage the warm and fuzzy route that Caroline seemed to have had in mind. "Listen... Caroline asked me to come and talk to you. She said you were upset."

"You are unbelievable."

It was said with such venom that it stopped Mark in his tracks. "What?"

Dee stood up, came to the bars and pointed a finger at him. "You were in the lab. You rescued me, and Baron doesn't know that, and I've spent the last week trying to pretend I know nothing about it. And then you just ignore me for days, like nothing happened, and then come down here to try and have a chat like it's all hunky dory, no explanation, no apology for sticking me in the middle of someone else's soap opera? Maybe I should just come clean, tell Baron what I know, and-"

"No! You can't!"

"Why not? What have I got to lose? If I tell them I can communicate with my wolf, they might actually let me out of this God forsaken cage."

"If you do, they'll kill me."

That pulled her up short. "As in...?"

"I'm not talking metaphorically, Dee. If they find out, they will execute me."

Dee's hand went to her mouth, shock written all over her. "Oh."

"And I haven't been ignoring you. I've spent the last three days trying to come up with any plausible excuse I can think of to come and see you. But Baron and Caroline are suspicious enough as it is, and I didn't want to draw extra attention to myself."

"Why would they kill you?"

"Breaking into a Noturatii lab without permission is considered an act of treason against Il Trosa."

"Then why the hell did you do it?"

Mark looked down, struggled to find the words to explain. "I was looking for someone."

"Who?"

"It's complicated. And I know this has screwed up your life, but that was never what I intended. I just saw you there, and I couldn't leave you to be killed. I'm sorry it hasn't worked out great for you, but please, don't tell Baron."

Dee stepped back, her anger fading as quickly as it had arrived. "Sorry. I don't blame you for this," she said, her voice small. "You saved my life, and it seemed ungrateful to rat you out without at least knowing why. But what am I supposed to tell Baron? Faeydir thinks you're the best thing since sliced bread, and I don't know how to explain that without giving you away."

"Faeydir? I guess the name stuck, huh?"

Dee shrugged. "She seems to like it."

"Look, the official story is that I came across you running about London after you left the lab and called in a capture squad. So tell Baron that Faeydir picked up my scent somewhere along the way and is just really grateful to have joined a pack of shifters, so she wanted to thank me."

Dee frowned. "That means I was in wolf form outside the lab. And I wasn't. The only time I shifted was before you killed the scientists."

"But Baron doesn't know that."

"What if someone saw me? You can't have a wolf running around the streets without someone noticing."

Mark's mind raced, trying to fit all the pieces of the puzzle into a story that seemed plausible. "The warehouse district is pretty quiet. Particularly in the middle of the day. Maybe you... I don't know... Faeydir led you to where there were more people, and then you turned human again to avoid any problems. Does that work?"

Dee considered the idea. "Yeah. I think I can work with that."

Mark sighed in relief. "So you're not going to tell him the truth?"

Dee shook her head. "No. I owe you too much for that."

"Thank you." They lapsed into silence for a while. Well, that had gone badly. He'd been sent down here to cheer her up, and instead, he was just scrambling about trying to cover his own arse. Some hero he was turning out to be.

"So what was it Caroline wanted you to talk to me about?" Dee asked, after a moment.

Oh yeah. Because this was supposed to be about Dee, after all. "About your family," Mark said awkwardly, not expecting Dee to want a heart to heart after that rather abrupt opening. "And adjusting to living in the Den. When I first came here, I was in a situation a lot like yours, and she thinks hearing about it will help."

Dee frowned at that. "A situation like mine? I thought most people came here willingly. No family, no ties, plenty of psychological trauma."

It was said wryly, and Mark smiled, despite the seriousness of the conversation. "True. I was something of an exception."

Dee sat patiently, waiting for a further explanation, while Mark felt his gut churn. It had been a traumatic period of his life, and given his current dissatisfaction with life in the estate, digging up a lot of old memories was not going to help his frame of mind.

"I had leukaemia," he said, deciding to just cut to the chase. "It started when I was fifteen. I joined Il Trosa when I was seventeen. So, two years of drugs and chemotherapy and hospital visits. All the way through I'd been determined to beat it, no matter how bad it got. But nothing was working. In the end I was stuck in a hospital bed, looking at the very real probability of my own death. At age seventeen. And then one day, this 'pastor' shows up, says he wants to talk to me about 'whether I had considered my future destiny'. I was expecting a lecture on God and heaven and all that, but instead, it was Simon, one of the shifters. He told me there was another option, offered me a new life, health, adventure, mysteries of the sort I could only dream of. But it came with a catch."

"You had to leave your family behind," Dee filled in, and then frowned. "Hold up... you had leukaemia, right? So, what, becoming a shifter is a magical cure for cancer? Publicise that, and you could make a fortune."

Mark shook his head. "It's not so much a cure, as a work around. Canines and humans aren't generally affected by the same diseases. If one side of your physiology is susceptible to a disease, the other half is probably immune to it, and will compensate accordingly. There are a few exceptions – rabies, for example. You should probably get vaccinated for that," he added as an aside. "But in practical terms, it means that shifters are immune to most diseases."

Dee looked fascinated at the news. But then she shook her head, focusing back on the story. "So you accepted his offer? You became a shifter, and left your family to think you'd died, when in fact you'd discovered a miracle cure."

Mark sighed. Nope, this was not the easy-fix solution that Caroline had expected. No surprises there. "They were going to lose me anyway. And I don't mean that as coldly as it sounds. But I was seventeen and I'd had a couple of years to come to terms with my own death. I was going to lose them, they were going to lose me. And then suddenly I was offered a world of blue skies and a strong body and crazy adventures. What seventeen year old wouldn't take it? And without looking too closely at the fine print."

"That comes up later, right?"

"Right. When you're lying in your bed, alone, and thinking that when you're fifty and your sister is forty-five and she's got children, and you've never even seen a picture of them, because all forms of contact with your previous family is forbidden. Yeah, it's the sort of thing that keeps you awake at night." Fuck, this wasn't the way it was supposed to go. He was supposed to be cheering her up, not making her more depressed. "So you've seen the down side, right up front," he went on, determined to make an effort to make this better for her. "But what you haven't seen is all the positives."

"Excuse me for sounding ungrateful here, but even if I was allowed to go outside, what are the perks, exactly? I get to turn into a wolf so that I can sniff who's pissed on which tree and run fast so I can chase rabbits? And spend the rest of my life hoping no one notices, or I might just get shot?"

She had a good point. "In the day to day details, it can be hard to see the big picture. But we can give you two things that most people spend their whole lives searching for. And some people never, ever find. Belonging, and purpose. As a shape shifter, you belong with the Den. And I don't mean that you're obliged to stay here, I mean that you *belong*. You were here less than a day, and Skip lent you her clothes. Caroline lets you stay, despite very real fears that you're a danger to us all, because she feels a certain kinship with you. A wolf in Romania would willingly spend three weeks researching a rare, ancient Greek text for you, for no better reason than that you're a member of Il Trosa. You belong with us, in a way that most people never feel they belong anywhere."

Dee looked sceptical. "I doubt some of your friends feel the same way. Silas refuses to even speak to me when he brings me food."

Mark let out a chuckle. "Yeah. He's a grumpy bastard. But if your life was ever in danger, he'd risk his own to save you without a second thought. He's the most loyal wolf I've ever known."

Dee made a disgruntled sound, her resolve cracking slightly. "And the purpose side of things?"

"Preserving our species. Shifters have always been big on record keeping. We can trace our history back to the ancient Greeks. There were shifters in Britain during the time of the druids, the Picts, the Celts, the Gaels. We had shifter advisors to some of the ancient kings. We have records of historical events that you won't find in any museum or history book anywhere in the world.

"We're suffering from some significant setbacks at the moment, but the Council insists that the shape of the modern world is all the more reason to preserve what we have. Since the technological age began, no one has ever seriously researched the potential of the shifter genome. We could hold the cure for cancer in our DNA. Treatments for devastating diseases. The potential to manipulate matter in ways that physics has never considered. No one really knows how we shift, in scientific terms, or what happens to our bodies when we do, because we've never had the chance to study these things without the risk of someone busting into our labs and shooting us all.

"So *that* is what you're preserving. That is what you can lay claim to, and as a shifter, you are an integral part in passing all that history and potential forward to the next generation."

Dee looked speechless as Mark fell silent. "I guess you have a point after all," she conceded after a moment. "And for what it's worth, you weren't the ones who took my old life away. The Noturatii did that. I could be a little more grateful that you're trying to give me a new one."

"That, at least, is something you have in common with everyone here," Mark acknowledged. "We've all got our own reasons for hating the Noturatii. We've all lost friends and loved ones to the war."

Perhaps he'd just revealed a little too much, as Dee suddenly looked up at him speculatively. "Who did they take from you?" she asked, and Mark felt a new wave of bitterness swamp him. For a moment there, he'd just about believed his own rhetoric on the value of the shifters' lives. But the stark reminder of what he'd lost dragged his mood straight back down again.

"Luke," he said, not looking at her. "About three weeks before you arrived. He was a good friend."

"I'm sorry."

"Yeah. Look, I have things to do, and Baron will be down for your lessons soon." He stood up and turned to leave. "I'm not really sure if that helped," he said as an afterthought, aware that he was leaving things on a rather grim note. "But however tough it gets, just keep in mind that we're all here to help you through it. You're not alone."

# CHAPTER ELEVEN

Melissa was in Jacob's office, standing firmly at attention, waiting for Jacob to finish reading the file on his desk. She'd been called into this office four times in the last few days, to make various reports or recommendations on the findings of the now-dead lab team and how to proceed with the experiments they'd been working on. And in that time, she'd come to respect Jacob's strict, no-nonsense manner, having had little to do with him before this current disaster had happened.

Jacob had been in charge of the British arm of the Noturatii for nearly ten years, and what he had achieved in that time was incredible, the expansion of resources, recruitment of new members, playing politics with the powers that be in order to secure their continued funding. He was something of a legend among the new recruits, and an object of awe even for more seasoned members.

But when he finally finished and closed the folder, Melissa's heart kicked up a notch as she saw her name printed on the cover. Her personal file. Was she in trouble? Had she done something wrong? But before her mind could get too carried away, Jacob spoke.

"I'm putting a team together to take over from where Andrews left off," he said, oblivious to her agitation. "Philip O'Brian is going to be leading it." Perhaps her surprise registered on her face, and Jacob seemed to misunderstand the cause of it. "The man's a wet blanket," he went on, "and a coward, but he's also a brilliant biochemist, and we don't have the luxury of being choosy." He placed a hand over the file, a smug smile on his face. "I'd like you on the team. It says here that you graduated with first class honours in biology. Impressive."

"Thank you, sir," she said, trying to pull herself together. Promoted? But she'd been with the Noturatii for only a single year, and by her own reckoning, she hadn't achieved anything of particular significance in that time.

"O'Brian will be running the trials – we want to see if we can replicate what Andrews did, convert another subject – but I want you in charge of reporting. Make notes, double and triple check everything. You have an eye for detail and a stomach for what is necessary." He looked her in the eye, with a hint of what she might dare to call affection, if she didn't know Jacob better than that. "Don't let me down."

"Thank you, sir," she said, positively glowing at her first real opportunity to contribute to their cause. But... "There is one other thing I'd like to discuss?" she said cautiously, not wanting to rock the boat, but knowing that this was too important to overlook. "I saw a report on the news last night. Subject 11. She's been officially pronounced dead, killed by an escaped serial killer. The story is completely fake. So that means she has to be alive."

"Our team picked up on the story," Jacob told her smoothly. "We're aware of the implications."

"I've done some thinking on how we could track her down," she went on, hoping she wasn't overstepping her bounds. But the idea of recapturing their escapee, yet another abomination they'd accidentally let loose on the world, was both urgent and exhilarating. "The most likely scenario is that she's been taken in by the shifter pack in northern England. I thought perhaps we should start-"

"Melissa." There was no anger in his tone, no reprimand for her distraction from the task at hand. But there was plenty of disapproval, disappointment, even, and Melissa felt the weight of that even more keenly than she would have felt his anger. "Miller and his team are already making enquiries, tracking her possible movements. They're trained soldiers. You're a scientist. Let them do the hunting while you invent miracles in the lab." It was equal parts praise and condescension, and Melissa willed herself not to blush as she was politely put back in her place.

"Yes, sir," she agreed obediently. "I'll start reviewing Andrews' notes right away."

"You have potential, Melissa," Jacob told her, as she headed for the door. "Don't get over-eager. This war has been raging for hundreds of years. It can wait another month or two."

"Yes, sir." She let herself out of his office, careful to close the door gently behind her. But as much as she respected and admired Jacob, she also disagreed with him. There was no time to lose, not one day they could wait while these abominations spread across the country, across the continent. Because with each new day, they could recruit another hapless victim, turn another innocent human being into a demonic perversion. And every single life was a life too many.

Energised by her renewed determination, Melissa headed for the lab.

She would read through Andrews' notes again. Prepare for the experiments to start over. So that when they caught the next wolf, the one they would use as a sire for the new converts they hoped to create... she would be ready.

Jacob had barely turned back to the report he was writing when there was another knock at the door, and Jack Miller stepped inside.

"You have news?"

Miller snapped a crisp salute – an old habit from his army days, though no one in the Noturatii had ever asked it of him. But then he hesitated before speaking. Unusual for him. "I do, sir. But there was also something else I wanted to mention."

"Go on."

"Let me firstly reiterate that I have the utmost respect for your abilities and insight into our cause. But in light of the recent breach in security, I have serious doubts about the wisdom of continuing to operate the lab here." Jacob didn't reply, which Miller took as leave to continue. "I realise that you've increased security, but the shifters know the location of this lab. And given the state of play between us, it can only be a matter of time before they return."

"You're absolutely right," Jacob agreed. "Our security systems were substandard, our guards were not adequately prepared, and the shifters are well known for being tenacious bastards. But to simply give up our position here would be overlooking an important opportunity."

"Sir?"

"Have you ever heard of the Satva Khuli?"

Miller was instantly on guard. Good. He had, then. "I've heard the term."

"What do you know of them?"

"Nothing, save a few rumours. It loosely translates as 'Blood Tigers'. Most people believe they're nothing more than stories told to keep Noturatii members in line. But they actually exist, then?"

"They do." The Satva Khuli were an elite branch of assassins, selected as young children and trained their whole lives to become the Noturatii's last, and most deadly line of defence. They were single minded, unencumbered by moral concerns and were taught from an early age to embrace the thrill of the hunt, the satisfaction of a kill. Few in the Noturatii had ever met one – and lived to tell about it – and they usually worked as lone operatives, hunting down rogue shifters or Noturatii members who had betrayed their cause. Their abilities were rumoured to border on the supernatural, and given the nature of their enemies, Jacob wasn't entirely convinced that was a bad thing. "I've contacted Headquarters in Germany. They were understandably disappointed with our recent losses, but they're eager to help advance the progress we've made. So they're sending one of the Khuli to join us."

Miller didn't reply, and beneath his carefully neutral expression, Jacob saw a tremor of fear – such was the reputation of the Khuli, that even a battle-hardened soldier like Miller should fear them.

"The shifters will return to this lab," Jacob went on, "either to burn it down, or to steal what secrets we've learned about them. It might take them weeks, months, or even years. But they will come back." Jacob allowed himself a grim smile, already imagining the bloodshed to come. "And when they do, the Khuli will be here. She's bringing a squad of assassins that she's trained personally. They will be our new security force."

"And what about the risk that they might murder us all in our sleep?" Miller blurted out. It was unusual for him to be so rattled.

Jacob laughed. "No guarantees. But that's half the fun, isn't it?"

Miller swallowed. "If you say so, sir."

"Now," Jacob went on, completely ignoring the soldier's disquiet. "What was this news you were coming to tell me?"

Miller pulled himself together quickly. "One of our informants in the police force sent through a report, sir. There's a lot of noise in the feed, so it took us a while to take notice of this one. About a week ago, a woman was snatched off a busy London street. She was described as small, brunette, wearing 'those green hospital clothes' and covered in blood. The witness was worried she was injured, and said she was taken by a large man in a white Ford Transit van. We ran the plates, and they're registered to a small blue sedan, to an owner in Cornwall."

"Our convert?" It was the first real lead they'd had on the woman.

"Can't guarantee it's her, sir," Miller replied predictably, never one to leap before testing the water depth. "But given the location she was spotted, it would be a good bet. North and slightly west of the warehouse district."

"And the van?"

"We're tracking it. Checking traffic monitoring cameras, CCTV, anything we can get our hands on."

"If you don't come up with anything useful, put out a news report. Girl gets kidnapped off the streets in broad daylight? Someone must have seen something useful. This girl is the greatest breakthrough the Noturatii has seen in years. I want her found."


Baron sat in the manor's expansive IT office, watching the video feed of the cages. The room was dim, one wall taken up with screens, some monitoring areas of the estate, some showing a continuous feed of the news channels, others connected to the computers, the nerve centre of Skip and Alistair's scheming and plotting. Three of the most powerful, most up-to-date computers money could buy sat on a shelf, processing data, running internet searches, monitoring the news for key words that would alert them to a breach in security, the need for Alistair to invent a story to cover their collective arses. In years gone by, most mistakes by the shifters could be dismissed as superstition, discredited with a little simple science. But now that everyone's phone was also a video camera, now that CCTV was everywhere and information travelled at the speed of light, they were forced to counter the outpouring of technology with a barrage of their own.

But for today, there was only one screen that Baron was interested in. On the screen that showed the cage room, the camera was zoomed in on Dee, and as he watched, she shifted into a wolf. It was a smooth transition, the crackle of electricity minimal, a rolling wave that started at her head and flowed back over her body. Once she was in wolf form, she pranced about a little, as if checking that each part of her body worked, glanced back to check on her own tail – eliciting a chuckle from Baron. Many a new convert had spent hours trying to figure their tails out, the appendage almost like an extra limb that the human mind had no immediate analogue for, with some falling into the trap of turning in circles again and again, trying to get a better look at it. And then being mortified as they realised that they'd been caught literally chasing their tails.

Dee didn't go quite that far, but she was certainly finding the thing disconcerting, and he wondered what kind of conversations she was having with her wolf about it.

And then, satisfied that everything was where it should be, she would shift back into a human, only to repeat the exercise again and again.

The door behind him opened and Caroline stuck her head in, then came all the way in when she saw what he was doing. She stood beside him, watching the video over his shoulder.

"Seems like she's got it down pat," Caroline said, after a minute or two.

"In private, yes," Baron agreed. It was for this very reason that new converts weren't told about the cameras. Knowing that they were being watched led to a universal case of camera shyness that had prevented new shifters from practising their shifting, stage fright leaving them self conscious and stunting their development.

"She still maintains that she and the wolf are separate entities?"

"That's right." Baron watched the video for a moment longer, then turned to face Caroline. "I'd like to let her out of the cage," he said without preamble. Actually, he wanted nothing of the sort, but a heated conversation earlier that day had left him with little choice but to suggest the idea. And to push for it, if necessary.

"She can't control her shifting, and she hasn't merged with the wolf,"

Caroline replied immediately. "It's too soon."

"She's been caged for nearly two weeks. She's not showing any signs of aggression or mental deterioration, she's learned to communicate with the wolf, and she's got a serious case of cabin fever."

Caroline raised an eyebrow. "Two weeks isn't overly long. You were caged for three weeks when you were converted." He must have looked offended, Baron realised, as Caroline's expression grew suddenly defensive. "What? I'm not saying that as a criticism. It's just a fact. Ergo, two weeks for an untrained lab-bred stray isn't too long."

Baron rolled his eyes. "All right, let's assume for the moment that her situation, however odd, isn't going to change," he suggested. "All indications are that, by some bizarre quirk of nature, she's not one person, but two. If that is the case, then what do you need her to do to prove that she's not a threat to the Den? That she's not going to go mad?"

"It's not about her going mad, at this stage," Caroline said. "If she was going to do that, we'd have seen signs of it by now. What I'm worried about is her wolf getting out of control. Okay, she can communicate with it, but she has no control over it. She's said as much herself. What if we let Dee out, she takes a walk down the road and shifts in front of the local farmers? Can you imagine the chaos and panic that would cause? The trouble with the Council? They could shut our whole Den down. What I want to see is some proof that she can control her shifts, some kind of assurance that her wolf isn't going to run off at a moment's notice and accidentally destroy our entire species."

"I'm not talking about letting her loose on the general public," Baron said. "But the wolf keeps insisting it wants to go outside. So we secure the grounds, lock the gates, and take her outside. See how the wolf reacts. If she can control it, great. If she can't, then we either cage her again, or if we're really lucky, we might stumble on a clue that will help her figure it all out. Either way, we're making very little progress the way things are."

Caroline didn't look convinced. "But if she does get out of control, we still have to catch her again. Most converts have years of training. They know the rules. They know what to do if they get into trouble-"

"But not all of them. Look at Mark. He didn't have years. He only had a couple of weeks to live until the leukaemia would have killed him. He had a week's training while he was lying in a hospital bed, and then suddenly he's a wolf, roaming the estate."

"And I wasn't alpha then," Caroline said sharply. "Just because it worked once doesn't make it a good idea."

"So, what, then? You're going to keep her in the cage for two years until she's finished her training?"

Caroline rolled her eyes at him, then went back to watching the screen. "Fine," she said finally. "But I want Silas out there with a tranquiliser gun and sentries at every gate. If she gets loose, it's all of our heads on the chopping block."

Baron turned back to the video feed. "I totally agree about the guards. And Tank and I will stay with her at all times. I don't want this going wrong any more than you do."

The door burst open, and Alistair rushed in, pulling up short when he saw the two of them standing there. And then he darted forward, switched on a lamp and plonked himself in one of the chairs in front of the computers.

"Sorry to interrupt, folks, but you're going to want to see this."

The main screen on the wall sprang to life, showing a news story that made Baron curse blackly and want to stab something.

"Police are asking for witnesses to a suspected kidnapping which occurred in London nearly two weeks ago," the newsreader was saying. "Investigations of preliminary leads have failed to yield results, and so now police are appealing to the public. Early reports state that a woman dressed in green hospital scrubs, with short brown hair was snatched off the streets around midday on the fifteenth, by a large man with dark hair. She was pulled into a white Ford Transit van. If you saw this attack, or have any information about this woman, please call the number at the bottom of the screen."

"Fuck!" Baron leapt up from his chair, causing the thing to sway dangerously.

"I'm already on it," Alistair said. "I'm going to need Skip up here. I've had a counter-story ready to go since Dee arrived. Shouldn't take more than two or three hours to get this wrapped up."

"You're a godsend," Baron said, equal parts relieved and infuriated. "Keep me updated. I want this sorted fast."

"You got it, boss. Just leave everything to me."

# CHAPTER TWELVE

"So you're saying these samples are completely useless?" Melissa glared at Phil, daring him to confirm what he'd just suggested. Two weeks after the disaster in the lab, they were back in operation, preparing and setting up for the next round of experiments. Among their other resources, they had discovered three pints of shifter blood stored in their fridge, enough for three more experiments. Or so she'd thought.

"The compounds unique to shifter biochemistry begin to break down less than half an hour after the sample is taken. Infusing a new subject with these samples would have no more effect than using regular human blood," Phil told her, peering at her over the top of a pair of spectacles, and out from underneath bushy eyebrows.

"Or it might just give them a case of blood poisoning," another scientist suggested, as grey and timid as the infamous Phil. What was his name again? Tom? Terry?

In total there were five scientists on the new team, the other two being a younger man and a woman in her forties called Linda who was more doctor than scientist. It was her job to keep the subjects alive long enough for them to be experimented on – a role that had been sadly overlooked by the last team. At least two of the deaths that had occurred in Andrews' experiments could have been prevented by appropriate monitoring of the subjects' vital signs during the infusions. If they'd been kept alive long enough for them to assess the results, then the team could be leaps and bounds ahead of where they were now, which was largely stumbling about in the dark.

"We still haven't learned how to use the machine Andrews invented," Tony said. Was it Tony? "We can create an electric field within the shielding, but we can't work out how the blood was fed in-"

"So the only way we can run more experiments is to capture another

70

shifter?" Melissa interrupted, trying to keep on track. Let these boffins start talking, and they'd be at it all day.

Phil nodded. "That's correct."

"Fuck." Melissa breathed the word softly. She was torn, equal parts impatient task master and respectful student. It had taken her only two days to realise why Jacob had assigned Phil to run this show. Because, despite the man's bumbling ways, he seemed to actually be something of a genius when it came to biochemistry. He'd deciphered Andrews notes, understanding nuances and details that had escaped Melissa, and had been the one to discover the necessity of the machine – the shock chamber, they were calling it – to apply an electric current across the mixture of shifter and human blood before the blood was infused back into the human's veins. That was the gist of the last experiment Andrews had done, the one that had been successful on subject 11.

But now the progress seemed to have ground to a halt as Tony tried to get the damn machine working again, and Melissa had gone in search of other avenues, preparing their supplies and equipment for their next subject.

"The German office called this morning," Linda told her, looking up from her charts and print outs. "The shifters have all gone to ground. Since we kidnapped the last one, it's like they've all vanished. We're going to have to search further afield if we want to catch a new one."

"How far afield?"

"Eastern Europe. Romania. Russia, maybe."

"Takes time to move a shifter that far," Melissa griped. Thanks to the Noturatii's long reach and plentiful resources, it was usually possible to move a shifter between countries without getting caught up with border security, but pulling that kind of manoeuvre took time, and paperwork. Lots and lots of paperwork.

"That's the damn security measures for you," Phil complained, tapping notes into a laptop. "Security cards for this, finger prints for that, iris scans, passwords. I met some poor sod at the door the other day as I was leaving. He'd forgotten his passcode and couldn't get in. And it takes three days to get issued a new one. That's how long it took me last time I forgot it. I saved the poor guy the bother this time. Who knows when it's going to be you next, right?"

Melissa looked up from her work. "Hang on… you're saying you let some random stranger into the building?"

"No! I checked his security card first," Phil said, sounding offended. "I'm not stupid enough to let just anyone in."

"What day was this?"

"Hmm… the fifteenth, I think it was. The day we had all that rain in the night. Unpleasant weather."

Melissa opened her mouth to call the man twelve kinds of idiot – that was the same day the science team had been killed, and she'd bet a year's salary that the 'forgetful' worker was in fact the shifter-spy who had wrecked such havoc.

But a moment later, she reconsidered her first impulse and closed her mouth. Turned back to her laptop and pretended to concentrate on the screen. Now what was she supposed to do?

On one hand, it was simple. The man had screwed up, and that should be reported. Jacob had no patience for this kind of stupidity, and rightly so. Losing Andrews had set their research back weeks, if not months.

But on the other hand, Phil was now the crux of this new team, the most senior and most knowledgeable of all their scientists. And if his mistake was known, he would almost certainly be removed from the project. After which, he would conveniently 'disappear'. But without him, they would be hard pressed to recreate Andrews' experiments. In their quest to undo this hideous mistake of nature, someone had finally come up with the idea that to know how to un-make a shifter, they first needed to know how to make one. And the race to start their experiments had begun.

Melissa's primary goal, the reason she had joined the Noturatii in the first place, was to stop these creatures from existing. So sabotaging the best and most promising chance they'd had in a decade or more made little sense to the ultimate goal.

Damn. She'd have to let it lie for now. This project was too important. If Jacob found out some other way, then so be it, but for the moment, she was going to keep her mouth shut. At least until she learned more from Phil about how these experiments worked.

"Speaking of Head Office," Phil piped up again. "Have you heard the news?"

Melissa had, a cold wave of fear spreading through her as she remembered it. "They're sending an assassin," she said, trying to sound unconcerned. As the youngest and newest member of this team, the last thing she wanted to do was come across as a wet weakling.

"The Satva Khuli?" Linda said it in a whisper, as if the notorious killer was likely to leap out from behind a cabinet, summoned by the mere mention of her name. "They're sending a Tiger to guard the lab."

"Insanity," Tony muttered, fiddling with the shock chamber. "The Khuli are insane. The last thing we need is one running around the lab. It'll be like having a live cobra roaming the place."

"They're on our side, though," Melissa pointed out, putting her hands in her lap so they wouldn't shake. "It's not like she's going to kill *us*, right?"

Four sceptical stares met her gaze. "Keep telling yourself that, sweetie," Linda said, her voice low. "The Khuli are the ones sent to kill operatives who betray the Noturatii. They have no loyalty, make no distinction between friend or foe. Tony's right. I'd sooner trust a live cobra than a Khuli."

Melissa turned back to her work, trying not to let herself be rattled by the news. Half of what these twits said was likely to be nothing more than rumour and superstition anyway. Jacob was a capable leader and a keen strategist. There was no way he'd bring in a Khuli if it was going to pose a threat to his team. After all, he saw the vital need for their work to be completed, was as committed to this war as any of them. Wasn't he?

"I'm sick of being in this cage!" Dee complained loudly, as Baron came into the cage room. "I feel like I'm turning into a vampire down here. I want to see some sunlight! Breathe the fresh air. Go for a run in the wet grass like I'm a cheetah on the Serengeti." She was lying on her bed, head hanging over the side, and delivered her complaint with all the melodrama of a fifteen year old in a high school play.

Baron merely cocked an eyebrow at her as he arrived in front of her cage. He glanced down at the bowl of meat on the floor. Despite bringing fresh food for the wolf each day, Faeydir had never once touched it. "So you still haven't convinced Her Majesty to eat anything?"

Dee huffed out an exaggerated sigh. She clambered around until she was upright and rolled her eyes at Baron. "She doesn't want it. She says the dog bowl is insulting."

"Would she rather I tip the food straight on the floor?"

Dee sent that mental picture to the wolf, and received a clear image in reply. "Firstly, she now wants to piss on your shoes. But food-wise, she says she'd rather eat something she dug up in the back yard." Dee caught a whiff of scent, and winced. "Apparently a rather old something, if I'm reading this right." She'd barely noticed that Baron had retrieved the key and unlocked the door until he propped it open and stepped back. Dee looked at him in confusion. "What...?"

"A small reprieve. Caroline has agreed to let you go for a run. But there are some rules to follow," he added, before she could get too excited. "You're allowed around the estate, but not past the gates. They're all shut and locked, but don't go getting any ideas. Once we reach the lawn I want you to wait three full minutes before you shift. Tell that to your wolf, because if you shift before that, you're going straight back in the cage."

"Why three minutes? I'm not arguing," Dee added hastily, seeing Baron's grim expression. "I just want to understand what you expect of me."

"Caroline wants to know that you have at least a rudimentary control over the shift. Your wolf can go out, but only on our terms. That's the deal."

Dee nodded. She turned her thoughts inward and tried to convey the details of it all to the wolf.

"Silas will be tracking you," Baron went on, "and he has a tranquiliser gun. He'll only use it if it's absolutely necessary. And the rest of the Den is out and about. Some of them are there to guide you, some to stop you if you cause trouble. So tell Faeydir she's going to have company out there."

The wolf seemed happy with the idea, replying with a tail wag as Dee sent her the image of other wolves running alongside her. She made sure to include a big black wolf in the picture, certain that Baron wasn't going to let her out of his sight.

When they emerged through the hidden door into the sitting room, Tank was waiting just outside, along with Caroline and two wolves. Dee hadn't paid much attention to this room the last time she had been here, just after she'd arrived on the estate, and she took the time to look around now. It was roughly square, furnished with antique sofas, wooden side tables and thick, gold coloured curtains. A large fireplace set into one wall gave the room a rustic, homey feel, and along the walls, bookshelves were filled with books, statuettes and vases. It was like an antique showroom, beautiful and elegant yet still retaining a warm, welcoming feel.

As Baron closed the door behind them, Caroline folded her arms and glared at her. "Baron's explained the rules?"

"Yes."

"We're largely going to let the wolf do her thing this time around. No time limits, no restrictions on your behaviour. The basic rules are don't try to escape, and don't start any fights, but that's it."

"Let's get this show on the road, then," Baron said, and led the way out of the room. The foyer was expansive, with a hardwood floor, Victorian chandeliers, gold rimmed mirrors on the walls. The front door was made of thick wood, a rustic design that perfectly suited the antique décor. Outside, stairs led down to a gravel drive, a sweeping arc that disappeared around the side of the manor, and to Dee's delight, she saw there was a formal garden on either side – potted flowers and herbs, low shrubs, coloured pavers and a fountain with stone statues around it.

And then further on past the driveway was a wide lawn than ended abruptly where a thick forest began. Ferns and creepers clogged the understory, the forest itself made up of tall elms, thick oak trees, hawthorn and holly, hazel forming impenetrable barriers in places. A hotbed of mystery and delight for one wanting to express the wilder side of themselves.

As she followed Baron down the stairs and across the drive, she felt her nose tingle in the cooler air. Autumn was well underway, turning the leaves yellow and orange and lending the estate a rather desolate air.

A small crowd was gathered on the lawn, both humans and wolves, and

Dee felt her face warm, aware that she was the centre of attention for the moment, and wishing she could downplay whatever it was that was about to happen. She had the sneaking suspicion that some of the people were not there because of security concerns, but out of simple curiosity, and she wondered exactly what they had been told about her.

She glanced at Baron, to find him checking his watch. Three minutes. They headed further out onto the grass, a strong sense of anticipation rising in her. Caroline and Tank had joined them, extra guards to keep her under control, no doubt, though in all honesty, Dee didn't mind the extra company.

To pass the time, she turned around and looked the manor over. Three storeys high, it was built of grey stone, chimneys rising elegantly from the roof, light shining from behind some of the square windows in a way that made it look warm and inviting.

A slight movement caught her attention, and she noticed a young man, hardly more than a boy, actually, standing near the group of restless shifters, but not daring to get too close to them. He was thin, weedy, arms wrapped around himself as he looked nervous and out of place. A human who hadn't been converted yet, she wondered? Faeydir caught the direction of her attention and Dee felt her reaching out, sensing the boy... Nope, he was a shifter, Faeydir informed her firmly.

Baron stepped into her line of sight suddenly, and she glanced up at him, wondering if her time was up... but the cold glare on his face pulled her up short.

"Sorry," Dee apologised, not even knowing what she was apologising for. "Did I do something-"

"John's not your business," Baron said darkly, putting a hand on her shoulder and gently pushing her in the other direction. "You just focus on yourself for the time being."

"How much longer?"

"Thirty seconds."

It seemed much longer, as the seconds ticked by, and she waited nervously, hoping that Faeydir would wait the allotted time without causing a fuss.

"Time's up."

Dee breathed a sigh of relief and gave Faeydir a mental nudge. Time to go running.

The wolf, true to form, however, had her own agenda, and as Dee retreated a little, prepared to give the wolf the freedom she craved, she was startled and dismayed as absolutely nothing happened.

"Well?" Baron asked after a moment. "You can shift now."

"I would," Dee said, embarrassed and concerned. "But Faeydir won't come out."

Baron gave her a look of pure disbelief. "Why not?"

Dee showed Faeydir another image of themselves, running through the forest, wolves beside them... And the wolf returned a swift image in reply. A large, beautiful grey wolf with golden eyes, running right beside her. *Who?* Dee asked, not recognising the animal. Faeydir showed her another image. Mark, eyes golden and watchful, who then shifted into the wolf she had shown her.

"Oh, you've got to be kidding!" Dee said out loud. This obsession with the man was going to get them both into trouble.

"What?" Baron asked, more curious than annoyed.

"She wants Mark to come running with us," Dee said, feeling even more embarrassed.

"She's fairly intent on getting her own way, isn't she?"

Dee threw her hands up in defeat. "I'm sorry. I'm trying to reason with her. But she's flatly refusing to come out unless Mark comes for a run." She scolded the wolf mentally, showing her an image of the cage. She sensed Faeydir putting her ears back, a soft whine in her mind, an apology of sorts, but the faint image of Mark came up again, accompanied by a hopeful wag of her tail.

"All right," Baron said with a sigh. "In the interests of actually getting somewhere today..." He glanced around the group of shifters and spotted Mark. "Mark! Get over here."

Dee smiled at him as he headed over, but the smile faded quickly when she saw the expression on his face. Dark, grim and brooding, and she was suddenly dismayed at Faeydir's request. Maybe he didn't want to see her again?

"You're running with us," Baron said, a command, not a request. Mark looked completely baffled.

"Faeydir wants you to come," Dee said apologetically. "She's being a little stubborn about it."

Strangely, Mark's mood seemed to improve at the news. "Okay. Yeah, if you think that'll help."

Baron looked satisfied. "Now, is there anything else your precious wolf wants-?"

Faeydir wasted no more time, not even to let Baron finish the sentence, and she surged forward in Dee's mind. Dee retreated, gave the wolf room and embraced the rush of electricity through her body.

Faeydir paused once she was in her wolf form. Shook herself all over. Waited a moment longer while the four wolves around her took form.

And then she took off.

# CHAPTER THIRTEEN

Mark had been surprised when he'd been ordered to accompany Dee on her run. He'd been in a foul mood, an idle glance at the calendar this morning reminding him that today would have been Luke's birthday, so when he was told that today was the day Dee would finally be let out of the cage – on a trial run only, it had been emphasised – he'd found himself unable to summon even the most rudimentary enthusiasm. And then he'd been called over to her, expecting that Baron was about to send him on another useless errand, or tell him to go back inside so as not to distract Faeydir with his presence. So the invitation to join the run had been a pleasant surprise.

Given Faeydir's past behaviour, Mark had been expecting the unexpected where she was concerned, so when she took off, he was ready, following on powerful limbs with a long stride that easily kept up with the smaller female.

Baron, Caroline and Tank were right beside him, keeping pace as Faeydir set off on a sprint, tongue lolling, seeming to enjoy the freedom in a way that had even Mark finding a measure of joy in it.

At the start, the more experienced wolves simply let her run, knowing she'd been locked up for a long time and needed to let off a little steam. A sly check over her shoulder, and the wolf slowed, invigorated by the first mad dash, and perhaps ready to look around at a more sedate pace-

She darted right suddenly, under a bush, and her four guards followed, razor sharp reflexes responding in a split second. Over a rock. Under a fallen log. And Mark didn't start to worry until they reached a clearing, and Faeydir led them in a flat out sprint across the open space. His feet scrambled on the loose litter as she changed direction again, and beside him, he heard Baron growl. She was trying to lose them! There was going to be hell to pay if she escaped. She was already gaining a significant lead, and when she disappeared into a thick stand of bracken, he was forced to slow, following her by scent and sound, until he burst out the far side...

Faeydir was nowhere to be seen. Caroline charged into the clearing, nose to the ground-

Faeydir leapt out of a hollow log, skidding to a halt scant inches from Mark, and he turned on her instinctively, teeth bared, prepared for an attack...

Faeydir spun and leapt away again, racing back towards the log and leaping up on top of it. Down onto a rock. Back over to Mark, shoulders bent low, tail up and wagging. And he suddenly had to rethink his entire take on the run. She wasn't escaping. She was... playing!

Faeydir whined another invitation, then she was off again, darting around Baron, racing past a growling Caroline, and barrelled right into Tank, who seemed to have caught onto her game. He rolled with her, regained his feet and lightly nipped her flank as she shot past him, then gave chase.

Mark let out a huff and realised his tail was already up and wagging. If he was human, he would have been grinning from ear to ear right now. And why the hell not? The simple joy of the game surprised him, lifting him out of his darker mood, and he took off after Faeydir, took a short cut and surprised her by leaping out from behind a boulder, right in her path. She skidded to a halt, looking as startled as he had hoped... and then darted off again.

She led them on a merry chase, through a stream, up the hill, then found a tall outcrop of rock. She leapt up on top of it, panting, and looked around as the rest of them caught up, gathered at the base of the rock. Baron and Caroline had both refused the game, merely keeping pace and tolerating her mischief, and now that she had decided to play 'king of the castle,' Caroline was looking less pleased than ever. She took a step forward, and Mark knew that that was exactly what Faeydir wanted, a last ditch attempt at getting the sombre, grumpy wolf to play.

Caroline wouldn't take the bait, though, and merely growled, hackles up, tail high. Deprived of a playmate, Faeydir cocked her head, sniffed the air... and then threw her head back and let out a spine-tingling howl-

Baron charged into her at full speed, toppling her off the rock. She landed in a tangle of limbs, her fall only partly cushioned by the thick bed of leaves, and Mark dashed forward, knowing she wouldn't understand her mistake.

One of the firm rules of the Den was 'No Howling.' While dogs were known to howl and an occasional slip would be dismissed by the neighbours as simply a domestic pet, the risk on the estate was that one wolf howling tended to encourage all the rest, regardless of their discipline and training, and there was little explanation for a dozen full-throated wolf howls echoing across the landscape.

But, new as she was to the Den, no one had remembered to tell Dee.

Baron leapt down from the rock and circled around the fallen wolf... and Mark charged between him and Faeydir. Acting on pure instinct, he bared his teeth and let out a long, low growl, while at the same time wondering what the hell he was doing. As alpha, Baron had the right to discipline the rest of the wolves, and the responsibility to protect them from mistakes, but all Mark felt was the undeniable need to protect Dee from his attack. It was an act of pure lunacy – he couldn't best Baron in a fight, and blocking him was an act of insubordination. But it was the same instinct that had had him killing scientists in the lab and thinking up excuses to visit Dee in the cages, and it was as relentless now as it had been then. He was aware that his body language was a mess of contradictions, tail tucked, ears flat back despite his challenge to the alpha – an all too clear indication that he was uneasy about going up against the lead male of their pack. But the need to protect Dee was stronger, and he stood his ground, waiting for Baron's reaction.

Which came in the form of a deep growl, bared teeth, a move towards him, and Mark took a step back, preparing himself for a fight.

Faeydir rose cautiously to her feet, keeping her head low, her tail down, and edged towards Baron, clearly taking the submissive route. It was entirely appropriate, the type of exchange that might happen a dozen times a day between various pack members of different rank, but something about it rankled Mark now, something that rebelled against seeing her acting so submissive. But then she nudged his shoulder, a whine in her throat, and slunk past him. Keeping her body low, she approached Baron and lay down at his feet, a clear surrender, an attempt to appease the dominant member of the pack.

Baron's growl faded away. He stood a moment longer, then turned his back on her and walked away. Faeydir sat up and Mark couldn't help but give her a cursory sniff, checking whether she was injured. There was no scent of blood, no sign of pain when he nudged her gently with his nose. She rose to her feet, rubbed her head briefly against his shoulder, then moved further into the clearing after Baron. The alpha male had apparently decided they'd had enough for one day, and he turned towards the manor, gave a huff that was part irritation, part command, and then headed back through the undergrowth. Playtime was over.

Dee fell in behind him, Mark immediately behind her, while Caroline and Tank spread out on either side of them. There would be consequences for this later, he knew, both for his own actions, and for Dee's. And questions about why he would dare to get in Baron's way over what was really a minor incident.

And now that the heat of the moment was over, Mark didn't have a clue what he'd been thinking. He had no business butting in the way he had. All he knew was that something about Dee brought out a protective urge in him that would not be refused.

Dee was aware of her wolf arriving back at the manor, and pressed herself forward, anticipating the need to shift, to give a report on the outing.

Baron led the way along the drive to the base of the stairs. Caroline shifted before she'd even stopped, a seamless change in which one stride was on grey paws and the next was on black boots. Dee found herself envying her skill. There were still times when she had trouble keeping her balance after a shift, even when she was standing still. Tank and Mark followed suit, and Dee was just gathering herself for her own shift when Caroline seemed to run out of patience.

"Dee? Human form. Now."

Sheesh, Dee thought, registering a wave of irritation from Faeydir. The wolf was inclined to stay, just to piss the woman off, until Dee reminded her of the cage that was waiting for them both. And then Faeydir thrust Dee forward so quickly she landed in a heap on the ground, hardly knowing which way was up.

She looked up, seeing Baron looming over her, huge and black with a very human intelligence shining in his canine eyes, and she scooted back involuntarily. He looked so much bigger from this angle.

For a moment the two of them just stared at each other. And Dee realised she'd never really taken the time to look properly at the black wolf. His fur was thick, almost shaggy. There was a faint streak of white over his left eye. His shoulders were wide, his neck thick, though half the bulk of him was probably just fur. But even so, he was a wolf of formidable size.

After reorienting herself, Dee stood up, her legs trembling a little, and turned to face Caroline, since Baron seemed to have no inclination to shift forms.

"Not bad for a first try," Caroline said, which Dee took to be high praise. "How much of that was you, and how much was the wolf?"

"All wolf," Dee answered, feeling the instant disappointment in the woman. "I was watching, listening, even making suggestions at times, but in truth, I wasn't controlling anything back there. Just as well, I think," she added, with a glance at Baron. He was still sitting there, panting, his teeth long and sharp and white. "I wouldn't have known what to do when Baron told me off," Dee admitted. "I think I would have just made things worse, if it was left up to me."

"We should have warned you," Caroline said, and Dee suspected that was as close to an apology as the woman ever got. "No howling. It draws too much attention from the neighbours."

"I imagine there are a dozen or more rules I should have been following," Dee said, trying to look at the incident lightly. "You can't teach me everything on day one." It had been terrifying, watching the huge wolf come at her, feeling the overwhelming strength of him, wondering how Faeydir would react. But in her mind, Faeydir merely shrugged. There had been no teeth involved, she informed Dee. No fight, no real aggression, just a warning that was ultimately for the pack's good. As far as wolf relationships went, it was a mild incident hardly worth mentioning.

Baron finally decided to shift back into human form, and he stood for a long moment, silently assessing Dee. "Tank?" he said finally. "Could you watch Dee for a little while? I need to talk to Caroline."

"Sure thing," Tank said, shooting a cheeky smile Dee's way.

"And Mark? You're coming inside for a little chat as well," Baron said, then he headed up the stairs without a backward glance.


Caroline waited silently as Baron asked Mark to wait in the hall. They had headed for the library, a wide room full of history, genealogies, storybooks about Faeydir-Ul and the first shape-shifters. She would never admit it, but Caroline loved this room. It was warm and welcoming, the very atmosphere inviting visitors to stay, to take up a volume and sit, read, enjoy a moment's peace. In her rigorous training schedule and with the duties of running the Den, quiet moments were few and far between for Caroline – and all the more precious because of it.

Baron joined her and closed the door, and Caroline quickly banished all thoughts of warm, quiet evenings. This man was part boulder, part freight train, and far too prone to bludgeoning his way through things rather than stopping to think them through. They'd been butting heads ever since Caroline had become Alpha Female, and she was honest enough, with herself at least, to privately admit that some days she argued with him just to prove that she could. Other days, however, the arguments were based on sound logic and very real concerns for the wellbeing of their Den.

"Well?" Baron demanded, in his usual blunt fashion. Why couldn't he just ask a simple question, Caroline thought in irritation. Why did everything have to be a demand?

"That was interesting," she began, not wanting to put all her cards on the table too quickly. "It seems Dee was telling the truth. The wolf just wanted to run."

"She just admitted that she had basically no control over the wolf."

"And you said we would try this on the assumption that she and the wolf are two separate minds. So on that basis, I wouldn't expect her to have much control. But she didn't cause trouble, so that, at least, is a step in the right direction."

"The wolf flatly refused to come out until she got her own way."

"Which was entirely within the limits of the rules we set. We said she couldn't shift for three minutes. We didn't say she had to do so immediately when those three minutes were up. And you could have refused to let Mark come. There's no guarantee she wouldn't have cooperated, given the right motivation. And," Caroline added, enjoying finding the fuel to argue with him, "she shifted back again when she was told to – albeit a rather rough transition, but I'm not going to hold that against her."

Baron watched her silently, the same way a wolf watches a deer it wants to eat, and she got the feeling he was going to try and force her hand, one way or another, so she decided to simply pre-empt the manipulation and jump in feet first.

"I don't see a need to cage her again immediately," Caroline said, with an air of nonchalance. "I would agree to a trial period for her to be let out around the estate."

If Baron was surprised then he hid it well. "That's quite a turn around from the last discussion we had on this."

"And that was the purpose of this trial, wasn't it?" Caroline snapped. "To convince me that it's all going to be hunky dory for an untrained stray to wander the grounds? Well, mission accomplished. What I wanted was evidence that the wolf is willing to follow basic rules. And from what I've seen, it looks like she is."

Baron's expression was unreadable. Bastard.

"So what about Mark?" Caroline went on, not interested in playing the waiting game. "Are you going to fight him?" As an issue of dominance between two males, it technically wasn't her business. But even so, it was a wise policy for her to keep an eye on any potential conflicts within the pack.

"I'm willing to try talking some sense into him. But I doubt it will go down well. So then we'll fight. A challenge like that doesn't just slide under the carpet. But I wanted to run something past you as well." Baron paused, choosing his words carefully. "Letting Dee roam loose by herself is unwise. Having Tank babysit her all the time is inconvenient." That was an understatement. Tank was a major part of their security force and often acted as bodyguard for any shifter who left the estate. He had enough to do without having to watch Dee twenty-four hours a day. "So how about this: Dee is allowed to go about unaccompanied inside the manor, but to go outside, she has to be chaperoned. And since Mark insists on sticking his nose into her business, let him be the chaperone of choice. He'll have to make himself available for at least an hour each day, and he'll be responsible for her behaviour while she's out."

Caroline laughed – actually laughed. "I don't know whether you're trying to piss Mark off, or do him a favour. You know he has his eye on that girl."

"I'm aware of it."

"And you're still willing to let him play babysitter? When he's clearly biased in her favour?"

"Mark's not going to let her do anything stupid. He's loyal to Il Trosa. Always has been."

"Fine," Caroline conceded. "Mark can play chaperone. But if Dee breaks any of the rules…"

"If she causes trouble of any kind, then she can go back to her cage," Baron agreed to her unspoken condition. And that was one of the things she respected about him. When push came to shove, Baron always put the wellbeing of the Den first. Every time.

# CHAPTER FOURTEEN

After getting back from her run, Dee had been escorted to the sitting room while she and Tank waited for Caroline and Baron to finish talking. Still feeling restless from her prolonged captivity, she found herself unable to sit down, so she paced the room, looking at the collection of books, the paintings on the walls, all the while aware of the sound of people coming and going in the foyer.

After a while, she crossed the room to look outside again. Faeydir was being quiet, content to sit back for a while after an afternoon of fun and exercise, but when Dee caught sight of the gathering of people on the lawn, the wolf sat up attentively.

"What's happening out there?" she asked Tank. It didn't seem like they were simply loitering after her outing – there was a tenseness and restlessness to the group, like they were waiting for something to happen.

Tank came to stand beside her, unsurprised by the sight. "I suspect they're gearing up for a fight. That sort of thing tends to draw spectators."

"Who's fighting?"

"That would be Baron and Mark."

Dee spun around in shock. "What? Why?"

Tank raised an eyebrow. "You don't know?" he asked, in a tone of voice that suggested she already did.

"Because of that incident in the forest?" Dee was dismayed. "That was a tiny thing! A minor scuffle. Why should they have a fight over it?"

Tank turned back to the lawn, where Baron and Mark were taking their places in the centre of the circle of onlookers.

"Status. Dominance. We're not human," he reminded Dee wryly. "We don't play by human rules."

"So the instant anything goes wrong, you beat each other up? That's barbaric. And stupid."

"It's not that simple. Baron would have had a chat with Mark first, see if they can resolve things peacefully. We're not total barbarians," he said with a grin, and Dee was annoyed that he was taking her protest so lightly. "But if that doesn't solve the problem, then a fight is the next step."

"Yes, but why?"

"Mark challenged Baron's status. So he's making a public demonstration in return to prove he still holds it."

Dee rolled her eyes. "That has about as much logic as a classroom brawl between a bunch of ten year olds. You're telling me that if Baron didn't fight Mark, the entire Den would revolt against him?"

"No. They follow him because they trust him to lead us with wisdom and intelligence. Status here is as much about personality as it is about strength. If he couldn't hold a following on a social level, he would never hold one by sheer force alone."

"So if people respect him, why do they need to fight?"

Tank shook his head. "They need to fight *because* people respect him."

Dee sighed in irritation. "That makes no sense."

"Not yet," Tank agreed. "But wait a few months." Another one of those annoying grins. "You'll get the hang of us. Where are you going?"

Dee was on her way to the door, determined to see if she could talk some sense into the pair. After all, she had been the one to cause the problem in the first place. Or, at least, Faeydir had. "Outside."

"Nope." Tank moved faster than she would have thought possible, planting himself firmly between her and the door. "You stay in here."

"I want to see Mark. To stop this stupidity."

"Not your call."

"Tank!"

"Nope."

She reached forward and gave him a shove... and found it as effective as trying to move a brick wall with her bare hands. "Let me past."

"Look, kid. I have one job here, and that's to keep you where you can't get into trouble. And I take my job very, very seriously. I can be a real nice guy about it, but push me again, and you'll find yourself with a one way ticket into a nice, cosy cage."

Dee glared at him for a moment longer, then, having to admit that she was on the losing end of this particular argument, went to stand back at the window, arms folded, a scowl on her face.

The fight was well underway by now, and though Mark seemed to be holding his own, his wolf large and fast, she assumed it was a foregone conclusion that Baron would win. His wolf was a third as big again as Mark's, and he had far more battle experience.

"This is stupid," she said again, as Tank returned to stand beside her, and he chuckled, giving her the impression that he was actually enjoying the fight.

"Welcome to your new world."


John watched from the sidelines as Baron and Mark thrashed out their differences on the wide lawn. This kind of fight was rare – a high ranking wolf rarely had to do more than growl at one with a significantly lower rank to pull them into line. But on the other hand, this was also more for show than anything, designed to make a point but not to do any serious damage, and much of the 'fight' consisted of little more than posturing and growling.

It had been going on for ten minutes or more, and John knew the match was only lasting so long because Baron was toying with the younger wolf. If he'd wanted to, he could have had him pinned to the ground and gasping for air in less than thirty seconds.

Half the Den had gathered around to watch, news having spread quickly that Mark had challenged Baron while out on their run, and while he didn't know the details, John had heard rumours that it had involved Dee.

Damn, he felt sorry for the girl. Snatched out of her life and thrust into this one, with no hope of ever going back. John's own conversion had been just as rude and abrupt, but at a much younger age. He'd hardly known any life of his own before he'd been sucked into the grim world of shifters and the Noturatii, and after that, it had been one long battle for survival. Until Baron had found him.

He watched the fight with disinterest. Baron would win. The rest was just details. But even so, he would likely have a few scrapes and cuts as a result of the fight, and since a wolf couldn't apply his own first aid, that would be John's role. His duty. So even though he would rather be curled up with a book somewhere, minding his own business, he was out here on the lawn, bored and getting colder by the minute as the sun slid towards the horizon.

Mark was tiring, panting harshly, bleeding from a dozen shallow cuts, while Baron still looked fresh and keen. He put his tail up, bared his teeth and attacked again, the two furry bodies rolling over on the damp lawn, a flurry of teeth and tails and paws.

There was a sharp yelp, and Mark scrambled out of the fray, limped away to the side, holding one front paw off the ground. He circled around Baron, head down, ears back, a soft whine coming from his throat.

Baron pounced, landed right on top of his smaller opponent and pinned him to the ground, teeth around his throat. A deep, rolling growl filled the air, and the watching crowd waited...

Mark lay still, conscious, but utterly submissive to his leader. A surrender that marked the end of the fight.

John sighed and rubbed his arms. Thank fuck for that. Now maybe he could go inside and get warmed up again.

Baron climbed off Mark and shifted back into human form. Mark shifted where he lay, then staggered to his feet, exhausted. Baron didn't offer him a hand up.

"Come see me after dinner," he ordered shortly. "There's something we need to discuss." Without waiting for a reply, he turned and stalked away towards the house. On his way, he caught John's eye and tilted his head in a 'come here' gesture. John followed, silent and obedient.

The fight had seemed to go on for ages, and when it finally came to an end, Dee realised that she was standing with her face and hands pressed against the glass, biting her lip anxiously, heart in her throat as Mark got pinned to the ground.

"He's not going to hurt him," Tank said gently. "This is for show only. They're not going to do any serious damage."

Dee tried to relax, both at the news, and at the fact that it was over now. She watched as Baron strode toward the house, John tagging along behind, and then waited while Mark picked himself up. Oddly, several of the shifters outside paused to shake his hand, pat him on the shoulder as if congratulating him, and then he had a brief chat with Alistair, the pair of them turning to head towards the house. Dee took two steps towards the door, then froze, glancing back anxiously at Tank. "Can I go into the foyer to talk to Mark?"

Tank nodded, then followed on her heels as she hurried out of the room.

The front door opened only a moment after Dee reached the foyer and Mark strode in, pulling up short when he saw her waiting for him. Alistair took one glance at her, and headed for the stairs. "I'll see you up there," he told Mark, then took the stairs two at a time, disappearing along the landing at the top.

Dee glanced sideways at Tank, feeling self-conscious about having an audience for this conversation, but knowing there was no way around it.

"Are you okay?" she asked Mark, not sure if her concern was misplaced.

He shrugged, but didn't seem too unhappy about it. "I've had worse."

"I'm sorry," she apologised awkwardly. "It was my fault you got into trouble."

To her surprise, Mark laughed. "Nope, I think I managed that one all on my own."

"Tank said that you and Baron talked things over beforehand. Why was this necessary?" she asked in dismay, flinging her arm at the door, trying to encompass everything that had happened outside.

"Baron said that he had the right to protect his Den from mistakes that could jeopardise us. I said he was right," Mark explained, then went on, before Dee could voice her confusion about the apparent agreement. "But I also said that I felt the need to protect you from punishment for a rule that no one had even told you about. And after getting my arse kicked from one side of the lawn to the other, I still feel that way."

Dee fidgeted under his intense gaze, unused to having anyone stand on her side quite so resolutely. "Well, thank you. But I'm still sorry you got hurt."

A smile quirked the edge of his lip. "It was worth it." Then he carried on up the stairs, leaving Dee staring after him.

Beside her, Tank let out a soft laugh. "Sounds like you have an admirer," he observed, making Dee blush.

"Dee?" Caroline snapped from the library doorway, sticking her head into the room. "In here. We have some things to discuss."

Dee slunk into the room, wondering what news was to follow, and what it would mean for her future in the Den. Things had unfolded rather rapidly in the last twenty-four hours, and she hoped that, despite the howling incident, she'd behaved well enough to be let out again on occasion. The cages were getting rather lonely, after all.


Baron was already halfway up the stairs when John got inside, and he followed, but not in any particular hurry. Trudged his way up the stairs to Baron's bedroom – still Baron's room, though John had been sleeping in there for years – and closed the door behind him when he got there.

Baron was already in the bathroom, setting out disinfectant, swabs, tweezers. Wolf bites had a nasty tendency to get infected, and while his scrapes were minor, not even worth bothering about had they been in the field or on a mission, it was simply careless not to take care of such things when the time and resources were available.

Baron glanced over his shoulder as John arrived, then simply shifted into wolf form. No more of an explanation was necessary, this scene having played out dozens of times since they'd met and moved in together. Or rather, since John had been conscripted into Baron's bedroom.

John stepped around the wolf and picked up the swabs. Poured disinfectant onto a wad. Picked up the tweezers, then sat down on the floor. Baron presented his flank for inspection, and John began searching through the thick fur for the inevitable cuts.

Shifters had an unusual advantage over ordinary humans – or ordinary wolves, for that matter. To a large extent, the injuries that one form sustained were undetectable on the other form. A wolf who had been shot and was bleeding profusely had only to shift into human form to be whole and uninjured again, able to go about their business until appropriate medical care could be found, at which point they could shift back into wolf form and have their injuries treated. Because of this strange quirk of nature, there were rumours throughout the various myths and cults of history that the shifters were immortal, unable to be killed through normal means. It wasn't really true – it was just that they needed to be mortally wounded not once, but twice. Of course, if one of the forms was actually killed, then the whole shifter died. There was only so much damage the magic could disguise. No one had ever been able to explain to John how the whole thing really worked, but on the other hand, no one was complaining about the strange benefits that the magic afforded them either.

Baron flinched momentarily, and John realised he was being a little too rough as he swabbed a wound. It was seeping blood, and the disinfectant had to sting. But Baron never made a sound. He was a tough bastard, which was a lot of the reason they got along so well. Tough, but fair. Stern, but caring. Gentle and brutal. Stubborn, and yet able to compromise, always able to see the bigger picture.

Except where John was concerned.

John finished cleaning the wounds and sat back. "Any others?"

The wolf shook his head and padded out into the bedroom, leaving John to clean up. Once the disinfectant was put away and the swabs tossed into the bin, John headed out as well, not at all looking forward to the conversation they were about to have.

Baron was standing at the window, hands in his pockets. He'd taken his coat off and his broad shoulders were now covered in a thick woollen jumper, lending him a deceptively cosy look. But there was nothing cosy about Baron.

"Well?" Baron prompted, without looking around. "You've heard the verdict. Dee is to be allowed free roam of the estate. That must make you happy."

It had been a huge relief when Baron had made the announcement, but the fight had prevented him from saying anything at the time. "Thank you," John said, meek and quiet. For all Baron's even tone of voice, it was plain as day that he wasn't happy.

He turned around slowly, face carefully neutral, and John couldn't help but duck his head, eyes downcast. "Thank you?" Baron repeated. He took a step closer. "Thank you?" This time he mimicked not just the words, but the tone, weak, light, ethereal. "You fucking accuse me of torturing the girl, I risk the safety of the entire Den to let her prove she's not a total liability, and all I get in return is a piss-weak two-word back-chat?"

Fuck. What was he supposed to do now? Twenty-four hours ago, he'd been full of fire, outraged at Dee's continued captivity, starting to get nightmares of the time he'd been imprisoned himself, and more than ready to go toe-to-toe with Baron to get the girl another option.

But the trouble was that his anger, like his courage, could flare up in a heartbeat, only to vanish again the instant the crisis was over. "I didn't say you were torturing her."

"You compared her captivity to yours. And I fucking well know enough about what the Noturatii did to you to take that as an insult."

"I'm sorry."

Baron growled, a distinctly canine-sounding noise. "So. Are. You. Happy. Now?"

"Yes. Thank you." John forced himself to lift his head, to meet Baron's eyes, forced his lungs to push the words out firmly and clearly.

"Excellent," Baron said, standing no more than a foot away now, sarcasm dripping from his voice. "Because I now have a deluded newbie roaming my estate, Caroline is *agreeing* with me, when I was rather counting on her insisting Dee got shut back in her cage, and now that Mark has had his arse kicked, there are going to be half a dozen status fights in the next forty-eight hours as every wolf in the house tries to reaffirm his own place in the pecking order. Fuck, John, do you have any idea how much I do for you?"

John knew. God, how he knew, and he thanked whatever higher power was watching over him every single day for the second chance he'd been given.

And there was only one real way he had ever been able to express that gratitude.

He closed the distance between them, grabbing Baron's head and slamming their mouths together in a kiss that was more brutal force than passion.

Baron's reaction was entirely predictable. He wrapped his massive arms around John's torso, lifted him off the floor and carried him to the bed. Dumped him on top of the duvet and followed him down, his superior weight pinning John to the bed in a way that was both terrifying and exhilarating.

Hands were everywhere, moans and growls as clothing was stripped off and sent flying, and then John was submitting to his Alpha in an entirely different way...

# CHAPTER FIFTEEN

Dee stumbled up the stairs to her room and paused to glance at the big old grandfather clock that sat in the first floor hallway. Nine o'clock. It felt like later.

The meeting with Caroline in the library had gone better than Dee could ever have hoped. She was to be let out of the cage – not just on occasional excursions, but permanently! On condition that she behaved, of course, or her freedom would come to a very sudden end, but... Freedom!

And then there had been a list of rules – a really long list – about all manner of daily activities around the estate. Rules about where she could shift and when, how to treat other members of the pack, how meals were organised, the sections of the garden where her wolf was allowed to dig and where she wasn't, rules about howling and that she was expected to obey both Baron and Caroline as leaders of the Den. For safety reasons, she was to remain inside the house unless accompanied by an escort – and for everyday purposes, Mark was her nominated chaperone. That had been a surprise, and she'd longed to ask why he in particular had been chosen, or what he thought of the arrangement, but Caroline had charged on through the list of rules and regulations without taking a breath, so there had been no opportunity to ask. The idea was both exhilarating and daunting. Mark was gorgeous, fit and toned with a brooding air that Dee found hopelessly appealing, but also prone to dark moods that left her a little apprehensive about how he'd react to the task.

After that, there had been a tour of the house, to the bedroom that would be hers for the foreseeable future, the industrial style kitchen, the long table in the formal dining room, the television lounge... it had gone on and on, and then back down to the basement to collect her things, and then she'd had dinner with Caroline in the library, going over more rules, more regulations, details on the Council, what to do if a stranger came onto the estate. For all that Dee's days had already been filled with lessons, there was a vast amount that hadn't been covered, and she suddenly understood why a mandatory two year training period was the norm.

And then Caroline had dropped the bombshell that had really rocked Dee's world. The decision to let her out of the cage was not just a reprieve for good behaviour. It was an official invitation to join the Den.

Dee's jaw had dropped and she'd sat there, speechless. "I'd be honoured," she'd said, meaning it from the bottom of her heart. This place was a small miracle. Baron and Caroline, as different as they were, somehow made it work, kept their eclectic family together, maintained order, kept the world at large ignorant of their existence and still had the energy at the end of the day to welcome in wandering strays like herself.

Finally, though, exhaustion had set in, despite the relatively early hour, and Dee had begged off another lesson in shifter culture in favour of a hot shower and a long sleep.

But rest was not to come so easily, she realised as she rounded the corner into the hallway that led to her room. There was a group of four men outside her door, and by the way they stood up when they saw her, it seemed they were not there just to shoot the breeze. They had been waiting for her.

Silas was at the front of the group, and Dee was dismayed to realise that she didn't recognise the rest of them. If Mark or Tank had been among them she might have assumed it was something civilised, an impromptu get-to-know-you maybe, to answer some of the questions the Den must have about her.

But this welcoming committee had a distinctly sinister feel to it and it took a fair bit of courage to not turn tail and run back down the stairs.

"We don't mean to scare you," one of the men said. He stepped forward and Dee gasped as she saw he only had one eye. The other was a puckered mess of scars. "I'm Caleb," he said, ignoring her fear and offering his hand. Dee shook it automatically, even as she backed up another step. "This is Kwan," he said, pointing to an Asian man, "and Aaron," a nerdish looking man with glasses. They both looked to be around her own age. "Also known as 'KwanandAaron'. Where you find one, you'll find the other. And you've already met Silas."

Dee glanced at the silent, brooding man, still not sure what they were all doing here.

"Look, we're not here to make you uncomfortable," Caleb went on. "We just wanted to say welcome to the Den, and... well, if anyone gives you trouble, any one of us would willingly step up for you."

Somehow the offer wasn't reassuring. "Is anyone likely to give me trouble?"

Kwan snorted. "Hell yeah," he said, earning a scowl from Caleb.

"There are eighteen people in this house," Caleb explained. "Nineteen, now, including you. And most of us come from chequered pasts. So not everyone gets along. You'll figure out who's who soon enough, but you need to understand that social dynamics here work the same way they do in a wolf pack. There's a pecking order, and Baron and Caroline basically leave it up to us to fight it out amongst ourselves. But it'll take you a while to find your feet, so until you learn which way is up… I'm just saying we'll be keeping an eye out for you."

Dee didn't quite know how to take that. She cast a wary eye over Silas. So far he'd seemed like a cut-throat killer, eager to either be away from her, or put her out of her misery. She longed to call him out on his odd behaviour now, but some subtle instinct told her not to. That was a mystery that would have to wait for another day.

"Thank you," she hedged finally, not knowing what else to say.

"Goodnight then." The men filed away down the hall, and Dee quickly let herself into her room, closing the door softly and turning the lock.

Okay, she thought, as she surveyed the Victorian style room. Time to catch her breath and take stock of the situation.

The room was decorated as much of the house was, antique furniture, thick rugs on the floor, a modest fireplace, though there was also modern heating in the room. There was a wide bed – definitely modern, though the wooden frame fitted into the style of the room nicely. A dresser, a chair, an old wooden wardrobe and a gold-framed mirror set in one corner. There was a wide angle photograph on the wall above the bed, a pack of wolves running through a snow-covered forest, and she wondered whether it was a generic, commercial shot, or if this Den had actually posed for the photo.

Faeydir perked up then, though she'd been silent for a good long stretch of the afternoon, and growled her approval at the scene. She'd like to run in the snow one day, she informed Dee, and Dee just rolled her eyes. She could already imagine the fuss Faeydir was going to make come winter. The first hint of snow, and she'd be clamouring at the back door.

But her eagerness to run with the wolves again made Dee stop and think. Would she one day run in a pack like that one? A fully fledged, knowledgeable, useful member of the team? She'd been accepted into the pack today, a huge leap forward and a weight off her mind, but given the warning from the crowd outside her door, it seemed that the adventure was only just beginning.


It was mid morning by the time Dee made it downstairs for breakfast, and she headed for the smaller kitchen where each member of the Den made their own breakfast and lunch. Dinner was prepared daily by a shifter called George – Dee hadn't met him yet – but for the rest of their meals, it was each man for himself.

But the instant she stepped into the kitchen, her plans suddenly changed. Silas was sitting at the old wooden table cleaning his rifle, the gun in pieces and various cloths and tools lying scattered about. And his strange behaviour from the night before had been niggling at her all night.

She took a breath, preparing herself to just ask him why he'd suddenly changed his tune on her, but then the door opened and another man walked in. Simon, Dee thought his name was, though she couldn't be certain.

One thing she was sure of, though – Silas would not appreciate an audience for this particular conversation. But how to make sure they wouldn't be interrupted?

An idea occurred to her, one that might be a long shot… but then again, stranger things had been happening to her in the past few days. Why not continue the trend?

"Silas?" He grunted, not taking his eyes off the gun. "I was hoping to go outside for a walk, but I'm not allowed to without a chaperone. I was wondering if you might have time. For just a short one."

"No."

Bugger. "Please?" Simon found whatever it was he was looking for and left the room again, the door thudding shut behind him. "I wanted…" She glanced at the door, checking no one else was about to interrupt them. "I wanted to talk to you about yesterday."

"There's nothing to say."

Christ, he could be stubborn. But so could she. "Please?"

Silas rolled his eyes. "Oh, for fuck's sake." He tossed down the gun and stood up, wiping his hands on a rag. "Fine. Lead the way."

It was rather intimidating, having him so up in her face again after he'd been almost polite to her yesterday, but after a night's worth of pondering, Dee was working on the theory that a lot of his aggression was just for show, saving face and maintaining his reputation, and that he had a softer side, if only the opportunity arose for it to show itself.

There was a side door leading directly out of the kitchen, and she led them out and around to the left, where the formal garden gave way to wide rows of roses. Faeydir was bouncing around in her head already, wanting to play, but Dee told her she'd have to wait. Playtime later, she promised, having learned that compromise was her best path to success, assuring the wolf that she understood her needs, but for right now, she had important things to do as a human.

"I thought you hated me," she began, preparing to explain her disquiet, but she didn't get the chance.

"I don't hate anyone," Silas told her flatly. "I just don't particularly like them, either."

"But yesterday evening you said you would help me," Dee persisted. "And I'm trying to understand why-"

"Look, you silly little chit," Silas snapped. "I didn't say I would take you on walks through the flowers and frolic on the lawn with you. I said I would happily beat the shit out of anyone who causes you trouble. So don't go thinking I'm suddenly your best friend."

"But why? There's no audience here to make you look weak or sappy, and I swear, my lips are sealed. So tell me why you'd offer to do that for me."

Silas fell silent. Looked away. Shoved his hands into his pockets and scuffed the toe of his boot against a weed poking out of the pavers. "There are... stories," he said finally. "Myths. In the history books."

"That say what? That you have to be nice to the new girl or she'll put a curse on you?"

Silas actually recoiled at her words. "There's a prophecy."

Now that got Dee's attention, but probably not in the way that Silas had intended. She tried to smother her laughter, but failed miserably. "You think I'm the focus of an ancient shifter prophecy? A myth come to life?" Laughter bubbled over again, while Silas merely rolled his eyes and waited for her to get control of herself again. "Sorry, but I'm just a run of the mill office worker who fell down a rabbit hole." She held out her arms, indicating her short stature. "There's no mythology here."

Silas shrugged. "That remains to be seen." Dee's laughter died out as she realised he was serious.

"You're scared of me," she blurted out, only a moment after the idea occurred to her, and wasn't that a damn fool thing to say, accusing this badass of being a coward. Silas folded his arms and looked away. "What is it that I'm supposed to do?"

"Look, I'm not your tutor," Silas snapped, running a hand over his bald head. "You want an education in shifter history, go read those great fat tomes in the library. Otherwise, mind your own damn business. And for that matter, I'm not your babysitter, either. So are we done here, or do you want to smell a few more roses? Quietly."

Not the conclusion to their chat that she had been hoping for. "We're done." She led the way back towards the kitchen, noting the rolling clouds that promised rain later in the day. But at least he hadn't punched her in the face. Or shot her with that rifle of his. So, all things considered, it could have gone worse.

Baron sat in front of the TV in the lounge, cracking his knuckles compulsively. On the television was a news report – the Den's official response to the kidnapping story the Noturatii had put out. And it was a work of art. The Noturatii had its share of police officers in its pocket, detectives, sergeants, even captains all willing to lie for them. But then again, so did Il Trosa. Some sided with them voluntarily, others needed to be bribed, but Baron had no qualms about the methods they used so long as they got results. The end result in this case was that a couple of detectives were going to make this story go away, and the Noturatii were going to be reminded that Il Trosa could parry just as well as they could.

Skip was front and centre on the screen, a wig, coloured contact lenses and an expert make up job making her look very different from her true self. She was looking tearful while two officers stood nearby, trying to appear supportive. "I'm just so grateful for the help from everyone who called in," she said to the journalist interviewing her – and from all appearances, the journo was lapping it up, believing every word. "I thought I was going to die. And the police, I just can't thank them enough."

The camera cut back to the reporter in the studio. "A good result all round, and once again, thank you to everyone who called in with information about this kidnapping. Police have arrested two suspects, and as we just saw, Helen Grange has been recovered unharmed and is on her way for a medical assessment."

Baron hit the mute button and glanced over at Alistair, standing by the sofa looking smug, and Skip, perched on the arm, grinning and swinging her legs like a child. "You do good work, Alistair," he said, genuine appreciation in his voice. "I'm impressed. But keep a close eye on the news stations for the next few days. The Noturatii don't like to be outsmarted, and something tells me this little episode isn't quite over yet."

# CHAPTER SIXTEEN

Jack Miller slowed the dark blue Range Rover he was driving, and turned carefully onto a gravel road. They were in a small village in the north east of England, following up on one of the few useful leads that had come in before the shifters had cut off their investigation by 'finding' the kidnapped girl.

Sitting beside him in the car was Aliya, a woman in her late twenties who was a new recruit to the Noturatii and had finished her six month training and initiation just weeks ago.

The lead was an interesting one. After seeing the news report on the kidnapping, a lady from this village had called to report 'strange goings on' as she'd called them, at a nearby farmhouse. Howls in the middle of the night, large dogs guarding the property, a series of vehicles coming and going, and the owners of the house were very antisocial – which might be normal in the city, she'd said, but this was the sort of village where everyone knew everyone else. And a white Ford Transit had arrived the day after the kidnapping. It was the reason she'd been looking for to report the 'weirdos'.

The farm in question was down a long gravel road, overgrown to the point where the Range Rover only just fit through the gap. They crossed a small stream, climbed a steep slope and came to a gentle stop in front of an old farmhouse… with a white Ford Transit parked in the driveway.

"Keep your eyes open and try not to say too much," he cautioned Aliya as they climbed out of the car. New recruits, in his experience, were prone to pushing too hard, being too eager to get results, and that tended to cause a certain defensiveness in the people they interviewed, rather than eliciting useful information.

As they approached the house, a pair of dogs around the side went nuts, a volley of barking announcing them to the owners even before they reached the door. The farmhouse was rundown, one window broken and boarded up, the door frame cracked. Weeds grew up through the gravel and old planks of wood were stacked haphazardly against the side of the house.

A middle aged woman opened the door, wiping her hands on a tea towel, and Miller got the immediate impression of a Betty Crocker wanna-be, so wholesome it made your teeth ache. "Good afternoon. What can I do for you?" she asked, with a strong American accent.

"Ma'am. I'm Detective Ashton," Miller said, pulling out his fake police badge. "And this is Detective Lewis." One of the reasons he'd brought Aliya along was as a form of social reassurance. As a black man from a military background who stood six foot three in bare feet, Miller was aware that he invoked an automatic anxiety in a lot of people. Showing up with a woman as his 'partner' went a long way towards alleviating those fears, which tended to land him better information from his enquiries. "Do you mind if we ask you a few questions?"

They didn't get the chance. "It's one of the locals causing a fuss again, isn't it?" the lady said, not sounding terribly put out by it. "Look, they took a dislike to me and my Harry when they found out we're American. This place is old. It's run-down, we haven't had a chance to fix it up yet. But there's a keep round the back, lots of history – a few notable families lived here back in the day. They think it should be owned by someone British, not a foreigner."

"How long have you lived here?"

"On and off for four, maybe five years. We bought it before we moved here, then business back home – in America – kept us away for longer than we'd planned, and by the time we moved in full time, I suppose a few rumours had started. Let me guess," she said indulgently. "Strange sounds at night, lots of odd people coming and going, witches, warlocks, lightning striking the house on Halloween?"

Interesting. "That's not far from what we've heard," Miller said, giving the lady an indulgent smile. Sometime, just letting people talk gave you the most information, and he was in no hurry to shut her up.

"We've been getting the roof repaired. Leaks from lack of maintenance. But it's all historical this and protected that, so we've needed quotes, and experts and biologists and historians. So there's been a fair bit of coming and going, but if people get upset about it, they're just seeing what they want to see, when there's nothing to see in the first place."

"That sounds perfectly reasonable," Miller said politely. "None the less, would you mind if we take a look inside the keep? And inside the van. It's just that if we receive complaints, we're obliged to follow them up."

The woman sighed. "Oh, if you must. The van's unlocked." She led them over, opening the back door, and Miller climbed inside. Nothing out of the ordinary, but...

"Do you ever take your dogs out in the van?" There was fur on the back seat.

"Occasionally. Trips to the vet and that sort of thing. They tend to stay on the property mostly."

He climbed out of the van again. "And do you ever get complaints from the neighbours about the barking?"

"The neighbours are too far away to hear much from our set. We've got three. German Shepherds. Just for company. They're loud, but they'd never hurt a fly."

"Shall we see the keep then," Miller prompted. "And I'm sorry, but I didn't ask your name."

"Helen. Helen Coombs."

The keep was far less remarkable than he had hoped. "We use this place to store some of the furniture while we're getting the house repaired," Helen said, showing off a room that was surprisingly neat and clean. A quick peak underneath the white sheets confirmed her story – a wooden bookcase, an antique dresser, nothing more remarkable than that, and soon enough, Aliya and Miller were heading back to the cars.

"We did hear one report that was intriguing," Miller said, when they reached the drive again. "Lights in the forest at night. Shadows moving back and forth, people and dogs…" Actually, they had heard no such report, but it would be interesting to see what she said.

"We like to go for long walks in the woods, that's all." Helen was momentarily uncomfortable, but hid it quickly. "Sometimes we get back late, so I take a torch with me. Like I said, people see what they want to see."

"True enough," Miller agreed, before thanking the woman for her time, and excusing them both. As they reached the car again, he glanced back and saw someone at the window watching them. The moment they saw him looking, they darted out of view, the curtain falling back into place.

"Did you notice the woman at the upstairs window?" Aliya asked him softly, when Helen was out of earshot. "She was watching the whole time."

"And another woman in the far corner of the garden. Hiding in the trees," Miller added. "Suspicious, but not enough to run with. The dogs are a good excuse for the howling, at least." He'd often wondered how shifters and domestic dogs would get along, though there was no information in the Noturatii's files on the subject. "But no sign of the girl from the lab, unfortunately."

"The wolves have humans working for them, you know," Aliya said knowledgably. "I read that one of their lackeys turned informant a few years back. Whole families brainwashed into helping them."

Actually, according to what Miller had read, the shifters tried to minimise contact with humans. After all, the more people who knew your secrets, the more likely it was that they would be leaked. It had never been proven, but he suspected that the 'informant' had been a plant, sent to feed them false information.

"I think it would be wise to keep them under observation," Miller concluded, "but we've done all we can for the moment." 'Observation' in this context meant the family would have their phones tapped, their mail monitored, their internet connection hacked. And the instant he sent his report back to headquarters, 'Helen Coombs' would have her full history checked, including her supposed migration from America.

"The forest runs right up to the back of this property," Aliya pointed out. "The girl's got to end up there one way or another, even if she doesn't come through here."

Miller glanced back at the house. The owner was still watching them from the doorway. And he decided to test out a theory. It was one he'd been working on for a year or two, and discussing it with seasoned operatives tended to get him nowhere. It would be interesting to see what a newbie had to say about it. "What would you think of the idea that there are two packs in England, not just one?" he asked, as they both climbed back into the car. "There's a certain amount of evidence that the second one is further west. What's to say she couldn't end up there?"

To his disappointment, Aliya snorted. "There's no second pack. The idea is just a clever decoy, designed to make us waste more time searching for them."

"But according to the database, there are two distinct patterns of behaviour from the shifters," Miller persisted. "One group is reclusive to a fault, but the other is the one that pulls stunts like 'solving' that kidnapping story. At the very least, there's got to be two different sub-cultures within the group-"

"I've read all the official documents," Aliya interrupted, sounding a touch defensive now. "All the senior operatives agree that there's only one pack. The rest of it is just tricks to throw us off target. I read a report from Jacob himself that said as much. And I'm absolutely sure the woman we just saw isn't one of those animals," she went on confidently. "Too sweet and polite. The wolves themselves are vicious killers. Antisocial, brutal and uncultured. They'd never stand around and chat like she was."

Miller made a non-committal sound and started the engine. It seemed Aliya, like most of their operatives, had been brainwashed by the 'official' propaganda. It was becoming more and more difficult to find people willing to think outside the square, to question the Noturatii's official modes of operation, and he was of the firm opinion that their organisation was weaker because of it.

Miller himself had read a vast array of reports, dating back years, if not decades, into the Noturatii's interactions with the shifters. And in many cases, their official view point on the shifters' behaviour was correct – in confrontations, the wolves fought viciously, using the full advantages of both animal and human forms and were to be treated with a shoot first, ask questions later policy. But there were also a dozen or so other stories he'd read. He'd had to read between the lines, the reports being coloured by bias, of course, but in each one, a distinct and worrying pattern had emerged. Far from being aggressive beasts bent on death and mayhem, each of those dozen reports had stated that, until the Noturatii had attacked them first, the shifters had only been trying to run away.


Helen – or Rintur-Ul, as she was known to the Grey Watch – watched the Noturatii leave, fighting to keep the polite smile on her face until they were out of sight. And then the wholesome housewife image vanished, dark curses on her lips as she strode into the house.

Genna, their newest recruit, a twenty-one year old who had yet to be converted, was still in the kitchen, doing her best to murder the dough she'd been making for bread. Rintur paused mid-stride, almost giving in to the impulse to go and rescue the poor stuff from the pounding it was receiving, before deciding she had more important matters to attend to.

Genna was typical of much of the younger generation, born with a sense of entitlement and slow to pick up responsibilities. They couldn't afford to be too choosy, though, with less and less women prepared to forgo the luxuries of modern life, even with the perks of becoming a wolf, and an intensive training course was their way of dealing with undesirable personality traits, whereas in the past, the women who joined them had been given time and space to discover the joys of the natural world at their own pace. Such were the demands that modern society placed upon them.

But try as she might, Genna was not a natural cook. As it was, she had burnt the eggs, set fire to the salmon and her bread had turned out as a solid, inedible brick. And this latest crisis was not likely to help her attempts to adjust to the Watch's way of life.

She pulled out her cell phone and dialled Sempre-Ul, praying that she answered. Rintur had been a wolf for just over fifteen years, but Sempre, their alpha, had been converted when she was barely twelve years old. Now in her forties, she knew things about their magic that made Rintur's skin crawl.

"We've just had a visit from the Noturatii," she said, as soon as Sempre picked up the phone.


Genna regarded the dough with a frown. It was sticky, clinging to her fingers and the kitchen counter, white flour sprayed about like a miniature snow storm, and no matter what she did, she couldn't seem to make it turn into the neat, round ball that Rintur's had become.

She picked up the lump and dumped it into the bread pan, doing her best to pat it down to fit inside. Damn cooking. She'd signed up to be a wolf, for Pete's sake. No one had told her that she'd have to learn to cook! Wolves ate their food raw, after all. But Rintur had lectured her on the need to be self sufficient – the Grey Watch kept a supply of the basic staples – flour, eggs, herbs and spices – but running down to the shops for groceries if they ran out of something wasn't an option, so here she was, battling it out with a wet, sticky dough monster that would no doubt turn out just as hard and inedible as her last three attempts.

No one, but no one, Rintur had emphasised, was allowed to be a burden on the pack. So if Genna wanted to live with them, she had to learn a lot of home crafts from scratch. Making candles from tallow. Repairing her own clothes. Cooking.

Bleh.

She covered the pan with a tea towel and made a cursory attempt at scraping the wet dough from her hands. She was about to head for the sink and lots of soapy water to clean up, but then thought better of it. Rintur would want to check the dough first, and if she hadn't done it well enough, she would make her fix it. So no point cleaning up until she'd gotten the all clear.

She headed for the study, where she'd heard Rintur go after she'd come in from outside.

The woman was on the phone, her back to Genna, so she waited, trying to be patient. Or rather, she was simply in no hurry to rush off to her next assignment. Feriur was upstairs waiting to give her a lesson in sewing, and if there was one thing Genna found even more boring than cooking, it was that.

"It's that damned Il Trosa again," Rintur was saying, her tone shrill and tense. "Every time they pull one of these stunts, we get the blame. There was some woman they kidnapped. The Noturatii got onto it and now they're stirring up trouble again." She paused, hand on her hip, staring out the window. "Of course it was Il Trosa," she went on a moment later. "There was a news report a few days ago... Oh, for fuck's sake, watching the news on television does not make me a heretic!"

Oh yes, Genna remembered. That was the other down side of this new arrangement she'd sign on to. No technology. No radio, no internet, no television.

"A woman was snatched by a man in a white van in London," Rintur went on. "White Ford Transit van, weird events and Noturatii types showing up here equals Il Trosa doing some fool thing and drawing way too much attention to themselves. We've both been around long enough to know how it works."

Another pause. "If they'd just sit down and shut up, stop poking the beast, then the Noturatii wouldn't even know we were here. We avoid them, hide in the forest, keep our heads down – like we've done for centuries – and then they come knocking on our door because Baron and his mob of mongrels can't keep it together for five minutes. But not much we can do about that now. Can you send Sven? We'll have to convert her tonight." Rintur turned around at that point and saw Genna watching her. She looked alarmed for a moment, then shrugged it off, returning to her previously resolute expression. "We'll head for the camp as soon as it's done. All right. Bye."

She hung up. "Change of plans, Genna. Sempre is sending a male to convert you. We'll have to finish your training in the wild."

# CHAPTER SEVENTEEN

The Den was a mess of activity. After the announcement that Dee was to officially join Il Trosa, Caroline had told her this morning that there was to be a celebration in her honour.

Dee had offered to help several times, but when everyone had simply told her to go and relax, she'd found herself at a loose end. And so around midday, she headed for the library, deciding to do what Silas had suggested and look through some of the history books for stories, myths, anything that might be linked to his odd behaviour towards her.

She'd found the story of Faeydir-Ul and her human conspirator, reading the story with rapt attention. And then a variety of historical accounts, shifters in ancient Greece and Rome, those revered by the druids, and finally she'd come across a number of prophecies of warriors who would return from the dead. Did Silas think she was one of those? But in this particular book, every prophecy she read about involved a shifter male, not a female. So no luck there. She had just reached the chapter on mystical powers that shifters might possess when she felt an irritated nudge at the back of her mind.

*What?* she asked the wolf. *You'll have a run later.*

An image of a clock appeared in her mind, and Dee glanced at the wall, shocked to see it was three o'clock already! Had she been reading for so long?

Another image in her mind, of Faeydir running outside in the forest, and Dee nodded. "Absolutely," she said out loud. "Sorry. I got a little carried away there."

She opened the library door, feeling apprehensive about bothering Mark for a trip outside. She still didn't know what he thought of being on babysitting duty, and his dark, brooding air did little to reassure her.

After checking the house with no luck, she learned from Caleb that

Mark was out in his workshop, and he agreed to escort her there – it was a short, thirty metre walk from the front door, but Caroline had made it clear that the rule of 'no going outside alone' would be broken if she was to set so much as a single foot outside the door unaccompanied.

Mark was sitting in the far corner working at a sawhorse when she arrived, firm muscles standing out on his arms as he worked on a piece of wood. He glanced up, then straightened when he saw who it was. "Hey. Come on in."

Dee felt the same thrill of attraction she felt every time she saw him, the sort of girlish excitement she might feel if she'd just walked into a room where Brad Pitt was waiting, and she tried to get a handle on her runaway hormones. Crumbs, she was behaving like a love-struck teenager. To cover her nervousness, she tried for an air of nonchalance as she stepped forward. "I'm sorry for interrupting you," she said. "But Faeydir really needs to go for a run."

"It's okay," Mark said quickly. "I need a break anyway." He tossed down his tools and brushed wood chips and sawdust off his jeans. To distract herself from the view of those long, lean legs encased in worn denim, Dee glanced around the room, and her eyes opened wide at what she saw. "Wow."

Mark looked up in surprise. "What?"

"This is beautiful." A set of chairs were lined up against one wall, smooth, dark wood, an oiled finish, each one a work of art. She stepped closer and saw intricate designs etched into the frames, swirls and curves that had a Celtic feel to them. "You made these?" He was talented as well as gorgeous, and it was doing nothing for her sense of equilibrium.

"Yeah. It makes a little extra money for the Den. Some of us work for the estate itself, house repairs, bookkeeping, or whatever, but most people have some form of job to help pay the bills."

"This is really beautiful," she repeated, surprised that Mark didn't think so.

He came over and ran his hand over the back of one chair. "I've made this exact same chair over a hundred times. And that one over there," he pointed to a slightly different design in the corner, "about eighty times. At the end of the day, it's just slapping a few bits of wood together and sanding off the edges."

Dee found his resentfulness odd, given the effort he clearly put into each piece. "Is it just tables and chairs you make?"

"Pretty much."

"So why do you do it, if you dislike it so much?"

He ran his hand over the chair again pensively. "I liked it when I started. When I was a kid, I wanted to be an engineer. But then I joined the Den, and a full time university degree doesn't really fit in with being shot at on a daily basis and having a wolf in your head that needs constant care. So no degree. But I liked building things and designing things." Another stroke of the chair. "So I learned to do this."

"And now?"

He shrugged. "It pays the bills."

"Do you still like designing things?"

"Yeah. But working with wood was never my first choice. I'd prefer to work with metal, but..."

"So design something else. A wardrobe. A bookcase. A computer desk. Whatever you like."

"I make what people order. And what they order is dining sets."

"Oh, rubbish," Dee scoffed. "People order whatever you make them want. And if they're all ordering dining sets, it means you're doing a fantastic job of marketing them, but you're not marketing anything else. There are plenty of younger people who want modern looking furniture that's also unique. There are people who make bookcases out of scrap metal, or bed frames out of pallets, or coffee tables out of recycled bricks. There's no reason why you couldn't branch out into... Oh heck, I'm so sorry," she interrupted herself, mortified that she was giving him a lecture on how to run his business. "I'm sorry. I barely know you, and I certainly have no right to be telling you how to do your job. I'm sorry."

Mark was looking at her with an unreadable expression. "You think I could make a coffee table out of scrap metal? And have someone want to buy it?"

"Well, yeah, I guess so," she said hesitantly, hoping she hadn't just made a fool of herself. "There are plenty of pictures on the internet of people who make recycled furniture. And some of it sells for a fair bit of money."

Mark stared at the chair against the wall. Then over at a pile of off-cuts in the corner. "I'll have to look into that."

"It's just an idea," Dee said apologetically. "I mean, you don't have to-"

"No, I actually like that," he said, sounding not exactly enthusiastic, but certainly more animated than the dull, flat tone he'd had before. "I'll do some research, see what I can find."

"Oh. Okay. Good." And then, "What?" she asked, when she saw him staring at her.

"You are turning out to be quite unexpected," he said softly. When she laughed and shook her head, he want on. "You've had a hell of a lot to cope with coming here, and you've dealt with it all with incredible poise. And with Faeydir as well. Even as a shifter, you've got more complications than most of us have. I like Faeydir, by the way, just in case she wants to take that as an insult."

Faeydir was perfectly happy with him, a persistent feeling of eagerness just at being in his presence. "No, she's quite okay with that," she told him.

"And now you're seeing potential where I see none," he went on, his speculative look turning a touch warmer. "We don't have many women here. Which makes it hard to... Well, I just think that when something special comes along, sometimes it seems all the more special, just because it's rare."

Dee could recognise flirting when she saw it. But along with a sharp spike of pleasure at his interest, she also found herself suddenly on the defensive.

It wasn't that she didn't find Mark attractive. She most certainly did, but in the sort of way one might admire a rock star or a movie star – from a distance. In a lot of ways, he was *too* attractive, too athletic, too self-assured, too dangerous – as proven by his willingness to kill a room full of scientists to save her life. Put simply, he was out of her league, and the realisation was disheartening. She was certain that his interest in her would wane once he got the chance to scratch the surface a little more, and discovered that she was really quite ordinary.

Dee's taste in men usually ran more along the lines of book worms and computer nerds, intellectuals who were undoubtedly interesting people, good company but far less threatening than the roguish, athletic men who never seemed to take an interest in her anyway. She was too short, too curvy and not nearly wild enough to attract their attention. Or at least, she had been, until she'd become part wolf.

Mark must have noticed her discomfort, as he immediately backed off. "Sorry. I'm a little out of practice at this."

"You don't have a girlfriend, then?" The question came out without her really meaning it to, and she immediately regretted it, thinking it was far too personal a question.

"No. I've tried things out with a few shifter women in the past, but it never worked out." He paused, then gave her another contemplative look. "If I may ask... did you have a boyfriend before you came here?"

Dee fought not to blush. Because no, that wasn't an awkward question at all. "Um... no. My last boyfriend broke up with me a couple of years ago." After deciding that her career plans were too 'safe', that her tendency to plan ahead lacked the spontaneity that made life 'interesting'.

"Ah." Damn, but he was hard to read sometimes. The question itself implied a certain interest in her, a subtle hope, perhaps, that she was single. But once he had his answer, there was no further attempt at pursuing the idea. No subtle hint that he might like to fill the role. Just a flat acknowledgement of the situation. What was she supposed to say to that?

The problem was solved a moment later when Faeydir gave her another nudge. "I don't mean to change the subject all of a sudden," she said, rather grateful for the interruption, "but Faeydir really needs to go for a run."

Mark nodded. "Of course." He led the way out of the workshop, then headed to the left, around the side of the house and across the lawn, towards the edge of the forest. "Anywhere in particular she'd like to go?"

"Just into the forest. I think she just wants to explore for a bit."

"No problem." Mark shifted, then looked up at her expectantly, and Dee had to laugh suddenly, Faeydir bouncing around in her head like a six year old who'd just been told she was going to the beach. She retreated and let the shift wash over her.

This time, instead of the frantic chase of her last run, the almost desperate embracing of freedom, Faeydir ran just for the pleasure of it, muscles stretching and loosening, fast, but not furious. There were tracks through the undergrowth, faint scents informing them of the wolves who had come this way recently, a few distinct territory markings from Baron, a blood smear where someone had caught and killed a rabbit.

After a while, they came to a small stream, running down from higher up the hill, and Faeydir decided to follow it. They headed up the hill, through ferns and under bushes, over a hollow log, always keeping beside the water, and Dee felt an odd sensation in her mind. A strange sense of disconnection, like déjà vu. Or almost like she was dreaming.

Could she be dreaming? Was all this just a figment of her imagination, the kidnapping, the Den, becoming a wolf? Was she actually lying in bed in her cosy flat, soon to wake and sigh with relief as she realised that the jarring changes to her life were no more than a particularly vivid nightmare?

They came to a level clearing, a wall of ferns surrounding a small pool, no more than a trickle, but it cascaded over rocks in a small waterfall before falling a foot or so into a pool below, and the surreal feeling got stronger.

Faeydir moved closer, sniffing. There was a scent here, one she liked, and yet it also made her tense, anxious. She whined a little, looked around for Mark, then edged closer to the pool again. An image flashed in Dee's mind of a much larger pool, a forest clearing, other wolves and several humans standing around. The sound of chanting filled her ears, but there was no chanting here. She and Mark were alone.

Electricity tingled up Dee's spine, a creeping sensation that set warning bells ringing in her mind. She tried to ask Faeydir what was wrong, tried to tap into the wolf's mind to see what she was thinking. An overwhelming surge of light shot back at her, a sense of hovering over a vast, empty space, a feeling of being flung backwards through time to a much, much more primitive place... and then everything went black.

# CHAPTER EIGHTEEN

Dee came to slowly. She could hear voices around her, two people arguing, other voices, low and gentle, someone scolding the ones arguing. She felt the crackle of electricity along her skin and then a sharp jolt. Her body felt odd, like it was floating, and then she heard shouting. Tried to make out the words...

"Caroline! Get over here. She's doing it again."

More electricity, then warm hands on her face, her neck, and the static died down. A whining sound in her head, dizziness... she tried to open her eyes and felt the room spin.

"Lie still," Mark told her, gently but firmly, pressing her back onto the pillow, and she realised that she was back in her room, lying on the bed.

"Lie still!" Caroline was standing over her, trying to hold her down, and it was only then that Dee realised she was trying to get up.

She lay back, feeling static electricity build up again, then fade out. "What happened?"

"We went for a run in the forest," Mark said, concern all over his face. "And then you passed out and started shifting uncontrollably. Baron carried you back here and Caroline's been trying to keep you in human form. Your wolf was having convulsions for a while there."

"What's the last thing you remember?" Baron asked, stepping forward. Behind him were Skip, Tank and Heron, an older lady who had spent time with her in the cages, and outside the door, she caught a glimpse of Kwan and Aaron. Great. She'd managed to become a circus side show again. She glanced at Mark and felt him squeeze her hand. The gesture seemed surprisingly intimate, and for a moment it distracted her from her nausea and unease.

"I was in the forest, like Mark said. By the stream. And then..." And then what? She checked in with Faeydir, only to have the wolf whimper and

109

snarl at her. "And then Faeydir remembered something. A waterfall. A pool in a clearing in a forest. There were two tall trees on either side of the pool, and three jagged rocks sticking out of the water." She looked up at Baron. "I think it was where she lived before she and I were joined..." She trailed off as every jaw in the room dropped.

"You saw what?" Baron asked, and it was a rare thing to see him so off guard. "That's... Have you ever been to France?"

Dee's eyes widened. "No. Never."

"Wow." It was Caroline who breathed the word, and then she had to concentrate as Dee felt another shift coming on. Caroline managed to control it, her hands still on Dee's shoulders, but she could tell the effort was wearing on her. How long had she been out?

Dee tried to focus, tried to find out if Faeydir knew what had caused this, but the wolf was off in la-la land, clawing at the edges of Dee's mind. The instant she offered to let the wolf out, Faeydir retreated, whimpering in fear. "What's France got to do with anything?" she asked, when she got nothing sensible from the wolf.

"There's a forest in the mountains," Caroline said, awe in her voice. "A sacred clearing where conversions were performed up until only last century. The landscape creates a natural focal point that attracts lightning – which was vital for a conversion until we learned how to use electricity to the same effect. Hundred of shifters have been converted in that exact spot. That Faeydir has seen it... I don't even know what that means."

Baron was looking rather shaken. "We've always worked on the assumption that the wolf side of us is born, or created, when the conversion takes place. But if your wolf was around beforehand... Fuck. Like Caroline said, I have no idea what that could mean."

"Is Faeydir angry about being with you?" Skip asked shyly, peering around Baron. "Has she said anything?"

"No. I mean, she's been angry about things, frustrated with different people and situations, but she's never complained about being stuck with me. I think she actually likes it."

Baron and Caroline exchanged a look that Dee couldn't read. And then Baron shook his head ever so slightly, an answer to a silent question that only made Caroline scowl all the more.

"Do you think you can control the shifting now?" Caroline asked, more gently than her usual harsh tone, and Dee nodded. She sat up cautiously, allowing Faeydir to retreat to the back of her mind.

"I think I'm good."

"I'd suggest you stay in bed until the festival tonight."

"And when you're feeling better," Baron added, "we're going to have to talk about this."

"Faeydir's terrified," Dee blurted out. "I don't know if she's going to want to discuss what happened."

"You come with a fair dose of weird, Dee, and for the most part we accept that," Baron said sharply. "But this is totally off the radar. So like it or not, sooner or later Faeydir's going to have to face up to who – or what – she is. Now," he said, turning to the rest of the room. "Everybody out. Let Dee get some rest. Heron, can you stay with her for a while?"

"Of course," Heron said, pulling up a chair next to the bed. "No problem at all."


By the time six o'clock came around, Dee was feeling a lot better. She showered and changed, then followed Heron downstairs and out onto the patio. The need for an immediate chaperone was waived for this one night due to the fact that the entire Den would be out with her and she would be the centre of attention for much of the evening.

Most of the shifters had already gathered on the back patio when they arrived, and Dee felt immediately self conscious as everyone turned to stare at her. Heron squeezed her hand reassuringly. "Don't worry. Usually when we do this ceremony, we've had a few years to get to know the convert. With you, everyone's just a little more curious than usual."

"Then why are people glaring at me?" Dee asked in a whisper.

"They're not sure where you'll fit into the pecking order. There are two sides to the social aspects of the Den. The human side is thrilled to have a new member, someone to strengthen our numbers. But each person's wolf side feels that you threaten their place in the ranks."

"But no one's allowed to challenge me to a fight tonight, right?"

"That's right," Heron said. Caroline had mentioned that in one of her training sessions – once Dee was a fully fledged member of Il Trosa, she would be expected to fight the other wolves to establish her place in the pecking order. The fights were controlled, designed to display strength and skill, but not to seriously injure anyone, but none the less, Dee was rather nervous about the idea. "But tomorrow," Heron went on, "you'll be considered a regular member of the pack. And that means you'll either have to accept the disadvantages of being the omega wolf, or start fighting for status."

The light was fading quickly, but a dozen torches were lit around the edge of the patio, providing more than enough light to see by. There were long tables covered with dishes of food, cold salads, steaming vegetables, a massive tray of meat, and at one end of the table was a large dish full of beef bones and chicken carcasses – food for any hungry wolf, no doubt.

Dee glanced up, seeing that the sky was clear, only a few faint wisps of cloud marring the stars, and a quarter moon was lending a silvery light to everything in the garden. It was a beautiful, almost magical scene.

Suddenly a loud, full throated wolf howl broke into the night. Beside the bonfire, Baron and Caroline both stood in wolf form, heads thrown back, howling at the sky.

"I thought that wasn't allowed," Dee whispered to Heron, none the less enchanted by the sound.

"Tonight is an exception. For ceremonial purposes. Only those two, though, and only once."

The howls died out, leaving Dee with shivers down her spine as a thick silence descended on the estate.

Baron and Caroline both shifted, electricity crackling over their bodies in the dark, giving them an ethereal, mystical quality. Then Baron took up one of the torches and lit the bonfire. It took quickly, flames leaping up to engulf the pile of wood.

He looked even bigger than usual, and Dee realised that he had a thick fur thrown around his shoulders. Deer, maybe? Or... it couldn't be a bear skin, could it? Caroline was similarly adorned, her fur identifiable as a large cat of some sort, and they made their way to the middle of the group, coming to a stop directly in front of Dee.

Baron addressed her first. "Dee Carman. Faeydir. For three thousand years, the shifters have bridged the gap between human and animal. Between wilderness and civilisation. For six hundred years, Il Trosa has held sway over the European continent, preserving our species, protecting our kind from humans, maintaining our history and our secrecy.

"Now you, too, carry the wolf within you. You are hereby called upon to swear your oath of loyalty to your brethren. Loyalty to us earns our loyalty to you, assistance from any wolf in Il Trosa, access to any resource or knowledge that we can lay claim to. Tonight, you become one of us."

Baron stepped aside, and Caroline took his place. "Your oath to Il Trosa is a sacred responsibility. Should you ever betray us, then every member of our species is charged with your execution. You will be hunted from shore to shore, country to country, continent to continent, until your betrayal is repaid. Likewise, you now take on the responsibility of hunting anyone who betrays Il Trosa, be they friend, lover, brother or sister."

She stepped back, standing side by side with Baron. "Do you understand these privileges?" Baron asked. "Do you understand these responsibilities?"

"I understand them and call them my own," Dee responded, as she had been instructed.

"Then repeat after me. I, Dee Carman, renounce my human life." Dee repeated the words, wondering what Faeydir thought of all this. She hadn't had much to say since the shocks of the afternoon, and Dee found it curious that her wolf wasn't being asked for any pledge of loyalty. "I renounce my human family," Baron went on, Dee repeating his words. "I renounce my worldly possessions and take on the mantle of Pack Member, Shape Shifter, Wolf. I pledge my allegiance to Il Trosa, vow my loyalty to my Den, swear my obedience to the Council, and forfeit my life should I break this vow." Even as she said the words, Dee couldn't help but think of Mark. He had broken this vow – she wasn't sure of all the details involved, nor of his exact reasons for his actions, but a sense of foreboding filled her. By staying silent about his visit to the lab, she was breaking her own vow – only just having made it.

The recitation ended, and the gathered crowd was silent.

"Is there anyone here," Caroline asked, loud and clear across the hushed audience, "who knows of any reason why Dee should not be accepted into Il Trosa and made a member of this Den?"

"I have reason." Two voices spoke up at once, and though she had been warned of this possibility, Dee felt her heart lurch. She was fast running out of options here. She was already dead, according to the human world. She was on shaky ground as a shifter, Faeydir an anomaly even amongst the shifters, and then there was that odd conversation she'd had with Silas. And he wasn't the only one to fear her, she was learning. And now there were members of the Den objecting to her joining them…

"Explain yourself," Baron demanded of the first man – Dee didn't know his name, but he was in his thirties, wore glasses and had a geekish look about him.

"All indications say that Dee hasn't been able to merge with her wolf, that the so-called Faeydir can't be controlled. What assurance do we have that this doesn't pose a threat to our Den?"

Baron regarded the man with a derisive scowl. "Simon. If I believed for a moment that you had a genuine concern for your safety, I just might take that seriously. But I have a sneaking suspicion that you're referring to a rather obscure myth instead. Am I right?"

Simon glared back at him. "Our mythology informs us of our origins, our place in this world and our future. I know there are those here who don't take those myths literally, but others of us do. My objection stands."

A murmur spread through the crowd, some agreeing with Simon, others mocking him, and Dee felt a tremor go through her body. She could be in serious trouble here.

"And you?" Caroline asked next, addressing a dark-skinned woman in her forties, the second to have voiced an objection, and Dee assumed that this must be Raniesha, the only female wolf she had yet to meet.

"Dee's sire is unknown," Raniesha said coldly. "Il Trosa has gone to great efforts to trace our lineages. Almost every member can list their sires back ten or twelve generations, trace their line back all the way to the Four Mothers. Why should we accept someone with no breeding?"

It was a valid question as far as Dee was concerned, and she wondered what Caroline would have to say to that. But before the alpha female could form any kind of answer, a deep growl broke the quiet, and everyone turned to see John, teeth bared, skin crackling with electricity, eyes fixed on Raniesha.

"Oh, fuck, I wasn't talking about you," she snapped, her voice full of disdain for the younger man.

"Then maybe you should think before you speak," Baron snarled, stepping forward. "And then maybe remember who you were before you came here, and that might get rid of that sense of entitlement you seem to have."

Raniesha paled at the insult – Dee had no idea what Baron was referring to, knowing nothing of Raniesha's life before she became a shifter, but it was clearly an issue of some significance. "I wasn't talking about John!" Raniesha protested again, though she was sounding less assured now.

Baron stepped back, tugging a still snarling John with him, then addressed the crowd. "More than half of you have witnessed Dee shift. Does anyone who has seen her do so have any reason to believe she is not a full blooded wolf?"

A chorus of 'no's' rumbled back at them.

"Then let us take the vote," Caroline announced. "The affirmative vote will be cast to my left, the negative to my right. Proceed."

Dee watched, heart in her throat as the members of the Den split. Baron and Caroline moved first, placing their vote to the left. Mark followed them, along with Heron, Skip and John, and Dee was a little surprised to find Silas heading that way too. His surly attitude had rather made her expect him to try and get rid of her at the first opportunity.

But Raniesha and Simon headed for the right, along with another man Dee didn't know, and then Caleb, of all people. After his promise to support her, he was now trying to kick her out?

A few others took longer to decide, Alistair the last to move. He stood in the centre of the patio, staring at Dee intently. And then he finally took a step to the affirmative side.

"The vote is called," Baron announced. "Twelve for, six against. Dee Carman," he said, shooting her a sly grin. "Welcome to Il Trosa."

Relief filled her, a shaky smile growing as the sentiment was echoed by a dozen voices. She was dying of curiosity about whatever this myth was that was causing so much trouble, and she resolved to look it up in the library at the first opportunity. But for the moment, there were other things to be attended to, and she made an effort to put the issue from her mind.

"Let the introductions proceed," Caroline announced, kicking off the next section of the ceremony… but then another voice interrupted.

"No one has performed the Chant of Forests," Mark said, loudly and clearly. "Should we cast aside honour and tradition because Dee was brought to us in unconventional ways?"

A murmur went through the crowd. "The Chant of Forests," Silas seconded the idea, a few other voices agreeing with him.

Caroline looked almost embarrassed. "Of course. Thank you, Mark, for reminding us," she said, sounded pained by the admission. "Dee? If you would stand over here, please?"

"What's going on?" Dee whispered, as Caroline led her to the centre of the patio. The rest of the shifters gathered in a large circle around her.

"The Chant welcomes a new wolf into the world," Caroline told her quickly. "It's usually performed at a shifter's conversion. But for you, we'll do it now."

A quick check-in with Faeydir reassured Dee as Caroline joined the circle. The wolf wasn't familiar with this particular ritual, but similar ones had been performed throughout history, she informed Dee, sometimes chants, sometimes dances, sometimes a presentation of gifts, but all with the same purpose – to affirm the birth of a shifter into their unique world and culture. And it was an honour to be a part of one now, she asserted with a sense of satisfaction.

A heavy silence fell over the Den as everyone stood still, hands clasped behind their backs, heads bowed, and Dee felt awkward and conspicuous, as no one had told her what was expected of her. She waited, trying not to fidget.

And then a single voice broke into the silence. "Hama Yukú Laethi-Ká." Dee realised that it was Tank who was beginning the chant. And that he had the most beautiful baritone voice she'd ever heard. And then everyone else joined in, their voices creating a rich, haunting harmony. "Hama Yukú Laethi-Ká. Hama Laethi-Kaánah. Veeshee ahnis sendigah. Hama Laethi-Kaánah." The words were in a language Dee had never heard before, but unspeakably beautiful none the less. But the most astonishing thing was that, as she looked around the circle, every single person was looking her dead in the eye. Still, focused, seeming to mean every word from the bottom of their hearts, even if Dee couldn't understand them. Even those who had voted against her – Raniesha, Simon, Caleb – even they seemed to take the chant as a solemn vow, and Dee knew she was going to have to find out what it meant, later.

After long minutes, the voices ended, the last notes of the chant drifting off into the cool night. "Let's move to the introductions, then," Caroline said after a moment's pause, and that, it seemed, was that.

Dee watched as the entire Den formed a single, orderly line, with no fuss, no question as to who would go first or last. Caroline had told her that she was to be personally introduced to each and every member of the Den, in both human and wolf form, but had failed to mention that it would be done in order of rank. The head of the line was Tank, and down the end was a elderly man who Dee could only assume was George, and it was fascinating and informing to suddenly see where each and every member stood. Natural wolf packs had a pecking order, from alpha down to omega, the lowest ranking wolf, with food, mating rights and other privileges being decided based on each individual's rank. And it made an odd sort of sense to see it carried over into their human lives as well. After all, humans were equally known to care about rank and status, it was just less obvious in modern times than it had been in the past, when kings and nobles held sway over peasants and commoners.

"May I introduce Henry Grounder, aka Tank," Baron said, a formal introduction regardless of how often he and Dee had met before. Tank grinned, shook her hand, and then stepped back. He shifted into a huge white wolf, and Dee couldn't help but smile. He was a beautiful animal, bright blue eyes, thick, snowy coat and a look on his face that promised mischief. He eased forward and gave Dee a thorough sniffing, then huffed and moved away along the patio.

"Caleb Anderson," Baron said next, and the ritual was repeated.

As they worked their way down the line, Dee made careful mental notes on each name and each wolf. She tried to identify characteristics that would be easy to remember – a dark patch over the eye, one foot a different colour, an ear that flopped instead of standing up straight.

And aside from that, she tried to control her surprise at the ranking of each member of the pack. Silas was near the head of the line, just behind Caleb. Skip was fifth from the bottom, though Dee had assumed that her outgoing personality would have let her climb the social ladder a little more. Heron was just below Silas, the woman's age apparently no barrier to her holding a high rank.

But John was a surprise. She'd expected the small, reclusive man to be near the bottom, but he was fifth, just after Heron. Small but fierce, Dee supposed, as she shook his reluctant hand. And then, when he shifted into his wolf form, Dee took an involuntary step back. The wolf was savage – that was the only way to describe him. Scars covered his face and chest, a bald patch over his left shoulder that looked like it had been burned, then scarred over. And his eyes were a dark grey, cold and steely, dark loathing pouring out at her.

And she was right to be nervous, she surmised, when Baron took a step forward, keeping his eyes firmly on John. John raised one lip in a silent snarl, then lowered his head and edged forward. He took a cursory sniff of Dee's leg, then hurried away, retreating to the far end of the patio.

Raniesha was next, surprisingly calm and composed given her earlier outburst, but while Dee was willing to bridge the gap between them and attempt to make peace, it seemed that Faeydir had taken exception to her insinuations. The wolf rose suddenly and sharply, and Dee fought her down, knowing that to shift now would be completely inappropriate. For all the casual air of it, this was a sacred ritual, one that had been performed for each and every new member of Il Trosa for hundreds of years.

Caroline noted her distress – she could hardly miss it, the way Dee was swaying and turning green – and took a discreet step closer. One small electric shock was all it took, and Faeydir was retreating with a snarl and a promise that tomorrow, there would be a fight.

Something else for Dee to look forward to.

She shook Raniesha's hand, stood to be sniffed by her wolf, then tried to concentrate on the rest of the ceremony.

# CHAPTER NINETEEN

In the living room of the Grey Watch's training house, Genna sat on an antique sofa, her back ram-rod straight as a group of shifters filed in the door. There were the three women who'd been training her – Rintur, Feriur and Vash, all looking grim and severe, along with two others who had arrived just minutes ago whom she hadn't met before. And trailing after them, head down, eyes on the floor, was Sven, the shifter male who was to convert her.

She tried to keep her eyes off the man, having been lectured at length about Grey Watch protocol when it came to males. They were fit for only two things, she had been told firmly – one was converting women into shifters, an unfortunate glitch in shifter biology meaning that members of one gender could only convert the other gender – and the second was sex. A handful of males were kept in the camp for the sexual pleasure of the women, though the opportunity to mate with them was determined by rank and seniority, so it would likely be years until Genna herself got the chance – and in the absence of either of those two immediate concerns, males were to be ignored.

But the Watch chose their males well, she had to admit. Sven was tall, muscular and blonde, the sort of man who would usually be found on the cover of a sports magazine. He wore buckskin trousers and a black jacket over his bare chest, the males of their pack denied the right to wear the usual grey robes of the Watch, and he had a collar around his neck.

"My name is Lita," one of the newcomers said, an aging woman who walked with a slow, shuffling gait. "You've been told what is to come?"

"I have," Genna replied. The conversion itself, when Rintur had explained it to her, had sounded terrifying, but the night to follow was by far the worst part of the situation. "I'm ready."

"Let's get this over with then. Sven, present yourself."

Without a word, Sven came forward, removing his jacket to reveal a hairless, muscular chest. Then he stripped off his trousers with the same cool disinterest and stood before her naked.

It was not the first time Genna had seen a naked man, but the sight of him now left her trembling. And not from desire. He stood in the middle of the living room, accepted a knife from Lita and without any preamble whatsoever, cut a long slit into his own wrist. He handed the knife to Genna, handle first, and she took it, pushing down the wave of fear she felt.

She stood up and removed the grey robe she had been given just an hour ago. Beneath it, she too was naked, and she felt the disapproving eyes of all the women upon her.

Determined to prove her worth as a shifter, Genna lifted the knife and pressed the tip into her own wrist. She had been expecting pain, had been bracing herself for it ever since she'd been told her conversion was to happen well ahead of schedule, but it was worse than she had anticipated. She pressed deeper, drawing blood, tried to cut a line up her wrist, but had to stop, clamping her jaw shut to keep from crying out. From the side of the room, Rintur made a sound of impatient disgust.

Taking a deep breath, Genna decided that she should treat this like ripping off a bandage. She took a moment to gather herself, then cut her arm quickly, a strangled sound of pain escaping her as her blood welled up.

Sven stepped forward, ignoring her pain, and took her arm, pressing the two cuts together.

Lita came forward next, holding an electric cord with a bare wire at the end. She plugged one end into a power socket on the wall, then flicked a switch halfway along. Electricity was the key to conversion, Genna had been told, and this device, crude as it was, got the job done. Part way along the wire was a heating element, designed to prevent new converts from being electrocuted, but that was the limit of the niceties. Lita stepped over and Genna braced herself again, every muscle taut as-

She screamed as a sharp current shot through her, Lita jamming the live wires directly into her and Sven's joined wounds. Genna felt her body convulse, muscles jerking uncontrollably as she hit the floor. Loud complaints, words flung out with disdain echoed around her as she tried to get her bearings. There was something different about her body now, a tightness, a tingling sensation as a new presence seeped in from her arm, up into her chest, electricity crackling along her skin though Lita had already started packing the cable away. Genna struggled to stand up, knowing that weakness in any form was not tolerated amongst the Watch. Sven was still standing, she realised, and wondered dimly how often he had been through this. There was blood on the wooden floor, thick drops dribbling down her arm, through her fingers, and Genna fought to still her shaking. The night was far from over yet.

"Complete the ritual," Lita snapped, and that was all the recovery time Genna was going to get. Sven came forward, his penis already erect, and Genna, overwhelmed and off balance, simply let him. He took her shoulders and pushed her down onto the floor. Spread her legs and put his hand between them, and began what would, in other circumstances, have been called foreplay.

Genna had been told that this was part of the ritual, a mandatory mating with one of the Watch's males, and when she'd been told, she'd been excited about it. Sven was a masterpiece of male perfection, chiselled jaw, rough stubble on his chin, powerful thighs, narrow waist, and for the month since she'd started her training in earnest, she'd been looking forward to the chance to get it on with the kind of man who would never have taken an interest in her in the normal course of things.

Now, though, her body was still thrumming from the near-electrocution and the conversion, her attention taken up with the baffling sensations of having a wolf invade her mind, and any romantic expectations she'd had about a gentle and beautiful initiation into a world of hedonistic pleasure vanished.

But this was necessary, she reminded herself, feeling the off-putting sensation of Sven's wet mouth on her breast. This was the rite of passage she must endure that would allow her entry into a world of wonder and mysticism, an escape from the cold drudgery of life as a supermarket checkout girl, and she submitted, telling herself that the reward was worth the indignity of it all.

Long minutes later, while Genna was still trying to fight off the wolf pressing for its first shift, Sven thrust inside her, and Genna registered that he must have used some sort of lubricant, as she was not the slightest bit aroused herself. But, to satisfy the demands of the pack, she spread her legs, wrapped her thighs around him and clung to his shoulders as he thrust into her again and again.

She closed her eyes, trying to block out the fact that there were five women watching this, trying to ignore the sick feeling of being used, not by Sven, but by the women, by the Grey Watch, by a degrading tradition that served to bind her more closely to the shifter world.

Finally, it was over, Sven climaxing without a sound, and then he climbed off her, retreating to stand at the side of the room like the trained dog he was.

Genna stood up, her legs fighting to keep her upright, and registered that she was smeared with blood, the wound on her arm still seeping, and with other fluids. But cleaning up right now was not an option.

"The wolves are waiting outside," Lita said, and for the first time, Genna recognised the undertone of malice in her voice. Her trials for this night were far from over.

Outside, once more dressed in her grey robe, Genna looked out into the darkness and saw dozens of pairs of eyes glowing in the dim light. The Grey Watch. In wolf form.

"Behold Genna, the omega," Rintur called loudly, the women having followed her out of the house, and Genna tried to hold herself up tall, attempting to appear strong and confident. "If she has the strength to reach the camp before dawn, she will become one of us. If not…" Rintur turned to Genna with a leer, "then she will return to the dust from whence she came. Let the run begin."

The wolves came out of the darkness, a horde of black shadows, and Genna reached inside herself desperately. Her first shift, unassisted, on a frightening deadline, and she had no idea how to proceed. She held the image of a wolf firmly in her mind, imagined her limbs shortening, her muzzle lengthening… and bloody hell, it seemed to work. She felt static crackle over her skin, and then she was no longer Genna, non-descript supermarket worker, but a wolf, small, bedraggled and struggling to manage her four legs, rather than the two she was used to.

The instant she was in wolf form, the wolves were on her. Their task was simple - to harass, to intimidate, to wound, but not to kill. They were to do anything in their power to stop her from reaching the camp before the night was over.

Weakness, Rintur had told her again and again, was a liability. A weak link was the one that was going to allow the Noturatii to wipe out their pack, if not their entire species. So new recruits had to prove from day one that they were worthy of the gifts bestowed upon them.

Genna had been given a map of the local streets, the forest, and the location of the camp, and had had no more than an hour to memorise the entire thing. The rest of it was up to her.

Death was not an appealing option, Genna feeling suddenly angry about the brutality that these women seemed to think was so necessary in their daily lives. She had been short changed five of the six months of her training, converted in a rush, mated just as quickly, and now they wanted to bully her into giving up?

Not too fucking likely. With a snarl and a show of teeth, Genna threw herself at the nearest wolves, charged through the ring of bodies surrounding her… and then she was off.

# CHAPTER TWENTY

It had taken Dee nearly half an hour to meet the entire Den. After the round of introductions in human form, she'd been asked to shift and everyone had had the chance to meet her wolf. She'd been worried that Faeydir wouldn't cooperate, but the wolf had come out easily at her request, and had taken a genuine interest in her new pack. She'd memorised everyone's scent, had snarled at Raniesha – an entirely appropriate challenge, Baron told her later – and she'd bowed her head to John and the higher ranking members of the pack. That had intrigued Dee. Apparently Faeydir saw something in the boy that Dee herself had yet to pick up on, offering him unquestioning respect and deference. The only slight incident had been when Faeydir had nipped George on the leg. As the newest member of the pack, Dee was automatically the lowest ranking member as well, and Faeydir was clearly impatient to start moving up the ladder. A stern growl from Caroline had set her straight, and she'd whined an apology, licked the man's hand and wagged her tail.

After that, there had been a few more formalities, speeches made, incense burned and a prayer to Sirius spoken over a bowl of burning herbs, but finally, the rituals of the night were over. Baron shouted for everyone's attention, welcomed Dee to Il Trosa one last time, and then declared the feast to have begun.

Dee found herself quite hungry, and she made herself a plate of salad, potatoes and roast chicken with a heavenly scent to it. She followed Skip across the patio to where the chairs were set out and they both sat, watching as the others ate, drank, squabbled over bones in wolf form or ran off to play on the lawn. Skip had helped herself to a plate twice the size of Dee's, but she set about ploughing through it like she hadn't eaten in a week

As usual, she was wearing a collection of childish jewellery, a necklace of bright pink and yellow, an electric blue bangle around her wrist as thick as her thumb, studded with plastic diamonds. As she ate, she fiddled with the beads in between each bite and seemed to draw comfort from their presence. Perhaps one day, Dee pondered, she would know the girl well enough to feel comfortable asking for the explanation for her obsession with the jewellery.

Turning back to her own meal, Dee bit into her chicken leg. It had been flavoured with lemon and ginger, the meat tender and delicious, and she almost felt guilty, knowing that tomorrow she would be challenging George to a fight. He was an excellent cook, an asset to the Den, and it was only when Skip had explained that he preferred to hold the bottom rank that Dee had managed to relax. Position came with responsibility, Skip said, and George preferred a quiet, peaceful life. And if the price for that was a drafty bedroom and the seat at the bottom of the table, then so be it.

Grateful for a peaceful moment now that the ceremony was over, Dee took the time to just observe the people around her. Tank was arguing with Caroline, something she'd seen him do with startling frequency. Baron was having what looked like a heated discussion with John on the lawn. John had his arms folded, head up defiantly, glaring at the alpha, but the way Baron dwarfed the smaller man was almost laughable. He probably weighed three times as much, and stood head and shoulders taller than him. But he looked fiercely angry, and Dee dreaded to think what John had done to warrant such an ear-bashing, as Baron continued lecturing him on whatever it was that had him so riled up.

"Would you like a brownie?" someone said suddenly, and Dee looked up, surprised to see George standing beside her, offering her a plate.

"Thank you," she said, taking one. "The food is all delicious."

That put a smile on George's face, and it was hard to tell in the dim light, but he seemed to blush. "It's a pleasure to prepare it. I never had anyone much to cook for before I came here." There was something diffident about his manner, as if he expected to be trodden on, and accepted that as his place in the world, and Dee could feel Faeydir growing more aggressive, sensing a weakness in the man and wanting to challenge it-

*Sit down and shut up*, Dee snarled at her. *He's friendly and polite, and doing you no harm. If you paid attention instead of snarling at him you might learn something about manners.*

Faeydir huffed in the back of her mind and relented, though Dee suspected there might be an ongoing problem between her and George. Which was a shame. She rather liked the man.

George wandered off, taking the plate of brownies to the next cluster of hungry humans, and then Dee suddenly looked down at the treat in her hand with concern. "Hey, isn't chocolate bad for dogs?" she asked Skip, who already had a mouthful.

"Yeah," Skip said, not bothering to swallow first. "But you're not a dog. And the wolves are smart enough not to eat them." At Dee's quizzical look, Skip rolled her eyes and finished her mouthful. "There's very little link between what you do physically and what your wolf does. You wear clothes, but they vanish when your wolf comes out. Your wolf could go for a swim in the pond, be soaking wet, but after you shift, you, the human, will be dry. So eat the chocolate, but don't feed it to your wolf, and everything will be fine. Have you kissed Mark yet?"

"What?" Dee squawked, the brownie already in her mouth, and she spat out the lump of it and coughed.

Skip just laughed and took another bite of her food.

"Where the hell did that come from?" Dee asked in a squeak. "I haven't... I've just... I barely know the man!"

Skip grinned. "Yeah. But he's been watching you ever since we sat down, and he fought Baron for you yesterday." She signed melodramatically. "That's so romantic."

"Mark's not... he hasn't... I don't..." The protests died on Dee's lips. Mark had tried flirting with her this afternoon, after all, so she could hardly claim that he wasn't interested. And saying that she wasn't attracted to him in return was a lie. But the idea of anything more at this stage was still rather intimidating, even a little surreal. She glanced over at him, standing with a beer in his hand, talking to Alistair, and felt her heart speed up a little. Damn, the man was gorgeous, the light from the torches making his skin glow golden, his dark hair giving him an untamed look. Gorgeous... and complicated.

"I don't think we'd work together," she said finally, needing to deny the idea one way or another.

Skip regarded her seriously, then sighed, a more heartfelt sound this time. "That's too bad." She glanced over at Mark, then down at her plate. "He's changed since you came here," she admitted quietly, and there was something in her tone that made Dee pay attention. "Well, kind of, at least. He used to be fun. Quiet, independent, but still fun. He and Alistair and Luke... you never met Luke-"

"Mark told me about him. Apparently he was... he was killed."

"Yeah," Skip confirmed sadly. "So anyway, the three of them used to hang out. They were good friends. But then Luke died and Mark kind of stopped living for a while there. Stopped talking to people, stopped playing, just started going through the motions. I mean, we all get that, the grief and all. We've all lost people to the Noturatii. But he took it harder than most. But since you arrived he's been more... I don't know. More interested. More motivated. Just... *more*. So I thought maybe..." She shrugged. "Or maybe not."

On reflection, Dee agreed that Mark had seemed a rather solemn sort.

Interesting to know that wasn't his normal self. But even so...

Their conversation was interrupted suddenly by Baron's voice, a loud string of curses that could be heard across the entire gathering. He was standing on the lawn still, glaring at Tank, who had apparently just asked him a question, and by the sounds of it was getting a right dressing down for whatever he had said.

"Baron seems rather unhappy today," she said, when the moment passed and the conversations started up again. John was sulking a short distance away from the alpha, and from their body language, it was clear that their argument was far from over. Tank, on the other hand, merely shrugged at Baron's outburst and headed back toward the food table.

Skip snorted. "Yeah. He had a fight with John earlier. Not this little quibbling stuff," she added, wiggling her fingers dismissively at the standoff on the lawn. "I mean a real fight, teeth and claws and all. I don't think you were around at the time, but if you ever hear them yelling at each other, just duck and run for cover. Don't even think about getting in the way."

Dee felt her eyebrows lift. "John doesn't look big enough to fight with Baron."

Beside her, Skip sighed, a melodramatic sound that promised a story of intrigue. "Ah, good ol' Johnny boy. There's a tale and a half. But," she added, lowering her voice quickly, "if anyone asks, you didn't hear it from me."

Dee nodded her agreement. John was just a scrap of a boy, and Baron was a larger than life brute who seemed to run the Den with an iron fist at times. So how, and why, were they fighting?

"First, let's get a few things out in the open, okay?" Skip said conspiratorially. "Baron and John are sleeping together. Now, I phrase it that way on purpose. They're not dating, they're not in a relationship, they're not partners. They just share a room and bump uglies on a regular basis. Capisce?"

Dee felt her jaw drop. "I hadn't realised Baron was gay."

Skip shrugged. "I'm not entirely certain he is. You don't have to be gay to sleep with another man," she added, to Dee's quizzical look. "Some guys are bi. Or curious. Or, in Baron's case, I think it's more about dominance and reminding John who's in charge. Hey, no one said it was a healthy relationship," she speculated flippantly. "But John seems to accept it, and while there are plenty of us who have our doubts, none of us are game to step in and try to change anything."

"You think he's abusing him?" That Baron would allow such a thing, never mind participate in it, was quite a shock. Sure, the man was tough, strict, forceful, but also kind and always willing to put the welfare of the Den first.

Skip lost some of her cheerful flippancy for a moment. "John shows up with bruises now and then. He'll never say where he got them, so who's to know, but you couple that with a lot of yelling in their bedroom and the way their furniture gets knocked about, and it's an easy conclusion to come to. Hey, we've all got a story," Skip said a little more sharply, at Dee's horrified look. She fingered her gaudy necklace. "Most of us were abused, lost, in jail or dying before we came here. So remember, you point a finger at them, and there are three pointing back at you."

There was a sharp retort on Dee's lips... until she remembered that, if not for Mark's interference, she would likely have ended up murdering a room full of scientists in her own bid for freedom. She looked away, not at all liking Skip's assessment of the situation. But what was she going to do? Go fight Baron and force them to change their ways? Not likely. "So what's the story with John?" she asked, working hard to keep her voice even.

"John's story?" Skip snorted. "No way. Ask him about his childhood, and be prepared to die young. But after he joined the Den?" She shrugged. "When he first came here he was a load of trouble. Got into fights with everyone, couldn't control his wolf. God knows why Caroline let him stay. She's usually pretty quick to boot the troublemakers. But she and Baron seemed to reach this weird agreement that he was worth the trouble. He was out of control, though, and the Council got called in at various points, helped them work it out. So John got to stay, but Baron decided something needed to be done to keep him under control. Took him up to his room for a 'discussion'." Skip held up her fingers in quote marks as she said the word. "Then the next thing you know, they've moved in together and they're rocking the furniture every night."

"So you think Baron is using sex as a form of discipline?"

"Who knows? And frankly, I don't want to know. The nuts and bolts of it is that Baron's the only one who can reign John in when he gets in one of his moods, and for as long as John himself isn't crying foul, then the rest of us are willing to let it slide."

Okay, this was getting creepy. Time to change the subject. "What about Tank? What's his deal?" After talking to Baron, she'd watched Tank return to Caroline and tell her something, only for her to then march over to Baron, stride long, head up, shoulders back, ready to start a small war.

"Tank is the highest ranking male, after Baron. It's a tough spot to be in. He gets along plenty well with Caroline – or at least, as well as anyone can, she's a bit high strung – but he likes to play them off against each other."

When Caroline reached Baron, the two alphas had a short, but heated argument, which concluded with Baron looking at Tank with open amusement, and Caroline stalking off back to the patio, shoving Tank out the way as she went.

"And before you go thinking he's just causing trouble for the sake of it, that's his job. He makes sure the leaders of the pack are still strong enough to lead. On the one hand, he has to detect any weakness in them and bring it into the light. But on the other hand, he's also trying to keep them sharp, to make them practice keeping the peace with small shit, so that when the big shit happens, they know how to deal with it."

"And if they can't?"

Skip huffed. "If they can't, then the long version is a big old shit storm starts up and everyone goes a bit nuts for a while, but the short version is that Baron gets booted, Tank becomes alpha, and the whole story starts again. And on that note," she said, hopping up suddenly, "I'm going to go occupy myself with one of those beef bones for a bit. Don't think I'm abandoning you, though," she added with a grin, "cos Mark has been eyeing you for the last five minutes, and the instant I'm out of the way, he's going to be over here like a shot." With a wink and a crackle of electricity, Skip had shifted and was gone, true to her word, straight to the bowl of beef bones. There was another wolf at the table already, and a brief scuffle ensued, which resulted in Skip shoulder-slamming the other wolf, grabbing a bone and running away with it. A half-hearted growl followed her, then the other wolf turned back to his task – far more interesting than chasing Skip – which was digging a chicken carcass out of the bottom of the dish.

Dee had her doubts about Skip's prediction, and picked up her wine glass, draining the last of the liquid, preparing to go and refill it, then perhaps have a chat to Heron for a while... until the seat beside her was suddenly taken again and she looked up to see Mark sitting there with a glass of beer in his hand, a half-smile on his face.

"How are you feeling?"

Dee felt her heart pick up its pace, feeling the nervous beginnings of what could become a serious crush. She made an effort to act calm and relaxed, even if she was feeling the complete opposite. "Much better, thank you. I'm sorry if I scared you."

Mark nodded ruefully. "Took a few years off my life. So long as you're okay, though."

"Faeydir's feeling better. She's been having fun tonight."

Mark nodded. "I wasn't sure you were going to make it there, for a while. It's always a little tense for a new shifter – after a conversion, we never know if someone's going to be able to merge with their wolf, and when you kept saying Faeydir was separate from you, a lot of people thought you were going to go rogue. So I'm glad you came through."

Dee felt her face warm, not so much from the words themselves, but from his tone, warm and just slightly husky, as if the sentiment carried too much weight for him. "What's it like for most people?" she asked, needing some way to redirect the conversation. "The conversion, I mean?"

"It's a beautiful ceremony. I'm sorry you weren't able to experience it like that. Usually we do it out in the forest. We have a machine that we use to create a field of static electricity. In the old days, of course, it had to be done in a lightning storm. Beautiful, but wet and cold and there was always the risk that someone was going to get struck by lightning," he said with chagrin. "These days, it's a lot more pleasant. The whole Den gathers. The chosen sire burns an offering of herbs and oil to Sirius. The alpha of the Den tells the story of Faeydir-Ul and the origin of the shifters. Then everyone is given a cup of spiced mead. The convert's cup also has some pain relief in it. The sire and the convert both step inside the machine. They cut their wrists, put the wounds together and get zapped with a small electric charge. It's not much more than getting an electric shock off a piece of metal, really. Then one of the senior shifters helps the convert through their first shift. We find that allowing them to shift straight away helps them accept the wolf better – and lets the wolf accept them.

"And then, once everything's under control, we perform the Chant of Forests. It's a kind of pledge, really, that we'll respect and honour the new wolf. Even if the shifter doesn't manage to merge with it."

"I've been meaning to ask about that," Dee said, remembering her earlier curiosity. "What does it mean? The Chant?"

"Some parts of it don't translate all that well – the language is ancient and there aren't many people who still understand it – but the gist of it is:

*I welcome you into the world, bold and wise, ancient and new.*
*I will look in your eyes and call you brother, sister, friend.*
*With each new dawn I will be by your side*
*And I will not sleep until you rest safely.*
*If you call me, I will come. If you fall I will carry you.*
*I will measure your steps each day that you run*
*And when the sun sets, I will wait for you in the Hall of Sirius."*

Mark stared into his glass, not quite able to meet her gaze, and Dee felt tears prick her eyes. So that's what they'd been telling her. That beautiful, haunting, solemn chant had been a pledge to protect her and honour her until she died.

Wow.

"Is that what it was like for you?" she asked softly, envious of the ceremony he had described. It was a far cry from a cold lab and an IV line.

But Mark surprised her when he replied, "No. Not for me." He sighed, scrubbed a hand over his face. "You know I had leukaemia, right? Well, by the time they brought me here, I was pretty close to dying. Actually, I was dying. I was crashing on the floor of the foyer. So there wasn't time for any kind of ritual. They just set up the machine around me, cut my wrist and bam, suddenly I'm a shifter. I'm not complaining," he added firmly. "At the time, just getting the job done was far more important than following the ritual. But I saw it later, when we converted some of the others. And wow… it's just beautiful."

"And was Baron your sire?"

To Dee's surprise, Mark let out a sudden laugh. "No. Male shifters can only convert female humans, and vice versa. And before you ask, no, it wasn't Caroline, either. Heron sired me. There are… wow, this is more history you don't know yet. Sorry if I'm overwhelming you with details-"

"No, I love hearing about this," Dee insisted, lapping up the information. "Please, go on."

"Okay. There are four official bloodlines among wolf shifters. The Council keeps tabs on how many of each bloodline there are, where they live, whether they're male or female, and they dictate who's allowed to convert new shifters on the basis of which bloodline has the most, or the least members. They try to keep everything in some kind of balance."

"So Heron sired you because she was from the right bloodline?"

"Exactly. Raniesha's of the same line, but Heron was the more senior wolf."

"Wow." She hadn't just walked into a new family. This was a whole new people, a tiny nation in its own right, complete with history, hierarchy, ritual and ceremony.

"Why are there so few women here?" she asked next. "It's hard to believe they don't want to become shifters. There have always been women interested in spirituality and mythology."

"It's not that we don't want them, or that they're not interested," Mark said with a sigh. "It's more a case of finding them. See, to invite a person to become a shifter means we pretty much have to already know that they'll accept. Otherwise they become a security risk and that means there's a very real possibility we'll have to kill them if they don't join us."

Dee swore softly to herself. "Does that happen often? That you have to kill people?"

Mark was silent for a moment. "Even once is too often for anyone's liking. It's only happened once since Baron became alpha. But some alphas aren't that careful. Anyway, in modern society, there are plenty of groups who run around pretending to be mythical and mysterious, medieval re-enactment groups, people who fancy themselves druids, witches, mages, but confront a lot of them with the reality of becoming part wolf and they run for the hills. The people who take us up on the offer tend to be a different kind of desperate. Criminals looking for a second chance. People with terminal illnesses. And we get our share of computer geeks – it's a stereotype, but it works for us. Adolescent boys who are smart, a little antisocial and with a passion for video games. It's a mindset that embraces elements of fantasy, and for some reason, they seem to accept the weird better than the people who think they really are weird. Plus, there's the added bonus that some of them can hack any database you throw at them. Skip was an exception – and an accidental one, at that. Not often we get a female hacker, but we rarely turn down interested women."

The patio had become quieter while they'd been talking, a lot of people shifting into wolves and running off to chase or wrestle on the grass. John was sitting off by himself, staring into the darkness. Baron was sucking back beers like they were going out of fashion, and Dee didn't envy him the headache he was going to have in the morning. Tank and Silas were wrestling on the lawn – both in human form, and from the jeering and cat-calls from their onlookers, Dee quickly concluded that it was just a friendly test of strength, rather than a more serious disagreement.

She glanced sideways and realised that while she had been watching everyone else, Mark had been watching her. She looked away, then glanced back at him bashfully. "What?" she asked finally, when he kept watching her.

"You're beautiful." It had been a long time since a man had told her that, and Dee felt her face heat, caught off guard by the blunt statement. "I know I wasn't in the best of moods this afternoon," he apologised, ducking his head. "It's been a little rough around here lately. But… Look, if I'm out of line, just say so." He looked up at her again, eyes seeming to plead with her. "But if you're… I'm just asking for a chance here. Take some time if you need to. Wait until we know each other better. But just so you know, it's been a long time since I met a woman like you."

Dee still wasn't entirely comfortable with the attention she was receiving. Mark was very different from what she was used to – not just his athletic form and wild air, but his directness was putting her off balance as well. She was used to her relationships starting with a lot of vague flirting and skirting around each other before one party or the other finally worked up the courage to say how they felt. It was unnerving, and oddly flattering, at the same time.

"I think… Um… no, you're not out of line," she managed finally. "I think…" Oh, what the hell. She hadn't had a boyfriend in a long while, and if she understood the shifter laws, then she didn't have a lot of options outside the Den. And if she was entirely honest with herself, she was starting to like Mark. Rather more than she had expected to. "I think I'd like to see where this could go."

The slow grin that spread across his face made her blush all over again, and she ducked her head, pleased, embarrassed. "Is that so?" She nodded, daring to glance up at him again.

He looked around the patio. To all intents and purposes, they were alone, the few shifters lingering nearby caught up in their own conversations and paying them no mind.

"Then could I…?" He leaned towards her, and it took Dee a moment to realise what he intended. She licked her lips reflexively, a tiny movement that suddenly had his gaze riveted on her mouth. And then he was leaning towards her, a slow, deliberate movement that gave her plenty of time to pull away.

She didn't. Instead, she leaned forward, meeting him halfway, and the kiss was everything she had imagined from a man like Mark, warm, firm, the taste of him wild and sublime and male in a way that she suspected she could very quickly come to find entirely addictive.

# CHAPTER TWENTY-ONE

Dee was in the kitchen in the morning, waiting while Faeydir ate breakfast on the mat at the end of the room. The wolf had woken up hungry, eager for a raw steak, and Dee, who'd been anticipating a plate of toast and eggs, had been a little startled as she'd realised all over again what it really meant to have a wolf living in her body. Equal time for both of them, and that included meals. Weeks of living in the cage with Faeydir refusing to come out at all had given her a lopsided view of what this new life would really look like.

She wasn't complaining though, as she watched Faeydir's progress with the meal, because it gave her time for a little reflection on last night. The ceremony. The Chant of Forests. And Mark.

She still couldn't quite believe she'd kissed him. Men like that simply weren't interested in women like her.

Except that Mark clearly was, his curiosity about her genuine, his affection cautious and yet passionate, and the whole idea was leaving her rather off balance. The kiss had been perfect, warm and firm, part heated desire and part playful teasing, followed up by Mark sliding his fingers through hers and a long, intimate chat, until Tank had come along, his white wolf standing out against the dark, and with a whine and a bounce, he'd invited them both to come and play.

Faeydir was just finishing the steak when a shriek sounded from the first floor, and the thud of angry footsteps came hurrying down the stairs.

Raniesha appeared in the kitchen doorway, her furious presence demanding the attention of every person in the kitchen, and she held up a handful of shoes. High heels, three of them, in black, silver and pink... and Dee's eyes opened wide as she realised that each of them had been thoroughly chewed by a set of canine teeth.

"Who did this?" the woman demanded, her face red, her eyes promising a slow death to whoever was responsible, and inside Faeydir's mind, Dee cringed. Though she hadn't been told specifically, she was fairly sure this kind of behaviour was against the rules of the Den, and surely there would be consequences for whoever had-

Dee paused, looking around the room in surprise at the rest of the shifters, expecting to see faces clouded with indignation on Raniesha's behalf, or possibly with guilt, from those responsible, but instead she saw... amusement. Eating his breakfast at the table, Alistair coughed, a clear cover for a chuckle. Standing at the cupboard choosing a box of cereal, Skip's face turned red and she buried her head in the cupboard, mouth clamped shut to avoid laughing. And next to Dee on the mat in wolf form, John, of all people, let out a snort. And then Silas walked in the door, no doubt curious about the fuss, saw the shoes in Raniesha's hand and quickly covered his mouth with his hand. Alistair was the first to break, letting out a strangled laugh, and that did it for everyone else. The room erupted in a burst of laughter that only made Raniesha more furious.

"Who. Did This?" she asked again, but the laughter only increased.

Mark was the next to arrive, followed quickly by Kwan and Aaron, who burst into laughter as they saw the problem.

But Mark wasn't laughing. Instead, a sardonic gleam appeared in his eyes, and he took one shoe from Raniesha, examining it carefully. "Looks like we have an untrained dog on the estate," he said smoothly, and Raniesha snatched the shoe back, her glare intensifying.

"If you had anything to do with this," she said coldly, but Mark quickly denied the accusation.

"I don't know anything about it," he said, his expression perfectly serious, and Dee couldn't tell if he was lying or not. "But you know the way it is around here. Strays, half-breeds... better keep the rest of your shoes locked up, if you ask me."

"Fuck you," Raniesha spat, then turned on her heel and stalked away.

The laughter died down after a minute or two, and once Faeydir had finished eating, Dee shifted, Faeydir announcing the fact with a short yip. In this part of the house, announcing a shift was mandatory, partly a simple courtesy, partly a security measure – unexpected shifting tended to alarm people, as it generally indicated an emergency. The only places inside the manor exempt from the requirement were the foyer, or inside a bedroom.

Faeydir was as curious as Dee about what had just happened, so she sidled over to Mark, who was pouring himself a cup of coffee. He winked at her as she approached.

"Did you do it?" Dee asked quietly, sure there were plenty of subtleties to the situation that she was missing.

But Mark shook his head. "Me? No."

"But you know who did?"

Mark glanced around the room, then tilted his head, inviting Dee to follow him outside, snagging his coffee on the way. They went out through the back door that led from the kitchen onto the lawn, and then he turned to face her. "I may have heard a rumour or two," Mark said slyly.

"But why would anyone do that?"

"Because Raniesha insulted you at the welcoming ceremony."

That was news to Dee. "She did? I mean, I know she objected to me joining the Den, but other people did too. So why pick on her?"

"She implied you were a half-breed. Brought shame on your bloodline. I know you don't understand all the nuances of our culture yet, but what she said was extremely rude. And I suppose some of the people here were inclined to make a statement about that."

That whole fuss had been for her? A strange display to defend her honour? "But how does chewing up her shoes prove anything?"

"It's a backwards sort of insult," Mark said, looking amused all over again. "The worst insult shifters can throw at each other is to call someone a dog. From a wolf's perspective, domestic dogs are considered to be quite stupid, not able to strategise or look after themselves, just dumb animals following orders. Calling someone a half-breed implies there's common dog in their bloodline. Chewing up her shoes is something only a dog would do, not a wolf, and certainly not a shifter-wolf." He grinned. "It's kind of hard to explain, but the gist of it is that Raniesha called you a dog, so someone decided to behave like a dog and chew up her shoes, but because of what she said last night, Raniesha becomes the butt of the joke, not the wolf who did the damage."

It made a twisted kind of sense, and Dee grinned despite herself.

"So who did it?" she asked, curious to know who would have gone out of their way to repay the insult.

"Can't say," Mark said mysteriously. "But let's just say that you and I weren't the only ones to take exception to her comments last night."

Back in the kitchen a short while later, Dee was finishing her cup of tea while the rest of the Den drifted in and out of the room, seeking out breakfast or coffee, more than a few of them still suffering the after effects of last night's party. But one man seemed nervous, lingering by the door awkwardly, and it was only when Mark nudged her and nodded pointedly at the man that Dee noticed George hovering.

It took only a moment's reflection to realise what was expected of her. He was waiting for her to challenge him to a status fight.

The very idea of fighting another wolf made her more than a little nervous, but she'd have to trust Faeydir to take care of that side of things. She was a capable wolf, after all, who was very much in favour of a round in the boxing ring.

Self-consciously, she stood up and stepped towards the older man. "I challenge you to a status fight," she said briefly, and George looked almost relieved at the news. The rules of the Den stated that any planned fight had to be authorised, and supervised by a more senior wolf – both for safety, if anything got out of hand, and to verify the truth of a change in status, so Dee turned to Baron, who had just wandered into the room. "Baron? Do George and I have leave to fight?"

Baron looked up at her blearily, no doubt only having gotten out of bed a few minutes ago. "Bloody morning people," he griped, pouring himself a cup of coffee. "Wait a minute, just let me get some caffeine sorted, and then you're good to go."

Minutes later, out on the lawn, a crowd gathered quickly. Any status fight in the Den tended to draw an audience, and in higher ranking fights, Dee had been told, it wasn't uncommon for bets to be placed as to who would be the winner. In this case, though, everyone was assuming Dee's win was all but a certainty, and the spectators were only really there to confirm that the fight had actually taken place, rather than for any particular interest in the result.

Watching from the sidelines, Baron nodded. "Proceed."

Dee retreated, letting Faeydir take over. The wolf assured her that she knew how to fight, and once George had shifted, the two of them faced off, both eager to get this over with.

"Begin," Baron announced, and Faeydir needed no more encouragement than that. The scuffle was brief and rather mundane, if Dee was honest about it. George put up a token resistance, then conceded defeat, lying limply on the grass, and there was brief applause from the crowd.

"Dee now outranks George," Baron announced, as they both returned to human form, and George gave her a nod and offered his hand for her to shake. Neither of them was injured, the whole thing having taken only a little more than two minutes.

"Thanks," George said, and it was hard to know whether he meant for taking it easy on him, or for getting this out of the way so quickly.

"No problem," she replied, then immediately felt Faeydir stir as she spotted the next wolf in line, a middle aged man called Eric. The wolf was nudging her insistently, so she approached the man and said, "I challenge you to a status fight."

Eric merely shrugged. "Fine. Baron?"

"May as well, while we're here," Baron said. "But I'm getting hungry, so don't think you can go challenging every wolf who's bothered to get out of bed this morning," he said, half in jest, half in warning, and Dee nodded.

This time, the fight was more serious, Eric putting up genuine resistance, as opposed to the token fight she'd had with George. He wasn't the fittest wolf, tiring quickly, but certainly not willing to just lie down and give up. But Faeydir was younger, stronger and more determined to win, and in less than five minutes, Eric was lying still on the grass, his surrender assuring Faeydir of one more step up the status ladder.

Back inside the house, Faeydir had more things to do, important things, as far as she was concerned, so Dee allowed a shift and Faeydir set about exploring the house. While Dee's tour had been largely a visual one, Faeydir needed to get to know the manor by scent, to find out who spent most time in which rooms, to see which rugs she could lie on, and which should be left for more senior wolves.

They started with the foyer, a fascinating room with hundreds of footsteps coming and going, a reminder of the scent of everyone who lived in the house. Then the library was next, the books old, the smell of them musty and comforting, and Faeydir learned that Caroline was an avid reader, her scent on more than a dozen of the thick volumes. John, too, liked to read, though he spent little time in this actual room.

Next was the dining room, with the long table where everyone had dinner, and Faeydir came upon a new scent here, one that was fading with time, in a seat about halfway up the table. *Luke*, Dee reminded her. *He died before we arrived. This must have been his seat.*

He had been a warrior, Faeydir informed her, his scent one of a strong male, without any trace of fear. A great loss for the wolf-clan.

Up the stairs was the next destination, Faeydir decided, but they'd barely set foot back into the foyer when Caroline came striding out of the kitchen, pulling her up with a commanding word. "Faeydir! Come here. I need to talk to you."

Faeydir tilted her head quizzically. It wasn't often the alphas wanted to talk to her, she mused. More often they wanted to talk to Dee, while pretending Faeydir didn't even exist. So despite the sharp order, Faeydir went, curious to know what had got the alpha's attention.

Inside the library, Baron was pacing the room — Dee was coming to realise that it was a rare moment when he was actually sitting down and relaxing. "This is for Dee as well," he said abruptly, when he realised who had just walked in the door. "But it affects you both, so I don't suppose it matters what form you're in." He hesitated. "Do you even understand human speech?" he asked of the wolf.

She did, picking up something of an instant translation through Dee's thoughts, but for a moment she was baffled about how to communicate that to a human.

*Move your head up and down,* Dee instructed, and, miffed by the idea,

Faeydir did, and was rather pleased when Baron returned the gesture, and said "Good."

"Do you want to sit down?" Caroline asked, gesturing to a rug, and Faeydir did, lying down sphinx style as she waited for Caroline to pull a chair over. "We've had a call from the Council," she began as soon as they were settled. "They've sent through a request which they've gone to great pains to stress is entirely optional. So please understand there is absolutely no obligation for you to agree with this. But at the same time, I'd like you to understand that it's a very serious request and that you would be doing Il Trosa a great service if you agreed." That sounded ominous. "The Noturatii have been kidnapping shifters from across Europe," Caroline went on, while Baron continued pacing the room. "Five have gone missing so far, and everyone's had to step up security because of it. The Council is doing everything it can to find them, but…"

"But we think one of them must have been used as a sire for you," Baron took over, and after seeing them at logger heads so much, it was odd to see the two of them finishing each other's sentences. And their sudden truce convinced Dee, more than anything else, of the severity of whatever it was they were going to ask.

Faeydir cocked her head. She had never met her sire, a thing of great sadness for the wolf, and it apparently held a significance both to her and to Il Trosa that Dee didn't yet understand.

"We'd like to try and find out which bloodline you come from," Baron said, and from his tone, the idea seemed a most weighty one. "Two of the kidnapped shifters were male. They come from different bloodlines, so if you match one of them, we can assume he was your sire. We'll know he ended up in London. And what his fate was."

"The process for discovering your bloodline is difficult," Caroline jumped in again. "And painful. And it can come with a few complications. It's not something we ask lightly. But it is very important."

Both alphas fell silent, giving Dee and Faeydir time to think that through. And it wasn't a great surprise when Dee felt a nudge from the wolf, and found herself back in human form. Faeydir was unperturbed by the request, perfectly willing to assist another wolf in harm's way, but Dee had questions. And to ask them, she needed to be in human form.

"What complications?" she asked first. According to what Mark had told her, it would have required a male shifter to exchange blood with her for her to become a shifter. So perhaps that's what they had been doing in the lab – trying to mix her blood with the shifter's in a way that got results. But after being confined in the lab, after being tortured there, subjecting herself to more pain, even for a good cause, was a daunting prospect. She had enough confidence in Baron and Caroline to believe that they wouldn't ask her to do this if there was going to be lasting damage, but…

Baron glanced at Caroline, then pulled up a chair, turning it around to straddle it. "If your blood matches one of the bloodlines, even if it's not one of the missing shifters, then your name will be recorded in the genealogy of Il Trosa and you'll be recognised as a pure blood. But…"

"There is a slight possibility…" Caroline paused as she took over the explanation, looking uncomfortable. "It's not very common, but there are a few unregistered bloodlines. People were experimenting with ways to create shifters back in the middle ages when we were being hunted to near extinction. They still pop up now and then, mostly out of the Grey Watch, and some of them…" She gave Dee an apologetic look. "A few of them made mistakes. Tried to convert wolves into shifters, but the wolves weren't purebred. They'd been mixed with domestic dogs. The results in a shifter can be messy."

"This is what Raniesha was talking about at the ceremony," Dee said, suddenly putting the pieces together. "You're saying that if I'm not from a registered bloodline, people will assume I'm a half-breed."

"Not all unregistered lines are half-breeds. Some of them did come from pure wolf strains. But yes, there's a certain tendency to jump to conclusions about your origins. And a certain stigma associated with not having a traceable lineage. So we realise that we're asking you to take a significant social risk in the possibility that your line can't be traced."

Faeydir had been quiet through all of this, and Dee gave her a nudge, wondering what she thought of this new possibility. Faeydir gave a mental shrug. She was a purebred wolf. She was certain of it. And if other people didn't think so, why should she care?

Dee had to smile at that. It was refreshing, to have her so unconcerned with social expectations. But Dee's other concern remained, the fact that the procedure – whatever it involved – would be significantly painful.

But then she thought of the other shifters' Dens. What if it was one of their own? Skip, or Tank, or Mark who got snatched. She liked to think that any other wolf who might be able to help track them down would do so willingly, and that was what made up her mind. The kidnapped shifters would have people who cared about them, who wanted to know what had become of them, and whether it might be possible to rescue them, if they were still alive. Despite her fears, she couldn't just leave them hanging.

"I'll do it," she announced. "So go on, hit me with the details. How much is it going to hurt?"

# CHAPTER TWENTY-TWO

Miller was typing a report on a laptop when the first alarm went off. A quick check with security revealed the problem – one of the sensors in the ventilation ducts had been set off. Likely a pigeon or a rat, they said, but they'd send someone to check it out, none the less.

Two minutes later, Miller's phone vibrated – an automatic message sent via the security system that informed him that one of the interior security doors was compromised. He wasn't officially part of the security team here at the lab, Miller's usual role consisting of acting as bodyguard for Jacob on his various travels or pursuing leads out of town, but while he was here, it was just as well for him to help keep an eye on things. He picked up his phone and dialled the head of security.

"What's going on up there?"

"Don't know," the reply came back to him. "Alarm system seems to have gone nuts. There's nothing in the air ducts, and the main security door is closed, but the sensor keeps tripping the alarm. Maybe some water got into the control box-"

The conversation was cut off suddenly as the fire alarm went off, sirens blaring throughout the entire building, and Miller watched as the staff around him began to pack up, closing laptops, locking filing cabinets, then traipsing in an orderly line out the door. For all their often ruthless policies when dealing with their enemies, the Noturatii still knew how to take a fire alarm seriously. And with the amount of potentially explosive chemicals stored in the labs, no one wanted to be taking unnecessary risks.

Miller slammed his own laptop closed, but rather than heading for the door with the others, he instead made a beeline for Jacob's office, next door to the administration area. "What the hell is going on?" he asked, barging into the room, not even bothering to knock. Jacob would have received automatic notifications of each alarm, along with corresponding updates from security.

"Get upstairs and help security," Jacob barked, tapping furiously at his computer. "The sensors have been triggered in nine locations. The external cameras just went offline... what the fuck??" More furious typing as Jacob swore softly to himself. "They've hacked the security system. They're setting off alarms at random, all over the fucking building!"

"Shifters?" Miller asked, drawing his gun and making sure he was standing between Jacob and the door. If anyone tried to get in here, they were going to have to go through him. But before Jacob could reply, another thought suddenly occurred to him. "Or the Khuli?" he asked suspiciously. "Head office said she was due to arrive tomorrow. What if she's come early and wants to stir up a little trouble on the way?"

"Why the fuck would a Khuli hack security?" Jacob demanded, then threw up his hands in disgust. "They've locked me out of my own fucking system! Get up to the server. Take it offline manually, just leave the local network connected. Then get up to street level and help security. There are only so many access points to the building. The intruders can't get too far."

Miller hurried out of Jacob's office and headed for the upper levels. The server room was on the first floor below ground, and he took the quickest route, knowing the hallways of this building like the back of his hand-

"Fuck." In keeping with the tight security the Noturatii insisted upon, there were security doors throughout the building, and he came to the first set leading up to the next level to find it locked. He tapped in his security code... and wasn't entirely surprised when nothing happened. Back down the hall and around the corner... and bloody hell, what the fuck was going on? The next security door was locked as well, but this time, a dozen staff were trapped behind it, caught between it and a fire door that had inexplicably become sealed shut. Two of the administration women saw him standing there and rushed over, banging on the door with their fists, yelling for him to help them.

There was nothing he could do from here, he realised. Whoever was hacking their system was an expert, locking doors, shutting down access routes, and he shuddered to think what would happen if this wasn't the Khuli and they were actually under attack. Their guards wouldn't be able to move through the building, or worse, they could get stuck in a very similar trap themselves. Damn it...

He set off again, at a fast jog this time, dreading finding out what other chaos their intruder had caused.

In the end it took him twenty minutes to make it to the server room, at one point actually having to climb into a ventilation duct and crawl over the top of a security gate – no doubt setting off more alarms himself in the process.

But finally, he made it to the right office, tapped in the access code and stood to have his retina scanned, relieved when the door opened. He strode over to the server cupboard and yanked the door open, quickly switching off the wireless router, shutting down that access route for a potential hacker, then he set about searching for the network cables to disconnect the system from the internet. He unplugged one wire and was reaching for the second... and then he froze.

He couldn't have said what it was that alerted him to the presence behind him. There was no noise, no stray rustle of fabric or exhale of air, no shadow cast where there shouldn't have been one. But the Satva Khuli was standing behind him in the office. He would have bet his life on it.

Deliberately, he relaxed his posture, standing up straight and easing back from the computer. And then, without turning around, he said, "I assume all the alarms are your doing?"

The laugh that floated back at him was young and girlish, and as creepy as hell for that very reason. "You're good. Even better than I was expecting." The voice, on the other hand, had nothing remotely childlike in it. It was the calm, even tone of a predator, slightly threatening, with just a touch of seduction to it.

"May I turn around?"

"You may." Miller did, slowly. The woman standing before him was nothing like what he'd expected. They'd been given next to no details on the Khuli that was to arrive – even a name had been absent, as the Satva Khuli referred to themselves as just that. This woman was to be addressed as 'Ma'am', or 'Li Khuli', literally, 'The Tiger'. But in trying to imagine the type of woman who'd dedicate her life to wholesale slaughter, he'd pictured a Russian mafia type, long black hair, poised and seductive, or perhaps an Asian warrior, straight out of a samurai movie.

The woman before him was short, maybe five foot two – much shorter than he'd expected for an elite warrior – with skin a shade darker than his own and tightly curled hair, cut close to her head. She wore a variety of weapons, knives, handguns, brass knuckles, but he had little doubt that she would be just as lethal if she were stripped completely naked and stuck out in the middle of a snowstorm. There was no sign of the team of assassins she'd brought with her, but that didn't mean anything one way or another.

"How did you guess it was me?"

"I assumed that an elite assassin would not just walk in the front door at the time everyone was expecting her."

"Clever. But your boss doesn't seem to share your insights," she said, with just a hint of disapproval, and Miller realised that she must have been eavesdropping on his conversation with Jacob earlier.

"Is Jacob...?" In danger, he wanted to ask, but wasn't sure how to phrase it without giving her ideas. Was he alive? Was he currently unharmed?

"He's safe and well in his office," the Khuli replied, picking up on his train of thought. "Just a little more pissed off, now that he can't actually leave it."

Miller nodded, not sure what else to say.

"Do you know," the woman went on, not taking her eyes off him, "that it took me and my team only a touch over fifteen minutes to lock down this entire building?" At his startled look, she grinned. "Oh yes. Every staff member is contained. Every security guard is neutralised – I haven't killed anyone," she said, when Miller's expression went from surprised to alarmed, "but not from lack of opportunity. Your security staff really are quite useless."

"My apologies, Ma'am," Miller said diffidently. "Clearly we need to do better."

"Clearly. You yourself were the only person to give me the run around. And yet here we are, face to face."

"Yes, Ma'am."

She stood there for a moment longer, seeming to weigh him carefully. "I think I'm going to enjoy working with you," she said finally, and Miller felt a cold thrill of fear run up his spine. And then she stepped to the side, removing herself from the path between Miller and the door. "You may go."

Miller nodded to her respectfully, not entirely convinced she wasn't going to behead him the moment he moved. "Ma'am." Back straight, head up, he walked quickly past her and marched straight out the door, without looking back.


Out on the manor's back lawn, the waxing moon was high, casting a faint silvery glow over the grass. The entire Den was gathered, making Dee the centre of attention again – something she wished would stop happening. They stood in a loose circle around her, Baron and Caroline front and centre. Heron and Skip stood beside them, Heron calm and poised, Skip looking a little green.

A low table was set up, nineteen small cups laid out, each containing a measure of spiced mead. Four of them, Dee now knew, also contained a small dose of opium.

Baron picked up one of the four cups set to the side and brought it to Dee. "May Sirius guide your days and guard your nights," he said as he handed her the cup. She took it, holding it carefully in her shaking hands. The ritual words and presentation were repeated as he gave a cup to Caroline, Heron and Skip, and then he stood back.

"May Il Trosa join us in our quest," Caroline recited to the rest of the gathered crowd. "Wake us with the dawn. Measure our steps each day. And wait for us at the setting of the sun."

In single file, the shifters each stepped up to the table, took a cup and stood back, forming a circle again.

"To Sirius and the perpetuation of the shifters." Baron lifted his cup, then drained the contents in a single swallow. Dee followed suit, along with the rest of the Den, and winced at the bitter taste of the opium, still detectable beneath the sweetness of the mead.

Baron stepped forward to take her cup, then gestured to the wooden chair at the centre of the circle.

Ignoring her rapidly beating heart, Dee seated herself and stretched out her arm over an archaic looking device. At first glance it appeared to be nothing more than a small table, but closer examination revealed a much scarier truth. There was a slit running the length of the wood, dark stains marring the colour, and a cuff at each end, designed to hold a person's wrist and elbow tightly.

Baron secured the cuffs, gently but firmly, and Dee experienced a moment's terror as it brought back memories of the lab, of being tied to the table...

"Are you sure you want to go ahead with this?"

Dee opened her eyes, not having realised she had closed them, and found that she was breathing quickly, loudly. She made an effort to control her breaths. "I'm sure."

"We'll begin with Caroline," Baron told her. He addressed the Den. "The Test of Sires begins. Caroline was sired by the line of Ranor. Her sire was Eric von Brandt. His sire was Eloise Franstead."

Baron took up a wicked looking knife and stepped up close to Dee. "Steady," he breathed into her ear, then reached down with a firm hand and pinned her wrist to the table. And then she let out a shriek as the knife cut deep. She tried to pull away, jerked her arm against the heavy wood and tears sprang to her eyes as the blood welled up and overflowed. Caroline stepped forward quickly, and Dee was barely aware that she'd cut her own wrist in the same manner. Christ, the nerve of these people.

Caroline placed her wrist parallel to Dee's, their blood mingling, and when she'd been told about this ritual, she'd asked a dozen or more questions about the hygiene of this. HIV, hepatitis, herpes, rabies, all manner of illnesses, but the answer had been the same each time. Shifters weren't subject to the common illnesses of humans. Mixing their blood did have side effects, but infection was not one of them. And everyone in the Den had been vaccinated for rabies, Caroline had added, when Dee brought that one up. There was no way she could catch anything from any of them.

Even so, something in Dee was still repulsed at the idea, a lifetime of caution and warnings reinforcing the idea that this was *wrong*, and she shuddered as Caroline pressed her wrist firmly against her own.

A slithering sensation pulsed against her wrist, causing her to try and pull away again, distaste curling her lips, then a spark of heat, and Dee closed her eyes, knowing that this was the part that was going to hurt.

The only way to test a shifter's sire was to attempt to mix their blood with another line. If there was no reaction, the two shifters had the same bloodline. But if they were different...

Dee screamed suddenly, as white hot agony burst through her entire body, the opium dulling the pain, but certainly not blocking it out completely. Her back arched, muscles convulsing, the heavy table actually rocking as her slight weight heaved against it. In her mind, Faeydir snarled, but seemed to be coping reasonably well. She pressed herself forward, not to shift, but to lend her strength to Dee, and she was surprised when it actually made the pain easier to bear.

Caroline withdrew quickly, tremors rocking her own form, though her reaction seemed less severe than Dee's. The fire in her veins faded slowly, then flared up again, just when she thought it was over, and Dee came to a minute later, slumped over the table, sweating, breathing hard, while the Den stood still as statues all around her.

God, no wonder John had refused to go through this, she thought dimly, seeing his impassive face in the crowd. He didn't know who had sired him, didn't know which bloodline he was from, and after it had been described to her, without a pressing reason for following through, Dee would have turned down the experience herself.

She glanced around the circle and found Mark. He was looking a lot less calm than John had been. Jaw clenched, hands curled into fists, his eyes were locked onto her, though he didn't seem to be seeing her. His lips moved in half formed words, but Dee couldn't make out what he was saying.

He'd been aghast when she'd told him she was going through with the ritual. Had tried to talk her out of it, tried to convince her that there was no shame in refusing, no obligation to endure this. His concern had been touching, a warm reminder of their newfound affection for each other... but none the less, she'd stood her ground and quietly explained to him that she had no intention of backing out. In her oath to Il Trosa, she'd been granted aid from any wolf in Europe, and agreed to lend the same in return. Honour, as well as conscience, decreed that she help in whatever way she was able.

Before Dee was quite ready for it, Heron stepped up next, her face blank, her shoulders back. Dee was still bleeding, not too quickly, but enough for another test, and Heron picked up the knife and cut her wrist, a tiny flinch the only sign of discomfort.

"Heron was sired by the line of Fellor. Her sire was Raven. His sire was Anstella of Inuell. Begin."

The same procedure. The same result, and at the end of it, Dee could hardly manage to keep herself upright. She leaned heavily on the table while Faeydir tried to offer comfort, feeling drained, weak as a newborn puppy.

And then Skip stepped forward, and she was about ready to beg off the final test.

Of the four bloodlines traced from the Four Mothers, only three were still used by Il Trosa. The fourth was the line of Grenable, reserved exclusively for the Grey Watch, and while it was unlikely that Dee would have come from them, the chance still remained. Or, of course, there was the possibility that she was not of any registered line. Given what was at stake here, they couldn't afford to make any assumptions.

"Skip was sired by the line of Harkans," Baron announced. "Her sire was Tank. His sire was Eleanor Renoir. Begin."

Skip flinched as she cut herself, grimacing as the blood began to flow, which made Dee feel better about the fuss she had made at her own wound. Quickly, as if to just get this over with, Skip darted forward and held their wrists together. Dee braced herself for another trip through the wringer… and a few seconds later, looked up at Skip in surprise. There was no reaction, no pain, no fire in her veins, just a faint warmth amid the slick seep of blood.

"The Den has witnessed this," Baron announced, as Skip withdrew. "Dee Carman is descended from the line of Harkans." He paused, and when he continued, his voice sounded a little tighter. "Her sire will be recorded as Jean-Luc Descoteaux." Dee recognised the name as one of the shifters who had been kidnapped. Jean-Luc was from the French Den, the only one of those kidnapped from the line of Harkans. But she was too worn out at the moment to really consider what it meant to know her sire. She had expected joy, maybe, or relief, or even sadness, given the circumstances of her conversion. Instead, all she felt was an overwhelming desire to get the cuffs off her wrist.

"Dee?" Baron was talking to her again, and she tried to concentrate. He crouched down in front of her and spoke in low tones. "There is one more test we'd like to perform. It won't hurt much, just one more little cut, but it will tell us whether your sire is… whether he's still alive."

They hadn't mentioned this before, and Dee fiddled with the straps with her free hand, wanting them off, not really listening to Baron-

He put a firm hand over her own, stilling her attempts to get free. "Dee? Listen. Please."

Dee forced herself to look up at him-

"Let her go," Mark spoke up, sounding strained. Baron growled loudly without even glancing up at him.

Dee shook her head. "How the hell can you tell if he's alive just by taking my blood? The mixing the bloodlines at least makes a bit of sense, even if it's totally gross-" Exhaustion was catching up with her, Dee thought as she realised she was starting to ramble. "But now you're just going to use my blood to conjure up a crystal ball to tell you if the guy's alive? That's not possible-"

"This is a world of myth and magic," Caroline said softly, and Dee was surprised to find her crouched down beside Baron. She hadn't noticed her move. "Science as you know it no longer applies, nor does the conventional sense of cause and effect."

"You're crazy," Dee said flatly. But then she felt Faeydir give her a nudge. An image of flames. An incantation echoing in her head. Bloody hell, even the wolf was against her.

"Let her go!" Mark repeated, and Dee glanced over at him. And wondered what it would feel like if he had gone missing, if she was sitting at home waiting for news of his fate.

She squinted up at Baron's rugged face, crease lines etched into the skin around his eyes, around the corners of his mouth, and he looked older in the dim light. Tired. Worn. "If he lives, we need to find him," she said, her voice strained. "If he's dead, then let his Den mourn for him properly." She felt completely wrung out, her muscles aching from the earlier tests, her head hurting, her eyes stinging even at the faint light of the torches. But she'd come this far. They may as well finish it now.

She barely flinched when she felt the next cut. Blood ran over her wrist, down onto the wood, pooling in a small silver dish beneath the platform. As Baron collected the dish, Caroline undid the straps and tended her wound, a few quick swipes with disinfectant and then a soft dressing, a fast and expert job of applying a bandage.

By the time she was done, Baron was over on the lawn. A large candle, at least four inches wide was set on the ground, and a strange scent was rising from it that made Dee wonder what it was made from. As she watched, Baron placed a metal stand over the flame, then lowered the dish onto the stand reverently.

Heron stepped forward, a bandage stained with red covering her own recently cut wrist. Electricity filled the air, and a low murmur rose around her. Dee felt herself sway as the sound got louder, and then she realised that the entire Den was chanting. Heron added a pinch of black powder to the dish over the flame. Two drops of oil from a tiny vial. A small leaf of some herb or other, crushed and then sprinkled on top. Then, startling Dee, she called out an incantation, the words loud against the chanting, the language beautiful, if incomprehensible.

The candle sputtered, the flame licking up over the sides of the dish. It turned vivid blue, engulfed the cup of blood in a bright burst of light… and went out.

Silence.

Baron closed his eyes briefly, took a deep breath to steady himself.

"The sire no longer breathes," he said, his voice strained, and Dee felt her lip tremble, tears pricking at her eyes. Her emotions were a mess, exhaustion, anger, and now a sudden and unexpected sorrow washing over her at the news that the wolf who had brought her into this world was dead. And for all her earlier indifference to her sire, she suddenly understood the hatred Il Trosa felt for the Noturatii. No longer a distant, impersonal threat, their activities now had a personal impact on her. And a moment's reflection was all it took to realise that, for all her shaky and involuntary introduction to this world, these people were now her family, her friends. Her comrades, in a war that had raged for centuries.

"May his body find rest in the earth. May his heart return to the forest. May his soul ride the night winds with those who fell before." The entire Den recited the mantra, then a thick silence engulfed the circle.

"Thank you, Dee," Baron muttered, eyes on the ground, his gratitude heartfelt, if laced with sorrow. "I'll contact the Council. And inform the Den in France."

# CHAPTER TWENTY-THREE

It took surprisingly little time for the laboratory complex to be restored to order. After her impromptu meeting with Miller, Li Khuli had released the security system back to Jacob's control, opened the sealed doors to let the staff out and presented herself and her team of five assassins to the Head of Security – not a polite introduction, but rather with a lecture on the inadequacies of their defences, and the need for a complete overhaul. After which, she had simply vanished.

Jacob was livid. It was hard to tell which annoyed him more – that Li Khuli had broken into the lab with such ease, or the fact that she had omitted to introduce herself to him at any point in the hours that followed. Jacob liked to be in control, liked to dictate how things ran, rather than having them dictated to him, and Miller had to wonder just how that was going to work out with a free-agent assassin wandering around. Li Khuli answered to no one but the CEO, an elusive figure in the German Head Office who ran the Noturatii with the refined control of a drill sergeant and the fanaticism of a third world dictator. So while she was here on Jacob's request and to serve his lab, that didn't mean she was going to do anything he said.

So when Miller finally had the chance to catch up with Jacob again, after an hour or two of restoring their systems and debriefing with the security team, it was no surprise to find him in a foul mood.

"You haven't submitted your report from your investigation up north," Jacob barked at him when he arrived in his office.

"I was nearly finished typing it when we were interrupted," Miller said politely, avoiding any direct reference to Li Khuli, as it was likely to just send Jacob into a lather again. "It would only take me a few minutes to finish it now-"

"Just tell me what the hell happened and stop wasting my time!"

Miller was not at all put out by Jacob's harsh attitude. If he was the type to get offended every time a superior officer yelled at him, he'd never have made it in the military. And would not have lasted five minutes in the Noturatii. "There was nothing particularly informative, sir. The house seemed suspicious, but nothing that could be immediately linked to the shifters. Once the report is finished I'll submit a request to put them under surveillance."

"The sooner the better," Jacob said impatiently. "These creatures are dangerous."

"The lady we spoke to didn't seem particularly dangerous," Miller countered hesitantly, knowing his views on this went against official Noturatii opinion. "She was polite, cooperative, pleasant enough. I would find it hard to believe she had any criminal intentions-"

"Have you ever met a shifter, Miller?" Jacob interrupted, impatience in his tone. "Ever seen one face to face?"

"Only once, sir. The day you showed me one in the lab." It had been a gruesome experience, Miller's first real introduction to the Noturatii's underground world, only an hour after he'd been told that shape-shifters were real, and not confined to video games and fantasy novels. The shifter had been more dead than alive from the torture, but that hadn't been what had shocked Miller. Seeing the man turn into a wolf...

He snapped back to the present, realising that Jacob was talking again. "...innocent face, a girl, maybe, some no older than eighteen or nineteen. And you can look into that face, wide eyes, tears, downturned mouth, and forget what they are. They are deceptive, above all else. They pretend to be one thing, while they're quite another. Do you know why I do this job?"

"No, sir."

"It's because the shifters are the biggest threat to national security – no, to the security of the human race – that we've ever seen. Can you imagine how easy it would be for them to carry out terrorist activities? They can travel through remote areas, endure conditions that would kill most humans. They could find their way through a forest to a major dam, let's say for example, set bombs to blow the place up, let the flood destroy a city downstream, then vanish into the wilderness as wolves, and no one, *no one* would ever find them again. They can cross international borders without a passport – any countries connected by land, at least. They could walk down the street and you'd never know the difference. That's what you have to keep in mind. The wolves are natural deceivers. They'll lie to your face, make you believe that black is white, turn your world upside down, and then kill you while you're trying to figure out what day of the week it is. So never, ever underestimate how dangerous they are."

"Yes, sir," Miller replied respectfully. For all his disagreement with Jacob's assessment, the man was his boss, after all.

"Now get that report finished and send it to headquarters. We've wasted quite enough time today already."

The ritual was over, the mood sombre as the Den filed away, back into the house, or out across the grounds, some of them shifting even before they got to the trees.

Baron and Caroline were standing nearby, having a tense conversation, and Dee supposed she could have waited for them to finish, asked them to help her back into the house, but a stubborn determination made her attempt to stand up by herself. Her legs were shaking, her arms supporting her on the blood-stained table, but it was only a short walk back to the house, after all, she told herself. Though getting up the stairs might be difficult-

Strong arms scooped her up suddenly, and Dee looked up in surprise, expecting to see Baron carrying her again-

No, not Baron. Mark had caught her, his face grim, mouth a tight, angry line as he carefully nestled her in against his shoulder. "You look exhausted," he muttered, as if that was *her* fault, and set a quick pace back towards the house.

"I'm okay," Dee said, trying to reassure him, but his scowl only deepened at the words.

"Baron shouldn't have asked you to do that. You're too young as a shifter. For heaven's sake, you've only been out of the cage for a few days."

It was tempting to argue with him, to insist that she was strong enough to look after herself, to make the point that she wanted to be useful to the Den, but given the fact that she didn't think she could even walk by herself at this point, she suspected the argument would be a hollow one.

"It was rough," she admitted. "But it was worth it. I know who my sire was, now. And his Den will know what happened to him. That's got to be worth something, right?"

They were inside the house now, Mark heading up the stairs, careful not to jostle her as he walked, and for a moment he didn't reply. At the top of the stairs, he paused, looked down at her, pain evident in his eyes.

"That was horrible to watch, you know that?"

Dee nodded. "I know. I'm sorry. But it was necessary," she said stubbornly, not regretting her decision to go through the ritual, despite the pain it had caused.

That pulled Mark up short. Then he shook his head, marching quickly to her bedroom, kicking the door closed and setting her gently on the bed. He tugged the blankets up over her and set a pillow against the headboard for her to lean against. Then he sat down beside her, watching her intently. "The surprises just don't stop with you, do they?"

"What do you mean?"

"You've been thrown in the deep end so many times in the past few weeks. You've been kidnapped, tortured, locked up, insulted… but I've never once heard you complain. And then Baron just keeps asking more of you, and you feel like *you* owe *us* something. Do you know how much I admire you?"

Dee shook her head. In her own mind, she hadn't done anything remarkable. Despite the bad circumstances of her arrival, this Den had been working overtime to help her, even when it had caused them plenty of problems of their own. Tonight had been a chance to prove that she had something to give back to them, however small it might be.

Unexpectedly, Mark leaned down and kissed her, hands cupping her face tenderly, his eyes shining in the dim light of the bedside lamp. "You are absolutely priceless."

Dee couldn't help the grin on her face. This fledgling romance with Mark was moving rather more quickly than she was used to. But then again, everything in her life in the last few weeks had seemed to be happening in fast forward. Her conversion, her 'death', her acceptance into the Den, the status fights – it was only a day after she'd officially become part of the Den, and already she was ranked third up from the bottom. Another two weeks, and God knew what more might have changed in her life.

But there was one nagging issue in her mind, one that, despite her best efforts, wouldn't leave her alone. "Could I ask you something that might be awkward?"

Mark nodded immediately. "Of course. Anything you like."

"It's about the lab."

Despite his eager agreement only a moment ago, Mark's expression turned guarded – not that Dee was surprised. The whole issue of the lab was rather a tough spot, after all. "Is this about keeping it a secret from Baron?"

"No! No, I said I wouldn't tell him and I won't. I do feel kind of guilty about that, but… Look, there was just… there's something I wanted to ask you."

"Okay," he said cautiously. "What is it?"

"When we talked about how you rescued me, you said you were looking for someone. I'd like to know who."

Mark grimaced and looked away. Dee didn't mean to upset him, but none the less, she needed to know. "My sister," Mark said finally. "You know we renounce our family ties when we join Il Trosa. But about a year ago, I just wanted to know where my sister was. How she was doing. So I did a little research. Which is completely against our rules, I know," he added, to his own chagrin. "I wasn't going to contact her directly, but I needed to know she was doing ok. And then… well, the short version is that I stumbled upon some information that suggested she'd been kidnapped by the Noturatii and was being held in their lab. I did a little digging, found out where it was, explored some of their security protocols so I could work around them. And then the other week, we were in London on other business, but I had a few hours to myself, so... I went looking."

Dee nodded. It explained a lot, why he'd been willing to take such a risk, how he'd known the layout of the lab to be able to find her. "Then you know what it's like to lose your family, and to need to break the rules to see them safe," she said softly.

Mark nodded slowly. "It's an act of treason. But in this case, the goal was worth the risk."

"I understand. And because of that... I'd like to ask you a favour."

"What is it?"

Dee held her breath, glanced around the room like she expected someone to leap out of the closet and yell 'gotcha!'. She lowered her voice to a mere whisper. "Would you be able to send a message to my family? To let them know I'm alive?"

Silence. And Mark's expression was suddenly and alarmingly blank.

"I would try to figure out how to do it myself," she explained, not quite sure why this was such a shock to him, given what he'd done himself, "but I'm not allowed to set a single foot off the estate. I don't mean to burden you with this, but I've got no other options-"

"No."

What? She'd expected warnings about the consequences, discussions on what it would mean to take such a risk, even anger that she'd ask Mark to put himself in danger on her behalf. What she had not expected was a flat refusal.

"What?"

"I said no."

"But you went looking for your sister! You didn't just send her a message, you broke into a Noturatii lab!" Even in her dismay and outrage, Dee managed to keep her voice low, harsh, angry whispers bursting from her lips.

"What I did," Mark said slowly, sternly, "was betray Il Trosa and my species. And for the record, I never, ever intended to directly contact my sister when I was researching her. I just wanted to know where she was, whether she was safe. If she'd been fine, working, dating some loser or making a couple of rug-rats for herself, that would have been the end of it. I went after her because I believed she was being tortured by the most evil organisation on this planet."

"And now?" Dee prompted, unable to believe he would refuse her like this. "Don't you still want to know where she is? Or have you just given up on her so easily?"

"If the Noturatii actually took my sister," Mark said, his voice tight, "then she is now dead. If they didn't take her, then wherever she is, it's none of my business. And either way, there is nothing I can do to help her." He looked up at her sadly, stark loss in his eyes. "Or you."

Dee glared at him, the hypocrisy of his refusal galling. "Get out," she said finally. "Get out of my room."

Mark stood up. "Give this idea up, Dee," he warned her softly. "We both renounced our family and our past when we swore the oath of loyalty to Il Trosa. And I can tell you from experience – there is no joy to be had in chasing ghosts that should be laid to rest."

Dee didn't reply. Mark waited a moment longer, perhaps hoping she would say something else, something to excuse or forgive his refusal to help her. But when it became clear she had nothing more to say, he turned and walked away.

# PART TWO – BATTLE

## CHAPTER TWENTY-FOUR

Three months passed in what seemed like the blink of an eye. Winter closed in, covering the estate with a blanket of white. Christmas came and went, Dee delighted and surprised when the Den celebrated in true pagan fashion, complete with a feast on the twenty-first, a yule log and a ceremony honouring Sirius.

Despite being confined to the estate, Dee found there was plenty of entertainment and enough people coming and going to keep her from feeling hemmed in. Caroline assigned her to administration duties, helping Heron keep track of the Den's finances, and much of the rest of her time was taken up with lessons, her continuing education in shifter history and culture, as well as hand to hand combat lessons with Tank and weapons training with Silas.

The one sore spot in her life was her relationship with Mark. After their heated discussion on her request to contact her family, their budding romance had cooled. After taking some time to reflect on it, Dee had come around to see his side of the argument, understanding that what she had asked of him was simply too great a risk, too much of a betrayal of the values and rules Mark had been taught to respect, but despite her apologising for it, the incident had left a lingering awkwardness between them that so far they couldn't seem to overcome.

If Dee was honest with herself, she would have to admit that she rather regretted the impulsive request. The more she got to know Mark, the more she found she liked him, moving past her initial shy crush to see him as a close friend. His dry humour was a welcome change from the serious attitudes of much of the Den, and their daily runs were a true delight, Faeydir free to explore the grounds and exercise her canine instincts in a way that Dee found to be both intriguing and, at times, quite hilarious. But even so, she missed the way he had looked at her during those first days, the shy hopefulness, the heated glances and subtle flirting. But try as she might, she couldn't find the courage to make an attempt at resuming their relationship, and Mark remained the perfect gentleman, warm and friendly, but with no hints of his earlier interest in her.

She'd been slowly climbing the ranks, now placed just below Alistair, and several bets had been laid that come spring, she'd be fighting for rank with Raniesha. The woman was quite intimidating – despite her preference for high heels and short skirts, Dee had come to learn that she was also an expert in explosives, and when she'd asked Silas about her one day, during her regular lesson in firearms, he'd snorted and said, "Don't underestimate her. She might look like a well-groomed poodle, but put her up against the Noturatii and heads will roll. There's pretty much nothing she can't blow up."

Dee had been informed that in a few weeks time, an emissary from the Council was to be sent to assess her as a new shifter – usually just a formality, but given her unique situation and the questions lingering about her conversion, the impending visit was hanging over her like a dark cloud. When pressed, Caroline had finally admitted that the emissary had the power to declare Dee a danger to Il Trosa and order her to be put down, which had caused no small measure of alarm. Baron had done his best to reassure her, telling her that that outcome was extremely unlikely, that the most severe result would most probably be that she was called to Italy for extra training, but none the less, Dee wasn't looking forward to the assessment.

Faeydir had adapted well to life in the estate, making friends with several wolves, becoming cautious rivals with others. The winter had been cold, snow falling thickly, and the wolf had revelled in the chance to run through the drifts. She'd dug tunnels, kicked snow at her fellow wolves, and had been on her first official deer hunt. The pack had brought down a young doe, one who'd been born only the year before, and a lot of snarling and snapping of teeth had ensued before Baron and Caroline had gotten down to the messy business of eating the carcass raw, the rest of the pack falling in to fight over what was left when they were done.

Dee had mostly hidden in the back of her mind during that day, not wanting to see the beautiful animal in such pain, not wanting to see the body parts strewn across the snow, red on white a terrible banner that reminded her of a disturbingly similar scene, blood painted across white tiles, body parts scattered around a lab... She'd retreated as far as she could go, hiding behind her wolf and letting Faeydir run the show, the Den none the wiser as to her difficulties in accepting this side of their life.

Early one morning, as spring was making its presence felt, the first buds appearing on the trees as winter began a reluctant retreat, Dee was called into the library. At first, she'd expected nothing more than another lesson, Caroline sometimes choosing one of the thick books and ploughing through the historical accounts it contained, so Dee was a little alarmed when she found herself face to face with not just Caroline, but a frowning Baron and a serious-looking Tank.

"Did I do something wrong?" she asked immediately. Faeydir had been behaving admirably, or so she'd thought, and she'd been working hard at her lessons, making an effort to obey the rules of the Den-

"No, you did nothing wrong," Caroline replied flatly, and Dee was by now familiar enough with her tactless manner to take the statement at face value. "You've actually been doing very well. Which comes as no small surprise, given how you started off here." It was a compliment dressed up as an insult, and Dee was in a good enough mood to just roll with it for today. "It's time we let you off the estate," Caroline announced without preamble, and Dee had given so little thought to the idea that it took a moment to register.

"What? Outside? I can go-"

"We're not talking free reign to go anywhere," Baron interrupted. "You'll still need to be supervised, and it'll be a long time before you get to go anywhere on your own. But it is time we started getting Faeydir used to the outside."

"We'll start small," Caroline went on. "A trip to the local village. Go to the supermarket, see how your wolf reacts to strangers and cars and whatever else you find. And if that goes well, then we'll need to take you to get vaccinated. You haven't had your rabies shot yet, and we have regular visits from wolves from various countries in eastern Europe where infection is still common, so it's worth doing."

"The local villagers know some of us," Baron took over again. "And they think we run a business retreat for an international company. It explains why some of us, like Tank or Alistair are seen around town a lot – ostensibly because they work here full time – and why others are seen on an occasional basis."

"Because they supposedly work in an overseas office and have just dropped in for a visit," Dee rounded out the idea.

"Before we came up with it, there were rumours about us being some odd sort of commune," Caroline said. "There aren't many reasons for twenty adults to be living under one roof together, so some kind of plausible explanation was required. We try very hard to keep ourselves off the 'weird' radar."

"Makes sense. And the locals believe this story?"

"They're more than happy to accept it, hook, line and sinker," Tank said with a dry laugh. "People like things to fit into neat boxes, and if there's a rational reason for something that otherwise seems a little out of the ordinary, that just means they don't have to spend time and energy worrying about it. They can put their blinkers back on and go about their lives."

"So when do we get to go?" Dee asked, suddenly eager to get out and about.

"Tomorrow, if the weather's fine," Caroline said. "And before we do, we have a fair bit of preparation to do. Starting with how your wolf is going to react to the butcher's shop…"


The following day was a Wednesday, and it dawned bright and clear, if still cold. Dee spent the morning with Caroline and Tank, discussing contingency plans, what to expect in the village, what to do if something went wrong. Tank was the default choice for body guard and Caroline was going in case she was needed to forcibly prevent Dee from shifting – though the act of preventing her would itself cause a disturbance, and was only to be used as a last resort.

Alistair dropped in at one point to help them invent some cover stories for the more likely problems they would encounter, and Dee carefully memorised and recited every one. If the villagers asked, she was working in Canada and had come here for a conference that was happening at the weekend. If she needed to make a quick exit from a situation, she should check her watch and suddenly 'remember' that she was expecting a call from overseas, and 'remind' Caroline that they needed to get back to the estate. If Faeydir played up and Dee turned pale or felt dizzy or any one of a dozen other symptoms, then she should complain about a 'migraine' and Tank would get her off the street and into the van as quickly as possible. If Caroline had to zap her, they could tell people she had epilepsy and had just had a minor seizure.

Dee found herself staggered at the degree of planning needed for what she really considered to be a minor excursion. Other shifters in the Den spent a good amount of time away from the estate – just take Alistair, for example. He worked freelance for a local newspaper, maintained a wide net of contacts in a number of industries, regularly travelled to London, Paris, Rome. He was a consummate extravert and Dee wondered just how many lies he told on an average day, and how he managed to keep track of them all. It gave her a whole new perspective on life as a shifter, a new respect for how closely these people guarded their secret, and made her dread the day when she would be ready to face the big wide world for more than an hour or two. The complexity of the whole thing was giving her a headache.

Finally, though, after a lunch of rabbit, eaten raw on the kitchen tiles, Dee and Faeydir were ready to head out. She'd explained the situation extensively to Faeydir, had talked through some of the wolf's concerns with

Caroline, each and every question and objection being taken very seriously, and Faeydir had finally understood that she was not to come out for any reason whatsoever once they left the estate. A short trip, Dee promised her, at her wary concern. Two hours, tops, and then they'd be back and Mark would take her for a run and she could be in wolf form for the entire evening. Mollified, Faeydir had agreed, and as she climbed into the van, Dee could feel her sitting front and centre, curious about where they were going and how they were getting there, and then, once they had pulled out of the driveway, Faeydir sent her a vivid image of the van window rolled down and Dee's head sticking out to catch the wind.

*No!* Dee said firmly. *I'm running the show here. Human time, remember?* An image of a pile of faeces showed up in her mind, and Dee just shook her head.

The village was bigger than Dee had expected, a row of shops that included a hairdresser, a butcher, a bakery, a clothing outlet, even a hardware store. The streets were active, but not overly crowded, and once they'd parked and gotten out of the van, Dee noticed several people waving at Tank. He was hard to miss, after all, and the locals must have been accustomed to him playing 'tour guide' for the 'business guests'.

The trip to the supermarket was more to expose Faeydir to the concept, rather than because they needed to buy anything, and Dee deliberately strolled past the meat display, testing the reaction of her wolf. But Faeydir had been warned about the abundance of food here, the smells and the variety, and she made no unexpected demands, much to Dee's relief. In the end they bought a small selection of fruits and a box of cookies, paid for the purchases, and headed back out into the crisp air.

Next they turned down the street, just a casual stroll past the shops. The smells coming from the bakery made Dee's mouth water, and then she had to pause outside a small café to inhale the scent of freshly ground coffee. There was a coffee machine at the Den, but it never tasted quite as good as one made fresh by a trained barista, and it was months since she'd been able to indulge that particular craving.

They reached the end of the row without incident and were about to turn around when Faeydir suddenly gave Dee an urgent nudge. Despite her insistence that this was 'human time', she'd gotten a lot better at cooperating with her wolf in the last few months, finally understanding that Faeydir saw life from a different perspective and could pick up on details that Dee might otherwise miss, so she pulled Caroline and Tank up with a sharp word and looked around for the cause of Faeydir's concern.

A dog was coming down the street towards them. He had no obvious humans with him, but a collar with a tag suggested that someone owned him. The breed wasn't immediately obvious – he was a medium sized creature of light brown that could have been part Labrador, part spaniel, or part German shepherd. He stopped a few feet away, sniffed cautiously, then sat down, wagging his tail at them.

Dee checked in with Faeydir again, not certain what the problem was. And choked back a laugh when she understood what the wolf wanted. "No, he can't come home with us," she said aloud – a habit she'd gotten into when talking to her wolf, and the rest of the Den had become accustomed to her talking to herself.

Caroline snorted. "She wants to keep it, does she?"

"I think she wants to feed it, look after it," Dee said, a little mystified. "I don't think she understands that it's not a wolf. She just registers that it's young and not capable of looking after itself, so therefore it must be a puppy. And puppies should be cared for."

Caroline let out a laugh, one of the few rare ones that Dee had ever heard from her. "That's priceless. Come on. It's time we got back."

"No, you don't understand," Dee said, not moving as Caroline and Tank both turned back towards the van. "She needs to know it's going to be looked after."

Caroline raised an eyebrow. "We're not taking it home."

Dee had a brief internal conversation with Faeydir, and got the feeling that the wolf was perfectly willing to press the issue. One way or another. "You've spent the last three months telling me that I need to respect my wolf," Dee said, trying not to sound defiant. "And what she's telling me is that she's concerned about the dog, and since she can't come out and look after it herself…" Dee emphasised the words, an implicit threat that Faeydir would do the very thing she had been expressly forbidden from doing, "… then she needs me to do it for her."

There was a moment's silence as Caroline and Tank absorbed the implications of that. Then Tank crouched down and held out his hand. "Here, boy. Come here."

The dog trotted forward, ears back, tail wagging, eager to please. Tank stroked his head and then snagged his collar, reading the writing inscribed on the tag. "There's no address, but there's a phone number." He pulled out his mobile and tapped in the number. "Hey there," he said, when someone answered. "I think your dog might have pulled an escape stunt. I have him with me at the end of High Street… Okay. Sure. Five minutes? No problem." He hung up. "The owners will meet us here in five. Is that good enough for your inner social worker?"

Dee consulted with Faeydir, and had to explain several times the concept that humans kept dogs as companions and cared for them, providing food, shelter and medical care. And in the end, Faeydir decided to accept the explanation, regardless of the fact that it made little sense to her. Real wolves would never delegate all of their care to human hands. And Dee had to remind herself not to be offended by the opinion. After all,

Faeydir spent a good deal of her time fending for herself, catching rabbits for food, drinking water from the stream that was still running. She'd even slept outside one night, building an impromptu den under a tree root, a pile of old leaves for insulation.

"No problem," Dee reported back to Tank, who was looking on expectantly. "Good call."

# CHAPTER TWENTY-FIVE

Mark stood in his workshop, screwdriver in hand, staring at the bookcase in front of him critically. It was crooked. Okay, so he wasn't an expert at welding. He'd been working from scrap, and the pieces of metal for the frame hadn't been the right length, the wood for the shelves was uneven, he'd had trouble finding feet that fit. But all that aside, he should at least be able to make something that stood upright. He felt like a rank novice again, trying to piece together his first chair, angry when the legs were different thicknesses and the seat was wobbly.

He stood back and stared at the bookcase again… and felt absolutely ecstatic.

He was learning. He had design problems he didn't know how to solve. He was being creative and challenged and frustrated for the first time in years. And the effect was exhilarating.

None of which would be evident to an outside observer, given the scowl on his face.

He became aware of the sensation of being watched and turned around, seeing Alistair standing in the doorway, leaning against the door frame with an air of nonchalance. Which didn't fool Mark for a moment. He waited, then, when Alistair didn't speak, asked, "Something I can help you with?"

"You've been working on that damned thing for more than a week."

Mark glanced back at the set of shelves. "And your point is?"

Alistair pushed off the doorframe, strolling casually across the workshop, his smart shoes tapping on the bare concrete. "What are you doing?"

"Trying something new."

Alistair managed to look both impressed and disdainful at the same time. More silence, and Mark's patience was wearing thin. "Is there something you need, or did you just come to complain about my work?"

Alistair turned to look him full in the face, and Mark suddenly wished he hadn't asked. "We're good friends, right?" he asked softly.

Mark shrugged. "I guess."

"You guess?" Alistair let out a bitter laugh. "You guess. Yeah, I suppose so. You know what we would have been doing a year ago?"

Mark shrugged again. "Same old. I'd be building furniture. You'd be concocting some bullshit media story. The Den would be fighting the endless war, same as it always does."

"Wrong. You, me and Luke would have been out on the lawn, practicing hand to hand combat with each other. We'd have been sitting in the lounge playing poker and drinking whiskey. We'd have been staying outside all night in wolf form, sleeping in a pile inside a hollow log. We used to have fun together, you, me and him." Alistair gave him a searching look. "What happened?"

Mark stared at him in disbelief. "You're not honestly going to make me answer that, are you?"

"You used to know how to live," Alistair continued, not flinching at the raw, tactless question. "And I got the brief impression a few months back that you hadn't entirely lost that."

He was referring to Dee. Which made him a complete and utter bastard. Although Mark should have known he'd have noticed. Alistair was observant – one of the reasons he did his job so well – but it could also make him a thorough pain in the arse. Mark's relationship with Dee was an ongoing sore spot, his interest in her undimmed, though he was at a loss as to how to express it without coming across as either demanding or sleazy. Dee herself had been giving him mixed messages. At times, she seemed eager and friendly, but at others, she would be quiet and withdrawn, leading Mark to conclude that she remained interested in simple friendship, but nothing more. But his hopes for a romantic relationship refused to die, and the ongoing frustration was making him tense and grumpy. "Things didn't work out," he said flatly.

Alistair gave him a calculating look. "Hm." Mark held his gaze, refusing to look embarrassed or disappointed or anything else that would give him more ammunition. "So you say," Alistair said smoothly. "But ask yourself this: How can one ever read the pages, if you refuse to let them open the book?" He turned and strode away, leaving Mark staring after him in consternation.

Mark was waiting in the foyer when the van got back from Dee's trip to the village, and he wasn't surprised when Faeydir came bounding in the door, bouncing up and down in excitement when she saw him. Dee had told him of her deal with the wolf – a run outside and plenty of time in wolf

162

form in exchange for the outing, and he grinned, shifting quickly as Faeydir was clearly eager to go for a run.

Outside, they took a fast race up to the top of the hill, Faeydir standing with her nose to the wind, revelling in the cold air on her face, then back down through the trees, a leisurely roll in the snow, a good sniff under the fallen oak tree, a vigorous dig around the base of the pines.

Faeydir had been quite insistent about spending the afternoon as a wolf, so Mark was surprised when Dee shifted, turning to stare up at the trees with a look on her face that was part contemplation, part longing.

Mark shifted beside her, then, when she didn't say anything, he asked, "What's up?"

"I want to climb a tree," Dee announced, sizing up the lower branches of the nearest pine.

Mark snorted in surprise at the out-of-the-blue statement, and he glanced up at the tree. The nearest branch was too high for Dee to reach comfortably, so he said, "How about I give you a leg up?"

Dee grinned at him. "That'd be awesome." He did, easily lifting her slight weight so she could pull herself onto the first branch, then hauling himself up after her as she began climbing.

Thick coats and gloved hands made the effort a clumsy, awkward shuffle rather than a graceful climb, but soon enough they were both up the tree, Dee picking a branch about halfway up to sit on.

Once they were both settled, squished together a little as there wasn't a whole lot of room, Dee took a deep breath of the fresh, cold air, and let her head fall back, grinning at the sky. "Well, this is cosy," she said with a hint of mischief.

It was, actually. The branches shielded them from the wind, the snow dulling any sounds, and for the moment, they were tucked away in their own little world. Dee was swinging one leg back and forth, a slow, lazy rhythm that brushed her calf against Mark's with each pass, and he automatically tried to wriggle away slightly to give her more room, searching for some simple comment to make, maybe on the weather, or a passing remark on how long it had been since he'd climbed a tree.

But before he could open his mouth, Dee shifted her grip on the branch, rearranging her hand so that her fingers rested over his, and Mark paused, reconsidering the situation.

Alistair was right, he realised. He'd been putting up walls around himself for the last three months, unwilling to let Dee get close enough to hurt him – on the excuse that she seemed to want to keep her distance, regardless.

Now, though, after it had been pointed out to him, he realised that this was a scene that had played out a dozen or more times in the past weeks. Dee would probe a little, try to get him to open up about something or other, or perhaps try a little subtle flirting, and he would shut her down, then blame her for being distant in the ensuing days, after he had firmly rejected her attempts at getting closer.

But up here, their bodies were pressed together, thighs touching, Mark's arm halfway around Dee as he held onto a branch to keep his balance, and he considered the idea that this wasn't quite so accidental as he had assumed.

Or perhaps it had started out accidental, he thought, as Dee fidgeted in a way that just happened to press her closer against him, but it was rapidly becoming much more interesting than a simple quest for a little adventure.

Dee was feeling rather warm, and only half of it was due to the exertion of the climb. Mark smelled heavenly, sitting so close next to her, and she wished she knew what to say that would allow her to test out his current feelings without embarrassing either of them. But flirting had never been her strong suit-

Mark's hand curled up and around her own, his gloved fingers stroking hers gently, and that got Dee's attention. Maybe all was not lost, after all?

She risked a glance over at him, pleased and embarrassed when she caught him looking at her with a warm, hopeful expression, before they both quickly looked away.

"It's warmer up here than I thought it would be," Mark said, moving his leg a fraction closer to hers, and this was more familiar territory for Dee, shy, fumbling attempts at flirting as each party tried to work out how the other was feeling.

"I guess the wolves have the right idea about this," she said, making her own attempt at flirting back. "Cuddling up close to keep each other warm."

"It has its benefits," Mark replied. Dee glanced at him again, and this time, let her gaze linger a little. They were like teenagers on a first date, and Dee let out the smile that was tugging at her lips.

On the branch above them, a squirrel suddenly burst out of its hiding place, dashing up the tree and dropping thick dollops of snow all over Dee in the process. She laughed, as a clump landed on her nose, but before she could reach up to remove it, Mark had moved first, gently wiping it away, then brushing some more out of her hair. And then his hand lingered, stroked a gentle line down her face. He had the sort of look that said he was about to say something, so Dee jumped in first.

"Yes," she said suddenly, and Mark looked at her quizzically.

"What?"

"Whatever you're about to ask," Dee clarified. "I'm pretty sure the answer's going to be yes."

That made him laugh, and then harder when Dee overbalanced, grabbing onto his shoulder to keep from falling.

And then, with no warning whatsoever, he leaned in and kissed her.

When he pulled back, Dee looked up at him in surprise. "What was that?" she asked softly.

"Well, you said the answer was yes."

Dee let out a chuckle. "Oh. Well, in that case, maybe I should have said yes sooner."

Mark grinned. "The fault is mine," he said, leaning towards her again. "I shouldn't have waited so long to ask."


Back at the house, and back in wolf form, Faeydir licked Mark on the muzzle as they reached the front door. He wagged his tail and barked a goodbye, heading for his workshop, while Faeydir went inside. The first port of call was the kitchen, where there was a particularly interesting lamb bone in the fridge, but she didn't get more than halfway across the foyer before Caroline pulled her up.

"I need to talk to Dee," she announced. "In the sitting room." Faeydir bared one long canine very briefly – not a threat or a challenge, just a comment that she wasn't happy with the request, and then she compliantly followed Caroline, shifting as they reached the sofa so that Dee could sit down, confused about the sudden meeting.

"We need to talk about today's outing," Caroline said, and Dee was a little surprised at the need for such an urgent debrief. Faeydir had behaved well, nothing had gone wrong, so what was the problem? "First of all, how are you feeling?" Caroline asked. "Three months is a long time to be cooped up in the estate. And sometimes getting out for a bit just makes the cabin fever worse."

"Cabin fever isn't the problem," Dee replied, resigning herself to sitting through the interrogation, while Faeydir waited impatiently to be back in wolf form. "Going out was fun, but it was exhausting. I constantly have to be aware of Faeydir, and what she wants, and what she can see and hear that I can't. She's willing to cooperate, but she lacks the impulse control to really be trustworthy. A five year old child can do the right thing 90% of the time, but they can still run out into the traffic without warning, you know?"

"Hm." Caroline didn't look too put out by the report. But then again, she didn't look particularly happy either. "And how did Faeydir feel about it?"

"Bored," Dee said succinctly. "She couldn't smell anything well enough for it to be interesting, she doesn't understand – or want to understand – why humans do half the things they do, and she didn't see the point of looking at all the meat in the shelves if she doesn't get to either eat or bury any of it."

"What about the dog?"

"She doesn't understand why a puppy would want to live with humans when it could live with wolves."

"It wasn't a puppy. It was a domestic dog."

Dee shrugged, trying not to look petulant about it. "I'm just telling you what Faeydir thinks. In her eyes, it was a wolf puppy. Who would have been better off coming with us." She paused, and then went on. "Actually, there was something I wanted to ask you about that. Why are there no children in the Den?" she said awkwardly. "Puppies, I mean. There are no puppies. Which means no children. I was just... wondering."

There were all manner of answers Dee had been expecting – the dangers of being hunted by the Noturatii, the shortage of women, the antisocial nature of many a shifter due to their questionable backgrounds. But what Caroline said came straight out of left field. "Shifters can't have children."

"What?"

"It's physically impossible. We reproduce by converting humans. We can't have children of our own."

Dee gaped at her as her mind worked to get a handle on that, and she must have looked rather horrified at the bare, blunt statement, because Caroline gave her a look that went at least part way towards sympathy. "This is something that's addressed with recruits before they're converted," she said with a touch of impatience. "Which is just another reason why your conversion was done badly."

"Yes, I do tend to think that being kidnapped and tortured is a bad way to start a new life," Dee snapped, a surge of anger bursting up at the woman's endless insensitivity. "Let me remind you that I never *chose* any of this, not the two personalities in one body, not being dragged off to your estate – oh, sorry, *rescued* by yours truly – not being caught up in a war with government agents who actually seem to be on the sane end of things by thinking that people who turn into animals is a *bad* idea. So forgive me if I have questions about things that are indelicate, and if I act a little shocked when I get answers I didn't expect!"

No children, Dee thought numbly, feeling the sudden urge to cry. She was never going to have children. She'd wanted two, a girl and a boy, and before her kidnapping had so completely altered her life, she'd been certain that it was only a matter of time before she found the right man and settled down and started decorating a nursery with butterflies and kittens.

Caroline seemed at a loss for words. "Ah. Well, I'm... Um... Perhaps now isn't the best time," she said awkwardly, seeming both baffled by Dee's shock at the news, and embarrassed by the way the conversation had gone. "I'll, uh... I'll let you think about that for a while. Perhaps we can talk about your outing later." She quietly left the room, leaving Dee staring after her in quiet dejection.

Later that evening, Dee sat on the couch in the upstairs lounge, Skip beside her, Heron seated in an armchair nearby. They'd found her in the sitting room earlier, still sitting dejectedly on the sofa, and after a few probing questions, Heron had ushered her upstairs and placed a glass of vodka and tonic in her hand and they'd sat down to talk things through.

"Not to dismiss your concerns," Heron was saying, "but the cold truth is that this very rarely comes up around here. Most of the women in Il Trosa have no desire for children. I'm not defending Caroline," she went on, as Dee looked up unhappily. "She could certainly have been more tactful about it. But it's something we just don't have to deal with very often."

"So no one else here wants children?" Dee asked, knowing that the answer was going to be no, but curious about the reasons why.

"No," Heron said gently. "Raniesha couldn't handle the responsibility – she's said as much herself."

"And could you imaging Caroline as your mother?" Skip interrupted with a sardonic laugh. "Any child of hers would be likely to hurl themselves off the rooftop. And Heron's too old."

Dee looked startled at what could have been quite a rude statement, but Heron just laughed, no doubt used to Skip's occasional tactlessness.

"And you don't?" she asked of Skip, only to receive a tense silence from both women. Skip got that hunted look she sometimes had, when anyone asked about her teddy bears or her jewellery or accidently touched her without warning. "I wouldn't want to inflict childhood on anyone," she said grimly, but it was the look on Heron's face that stopped Dee from probing any further. This was clearly not an appropriate topic of conversation for the girl.

"What about you?" she said, turning to Heron next. "You never wanted any when you were younger?"

A wistful look came over Heron's face, and Dee almost regretted having asked.

"There was a time when I would have considered it," Heron said softly. "But that ship sailed a long time ago. But there have been enough children passing through the Den to keep me from feeling I was missing out."

"Wait," Dee said, confused now. "What children? How-?"

"Ah, see, it's not all as clear cut as it sounds," Skip interrupted. "I mean, no, we can't have natural children, but sometimes the Council will let couples adopt."

"There are three children in the Italian Den," Heron filled in, "and two more in Germany. It comes with complications-"

"As everything in this lifestyle does," Skip interjected.

"-one of which is that the children must become shifters when they come of age. It can be quite a stressful time for their parents. Even for a child raised within Il Trosa, there's no guarantee they'll be able to merge with their wolf, and… well, you can probably imagine what it would be like as a parent, to see your child going rogue and being put down."

"Fuck." The bad news just kept on coming.

"But adoption is a realistic possibility," Heron repeated firmly. "Something to keep in mind down the track, if you decide to go that way."

"One detail to be aware of though," Skip added, as Dee considered the idea. "The Council has pretty strict rules for raising children, and one of them is that two parents are needed. Doesn't matter what gender they are – we're open to same sex couples – I mean, just look at Baron and John – but the two parent thing is non-negotiable."

Dee was taken aback. "That seems a little archaic. There are plenty of single parents in the world, both men and women, and they get by fine."

Skip shrugged. "It's kind of an insurance policy. Shifters have a fairly high mortality rate. Thank you, Noturatii," she added sardonically. "So having two parents means that if one dies, the other can still raise the children. It's kind of morbid when you look at it that way, but I guess there's a certain logic to it."

This was hardly the silver lining that Dee had been hoping for. A slim chance for adoption, if she could find someone to raise the children with her, followed by a lifetime of complications and worries… it was no wonder not many people decided to go down that path.

But what Heron said next was completely unexpected, a sly distraction to pull Dee out of her brooding mood. "I'm fairly certain that young man of yours would be interested in raising a family."

"*My* young man?" Dee asked, trying to play it cool, knowing she was referring to Mark. "I'd hardly say he's *mine*." The two of them had only just gotten things back on track this afternoon, after all. It was startling to realise that other people in the estate had noticed them dancing around each other.

"A little birdy told me that something interesting happened today," Skip said with a wink, as Dee felt her face heat, "Mark and Dee, sitting in a tree, K I S S I N G."

"Skip," Heron chided her gently, but Skip would not be deterred.

"I'm serious," she said defensively. "They were sitting in a tree. Out in the forest."

"That's not the point," Heron tried to scold her, but Skip just laughed.

"And they were most definitely kissing. So I'm not starting any unsubstantiated rumours here."

Despite her attempt at being stern, Heron looked like she was trying to smother her own amusement, so Dee decided to come clean.

"It's a fair call," she said, seeing the funny side to the situation. "And I know, I know, about time," she admitted, seeing the glee on Skip's face. She'd been trying to push the pair of them together for months, disappointed and impatient every time Dee had explained to her that she and Mark didn't think of each other like that. "But it's early days yet, and children is just too big a bridge to cross at this stage."

"It'll be a while until you could be granted approval anyway," Heron cautioned her gently. "Usually the Council won't even consider an adoption request until both parents have been shifters for two or three years. So you have plenty of time to think about it."

"And plenty of time to keep wooing Mark," Skip added gleefully. "First comes love, then comes-"

"Skip," Heron scolded her again, trying to look serious. "That will do, thank you very much."

# CHAPTER TWENTY-SIX

After Dee's visit to the village, there were two more outings. The first was a trip to a local café for lunch, more a test-drive than a social event, as Tank and Caroline were her chaperones again, both breathing down her neck when the slightest thing out of the ordinary happened.

But the second was far more fun. Mark, Skip and Tank accompanied her to a pub to watch a local band play. For her and Mark, it was like their first real date, a milestone in a relationship that had suddenly picked up its pace.

Aside from the outing itself, Mark had been trying hard to make her feel special, cooking her breakfast, watching movies with her in her room at night, lounging comfortably on the bed with a laptop balanced on the sheets. It was a long time since Dee had had any real romance in her life, and she was finding it quite addictive now. She had a love of old black and white films, and was pleasantly surprised when Mark took an immediate liking to them, finding them a welcome break from the mindless explosions of the modern actions films that were the usual fare of the Den's residents.

The pub was nothing out of the ordinary, the food pleasant enough, but Dee found the music absolutely enchanting, a blend of modern rock and Celtic ballads that had an upbeat, yet haunting quality to them. And the evening became even more enchanting when Mark discretely twined his fingers through hers and spent the next hour slowly stroking her hand in a way that was every bit as enticing as it was designed to be.

Back at the estate, they said good night to Skip and Tank, and Dee gave a brief report to Baron about the outing, the alpha pleased to hear there had been no problems from Faeydir, then headed up the stairs.

Her and Mark's usual routine was to say goodnight at her door, a few heated kisses closing off their evening's plans. But when they reached the door tonight, Dee found herself dwelling on the tantalising prospect of something more.

Mark leaned down to kiss her, a few slow minutes passing in a warm embrace. But when he went to pull away, Dee slipped her arms around his waist and tugging him back again.

"I really enjoyed tonight," she said earnestly. "Thank you for coming."

"It was a pleasure."

She was back to awkward fumbling, trying to figure out how to express her feelings. "So I was wondering… um… maybe… maybe you'd like to come inside for some coffee?"

Mark's eyebrows rose in surprise, and then he glanced automatically at her bedroom door. "Coffee?" he asked, in the sort of tone that said he knew exactly what she was asking, but needed to confirm that that was what she really wanted.

Dee nodded, feeling nervous and excited and embarrassed all at once.

Mark's arms tightened around her and his voice took on a slightly husky tone. "I would like that very much."


Mark followed Dee into her bedroom, eyes fixed on her curvy form. She'd dressed up for tonight, trading casual jeans for dress slacks and a pair of black boots with heels that made her legs look distractingly sexy, and he'd wondered more than once this evening how long it would be before they took this next step in their relationship. He hadn't expected it to happen quite so soon.

Not that he was complaining. Three months of slow frustration had given him more than a few fantasies about what would happen if they ever reached this point.

Once the bedroom door was closed, Dee turned around to kiss him, and he could already feel himself getting hard. Take it slow, he cautioned himself. They had all night. No need to rush…

"Are you sure about this?" he asked, feeling her fingers plucking hesitantly at his waistband, and she nodded.

"Very sure," she murmured, before tugging him down to kiss him again.

What followed was a slow waltz towards the bed, one step, a kiss, a few caresses, another step, until Mark felt the edge of the bed hit the back of his knees.

He jumped as Dee slid a questing hand beneath his t-shirt, stroking over his abs, then higher, and he tightened his arms around her waist, unable to resist the sweet temptation of her lips a moment longer.

"It's been a long while," he said, needing to warn her that perhaps he wasn't up to what she might be expecting, but she shook her head.

"It's fine. I'm a little out of practice myself."

For the next half an hour, they took things leisurely, removing one article of clothing at a time, exploring the new territory revealed along the way. At one point, they took a slow, comfortable tumble onto the bed, Mark landing on his back with Dee sprawled across him, and he kissed her through her laughter as they untangled themselves, the movement pressing the delicious heat of her thigh against his groin in a way that had him gasping for breath.

Dee noticed their position, and deliberately rubbed against him, causing Mark to groan, his hands cupping her buttocks to encourage her, then sliding inside the scrap of fabric that still covered her, captivated all over again by smooth skin and an almost staggering warmth.

But just as he was contemplating helping her remove that most tantalising item of clothing, Dee suddenly stopped. Sat up. Cursed beneath her breath. And Mark dragged his attention away from the enticing view of her breasts, held captive beneath a lacy bra, to try and focus on her sudden apprehension.

"What's wrong?" Mark was down to only his underpants, hard as a rock and so damn close to the edge… Fuck, if she wanted to stop now, he was going to have a heart attack. He would stop, of course. Absolutely. But it might just kill him in the process.

"I don't have… Um… I don't have any condoms," Dee blurted out, red faced, but clearly seeing this as an important priority, and Mark only just bit back the automatic 'So what?' that he had been about to say.

It wasn't any kind of disregard for her concerns. In the normal course of things, women had every right to be worried about diseases and pregnancy, contraception a totally reasonable priority. But as things stood now…

"We don't need one," he explained cautiously, then rushed on before she could get defensive about it. "Shifters can't have children," he reminded her, hoping the topic wasn't a sore spot. She'd told him about her tense discussion with Caroline on the subject. "And we can't catch STDs. Shifters are immune to them all." There was still the chance that she was simply going to object to the mess – though if they stayed here for much longer, there was a good chance there would be a mess, regardless.

"Oh." Rather than put out, Dee sounded relieved by the reminder. "That's right. I'd forgotten. It's just that we have the 'safe sex' message drummed in so often, it's hard to break away from that."

"I get it. And if you'd prefer to use one, the Den has a supply in the medicine cabinet." Though how in the world he was going to manage to go downstairs and get a box was beyond him. He doubted he could even walk at this point.

"No," Dee said simply, leaning forward to kiss him again, and that pressed her breasts hard up against his chest in a way that short circuited any further rational thought. His hands came up of their own accord to cup her through her bra, a gentle massage that grew firmer when she pressed into his hands.

"Here, let me," she said, then reached around and undid the clasp.

God, she was perfect. Curvy in all the right places, breasts full and firm, and he tumbled her over onto her back, urging her to relax when he felt her hands fumbling for his underpants. "Just enjoy this." He leaned down and kissed her breasts, first one side, then the other, and then drew one warm bud into his mouth, lapping his tongue back and forth across her nipple, thrilled at the small moan that escaped from her mouth. His hand captured the other breast, and soon she was squirming beneath him, hand stroking his hair over and over again.

"Could I...?" Mark reached for her underpants, tugging the waistband down just a fraction, and Dee eagerly nodded, lifted her hips for him, and after Mark tossed the fabric off the bed, he paused on his way back to her lips...


Dee was feeling giddy. The look of anticipation on Mark's face as he removed her last piece of clothing was eclipsed by one of total captivation, and she let her gaze drift downwards, returning the thorough inspection he was giving her. He was decadent – there was no other word for it. A light dusting of hair across defined pecs, a six pack that flexed in the most fascinating way when he moved, down to that distinct bulge in his underpants, and she had a sudden craving to peel away the fabric and get a good, long look at what lay beneath.

But then Mark began kissing his way back up one leg, starting at the ankle, the knee, then along the sensitive inside of one of her thighs.

None of her previous boyfriends had been particularly interested in oral sex – not on the giving end of things, at least – so Dee mostly expected Mark to give her a token kiss, or perhaps even bypass her most sensitive area completely, and simply continue on his slow, sensual path northwards.

But instead, he paused when he reached the junction of her thighs. Slid one gentle finger over her clitoris, rubbing back and forth... and then he leaned down, his tongue taking over where his fingers had been.

Dee momentarily lost the ability to breathe. Her head fell back and her legs parted involuntarily, and oh, the feel of that was just sublime. Her nerve endings were on fire, her hips lifting before she got control of herself. Perhaps he wouldn't like her pressing herself into his face?

But he seemed to take the move as encouragement, adding talented fingers to the task, and Dee moaned again, fist gripping the sheet as he stroked his tongue over her clitoris again and again, then delved lower, fingers sliding in and out, sucking then stroking in a rhythm that constantly left her guessing.

When he finally left off the pleasurable torture long minutes later, he was breathing fast, as was Dee, and he kissed his way slowly up over her abdomen, her belly button, one hand stroking tantalising lines over her ribs while the other kept up the teasing between her legs, and when he kissed her on the mouth again, Dee slid one hand behind his neck, opening her mouth eagerly while she wrapped one leg around his thigh.

"Okay?" he asked, when he pulled back, and Dee nodded emphatically.

"Better than okay." She lifted her hips again, feeling his erection hot against her inner thigh, and realised that he must have removed his underpants somewhere along the way.

Mark took the hint from her restless fidgeting. He moved to cover her, Dee's heart beating fast as they rearranged their bodies to suit, and then she felt the tip of him pressing against her entrance.

It seemed like forever since she had done this, and she groaned as she felt him press inside her. The warm, slick sensation was absolutely divine, the coarse hair of his legs scraping deliciously against her thighs, his body hot against hers.

He dropped his head onto her shoulder, breathing hard, and Dee stroked his back, drinking in the sensation of his heated skin against her own, her hips lifting with each thrust. He paused, shifted position, thrust again, his mouth seeking out her breast.

"Oh, fuck…" She heard the words as a breathless exhale, and then she felt him thrust harder, his whole body tense, a low moan escaping from him, and Dee would remember the sound of that deep, rumbling groan forever. It was the sexiest sound in the whole world, and for a moment, she didn't even care that she wasn't quite there yet, her body hot and throbbing, and insisting that she have MORE and NOW, even as she stroked Mark's shoulders and felt him relax against her.

"Sorry," he murmured, kissing her shoulder. "It's been a long time."

"It's no problem," Dee said, though her body disagreed. But so far he'd been a generous and thorough lover, so she wasn't going to hold a grudge-

Mark, it seemed, wasn't quite so willing to let it go. He pulled out, slid to the side and kissed her, and then that clever hand was sliding down her body again to tease her clitoris. He slipped one finger inside her, then another, and damn, she was so close. A moment or two more was all she could take, and then she slid one hand down, rubbing herself firmly while Mark's fingers were inside her, and that was all it took. She moaned, arched her back and dug her fingers into his arm as she went over the edge.

When she opened her eyes a short time later, it was to find Mark grinning down at her like he'd just won the lottery. And Dee had to laugh.

"Oh, don't look so pleased with yourself," she said with a grin.

"Why not? You seemed to enjoy that."

Dee laughed again, and tugged him down to kiss him. "I did," she admitted against his mouth. "Very much."

And then suddenly, a strange expression crossed his face. "Not meaning to break the mood or anything, but... what did Faeydir just think of that?"

Bloody hell. She'd forgotten all about the wolf, so caught up in the moment, and braced herself as she tuned into her other half, dreading what she might have to say, and bemused by the fact that their lovemaking had most likely just been eavesdropped upon by a most unusual third party.

Complete boredom was what came back at her, and Dee almost sighed with relief. Faeydir was more than happy to spend time in Mark's company, but the whole concept of human sexual relations was completely baffling to her, and she'd pretty much tuned out once the kissing started. Dee relayed the information to Mark, who looked equally as relieved.

He fell back onto the bed, letting out a groan of contentment. "Good to know," he said, sliding an arm around Dee's waist and tugging her closer. "Because as much as I like your wolf, I really don't fancy the idea of her interrupting this kind of thing."

Dee just grinned, reaching out to switch off the lamp and snuggling in beside him. She agreed – having Faeydir butting in on their lovemaking would be awkward, to say the least. But with her wolf as curious and independent as she was, she wasn't inclined to take anything for granted.


When Dee woke in the morning, it was to an unexpected sense of warmth and wellbeing.

The first thing she noticed was that she was naked. Her usual habit was to wear pyjamas to bed, and the feel of smooth sheets against her skin was unexpected.

The second thing she noticed was the incredible warmth in the bed.

Mark.

He was lying on his back, fast asleep, his arm and thigh pressing against hers, and the heat radiating off his body was like a living furnace. Dee snuggled closer, then froze as he stirred, not wanting to wake him just yet.

Wow. Last night had been fantastic. After the lights had gone out, he'd held her for a long while, stroking her hair, pressing kisses to her face, her hand, her shoulder, and after a comfortable silence, they'd talked. About nothing, and everything, philosophies on life and love and religion, Mark confessing to finding great comfort in Il Trosa's doctrine on Sirius the Wolf-God, while Dee found the whole thing rather outlandish, if she was forced to put a word to it. She had no objection to their rituals, of course, finding many of them quite beautiful and asserting that each person should be free to follow their own beliefs, but having been raised more or less as an atheist, she didn't feel she was about to commit herself to a spirit-wolf, no matter how comforting the myths might be.

Finally, they'd both fallen asleep, tired and satisfied and comfortably warm, with Faeydir a sleepy presence in Dee's mind, commenting that her sense of smell was sufficient, for once, the musky scent of Mark's skin a soothing balm that put the feisty wolf to rest.

Now awake, Dee simply watched Mark sleep, a surreal kind of joy filling her, one that made her question whether this was reality, or just a particularly vivid dream. Surely one person couldn't be allowed to feel this much contentment? How quickly life could turn around and surprise you.

Finally, though, Mark stirred, letting out a contented hum as he turned towards her, wrapping an arm around her waist before opening his eyes. And then a self-satisfied grin broke across his face. "Morning."

"Morning," Dee replied with a grin of her own.

"Sleep well?"

"Very. I dreamed about France. A shifter's initiation ceremony. It was beautiful."

Mark leaned in and kissed her. He craned his neck to look at the clock, then fell back onto the bed with a groan. "We should get up."

It was nearly nine o'clock. Dee moaned in protest. The bed was just too warm. "Do we have to?"

Mark let out a throaty chuckle. "Don't tempt me…"

# CHAPTER TWENTY-SEVEN

Two weeks later, the first real thaw of spring arrived. Melting snow turned the ground to slush, and every single wolf got an earful from someone or other about tracking mud through the house. Caroline yelled at Baron, Baron yelled at John, George yelled at half the rank and file – apparently cleaning the kitchen floor was one of his duties – and after that, it became a game, various members of the Den deliberately lurking in the foyer or the kitchen, waiting for people to come inside just so they could shout about the mess on the floor.

Spring was a dreadful time for house work – each member of the Den was assigned a room to clean on a regular basis, and spring meant not just mud, but fur as the wolves shed their winter coats all over the furniture, the carpet, the antique rugs. So when Dee was summoned to the library for a meeting with Baron, she wasn't surprised to find John in there, vacuuming the carpet and making a hell of a racket as he rattled the nozzle in and around the bookcases.

Tank and Caroline were sitting with Baron at one of the long tables and Dee took a seat, waiting for the latest news or instructions.

"It's time we got you vaccinated," Baron announced, once she was settled. "There's a doctor we use out east – sometimes it's better not to do these things too close to home- For fuck's sake, John, will you give that a rest!"

"What?" John yelled back, clattering the nozzle about more loudly.

"Shut that fucking thing off!"

"I can't hear you," he replied blithely, moving on to the next shelf.

Baron leapt up and yanked the cord out of the wall. "You can vacuum later, you fucking princess-"

John grabbed the cord and plugged it back in. "You said you wanted the fucking house clean, so I'm cleaning it-"

Baron yanked the plug out again. "That doesn't mean right this instant, you little-"

A tussle ensued, the sight almost comical as Baron's massive figure wrestled with John's slender form, and Dee watched with wide eyes, not at all sure whether this was a real fight, or…

Moments later, Baron had John pinned up against the wall, tongue down his throat, John almost hidden from view by his much larger opponent, and then Dee felt herself blush as a faint but distinct moan drifted across the room. Baron whispered something in John's ear. And then the younger man let out a chuckle, the first one Dee had ever heard from him, and lithely extracted himself from Baron's grip.

"No problem," he said sassily, and smoothly left the room, a smirk on his lips.

"If you two lovebirds are done?" Tank prompted, when Baron just stood there watching him go.

Baron cleared his throat and returned to his seat. "Where were we?"

"Vaccination?" Dee said meekly. Neither Tank nor Caroline seemed to find anything odd about the exchange between Baron and John, so she figured her best bet was to simply ignore the incident.

"Faeydir's been reacting well to her outings," Baron picked up the conversation. "Have there been any problems we need to iron out?"

"Nothing serious, no. So long as I prepare her properly first, she seems fine with having to behave for a little while."

"Good. Because this trip's going to be longer than the others. It's a two hour drive each way, and then there could be a fair wait in the surgery."

Dee immediately conveyed the information to Faeydir, who responded with consternation. Why were they going, she seemed to ask, and Dee tried to mentally express the sense of a terrible disease, which would be prevented by going on a long trip and seeing-

Faeydir recoiled at the image of a man in a white coat, a flat refusal, snarls and bared teeth in Dee's mind, and she gripped the table as a wave of dizziness took over. "No, Faeydir's not happy with that," she said quickly. "Not the long trip, I mean, that's fine. She doesn't want to see a doctor."

"It's a necessary evil," Caroline put in, not particularly helpfully, since Dee knew that already. "And an absolute necessity if you're ever asked to travel overseas for Il Trosa."

"Let me work on her," Dee said, knowing it was partly her own fault. Doctors didn't necessarily wear white coats these days, normal civilian attire far more common, but she'd been trying to explain a complex issue in simple images, and the stereotypical 'doctor' had been an easy, if misguided choice. "Let's talk about logistics," she rushed on, needing time to figure out how to explain the rest to her wolf.

"Tank will go with you. And Silas," Baron said. "Tank will need to go into the surgery with you, so the easiest way is if he poses as your boyfriend. Silas will stay outside – just for back up, in case you need it."

"That seems a little heavy handed," Dee protested, her mind a swirling mess of questions and emotions from Faeydir. "Are we likely to run into trouble?"

"The Grey Watch has a strong presence in the east," Caroline explained. "That's one of the reasons we go out that way. The Noturatii know they're there, and we try to maintain the illusion that all the shifters in England live in the same area. It creates a few inconveniences for us – like having to travel a few hours whenever we need something that the Noturatii might be tracking-"

"Rabies vaccines being on their list," Tank interrupted.

"But it also means that they're less likely to come sniffing around our back door. The less they know about the Den, the better. But that creates two problems. One, we're far more likely to run into Noturatii operatives out that way, and two, there's always the odd chance that you'll come across one of the Grey Watch. They tend to be very reclusive, but even they have to venture into town now and then to buy food, or the odd bit of clothing they bother to wear."

"Right," Dee said. "So hence the security detail."

"Right."


In the end, it took a full five days for Dee to convince Faeydir that a trip to the GP was a good idea. She spent the time looking up images of rabies-infected dogs on the internet, gave the wolf a list of symptoms, went through what was likely to happen inside the surgery in detail, and emphasised that this doctor was nothing like the ones in the lab. The injection might hurt a little, she admitted, but it was a much better option than contracting an infection that could kill them both.

Mark got on board as well, explaining to Faeydir that he'd had a vaccination himself, detailing what it had felt like, what the doctor's surgery had looked like, and generally trying to convey his approval of the idea – Faeydir still took his opinion more seriously than anyone else's, and in slow degrees, the wolf relented. But if anyone tried to harm them other than one single injection, Faeydir cautioned Dee strongly, then the wolf was more than willing to retaliate.

That was an issue of concern for Dee, and she brought it up with Baron. The risk of a forced shift in the middle of a town could be a complete disaster, and Alistair was called in to help. They concocted a story to give the surgery – Dee was terrified of needles, but she'd been offered a chance to work in a bear sanctuary in Asia, an offer too good to turn down, and vaccination was mandatory for the sanctuary workers. Tank was charged with conveying the drama to the nurse, the caring, concerned boyfriend here to comfort his nervous girlfriend, and hopefully they would be in and out with a minimum of fuss.

When the day for the visit came, the drive out was uneventful, Dee relenting to Faeydir's continued requests to feel the wind by finally putting the window down and letting the cold air blast over her face. Faeydir loved it, responding with impressions of wagging tails and playful bounces, and Dee promised her a repeat performance on the way home, if she managed to behave in the clinic.

All too soon, Tank was pulling the van into the clinic parking lot, and Dee took a moment to remind Faeydir of the rules, and the consequences of breaking them. Silas got out and surveyed the parking lot, then gave the nod to Tank, retreating to lean against a wall and fiddle with his iPhone – a pretence while he kept a sharp eye on the goings on around him.

Tank and Dee hopped out of the van, Tank's arm instantly around Dee's shoulder, a kiss pressed to her forehead. "You'll be fine," he said, already in character, and Dee simply concentrated on keeping Faeydir calm, grateful that her role in this charade was simply to look uncomfortable and nervous.

Inside the clinic, the waiting room was crowded, and Dee hovered in the background as Tank spoke to the receptionist. Arrangements made, they settled in to wait, Tank's hand taking Dee's as he casually scanned the waiting room.

As they sat there, the thought occurred to Dee that she had no idea what to look for in a Noturatii operative. How did one tell the difference between them, and any regular human being? What was Tank looking for? Weapons? Uniforms? No, that would be too obvious. Highly trained government operatives wouldn't give themselves away so easily. So the unsettling truth was that they could be sitting directly opposite one of their enemies and never know it until it was too late.

Then again, how did the Noturatii recognise a shifter? Did they have a way of detecting them, like the way Faeydir seemed able to sense the wolf in other shifters? Each shift was preceded by a burst of static electricity. Could the Noturatii detect the minute charges in the air?

"Caitlin Moss?"

"That's us," Tank whispered to her when Dee didn't move, the unfamiliar name lost in her swirling thoughts, until she remembered the false identity Alistair had given her, and stood up abruptly.

"Hey, take is easy," Tank murmured, taking her hand and leading her into the doctor's office.

The appointment went fairly smoothly, not that Dee was paying much attention. She was trying to concentrate, trying to remember far too many details about her fake trip to Asia, giving false answers to questions about family history, any medication she was on, while half her attention remained on Faeydir, the wolf alert and searching for any hint of betrayal or danger, to the point that when the sting of the needle finally hit, Dee hardly felt it.

"Now that wasn't so bad, was it?" the doctor said genially, and Dee managed to summon a weak smile.

"Thank you," she said politely, then glanced at Tank. "Are we done?"

"All done," the doctor told her. "Best of luck with your trip."

"Thanks. Thanks again."

Dee couldn't get out the door fast enough, Faeydir demanding they leave immediately now that it was over, and she took a deep breath the moment she stepped back into the cold air, so relieved that it was finished that she wasn't really paying attention. Silas pushed off the wall and moved towards the van, and as Tank was closing the door to the clinic, Dee paused at the roadside, waiting as a large SUV entered the parking lot. There weren't many spaces left, and the car stopped in front of her, blocking her view of Silas for a moment. She glanced back at Tank, the tension of the whole trip making her anxious and vaguely paranoid.

Tank shot her a reassuring smile, stepped out across the footpath... and his smile vanished. Behind her, Dee heard a car door slam, heard a shout from Silas, and Tank's hand disappeared into his coat, reaching for his weapon.

A hand grabbed Dee's shoulder and she spun around, finding herself face to face with a tall, solidly built black man who seemed as shocked to see her as she was to see him. "Dee?" he said, and that's when the panic really hit.

"Dee, get down!" Tank shouted, rushing forward, while Silas burst out from behind the SUV. Two rapid shots took out two of the men from the SUV, the guns seeming deafening in the quiet of the town even with the silencers on them. And then the gunshots were eclipsed by the 'thud, thud' of two bodies hitting the ground, but the black man stayed standing, until Tank barrelled into him, slamming the big body into the side of the car by using his own even larger frame as a battering ram. But there was another man in the car, Dee realised, and he had a Taser. Faeydir sharply remembered getting hit with one of those when Baron had first found her, and suddenly there was no more controlling the furious wolf. Static electricity burst over her skin and Dee knew she had just shifted, powerless to stop the change as Faeydir took control, and then they were off, bolting out of the carpark and along the road at a dead sprint.

Oh shit, they were in public, Dee thought frantically as Faeydir ran. They were in a town, people everywhere, and God knew if anyone had seen them shift. But Faeydir liked being around humans even less than Dee, and she took the first exit she could find off the street, a narrow path into a park, and then out the back into a small woodland.

Nose to the ground, she searched out the path that smelt the least like human, and then another turn, over a stream, under a fence, then a headlong sprint across an open field. Hopefully if anyone saw them, they would just think she was a large dog. Faeydir climbed a small rise, then jumped up onto a garbage bin, then a brick wall... there! In the distance, a forest. Trees. Cover. And the chance to kill those who pursued them.

Where they even being pursued? Dee wondered, trying to get her bearings. It was near impossible with the onslaught of scents, of sounds that Faeydir was processing, the memories running hard and fast of what an empty forest smelled like, of the sounds that meant safety and the scent of fresh leaves and moss.

Faeydir jumped to the ground again and took off, heedless of Dee's suggestions, then demands that they stop and reassess the situation. Faeydir didn't even know if they were being followed, she pointed out sharply, only to be shoved back, an image of a Taser vivid in her mind.

And it was only then that she realised Faeydir wasn't just angry at being attacked, wasn't just driven by the need to protect them both.

She was terrified. She'd hated the lab just as much as Dee had, she'd felt the frustration of being caged more keenly, she'd objected with sound logic to the trip to the doctor today, and in the wolf's mind, all of her concerns were now completely justified. They had gone to a place with men in white coats, and the Noturatii had tried to kidnap them again. So for the time being, she was done with listening to Dee.

# CHAPTER TWENTY-EIGHT

Baron was sitting at his desk working on his computer when his phone vibrated, and he frowned as he picked it up. There were few people who ever sent him a message – the Council would send occasional cryptic instructions or requests, more sensitive information handled via more secure channels, or any of the wolves out of the estate might send a message if they ran into trouble. Tank and Silas were late back from taking Dee to the doctor, but they were his two most capable fighters, so trouble was hardly likely to-

Holy shit.

*Due to complications at home, we have sent our package early. It is postmarked appropriately.*

It was from the Council. And as cryptic as usual. The only 'package' they should be sending was an emissary to assess Dee as a new recruit, and the 'postmark' could only be the Council brand that marked all of their operatives. The emissary hadn't been due until later in spring, but Baron was just as glad to get it over with now. Visits from the Council tended to be complicated. He'd tell Dee as soon as she got back-

"Baron?" John said from across their bedroom. He was sitting in front of a computer console playing some video game or other, a clear view of the front lawn from his vantage point. "There's some joker in a bad suit standing at the front gate."

Baron was out of his seat in a second, leaning over John and his slice 'em dice 'em character on screen to peer out the window.

"What the hell? How about a little notice, you pompous shits."

"Yeah, good luck with that one," John said disinterestedly as Baron dashed for the door, then he shifted on his way along the hall, bolting down the stairs in wolf form and making it to the ground floor in record time. He was in such a hurry he barely managed to shift back to human form before he was out the front door, and then it was a battle to know whether to run for the gate so as to keep the emissary from waiting, or to maintain a dignified walk, a show of poise that could just as well piss the guy off.

In the end, he opted for a brisk walk, greeting the man with a tight smile. "Morning, sir. Can I help you?" Text message aside, no one, but no one got through that gate without the proper authority.

The man didn't reply immediately. Instead, he held up his left hand. A pale brand sat in the centre of the palm, no more complex than three straight lines at an angle to each other, the sort of thing that could easily have been caused by a burn during a careless moment in the kitchen. But it was the official mark of the Council, branded onto each and every member chosen to directly serve the shifter version of aristocracy, and the mute display had Baron keying in the access code and opening the gate as fast as humanly possible.

"Welcome to England, sir. I trust your travels were uneventful."

"They always are," the man said, a wry quirk of a smile on his lips as he picked up his small travel case. It was a safe bet that it contained more weapons than clothing. "Otherwise I wouldn't be doing my job."

There was no point introducing himself. The emissary no doubt knew exactly who Baron was, and a small, childish part of himself was resenting this intrusion with all the passion of a two year old throwing a tantrum.

It wasn't the lack of notice. It wasn't even the high handed way the Council tended to deal with things. No, the thing that pissed Baron off was that for the first time in months – no, years – there was someone on the estate who outranked him.

It was a petty complaint, even to his own ears. Council emissaries were trained as warriors, not just in fighting as a wolf, but also as a human. The man standing before him would be an expert in not one, but two martial arts, capable with a sword, a pistol and a bow and trained in espionage until it was not a skill but an art.

Should Baron actually go toe to toe with the wolf in a fight, he would almost certainly come out the loser. But the thing that rankled him was not that he would lose. It was that he was forbidden from ever challenging the man. So the question of whether he was the more capable fighter or not would remain forever unanswered.

Council members themselves, of course, were not just fierce warriors, but diplomats, masters of strategy, patience, psychology and philosophy, charged with the sacred task of preserving their species for generations to come.

It was not a task that Baron envied at all.

"I'm Andre," the man said, giving Baron a smooth once-over. "Please forgive the lack of notice. Given the disturbances from the Noturatii lately, we're being more reticent than usual about our plans."

"I see." Fuck, things must be bad if even the Council was on edge. Baron returned the once-over, and if anything, what he saw only made him more tense. Despite the suit, there was no doubt that a warrior stood before him. Every movement was smooth, lithe, deliberate and efficient. Andre was scanning the estate in a confident, unhurried manner that implied he would obligingly kill anything that presented the least threat, and then his gentleman's air would make him apologise for the mess afterwards. A stiff British accent had been coloured by his time in Italy, but it was clear the man was originally from England – though he must have left a long time ago, as Baron had never met him in all his years at the Den here.

"I'm afraid Dee's out at the moment," he began, not knowing if this was going to be a problem or not. The Council was not known for its patience. "She had a doctor's appointment, and since we weren't expecting you-"

"I'm in no hurry," Andre said, his tone at once accommodating and commanding. "Perhaps, if you could show me to my room, I'll freshen up, and then you can fill me in on how the young wolf has been progressing?"

It was a polite request, a question, not a demand, and yet Baron still felt like he'd just been given his orders like a common servant.

"Of course. This way." He led the man towards the manor, sending a Den-wide message from his phone alerting everyone to Andre's presence. Strangers on the estate tended to be treated with a shoot first, ask questions later policy.

Caroline met them at the door, her characteristic scowl on her face, until she saw Andre. And then… well, in all honesty, it was hard to tell what she felt.

"Andre."

There was the briefest, and yet most telling of pauses. "Caroline."

"I didn't realise it would be you."

"You know each other?" Baron interrupted, not liking being left out of the loop.

"We met in Italy. Shortly after Caroline was converted," Andre explained. And then said nothing more, which really explained nothing at all.

"I see."

"Would you like me to show you to your room?" Caroline offered, sounding almost eager? God, who the hell was this man, to get that kind of reaction from their resident heartless bitch?

But if Caroline was off balance from the unannounced arrival, then Andre was utterly unaffected, no doubt having known exactly who would be meeting him. And Baron was itching with curiosity to know more.

"If you would be so kind," Andre answered, the perfect gentleman. "I'll catch up with you a little later," he said to Baron, a clear dismissal if he had ever heard one, and Baron fought to contain the glare he longed to shoot

Caroline's way.

"As you wish." He prowled out of the room, heading for the library, determined to wring some answers out of the alpha female later on.

Caroline was acutely aware of the man behind her as she led Andre up the stairs. Had it really been fifteen years? It seemed like yesterday.

"So you're alpha now." The smooth statement surprised her, and her foot caught the edge of the next step, a stumble quickly covered, and she glanced back at him.

"For the last five years. But I'm sure you know that already."

"I was briefed on the members of your Den, yes. And their respective histories."

They reached the top of the stairs and turned left. But before they could get any further, Heron appeared from out of one of the hallways, and she looked both startled and delighted as she saw Andre. "Heshna, Andre," she said with a smile. "It's been a long time."

"Heshna, Machia," he said respectfully, giving her a slight bow.

Caroline was briefly surprised by the exchange, until she remembered that Andre had grown up on this estate. As the adopted son of a shifter couple, he'd been raised here until he was fifteen, when he and his family had moved to Italy, and though he'd left long before Caroline had arrived, Heron would have been here throughout his childhood, would have watched him grow up, helped raise him, and 'Machia', the term he'd used to greet her, meant 'aunt' in the ancient language.

Heron let out a pleased little laugh. "Always the gentleman. I'll let you get settled in, but when you have time, we must catch up. I'm sure you have some fascinating stories to tell."

"It would be a pleasure." Heron continued on down the stairs, leaving Caroline feeling slightly jealous of the easy camaraderie between the pair.

There were a number of visitors' rooms permanently made up on the first floor, a precaution for exactly this sort of situation, and Caroline led Andre to one that would afford him the least disturbance and the greatest privacy.

"How's Italy?"

"Warm."

It was a hopeless attempt at small talk, and a far cry from the conversation Caroline wished to have, but one did not question a Council emissary, regardless of any shared history.

"This will be your room," she announced, opening the door and preceding him inside. "There are towels in the bathroom, wireless internet on a secure connection, and you'll find-"

"You've come a long way."

"What?"

Andre had closed the door and was standing just in front of it, the sudden change of topic throwing Caroline off balance again. And if he had been anyone else, she might have resented how easily he could do that to her. Then again, if he had been anyone else, he wouldn't have been successful.

Andre looked her over carefully, but the inspection was neither critical nor lewd. There was just a gentle curiosity and a hint of affection. The barest hint. His eyebrow twitched. A muscle tugged at the corner of his mouth, and Caroline found herself smiling almost bashfully.

"Yes. I suppose I have." It was quite the understatement. As a newly converted wolf, Caroline had been out of control. Too much anger and violence fuelling her actions, too little experience to temper rage with patience, and the only solution had been to send her to Italy for 'retraining'. She'd been terrified at the thought, imagining all manner of torture, punishment and strict rules to make her life hell.

Instead, she'd been turned over to Andre's care, a much younger, much less severe version of the man who now stood before her. Since then, of course, Andre had been through not just the Council's specialist training, but a large number of assignments, many of them dangerous, some of them no doubt quite painful, and that sort of thing tended to change a person.

There was a mere five years age difference between them, but at Caroline's conversion, Andre had been a wolf for five years already, and serving under the Council for three of them. To say he was naturally gifted was a gross understatement.

"Is there anything you need?"

Andre's calm gaze didn't waver. "No. Thank you."

"I'll leave you to unpack then."

"I'm glad you made it," Andre said softly. "For a while there, we weren't sure you were going to."

And that, at least, made Caroline smile, though it was her usual sardonic smirk that came out. "I hear that about almost every wolf we convert. And yet nine times out of ten, we somehow manage to pull through."

Andre's smile widened into a real expression, rather than the pale shadow of one he had been wearing. "It's good to see you again," he said as Caroline turned to leave. And if she felt her face warm as she closed the door… well, it was probably just the heating system playing up again.

# CHAPTER TWENTY-NINE

They were in a forest, Dee registered. Faeydir had been running for what seemed like hours, following God knows what path or scent, and after crossing a few paddocks and weaving through a few lanes, they'd entered the forest proper. And Dee was none too happy with proceedings.

It would be getting dark soon, and she'd tried repeatedly to pull the wolf up, to reason with her, even tried to force a shift, only to get shoved back with a snarl and an onslaught of anger.

The problem was that, despite being rather more intelligent and alert than the average wolf, Faeydir still lacked a lot of the human understanding of cause and effect. According to her, it was the doctor's fault that the Noturatii had found them. Men in white coats were not to be trusted. Dee had had no luck at all explaining that it was likely just a coincidence, and that the doctor himself had had nothing to do with it. The wolf simply wasn't listening.

Like a child, Faeydir was also able to plan ahead a little, but not always able to see the consequences of her decisions, and with the light fading fast, Dee was dreading being stuck out here come nightfall. The nights were still freezing, and while she was dressed warmly, she could still freeze to death-

Oh. The image in her mind was clear and vivid. A makeshift den, maybe under a tree root, or inside a fallen log. Faeydir's fur would keep them warm, and she might be able to catch a rabbit for dinner. They would be well taken care of, Faeydir told her, not at all offended by Dee's lack of trust. She didn't trust Dee any further, knowing full well that she didn't understand Faeydir's needs and desires as a wolf. And it was humbling, as well as eye opening, to suddenly be so completely dependent on the wolf's skills.

Dee had never really been able to get her mind around the other shifters' insistence that the wolf was an asset, and not just an ultra-fancy toy

to play with. Then again, Dee thought darkly, if she hadn't become a shifter, then she probably would never have been stuck out in the dark, in the cold, needing a coat of thick fur to survive the night. Still, she was not one to look a gift horse in the mouth.

This was a good place, Faeydir reported suddenly, coming to a stop at the edge of a mossy clearing. A brief exploration turned up a deep puddle to drink from, a cosy nook underneath an overhanging rock – perfect for a makeshift den – and the scent of rabbits on the ground. Faeydir took the time to scent-mark the area, then padded off into the undergrowth, Dee watching her progress with a newfound respect and a sharp curiosity.

"Where the hell are they?" Baron snarled, all but ready to hurl his phone across the room. Night had fallen, the darkness thick without a moon tonight, and he'd been trying for the last hour and a half to reach his Den-mates. Tank wasn't answering, his phone just ringing out. Silas's phone kept going straight to voicemail – which meant he was in wolf form, since no shifter out on assignment would ever turn their phone off – and Dee's phone was simply 'unavailable' since she'd been lent a spare just for this excursion and no one had set up the voice mail on it.

"Where's the van?" Every vehicle was fitted with a GPS tracker, and Skip had retreated to the office earlier to find it.

"Just south of Carlisle," she reported, arriving back in the library. "And it's stationary. Has been for hours."

"Fuck." He could feel Andre's eyes on him, no doubt assessing his capabilities as alpha depending on how he chose to deal with this crisis. Three wolves MIA and one of them an untested newbie. And that was bad enough, without the eyes of the entire Den on him. Once word had spread that the team hadn't come back, the shifters had gradually congregated here in the library, a silent audience that was equal parts anxious concern and eager ferocity. It was heartening to know that each and every one of them was willing to drop everything and rally to the cause at a moment's notice, but equally unnerving to have them all watching him, when he didn't know what the fuck he was supposed to do next.

Caroline was being unusually quiet. Normally she'd be tossing out ideas for finding them, sniping in his ear about how he could have let this happen, but she was sitting silently at one of the tables, legs crossed, her black leather making her look more of an assassin than the one the Council had sent to them.

"We need to search for them," Baron said finally. It was the obvious choice, but not without its own risks. "Simon and Skip can go get the van. Check it out for bugs, bombs, mechanical tempering, the whole bit. Caleb can go with them. And you, Caroline. I'll take Mark and Alistair and start at the clinic, see what we can find." Mark had been pacing the room, understandably more agitated than the rest of the Den, and he looked almost relieved at the announcement, no doubt eager to be out and *doing something*, rather than sitting around hoping his girlfriend magically came back on her own.

John, sitting in the corner ignoring the entire room, also looked up at the announcement, and Baron cast an uneasy eye over him. Should he...?

"John, you're with me. You're the best tracker in the Den, after Silas. We're going to need you." The predatory leer that appeared on John's face was not at all reassuring.

"What about me?" Andre asked softly, and Baron held back a groan. Fucking politics.

"If you would like to join my team, your help would be most welcome," he said, managing to be diplomatic.

"If I could make a suggestion? Perhaps you should leave Alistair behind. As I understand it, fighting is not one of his more refined skills."

Fucking asshole was calling one of his wolves weak? And in front of the man himself? Baron gritted his teeth. "Alistair comes," he said, glancing at the man with a reassuring nod. "He's a demon behind the wheel and he can drive the van while the rest of us do our thing. Everybody, be ready to leave in ten minutes."


Dee was torn between being terrified and fascinated. Now that Faeydir had promised to look after them both, Dee was paying more attention to what she was doing, and less to trying to get her to stop it. The scent of rabbit was strong – this was a path they used frequently, and up ahead they were likely to find a warren.

Faeydir crept along the path, her paws silent against the damp soil as she listened intently, focused on the scent trail, thoughts on a tasty meal...

Without warning, a large wolf leaped out of the undergrowth, standing before them in open challenge. And Faeydir realised a moment later that there were two more, flanking her, one on either side.

*Run!* Dee urged in her mind, terrified by their sudden appearance, but Faeydir paid the comment no heed. She simply stood there and watched the wolves come, hackles raised, teeth bared.

The three stopped, the leader coming to a halt just feet from where she stood, and Dee's racing mind reminded her that there weren't any wild wolves in England.

Right on cue, the wolf in front of her shifted, becoming a tall, black haired woman clad in buckskin and grey wool, a long knife in her hand only a moment after the shift was complete.

"Who are you?" she asked without preamble. "You trespass, and Il

Trosa has no rights here."

The Grey Watch. There was a tattoo on the woman's left cheek, another on her left hand, and no hint of compromise in her eyes. In the months that she'd been with the Den, Baron had warned her repeatedly to avoid the Watch at all costs, and Dee was already planning escape routes, weighing up whether Faeydir could fight the three of them all at once.

But Faeydir seemed almost relieved to have met them. An image came to mind of a warm den smelling of earth and wolf, of low tents and a fireplace, simple tools like knives and axes set out neatly.

*These wolves are dangerous!* Dee told her urgently. But Faeydir disagreed. Wild wolves, these were, living outside without cages and rules. Open skies. Cold winters. Wide forests. This was where Faeydir had wanted to come ever since they'd escaped from the lab, and Dee's heart sank as she realised that she'd be fighting an uphill battle to get them out of here.

Faeydir huffed at her, and Dee sighed inwardly. Well, okay. If she couldn't leave by force, then she might as well try to negotiate instead. She was getting rather a lot of practice at that, after all.

*I need to talk to them,* Dee pointed out, and Faeydir agreed. On condition that she be polite. These were friends, Faeydir insisted. A throwback to simpler times, more in touch with their wolf side than anyone in Il Trosa.

Oh hell, Dee thought as she shifted, her feet not quite willing to hold her steady as tiredness overtook her. Faeydir sounded like she wanted to stay, that she would try to convince Dee that this was a better option than her newfound friends at the Den. How the hell was she going to convince the stubborn animal that they needed to leave?

"I didn't mean to trespass," she said to the dominant female, cutting to the chase. "I was in town when the Noturatii showed up. I had to run away, and ended up here. I'm not even sure exactly where here is, but I assure you, I meant no offence." It was an effort to refer to herself as 'I' instead of 'we', as had become her firm habit, but Baron had told her often enough that most shifters were a single, cohesive unit, and given her enough warnings about the Grey Watch to make her think it would be a bad idea to admit to her unusual condition.

Though, now that she thought about it, he'd never mentioned exactly *why* the Grey Watch was to be avoided. Given all the weirdness that routinely went on around the estate, she had a hard time believing that Baron was simply reacting to rumour and superstition. But the lack of details was disconcerting.

"You're from Il Trosa?"

"Yes," Dee admitted without hesitation. "I joined them last autumn."

The two other wolves had so far remained in their animal form, but one of them shifted now, looked Dee over, and said something to the leader in a language Dee didn't understand. The leader merely shook her head.

"A new recruit?"

"I suppose so, yes."

"And yet you're already a wolf. My understanding was that Il Trosa did not convert their newlings so quickly."

Dee hesitated, wondering how much she should tell them. Her gut feeling was that honesty was her best policy, knowing that wolves were rather adept at detecting lies. "I was kidnapped by the Noturatii and converted in one of their labs. Il Trosa took me in after I escaped. They've been training me since then, but yes, I suppose I'm still rather new."

The second shifter said something else, and the leader nodded. "And what were you doing just now?"

"Hunting for rabbits. I figured I'd be here for the night, and I was hungry..." Were they about to punish her for hunting in their territory?

"Are you alone?"

Dee hesitated. Answering that question, either truthfully, or with a lie, could be equally dangerous. "Yes."

The woman stared at her intently, as if trying to weigh the truth of her words. "You cannot be allowed to wander the forest alone," she said finally. "Whatever your intentions were before, you'll have to come with us. You'll spend the night in our camp. But be warned," she snapped, pointing her knife at Dee. "We are many, and we are fierce. We will not tolerate being toyed with."

Dee nodded obediently. It was actually a relief of sorts to have met them. Okay, so being 'escorted' to their camp held a lot of risks in itself, but at least this way, if the Noturatii did manage to track her, she'd have help to fight them off. And Faeydir seemed happy with the outcome, eagerly shifting back into wolf form to follow the woman through the forest. It was a situation fraught with unknowns, a thousand potential mistakes and missteps waiting for her, but it was far from the worst situation Dee had ever been in.

She only hoped that come morning, Faeydir would see sense and agree to leave.

And that the Grey Watch would let her.

# CHAPTER THIRTY

Nine wolves had gathered out the front of the manor, and Baron was well aware that with this 'rescue' attempt, he was putting more than half his Den at risk. And if it all went south… goodbye Den. "Phones on silent," he instructed everyone. "If the Noturatii shows up, avoid them at all costs. If they've managed to take down Tank and Silas, they mean business."

"Movement at the gate!" John hissed suddenly, sending all nine shifters scattering for cover. Andre, Baron and Caroline all had guns, while the rest of them were reliant on close contact fighting skills, and Baron felt his heart race as a host of worst case scenarios flashed through his mind. If the Noturatii had captured Dee… she was no warrior. If they tortured her for information, there was no telling what she'd reveal.

A shadow moved at the gate again, nine pairs of eyes fixed on the spot, and there was a shuffling sound, a grunt, and then a wolf was running towards them, a dark blur against the night-

"It's Silas!" Baron couldn't have said who made the call, but a moment later his own eyes confirmed it, and he was out of cover, dashing towards the bloodied and exhausted wolf, catching him as he collapsed on the drive.

"What the fuck happened out there? Where are Tank and Dee?"

It took Silas a moment to manage a shift, and then a longer one before he could speak. He'd been shot, in both human and wolf form, though it looked like neither wound was fatal.

"Noturatii," he gasped out, confirming Baron's fears. "At the clinic. Dee ran off."

"And Tank?" If he wasn't with Silas, then… had they killed him? His loss would leave a gaping hole in the Den-

"The Noturatii took him."

A whole chorus of curses filled the night, and Baron was fairly sure he heard a few choice words in Italian from Andre.

"I got away, killed a few of the bastards," Silas went on, when he'd caught his breath a little. "But they tailed me in the van. I ditched it. You have to burn it. They'll have bugged it or planted a bombed in it. Find Dee. She's out there on her own."

"That'll do," Baron told him, helping him to his feet. "Caroline, get him inside. And forget the van. The Noturatii will be watching it. You'll just get yourselves killed. Andre? Mark, John? Ready to go?"

"What about Tank?" The obvious question came from John.

Baron glanced at Andre, who looked impassive as always. Rather than his suit, he was dressed for fighting this evening, camo trousers and combat boots, a trench coat that no doubt covered a multitude of weapons.

"There's nothing we can do for Tank right now. Let's see if we can get Dee back. Then we'll figure out what the fuck we do about Tank tomorrow."

Dee wasn't entirely sure what to expect from the Grey Watch camp. Baron's stories had depicted a people who loathed all human comforts, so she thought maybe it would be nothing more than a wolf den, a few bags of food or equipment scattered around a clearing that was otherwise devoid of human habitation.

So it was a pleasant surprise to find herself being led into a large clearing with a roaring fire and a wide tent, white cloth covering the walls. Wolves loitered around the clearing, each of them taking a keen interest in her when she arrived, but with the Watch leader as her escort, none of them made any move towards her.

She was led straight into the tent and was relieved to find an array of cushions and pillows spread out, a few wooden boxes containing tools and weapons laid out against one wall, a low table holding trays of food – nuts, dates, dried fruit. She still expected to spend the night in wolf form, if for no other reason than that Faeydir would be offended if she didn't, but the sight of a few human comforts was enticing.

The leader shifted into human form, and Dee followed suit. "My name is Sempre-Ul," the woman said. "And you are?"

"Dee Carman."

Sempre-Ul snarled. "Such a human name," she muttered. "Wait here."

She strode from the tent, confidence and authority in her stride, but the other two shifters remained with her, both in wolf form, and Dee supposed it wasn't unreasonable for them to leave her with a guard. She eyed the cushions, but decided against sitting down. So far her welcome had been none too warm, and it might not be a good idea to make herself too comfortable.

Genna had watched the newcomer arrive, her skin itching as she suppressed the urge to shift. She'd been in wolf form for three full days now, and the need to shift was getting harder to ignore.

Rintur had lectured her at length on these urges, Genna's perceived need to shift at least once a day, and had expressed her disgust at Genna's reluctance to remain in wolf form all the time. The Grey Watch embraced their wild nature, she'd said repeatedly. The wolf was stronger, able to hear more, to smell more, the far more capable side of their nature, and if Genna was ever to carve out a place amongst the Watch, she had to learn to suppress her human side.

Grey Watch rules on such things were strict and unyielding. She'd been harassed and derided repeatedly after finally arriving at the camp on her first night after a hellish run through the forest, both her back legs bleeding, her lungs burning as she'd burst into the camp only minutes before dawn.

But she'd made it, had become a fully fledged member of the Watch... only to realise that her trials were only just beginning.

She'd had to fight for food, every scrap a coveted prize by those stronger and more experienced than her. She'd been insulted when she'd tried to spend the first night in human form, laughed at and kicked out of the camp to sleep in the snow, alone. She'd been bullied and intimidated and belittled at every turn, and she'd learned to survive by simply keeping her head down and avoiding anyone's attention. It was a far cry from the life she'd imagined, when Sempre had first told her of the magic of the shape-shifters and the wonders of a life as a member of the Watch.

And now, here was this stranger – a member of Il Trosa, Genna guessed, as she'd never seen the female before – being led straight into the tent that Watch members were only permitted to use one night each month and allowed to wait in human form while Sempre set about deciding what to do with her.

Genna crept closer to the tent, curious about the woman inside, and resenting her easy acceptance of her human side. The Watch had little respect for those who didn't wholeheartedly embrace their wolf, and she was pained to admit that she was more than a little curious about Il Trosa. Shifters, like herself, but with an entirely different set of rules.

The senior wolves had warned her about them often enough, about the way they tried to keep one foot in two different worlds, about their indulgent use of technology, their denial of many of the shifter magics.

The woman in the tent looked nervous, dressed warmly as if she expected to spend time outdoors in human form, and she was on the small side – trim and toned, but short and none too muscular. Genna would be carrying more muscle than her, the rigours of daily life keeping her body fit and lean.

Satisfied that this woman was no more special than she herself was, Genna slunk away, heading for the tight circle of elders surrounding Sempre and eavesdropping on their conversation. Who the hell was this wandering female, and what was Sempre going to do about her?

"…unusual for a shifter so recently converted," Sempre was saying, as the three other senior females hung on her every word. "She found a den to spend the night, then went hunting for rabbits. She was in wolf form, behaving as a wolf, thinking as a wolf, but if what she says is true, she was converted only three or four months ago. There's no way she should have learned all that by now."

"Remarkable," one of the women said. "Do you think Il Trosa has some new training method?"

"Not likely," another woman snorted. "They're all about cosseting their newlings, handing life to them on a silver platter. There's no way their training could make a human embrace their wolf side this quickly."

"None the less, her abilities deserve some attention," Sempre said. "As well as this story about the Noturatii. I highly doubt someone like her could have fought them off on her own, so she must have had help."

"But you said she came here alone."

"Or so she claims. Lita," Sempre said, turning to the oldest woman in the group. "Could you track the others? And these Noturatii operatives?"

"With the girl's cooperation, yes," Lita replied. "The ceremony might worry her, so she'll need to be persuaded."

"Consider it done."

"And what about in the morning?" someone else said. "We're not just going to let her leave?"

Sempre smiled, an expression that Genna had come to fear. "Of course not. She's a liability. If nothing else, she could lead the Noturatii right here. And we don't have enough camps left to give up another one. But maybe…"

"Maybe what?" Lita prompted, when Sempre didn't continue.

"She's got some skills as a wolf," Sempre said thoughtfully. "And she seems comfortable enough making a go of it in the wild as one."

The other women looked astonished. "You're thinking of recruiting her?"

"She's only been with Il Trosa for a few months. And they have enough restrictions that she might be feeling a little chaffed by it all. So if we paint a rosy picture, there's a good chance she might see reason and join us. It's not like we're spoilt for choice as to our new recruits."

Not spoilt for choice? Meaning they'd settled for Genna, rather than deliberately choosing her. Genna slunk away, not liking the direction of the conversation. She'd done everything they'd demanded of her, fought, run, survived, denied her human half, and still she was treated as an afterthought, a nuisance necessary to boost their numbers, but nothing more.

She crept away into the darkness, glaring at the tent where the newcomer waited. Such insults were not to be borne. And the moment she had the opportunity to prove to them that this woman was nothing more than a thorn in their sides, she would leap at the chance.


The tent flap was pushed aside, and Dee sighed with relief as an aging woman limped inside, Sempre on her heels. The older woman was holding a bowl of stew and a thick slice of bread, and Dee accepted them both politely.

"I'm Lita," the woman said with a smile, reminding Dee of Heron. "You must be hungry."

"I am. Thank you."

"Here, sit. Make yourself comfortable."

The woman slowly eased herself down onto the cushions, and Dee sat beside her, conscious of Sempre lingering nearby, but her two guards disappeared at a nod from the leader, leaving the three of them alone.

"You'll have to excuse the rather abrupt welcome," Lita went on. "We don't mean to be rude, but with things the way they are, we can't be too careful. Sempre tells me you had a run in with the Noturatii?"

Dee nodded, and between bites of the stew – which was delicious – she told them of the encounter in the town, the visit to the doctor and the way the Noturatii had shown up out of the blue. It was only fair, she supposed, to warn them of the Noturatii's activities. Despite their differences, Baron and Caroline had agreed that Il Trosa and the Grey Watch were equal enemies against the Noturatii, and the enemy of my enemy…?

"My, my," Lita said when she finished the story. "And two of your comrades were with you? Neither of them came with you into the forest?"

Her tone was concerned, but Dee suspected that she was fishing for information just as much as trying to be comforting. "They were still fighting the Noturatii when I left," she admitted. "I don't know what happened to them."

"Ah, well then, you're in luck," Lita said, brightening suddenly. "Il Trosa isn't known for being particularly liberal with its rules, but you must have realised that there's more magic to the shifters than just the ability to shift. Some of us have particular abilities."

Dee nodded, thinking of Caroline and her ability to force a shift. "I'm familiar with the idea."

"Well then, let me help you. We don't deal much in technology out here, but we still have a few ways we can track people, keep tabs on what's going on around us. There's a ritual I could perform for you. It would require a small sample of your blood... Oh heavens, I'm sorry. You are aware that we sometimes perform blood rituals, aren't you?"

Dee nodded again. "I know. I've seen a few." The ritual to discover her sire was vivid in her mind, along with the knowledge that shifters were converted by exchanging blood. Shifter blood seemed to contain a particular magic all its own, so while she was by no means looking forward to another ritual, the idea wasn't too frightening. "How much blood?"

"Just a few drips. A small nick with a knife, and it's all over."

"I suppose I could manage that," she said cooperatively. "But why do you need my blood?"

"I need to retrace your path through the forest to the town, then I can focus on the other shifters with you and see what happened to them. If they're injured or in trouble, we need to know. And the only way I can focus on your energy is by channelling the magic through your blood."

That sounded reasonable enough. It was certainly no more strange than the idea of finding out whether her sire was still alive by burning her blood, and Heron had done that easily enough. "Okay. I'll help."

Lita smiled again. "Okay, my dear. Give me a few minutes to get set up, and then we'll call you outside."

# CHAPTER THIRTY-ONE

Baron was on full alert as he pulled the van up in the clinic parking lot. It was deserted, the faint glow from the distant street lights barely penetrating the darkness of the clinic's imposing building.

Andre was out of the van first, scanning the area for the faintest hint of trouble. Baron wasn't far behind, pride firmly leashed as he allowed the more experienced and better trained shifter to take point. For all that he'd love to go a couple of rounds with the guy on the manor lawn, right now, getting Dee back was his only priority, and if Andre was their best hope of achieving that, then so be it.

The parking lot was clear, no evidence of a fight, no tell tale clues to give them a direction.

"Silas said Dee ran off on foot. So we should be able to track her by scent," Andre said, and it was hard to tell if it was a suggestion or an order.

"You're suggesting one of us shifts?" It broke almost every rule of Il Trosa, and even if it was the most pragmatic idea, Baron was more than a little startled by it, coming from one of the Council's best and brightest.

Andre took a slow breath, contemplating the situation. "It's night. The streets are mostly deserted. Someone can shift inside the van, and then we're simply out walking a dog. It's certainly *bending* the rules," he added, seeing Baron's consternation. "But there's nothing illegal about walking your dog at night."

"No fucking way." It was John who spoke, an emphatic refusal that Baron knew the cause of without even asking. John was the best tracker in their group, and to accomplish what Andre was suggesting and still obey Council laws – as well as local animal control bylaws - the wolf would have to be collared and leashed. A tame pet, not a wild animal.

And nobody collared John. Ever. Not even Baron.

"I'll shift," Mark volunteered. "I know Dee's scent. I'll be able to find her."

Hardly a surprise, right there. This was one of the reasons he'd brought Mark along. There was the firm chance that he might do something risky or even downright stupid in the hope of finding her, but on the other hand, he would also be willing to put himself on the line in a multitude of ways to achieve his goal.

But just as he was agreeing with Mark's plan, it was Andre who really made him sit up and pay attention. "I'd like to shift as well," the warrior said, scanning the area again. "I can hear better that way. Keep track of who might be around."

A stunned silence met the statement.

"You'd have to be leashed," Baron said dumbly. Surely Andre would have already realised that. "And you don't know what Dee smells like."

A wry smile from the emissary. "Yes. That has occurred to me. But once Mark finds her scent, I should be able to follow it."

Well, what do you know. The Council's watchdog was willing to be collared like a dumb pet. And there was nothing funny at all about that, Baron realised, seeing the cool calculation in Andre's eyes. His respect for the man went up a notch.

Andre and Mark disappeared inside the van, then emerged a few moments later in wolf form. Baron snapped collars around both their necks, then leads. He tossed the keys to Alistair, who had, up until now, said nothing. "You drive. I'll call you and let you know where we're headed."

"No problem." Alistair was in the driver's seat in a flash. No, he wasn't the best fighter, or the best tracker, Baron admitted to himself, echoing Andre's earlier comments. But he was a genius behind the wheel, and if they needed to outrun a Noturatii vehicle, he had absolute confidence that Alistair would find a way.

"Let's go," he said, handing Mark's leash to John. "Which way?"

Both wolves put their noses to the ground, sorting out a hundred human scents from Dee's particular one. John and Baron just meandered around after the wolves, adopting that patient, faintly embarrassed look of dog owners waiting for their animals to relieve themselves and wishing they would get on with it.

And then, over near the edge of the parking lot, Mark suddenly tensed, nose roving over the concrete again and again, and then he let out a yip that had Andre at his side in a heartbeat, scenting the ground to learn Dee's smell.

The next few minutes were excruciating. The wolves could have followed the scent trail at breakneck speed, but Baron and John would never have been able to keep up, and there was always the need to maintain the appearance of normal people walking normal pets. In this part of

England, they couldn't afford to draw the slightest attention to themselves without calling the Noturatii down upon them. So they strolled along the road, through a park, down an alley, trying to stay patient when all Baron really wanted to do was unclip the collars and let the wolves run.

Finally they came to the edge of the town, wide paddocks opening up, then, in the distance, giving way to thick forest. At the end of Baron's leash, Mark put his tail up. Scented the air drifting in from the field and yipped a plaintive request. And Baron was all too ready to agree. Now that they were out of the guts of civilisation, they could all move faster as wolves. Baron pulled out his phone.

"Alistair? We're going to be out of range for a while. Heading north."

"That's Grey Watch territory," Alistair replied, scepticism heavy in his voice.

"And that's where Dee headed," Baron stated flatly, raising an eyebrow at Mark, who nodded in confirmation.

"No problem," Alistair said, shelving any reservations he might have had, and this was the other reason Baron had brought him. He thought fast, reacted well to sudden changes of plan and could improvise the pants off anyone in the Den. "I'll head out of town and rendezvous with you in the forest."

Baron hung up then glanced at John. Without a word, they both unclipped the collars on the wolves and pocketed the leashes. "Grey Watch territory, folks," Baron reminded the group. "Watch yourselves. These wolves be crazy." He shifted, with John following a moment later, and then all four wolves took off across the field.


Faeydir was in her element, Dee knew, when she was called outside some ten minutes later. Rituals were good, the wolf insisted. It showed that these wolves embraced their magic, unlike Il Trosa, who seemed only to want to control and restrict it. They slept outside. They lived simple lives. And Dee was struck by several images in her mind that made little sense, until she realised that Faeydir was remembering an ancient time, a past life, perhaps, when she had lived with a very similar group of shifters. Wild, free, primitive. They could do well here, the wolf suggested, at which point Dee sharply showed her an image of Mark in her head. That pulled Faeydir up short. Right, Dee thought with a touch of triumph. No Den, no Mark. It was enough to make Faeydir think twice, but not enough to change her mind completely. Wait and see what the morning is like, she seemed to say. But the small concession was enough to give Dee hope that she could talk Faeydir around. These people seemed nice enough, if a little on the defensive side, but it would take a lot more than that to convince her to live with them.

She followed Sempre through the camp, down a short slope and over to a small waterfall – barely big enough to qualify really, just a short drop where a stream ran over the edge of a boulder. A dozen shifters were gathered around, all of them in human form, and Dee was startled to see a rabbit in a cage set beside the water. Faeydir perked up immediately. Dinner, perhaps?

*No,* Dee told her firmly. But what?

Lita stood at the centre of the group, dressed in a long, flowing robe, and she smiled when she saw Sempre arrive. "I have said the prayers and cleansed the site. The ritual can begin," she said.

Sempre nodded. "Proceed."

"Dee? If you would come forward please?"

Dee did so, conscious of being the centre of attention. But at the same time, she realised that there were no men among the gathered shifters. Was that because men were forbidden from seeing this particular ritual? Or because there weren't any men here in the first place? While some women might prefer to live without men, it was impossible to maintain a pack without them. Only male shifters could convert females, after all.

"This will only hurt for a moment," Lita said, picking up a long knife, and Dee reluctantly held out her wrist. The knife was mercifully sharp, and she barely felt the cut, watching resolutely as her blood dripped into a small bowl. Then Lita handed her a short bandage and motioned for her to step back.

Chanting started up, and Dee tried to pay attention as she wrapped her wrist. Despite her reservations about the Watch, she was genuinely curious about this ritual. Aside from the one to reveal her sire, she hadn't seen any others at the estate, and this side of the shifter life was fascinating.

But then, to Dee's shock and embarrassment, Lita undid the ties on her robe and let it fall to the ground, leaving her completely naked. And aside from the nudity, Dee suddenly felt cold in sympathy for the woman. The air was frosty, her breath clouding in front of her, and Lita must be freezing.

The chanting grew in volume, and Lita lifted her arms, revealing a fine network of tattoos along her forearms. She turned in slow circles, head thrown back, eyes closed... and then she stopped suddenly. Threw her arms wide and howled.

Privately, Dee was amused by the sound. It lacked the deep resonance of a real wolf howl, the sound thin and shaky, and she could feel Faeydir scoff at the noise. A series of images flashed though her mind, and it took a moment to work out what Faeydir meant. *This one is as weak as a puppy,* she seemed to be saying. But Dee disagreed. Okay, so her howl was weak, but the woman herself... there was something odd, something disturbing about her that Dee hadn't picked up on before.

And then Lita stepped forward and opened the cage, taking out the rabbit.

It had been drugged, Dee realised immediately. It didn't struggle, didn't even fidget the way a normal, pet rabbit would have done. Instead it lay limply in her arms, eyes half closed, and a terrible sense of dread filled her. She suddenly wanted to be far away from here, anywhere but here, and she instinctively turned to Faeydir for support. They were going to kill the rabbit, not for food, but as a sacrifice for the ritual. And once again, Dee's abhorrence for death and bloodshed rushed to the fore.

She knew the moment the realisation hit Faeydir at what this was. And once again, her wolf completely surprised her. Suddenly the childish, demanding animal was gone, replaced with a sapient consciousness that seemed old far beyond her years.

Faeydir knew this ritual. Had seen it performed before. And while she didn't share Dee's disgust at the process, she disapproved of it for a number of complex reasons. This magic was forbidden. It came with consequences that were unpredictable and unwise, and Faeydir was instantly disappointed that these wolves had reverted to such measures. Out of ignorance? Desperation? Weak wolves, these were, she informed Dee. And she was rapidly rethinking her stance on wanting to stay.

Distracted by trying to translate Faeydir's ramblings, Dee realised that she had missed part of the ritual. Lita was now standing beside a stone tablet, a knife in her hand, the rabbit laid out in front of her. And part of her wanted to look away.

But another part needed her to watch. She needed to see this, to know that these wolves were not part of her pack, were not part of anything she wanted to be involved in. It was easy to believe that the Noturatii were the most dangerous threat to Il Trosa, the only real concern in an otherwise peaceful existence. But there were other monsters hiding in plain sight, she was starting to learn.

*Stay?* she asked Faeydir.

In response, she got a bright image of Mark in her mind. And the rather more frightening image of them racing through the forest, away from here… in the dark. What? Faeydir wasn't even willing to stay until morning now?

And then the knife came down and Dee felt Faeydir cringe. Blood rituals tainted the practitioner, the wolf explained in her usual mess of pictures and feelings. Yes, each wolf had their own magic. Far more than the Den allowed for. But this was cheating, reaching into mystical aspects which should not be tampered with, like an athlete who took drugs to enhance their performance. Or people who had plastic surgery to look more beautiful. How the hell did a wolf know anything about plastic surgery, Dee wondered, before Faeydir tossed up an image of a television show she'd been watching a few weeks ago about that very thing. Wow.

The wolf paid more attention than she thought.

But Dee had been through a blood ritual herself, she reminded Faeydir, to discover which blood line she belonged to. And she had willingly donated her blood to this ritual, she realised in horror.

Her own blood, Faeydir responded. Not another animal's. What she did with her own was up to her. This magic would not taint Dee. Only Lita. Only those who chanted.

The chanting had kept up all through the ritual, a soft, background noise that was almost hypnotic, and Dee watched with a sense of revulsion as the bowl of her blood was laid reverently upon the stone tablet. And then Lita began drawing intricate patterns with the rabbit's blood around the bowl.

She'd been worried about Silas doing something like this, Dee thought with no small amount of irony. Not a bunch of old women running about naked in the forest. The smell of burning reached her, the blood set alight, with a combination of herbs, from the smell. More chanting, and Dee stared at the trees, tried not to see the little furry body lying still...

"I have found the Noturatii men," Lita announced suddenly, startling Dee. She looked up, seeing that the rabbit blood had turned to black ashes on the tablet. Lita was studying them closely. "They have gone west, seeking fresh game. One of the shifters went with them... No, he has gone further. Far to the west." She looked up at Dee. "I dare say one of your companions has gone home to his Den." She turned back to the ashes. "The other shifter has gone south. And two wolves have come north into the forest." A sharper glance at Dee. "You told us you were alone."

Sempre stepped closer to her. "Where is the other? Who is it? Do not deceive me, girl."

Dee shook her head. "I'm alone. I swear to you, I came here alone. I was with two men and neither of them came north with me."

"You lie," Lita stated flatly. "I see two beings coming north. Both contain the shifter magic. Who have you brought with you!?"

Me, Faeydir told her. An image of them standing side by side – of course, two beings, though they shared a body. Bloody hell, how was she going to explain this one?

"Actually it's kind of complicated," she told them hesitantly. "My wolf and I, we didn't really... um... We never merged properly. Is that what you call it? That's what they call it at home. She's different. Her own personality, her own thoughts and desires, kind of like Faeydir in your legends. She and her human shared a body, but had separate minds..."

The shifters around her were gaping at her in astonishment. And wow, she might just have underestimated how big this news really was for them. But somehow she'd assumed that shifters who cast spells and killed rabbits to locate their enemies might have a better handle on the weird than this.

"Who is she?" Sempre demanded, and Dee opened her mouth to reply, then realised that Sempre wasn't talking to her, but to Lita.

Lita grabbed her cloak and wrapped it quickly around herself, looking far less welcoming than she had in the tent earlier. She picked up the knife again. "I will need more of her blood to find out."

"Collar her," Sempre demanded. "Tie her up. And bleed her. I want answers!" Dee suddenly found herself being grabbed, rough hands forcing her towards Lita, shouts and chaos all around her. But the one thing she focused on was that sharp command. Not 'tie her up', not 'bleed her', but 'collar her' was the thing that struck terror into her. It had been one of her first lessons with Baron about safety, about what to do in an emergency, about how to escape attempts to capture her. Never, ever, he had said, let anyone collar you. Most restraints were useless on a shifter, ropes, handcuffs, even a straight jacket rendered useless when the shift came on, the body rearranged and reformed around the objects, setting the shifter instantly free.

But a collar? That was the one exception, the one piece of equipment that could fit equally well on a human, or on a wolf. Even if she shifted, the collar would still be around her neck, her wolf captured like a dumb animal, as surely as her human self would be if she didn't do something fast.

"Stop! What are you doing? I can tell you whatever you want to know," she tried desperately to reason with her captors. "You don't have to tie me up!"

"Don't resist, child," Lita said sharply. "The legends contain more than one wandering spirit. Faeydir was the first, but certainly not the last who will come again in another form. We must know who you are."

Hand were tying her wrists, a thick press of bodies keeping her from moving, making Dee claustrophobic. The rough treatment reminded her of the lab, memories coming fast of scalpel blades and needles and bright lights.

And then she saw the thing she had been taught to fear. A thick, metal collar that could be secured with a padlock, a thick chain trailing from it, and a look of glee on the faces of those who brought it.

There would be no escaping once that thing was on her, no leaving in the morning, and even the sharp curiosity to know exactly who Faeydir really was, perhaps finally solving the mystery of why people in her own Den feared her, was a faint memory as she saw her own captivity stark and vivid in front of her.

Faeydir was livid, snarling in her mind at this betrayal from these wild wolves. These were nothing like the ones she had lived with, who had run free under the full moon and howled at the dawn. These were weak, traitors, abominations twisted by their own lies.

*Escape*, Dee commanded, her hands already tied, knowing Faeydir was their only chance for freedom now. *Escape!*

The transformation was different this time, not the smooth, easy blending of bodies as one retreated and the other emerged, but a hard, jarring jolt, and as her new limbs appeared, paws and fur and legs where arms had been, Faeydir twisted inside her, spun them around and broke free of the restraints in the split second that they were neither Dee nor Faeydir, and Dee found them on the ground, in wolf form, no longer tied to anything.

*Escape!*

Faeydir was up before she'd even thought the word, scrambling to find her feet, weaving between multiple pairs of legs, skidding on loose leaves, and then they were off, bolting through the trees in the pitch black, leaving the lamps and firelight and startled expressions behind.

But not for long. Moments later there was the crackle of feet on leaves, then the lighter footsteps of wolves, not humans, howls instead of spoken commands, and Dee shuddered within Faeydir's mind as she realised that the Grey Watch was coming after them, a dozen or more wolves, skilled, fast, deadly, who knew these woods a hell of a lot better than she did, and all hell bent on stopping her, at any cost.

Bloody hell. What had they gotten into this time?

# CHAPTER THIRTY-TWO

Baron reached the edge of the forest and slowed to a halt. He scented the air, the ground. No doubt about it, Dee had come this way. But the smell of unfamiliar wolves was thick on the ground, and he'd had enough run ins with the Grey Watch to last a lifetime.

Andre was circling around, tense and agitated, and then his head snapped up, ears twitching. Baron turned to listen… and there! Howling! Not the calm, relaxed sound of wolves on a moonlit night, or the haunting ceremonial echo he was familiar with. This was the sound of wolves on the hunt. They were moving fast, working together, and with one of his pack mates out on her own in unfamiliar territory, Baron wasn't inclined to stop and ask questions about what it was they were chasing. He barked sharply, then took off. John would have his back, should he run into trouble, and Andre might stick with him… then again he might go off and try some wolf-ninja shit so Baron wasn't taking anything for granted there. But Mark would break off and follow Dee, fuck the Grey Watch, even if it led him straight into the lion's mouth, so to speak. And since Baron was done with having his Den mates taken away, it took him only a split second to choose his course of action. He slowed minutely, let Mark take the lead, and then fell in behind him, a light yip letting Mark know that he was now running the show. As far as he could tell, Mark ignored him completely.

The trail led up a hill, through a stream, around a large boulder with a small cave etched out beneath it… and then a blood-chilling sound reached all their ears, and in a split second Mark had abandoned the scent trail in favour of following the much more urgent call.

Dee was struggling to keep up as Faeydir raced through the forest. She seemed to know exactly where she was going, taking sudden turns and

207

leaping over obstacles at a speed that was making Dee dizzy. She could hear the howling behind her, the Grey Watch communicating with each other to keep track of her location and each other. And then she heard light footfalls beside her, glanced back and saw a huge grey wolf leap out of the undergrowth.

It was a female, Faeydir detected immediately. One of the older wolves in the pack, strong and experienced-

Teeth in her back leg, and Faeydir spun, lashed out and kicked the wolf in the face. But the move only slowed her pursuer for an instant, and then she was back, snapping at her heels, more wolves closing in from the right.

The human presence in this wolf was weak, Faeydir informed Dee without breaking stride. The Grey Watch spent so much time in wolf form, let their wolves have such free reign that their human selves tended to have little control once the wolf was unleashed. It would be easy to…

*Easy to what?* Dee demanded, flinching as Faeydir was smacked in the face by a low branch.

Faeydir twisted, darted off to the side to buy them time, away from the gaining pack. An image in her head of a human lying dead, a live wolf beside her.

*Kill them?*

The same image repeated itself, and Dee knew she was missing something important. But, as with the last time she'd been offered a life or death choice by this wolf, she was out of options. *Do it,* she agreed, implicitly trusting Faeydir to get them out of this mess.

She felt Faeydir reach out with some kind of psychic energy, felt the wolf and the human in their pursuer as two separate beings, and it seemed like the most natural thing in the world for Dee to reach out with her mind, grab hold of the two distinct energies and yank…

A scream. Impossible to tell whether it was wolf or human, but the creature on their tail broke off, lagged and Faeydir used the opportunity to change course, leaping into a small stream and running along the bed for a short stretch, letting the water disguise her scent. It wouldn't fool the Grey Watch for long, but it would buy them precious seconds to make good on an escape.

More howling behind her, and then a sound that Dee had never thought she would be so grateful to hear. A long, clear, echoing howl sounded through the forest. That was Baron, she was sure of it. Baron's howl, one of the few Den howls she'd heard often enough to identify, since as a general rule, howling was forbidden, and oh, thank God, because that meant the Den had come for her.

Faeydir spun to a halt atop a fallen log. No pursuers in the immediate area, so she threw her head back and howled. She didn't know if anyone would recognise the sound, but it was worth a try.

More howling, closer now, and Faeydir was off again, heading west, heading for home, however far away it might be.

Baron tried hard to keep up with Mark, but a deep pocket of undergrowth swallowed the wolf, and when he emerged on the other side, Mark was nowhere to be seen. Baron's nose was instantly on the ground, following the scent, John behind him, and what do you know, Andre was right there, off to the right, keeping up while no doubt doing some of his 'special training' shit, like plotting the trajectory of each wolf and triangulating Dee's position – still assuming that it was Dee they were chasing, of course. Long hours had passed since she'd disappeared from the medical clinic, and God knew what had happened in the intervening time-

A howl. He knew that sound. And so did Mark, it seemed, as a sudden crashing sound in the undergrowth signalled a wolf changed direction suddenly. Baron took off in the direction of the sound, running flat out to try and catch up. They were closing in on the Grey Watch, and should there be a confrontation, Il Trosa well out of their own territory and the Watch already riled up over Dee's intrusion, then there could well be a vicious fight – blood would be spilled, for certain, and lives might be lost. And Mark on his own would be a sitting duck.

Dee couldn't really say when she became aware of the wolf running along side her. He was a distance away, a shadow off through the trees, keeping pace, and slowly edging closer.

It was a male, Faeydir informed her, which immediately suggested he wasn't from the Grey Watch. And damn, but she'd never gotten around to asking why they had no men with them.

More wolves behind them, and the male wolf angled closer, fighting to keep pace as Faeydir ran in a dead sprint, adrenaline giving her strength, as this could well be a race for her very life.

It was Mark, Faeydir said suddenly, and veered to the left, heading on a path that would connect with his own.

A huge wolf suddenly dropped down in front of them, a leap from a small cliff above them, landing in a heap that only narrowly missed landing right on top of them.

Sempre, Dee realised, recognising the leader. Faeydir sneered, skidding to a halt. Weak. Half-breed. Fight.

No shit, Dee thought desperately. Because the wolf hadn't just dropped in for a friendly chat. Faeydir bared her teeth, hackles up, tail held high as she and Sempre circled each other.

Mark attacked without warning, without a sound to give him away. One moment, Dee was facing off against an angry alpha, and the next, Mark had his teeth around her throat, going for the kill.

Four wolves burst out of the undergrowth, all of them falling on Mark in a tangle of teeth, legs and flying fur. And there was no way in hell Faeydir was going to stand for that. She braced herself, looked for an opening in the fight, and launched herself at the wolves.

They'd lost Mark, Baron was forced to admit after a minute or two, but what they'd found instead was more than enough to keep them occupied. He slowed to a halt as six, then eight, then ten wolves surrounded them. He, John and Andre went on the defensive, their backs to each other as they faced off against the angry Watch. The sound of fighting nearby indicated that Mark had found his own set of problems to deal with, but unfortunately for him, there was nothing Baron could do to help right now.

He stood up to his full height, hackles raised, making him look even bigger, and bared his teeth. Growls from John and Andre proved they were both more than ready for a rumble.

The attacking wolves showed no fear, their postures tall and commanding, but their hesitation to attack betrayed their nervousness. Even outnumbered three to one, Baron knew that the three of them were a force to be reckoned with. He felt no love for the Watch, having spent his ten years as alpha mopping up one problem after another of their doing. John, he knew, held no particular grudge against them, but was always eager for a fight, no matter the circumstances, and his wolf was a thing of nightmares to look at. Scarred, savage and relentless, the Watch were right to hesitate in a fight against John.

And Andre?

The Watch attacked before Baron could finish that thought, but the first hand evidence spoke for itself. Andre was every bit as lethal as his reputation suggested. The fight was brutal – for all of them – but Andre held nothing back of his vicious training, ripping one wolf's throat until she was bleeding profusely, causing her to retreat and shift into human form so as not to bleed out. He latched onto another wolf's shoulder and ripped, tearing the skin away in a long strip that had the wolf screaming and breaking off from the fight.

But despite the wins, Baron was soon forced to admit that they were simply outnumbered. More wolves arrived from out of the darkness, and at one point he found himself holding off three of them, big, experienced fighters, while he watched another three leap on top of John, the smaller wolf all but buried beneath the bodies for a moment before he managed to shake them off, drawing blood in the process.

Baron longed to know where Dee was, to join her and Mark in their own battle, but there was no escaping from the current fight at the moment. He felt jaws sink into his shoulder, spun around with a snarl that had his teeth connect in a satisfying way with the female's face, and felt blood drip down his leg as she let go.

They were wasting time and wearing themselves out. Another strategy was needed here, but how the hell was he supposed to communicate that to John and Andre when they were both...

A gunshot blasted through the clearing, and Baron spun around to see Andre in human form, gun in hand with a dead wolf at his feet. How he'd managed to shift and get a shot off fast enough to avoid being bitten was unbelievable, but the move worked – every wolf in the clearing pulled up short, gaping at the assassin in shock.

"I break no laws here," Andre announced, loud and clear. "The Council has sent us to cull your kind more than once in the past." He swung the gun around to point it at the other wolves, several of them attempting a stealthy retreat to the edges of the clearing. "I bear their mark..." he held up his hand, displaying the brand on the palm, "...and I am well within my authority to slaughter the lot of you." As a general rule, the Dens of any particular country and the resident Grey Watch pack lived in an uneasy truce – they avoided each other where possible, and were expected to render minimal aid to foreign shifters in distress, but nothing more. To outright shoot one of their pack could well be seen as an act of war.

Unless you happened to be a registered assassin for the Council.

The remaining wolves glanced at one another, fidgeting restlessly, and then one of them headed for the forest, back the way they had come. The rest slowly followed, growls and bared teeth all the way.

The last one out of the clearing stopped at the edge of it and shifted into human form. She glared at Andre, then spat at the ground. "You are a traitor to our species," the woman snarled at him.

"Unfortunately for you," Andre said evenly, "I'm prepared to live with that."

With one more sound of disgust, the woman followed the others back into the forest, shifting between one step and the next. Andre waited a moment, until he was sure they were gone, then he holstered his gun.

"Let's go find Mark," he said grimly, then was back in wolf form a split second later, the shift faster than Baron could believe, and Baron led the way off through the forest, tracing Mark's tracks and hoping that the thick silence ahead of them meant victory, and not defeat.

# CHAPTER THIRTY-THREE

Snow was falling, blood splattered red on white in a pattern that Dee was learning to dread. Mark was a beast, tearing skin and flesh, breaking one wolf's foot, biting the end off another's tail. Faeydir was no less savage, throwing herself into the fight with glee.

This was far different from the fights Dee had seen, or been involved in. In all the status fights in the Den, the goal had always been to make a show of strength or cunning over your opponent, but never to do lasting damage. In this fight, the wounds were deep and painful, the risk of permanent injury or death very real, and Dee was once again glad to have Faeydir along. The wild wolf knew plenty about fighting, and held nothing back as she faced off against her larger and stronger opponents.

But as the fight wore on, with odds of two against five, the harsh truth began to sink in – after a day of stress, first the Noturatii, then hours of running through the fields, the Grey Watch and then a breakneck chase through the forest, Faeydir was all but exhausted. She was determined, though, not willing to stand down until these weak, imposter wolves were defeated, not willing to abandon Mark to the fight for a single moment, but her strength was waning, and they were going to need to finish things here quickly if they weren't both to be killed.

The breakthrough came when Mark launched a new assault on Sempre, a violent tussle that resulted with Mark hanging from her shoulder by his jaws, Sempre snarling and snapping, but unable to get a good angle to fight back. Faeydir shoved the wolf she was fighting aside and leapt for Sempre, biting her hard on the back leg, sinking teeth through muscle and tendon, ensuring the wolf would be limping for days. Another hard bite through her flank, and Sempre went down.

She half expected Mark to kill her, the rage in his eyes unrelenting, as the other four wolves stood around nervously. Mark gave Sempre a quick shake, tearing the wound in her shoulder a little more, and the older female lay still in surrender. She was breathing hard, bleeding from a dozen wounds, and looked outraged at having been defeated.

A gunshot suddenly blasted through the forest, loud and haunting, followed by an eerie silence.

Mark released his grip and stood back, still snarling, placing himself firmly between Dee and the other wolves.

Sempre got to her feet, then shifted, glaring daggers at Mark. Perhaps she had been expecting back up, more wolves to finish what she had started, but the forest around them remained empty and silent.

"This is not over," she promised. "You trespass on our territory and then act like you own the place? There will be repercussions for this."

No doubt there would be. But for the moment, Dee was far more interested in getting out of here than in worrying about what would happen in the days to come. Once they were back at the estate, Baron would come up with a defensive plan. Tank and Silas would protect them. Simon would employ whatever was the newest, greatest security gadget, and Il Trosa would hold its own against the Watch.

Sempre backed away into the undergrowth, shifted, then turned and fled, her roughened voice calling the other wolves after her, and Dee and Mark waited a full minute to make sure they were gone.

A yip from Mark had Faeydir turning around, and he led the way quickly to the west, a brisk pace that was none the less slow enough for Faeydir to keep up. He was bleeding, but a quick once over revealed that none of the wounds were serious, so Faeydir was content to just follow him for now.

A few minutes later, they reached a road, a narrow track through the forest, and Mark stopped at the roadside, threw back his head and howled.

Three echoing howls came back at him, not too distant from their spot, and he sighed with relief. The sharp crackle of electricity followed, and then he was human again. He was still breathing hard, tense and restless as he scanned the road up and down, then glanced warily at the forest.

"Alistair has the van. When Baron arrives, Alistair can track us from the chip in Baron's phone. I have no fucking idea where we are."

Now that they weren't running or fighting for their lives, Dee took a moment to just be utterly and completely grateful that Mark had come for her. She was grateful to the whole Den, unreservedly, but that Mark had been the one to find her…

Satisfied that they were out of danger for the moment, Dee asked Faeydir to shift… and received a flat refusal. The wolf stepped closer to Mark and nuzzled his hand, and with a wry grin, Mark crouched down and ruffled her fur, half amused, half infuriated.

"You run off like that again, and you and me are going to have words," he told the wolf sharply.

Faeydir responded by wagging her tail fiercely and licking him all over his face, and then he checked her over, making sure the worst of her wounds weren't bleeding too badly. They would both need medical treatment when they got back to the estate, but for now, none of the wounds were serious. Only when he was quite finished did Faeydir retreat and allow Dee to take over.

The instant she was back in human form, Mark turned on her with a fiery glare, more angry than she had ever seen him, and as he stalked towards her, she involuntarily took a few steps back.

"I'm sorry," she blurted out, trying to explain her disappearance, and the fact that she had been doing a thousand things that the Den and Il Trosa expressly forbade. "I shouldn't have run off, but the Noturatii were there, and they were going to capture me again, and Faeydir panicked- Mmph!"

Mark grabbed her by both shoulders, kissing her with a passion that left her breathless. Then he released her arm and cupped a warm hand around the back of her neck instead, and how the hell did he manage to be so warm when they were standing in the middle of a snow storm? "You scared the shit out of me!" he told her sharply, then kissed her again, and Dee was no more prepared for it the second time around. It was heavenly, though, the warm, familiar scent of him, the heat of his chest against hers, the way his hands cupped her face so gently. "Are you all right?" he asked, when he finally pulled back.

Dee nodded. And then shook her head as a day full of chaos and fear and danger caught up with her all at once. "No. I'm really not."

"Are you injured?"

"No, not hurt. Physically I'm fine. I just..." She swayed on her feet and clutched at his coat for support.

"You're exhausted."

Dee shrugged helplessly. "It's been a long day." And if that wasn't the understatement of the century.

"We're going to get Alistair to pick us up. And then we're going to head home. And as soon as we're there, if you want to fall apart for a little while, you're perfectly entitled to."

Dee smiled despite herself. "I might just do that."

The light sound of wolf footfalls broke through the thick silence.

"Thank God," Mark muttered, still holding her close. "That'll be Baron and John. And Andre, if we haven't lost him."

"Who's Andre?"

"Oh right. You missed that bit," he said, almost to himself. "He's the Council emissary sent to assess you as a shifter."

Right. Because Dee didn't have enough problems right now. "Did Tank and Silas send you looking for me?"

Mark tucked her under his arm, letting his coat drape around her as they waited. "Silas did."

"What about Tank? He's not mad at me, is he?"

Silence. And then... "Tank's gone missing."

Dee pulled back and peered up at him. "Missing?" A cold weight settled in her chest. "You mean the Noturatii took him." It was not a question.

Mark sighed and stared at the ground. "Yeah."

"Then we have to rescue him!"

"What we have to do is get back to the Den and make sure you're all right. Let Baron and Caroline worry about Tank."

"But we can't just-"

"Dee! We're not going to abandon him! But right now you and Faeydir are both exhausted and you're freezing. Can we deal with one crisis at a time?"

If it hadn't been for that desperate kiss a moment ago, Dee would have thought Mark was angry with her, his tone sharp and cutting. But no, she realised, burying her head against his shoulder. It wasn't anger. It was fear. Fear for her, for Tank, perhaps even for himself, what with the Grey Watch still roaming the forest.

"I killed someone today." The words escaped without Dee meaning them to, as if the knowledge was too dark and evil to contain.

Mark glanced down at her. "One of the Grey Watch?"

"Yeah." She wasn't quite sure what had happened, but when she'd grabbed hold of the two parts of the shifter chasing her and pulled... she'd done something bad. Very, very bad.

Faeydir sent her an image of herself, lying dead on the ground, and her message was clear – if they hadn't killed the shifter, she would have killed them. The news was not comforting.

Thankfully, Dee got no more time to dwell on the situation as three large wolves bounded out of the forest towards them. In the dark, it took her a moment to recognise them – Baron and John, along with another wolf she didn't know – but it was enough time to get her heart racing and for her to shrink in beside Mark.

Baron shifted, then pulled out his phone without so much as a hello. "Alistair? Track us with the GPS chip. We need extraction asap... what? Yes. Thanks."

He hung up, then turned to Dee. "Are you injured?" It was Baron in mission mode, curt, laconic and impatient, but Dee knew him well enough to know that it was born of stress, not anger. Baron took his duties in protecting his pack extremely seriously, and for all that she might be safely back in their custody, they weren't out of the woods yet. No pun intended.

"Faeydir has a few scratches. I'm fine."

John and the other wolf – presumably Andre – didn't shift, just paced back and forth, ears twitching, alert for any danger, and Dee noticed that they were both streaked with blood. They'd been fighting. And perhaps that explained why there hadn't been more of the Grey Watch joining in the fight against her and Mark. They'd been caught up with three elite and very pissed off fighters on their tails.

What seemed like only two minutes later, the dull drone of an engine could be heard. The regulation white van pulled up beside the road, Alistair behind the wheel, and Dee wasted no time in scrambling inside. Mark followed, Andre and John leaping into the back with them, still in wolf form, then Baron took one last look around, climbed into the passenger seat, and they were off.

"Turn the heat up, would you?" Mark told Alistair, trying to keep his tone civil. It was toasty warm inside the van, but Dee was shivering, and Mark was having a hard time dealing with her suffering – even more so now that she was found, safe and well. Before, he'd had the necessary momentum of the rescue to keep him occupied, tracking scents, forming contingency plans, keeping an eye out for wandering humans. It had kept him from thinking too much. But now that they were safe – or relatively so, at least – his imagination had kicked into gear and was tossing out all kinds of fanciful and devastating endings to this little adventure. Dee could have been killed. She could have been re-captured by the Noturatii. She could have gotten lost in the forest and been left wandering in circles for days. She could have frozen to death overnight. He slid closer to her and put an arm around her shoulder, breathing in the scent of her hair. It was cold and damp from the snow, Dee's nose a small icicle against his skin, but he didn't care. She was safe. She was back.

Once they were clear of the forest, John and Andre shifted, announcing the fact beforehand with a short yip. John gave Dee a short half-smile and sat down, putting on his seatbelt without a word.

Andre gave her a more thorough once-over that had Mark sitting up straighter and attempting to shield Dee with his body.

"You're the Council emissary?" she asked timidly, and a whole new wave of concerns overtook Mark. He hadn't really given the situation much thought beyond rescuing Dee and beating the crap out of the Grey Watch, but this was probably the worst possible start to her relationship with the Council. Her first assessment, and she was getting caught up in every possible sort of trouble.

"Yes, I am," Andre said calmly. "But let's leave that aside for now."

"You were sent here to assess me?" Dee pressed, and Andre reached out and gently took her hand.

"We have bigger problems right now, little sprite. You're not responsible for the Noturatii attacking you, nor for Tank's disappearance.

None of this will be held against you."

As Mark watched, Dee seemed to sway a little, and her expression went strangely lax. "Okay," she said, her voice toneless. Good God, had he just hypnotised her?

Without really intending to, Mark snatched Dee's hand out of Andre's. And at the man's startled look, he bared his teeth, growled and slid closer to Dee. Who remained oblivious to his disquiet.

"I meant only to calm her," Andre said.

"Don't touch her," Mark snapped back at him. And when he thought about it later, he would blame the excessive stresses of the day for his sharp temper. Under normal circumstances, one simply did not speak to a Council assassin in such a tone.

"My apologies. I meant no offence."

"What did you do to her?"

"A little psychic calming. Just to help her relax. Dee's been through enough stress for one night, don't you think?"

Yes... yes, of course she had. "Yeah. Okay. Just don't touch her, okay?" Mark found himself calming down rather abruptly. Which was something of a relief, actually. It had been a very stressful day, and now that they were out of danger... yes, a little down time would be good. For both of them.

Mark glanced up to see John give Andre a sideways look, but the meaning of it escaped him.

The rest of the trip to the estate passed in silence.

# CHAPTER THIRTY-FOUR

It was after midnight by the time they got back to the manor. Alistair pulled up right beside the front steps, and Dee found herself rather surprised that they were back so soon. She hardly remembered any of the drive back. Maybe she'd fallen asleep for a while?

Mark was out of the van first, helping Dee out, her body stiff and tired, and the other men kept a close eye on her and on the surrounding area while he led her up the stairs into the house.

Once inside, Andre and John quickly excused themselves, Andre disappearing into the library, John heading up the stairs. But Baron lingered in the foyer, giving Dee a close, scrutinising look. "Do you want to talk about it?" he asked softly. For all Baron's usual gruff nature, Dee knew that the offer was a genuine one. Baron took care of his pack. She'd learned that much.

"I do, but maybe tomorrow?" she hedged. Then she shook her head. "They're crazy."

"That they are," Baron agreed.

"I thought they would be like us. Just wilder and with less rules, but..." Baron gave her a sympathetic look, and then Dee blurted out, "I think I killed one of them."

"Hm." Baron seemed to take the admission seriously, which was something of a relief when Dee had half expected him to dismiss her concern, perhaps with a quip about her distaste for violence. "Generally we try not to aggravate the Watch," he said finally. "But if they tried to harm you first, then you're perfectly entitled to defend yourself."

"But it was..." Dee glanced at Mark, standing close by her side, and felt a sudden reluctance to admit what she had done in front of him. The strange energy from Faeydir. The ripping sensation, as if she had torn not just the shifter's body, but her soul as well. Perhaps the rumours about her

218

were true, perhaps she was something to be feared. "We'll talk about it tomorrow. I'm tired and I need to think about things a bit."

"Get some sleep," Baron advised her gently. "We're not out of this mess yet."

Dee nodded and allowed herself to be led up the stairs.

Phil sat on a hard, plastic chair, watching the shifter in the cell with fascination. He was big – huge, in fact, tall and muscular, and quite intimidating, despite the fact that he was unconscious. Close cropped hair and combat boots gave the impression of a military type, which was not at all reassuring.

To be honest, this was the first shifter he'd ever seen up close, having spent the greater part of his career in a lab with blood samples and test tubes, rather than up close and personal with the real deal. Of course, they had yet to see the creature shift, the field team having drugged him as soon as he was captured – no way in the world they wanted a beast like that loose in the lab – and then he'd been chained to the wall, wrists and ankles cuffed so that he could stand up, but that was about it.

He was still out cold, though, and Phil peered up at Miller, standing beside him, looking every bit the military soldier. A mirror image of the man in the cell. He scared the crap out of Phil.

"How much sedative did you give him?" he asked meekly. The animal should have been awake by now, and he was terrified that if something went wrong on his watch – a drug overdose, for example – it would be his head on the chopping block.

"Enough," Miller said flatly. "Don't worry. He'll wake up."

They'd already taken a blood sample, the lab team setting up for the first experiment while Phil monitored their new captive. He'd gotten the call mid afternoon that a live captive was coming in, and it had been all hands on deck since then, the entire lab a flurry of activity, every scientists and security guard called in, despite the fact that it was now well past midnight. Jacob had arrived shortly before Miller and his captive, and the cold glee in his expression when he'd laid eyes on the creature had made Phil's blood run cold.

Li Khuli had come over for a look, stared at the unconscious man for a long time, before she'd made a sound of quiet disgust. "They'll be coming for him," she said with an air of finality. And that was both a relief and a terrifying prospect. A relief because once the shifters made their assault on the lab, this frightening assassin could leave, sent back to whatever gore and chaos was her usual way of life. And terrifying, because Phil had seen first hand the result of their last attack – dead scientists lying broken all over the floor – and he dreaded to think that that could be his own fate, next time around.

The animal stirred finally, eyes opening, a groggy look on his face as he peered around, but there was none of the initial panic that some of their captives had. No desperate struggling against his bonds, no questions about where he was and why. He saw the cuffs, saw the bars on his cage, and locked his eyes on Phil. Sat up, his face totally expressionless. Oh my, oh my, he was going to be a dangerous one.

"You're going to die," the animal said, and a cold chill ran down Phil's spine. "One way or another, your days are numbered."

It was 7am when Dee woke up, and the first thing she was aware of was the warm body wrapped around hers.

Mark.

He was tucked up against her back, holding her tightly to his chest, legs curled around to lay against hers.

And then a moment later, the day before came rushing back. The Noturatii. The Grey Watch. Tank. They had to rescue Tank. And she was suddenly wide awake, despite having gotten only about five hours sleep.

Mark stirred with her slight movements, sighed, and kissed the back of her neck. "Hey."

Dee wriggled around in the bed until she was facing him. "Morning."

Mark made a disapproving sound. "You're worrying already."

"We have to get Tank back."

"We will." He had a strange expression on his face, and Dee's face fell as she watched him.

"What?"

"We're going to get Tank. One way or another," he repeated. "But that means a hard-core battle with the Noturatii. You haven't seen one of those before."

"No. What's it like?"

"We don't call this a war for no reason. It means weapons. Battle formations. Strategies. Bullet proof vests. A lot of people are going to die when we go up against them, and some of us might be among that number."

Dee swore softly as the weight of that sunk in. "You're saying that by the time this is over, one or both of us could be dead."

"You don't have to go-"

"I'm not leaving him there," she said, cold determination in her voice. "I know what those bastards are doing. In vivid, screaming detail. I am not leaving him there."

Mark nodded, his eyes fixed on hers. "Good."

Dee hummed in satisfaction. Good to know she was a valued member of the team. But the possibility of one of them dying was very real. And if this was to be one of their last moments together…

She kissed him suddenly, pressing her body fully against him, and was gratified when he responded in kind.

"Baron will be waiting for us," Mark pointed out, but even as he spoke, one hand was sneaking beneath her pyjama top to stroke warm, smooth flesh, and Dee quickly removed the garment. Mark was already naked aside from a pair of underpants, and throughout long kisses and heated caresses, she gradually kicked off her pyjama bottoms until she was dressed as sparsely as he was.

"We don't have long," she gasped out, as his mouth found her breast, and he nodded.

"Then let's make this count."


Not quite half an hour later, Dee and Mark were curled up against each other, naked, warm and satisfied. "We should probably get up," Mark said reluctantly. "There's a lot to be done today, and-"

"Dee! Outside, right now!" Caroline's piercing voice filled the entire second floor, and Dee jumped in alarm. A moment later they both leapt out of bed, scrambling around for their clothes. The interruption had been inevitable, and Dee could only be grateful that it hadn't come a few minutes earlier.

They both dressed quickly, Dee in jeans and a sweater, Mark in the clothes he'd been wearing the night before. She was just pulling on her shoes when Caroline's fist pounded on the door. "Dee?"

She yanked it open. "Coming."

Caroline was scowling fiercely, and she cast a dismissive glance at Mark, not at all surprised to find him here. "Move it. Outside. To the front gate."

"What's going on?" she asked as they all but flew down the stairs. But as usual, Caroline wasn't giving anything away.

"Just move."

Dee hurried out the door, the cold a blast that ripped right through her woollen sweater, and immediately saw the gathering by the main gate. Baron, John and Silas were there, along with half a dozen wolves, all with their hackles up, teeth bared, and just outside the gate there were eight women, grey cloaks covering them from neck to toe.

Holy hell, it was the Grey Watch. A long way from home, and engaged in a rather heated argument, from the looks of things. Dee rushed over, dreading the confrontation to come, but knowing there was nothing she could do to avoid it.

But as she arrived, Sempre saw her coming, and turned pale, stepping back, eyes wide in fear.

"You keep that creature away from me," she demanded. "You bring death upon us all, Baron. We have tolerated all manner of stupidity from you over the years, but this goes too far. You harbour Fenrae-Ul amongst you. She'll be the death of our entire species."

Fenrae-Ul? Dee recognised the Ul part – likely a reference to her wolf, but the name didn't mean anything. No doubt one of their myths, as Faeydir had been.

Baron looked Sempre over, a cold, calculating look. "What evidence do you have for this claim?"

Sempre nodded to one of her pack mates, who strode over to a white van, parked beside the gateway, and threw open the back doors. Inside was a cage with a wolf in it. "You recognise Rintur?"

Baron shook his head, but Caroline stepped forward. "I recognise her."

Sempre seemed to soften ever so slightly. "Caroline. It's good to see you still run. You have magic of your own – use it now to see what harm your Fenrae has done."

Caroline opened the gate cautiously and stepped forward. "Can she not shift by herself?"

Sempre let out a harsh laugh. "See for yourself."

Caroline approached the wolf, who seemed confused, but not alarmed by the action. She reached into the cage, stroked the thick fur once, then the air crackled and she let out a jolt of electricity-

The wolf yelped, snarled, backed away into a corner of the cage, but there was no shift, no transformation into a human. Caroline stepped back in shock.

"She has separated wolf from human," Sempre concluded. "Rintur is dead, and yet her wolf lives on, devoid of any trace of the human who once shared her body." She turned to Dee, a cold, accusing look on her face. "You harbour death within your walls, and we demand that you put her down, for all our sakes. For your own safety."

"What does Fenrae-Ul mean?" Dee asked, needing to know just what they were accusing her of. Yes, she had ripped the human out of the wolf's body, but she hadn't thought it any worse than killing her outright – and Baron had already excused her for that.

"Destroyer-wolf," Baron answered, gaze still fixed on the wolf in the cage. "There's a prophecy in the journals. They speak of an ancient wolf who will return one day and herald the end of days for our kind. Able to separate man from wolf, she will return us to the natural order, one species or another, reversing a creation that should never have been made." He turned to face her finally, sadness in his eyes. "The undoing of the mistakes of Faeydir-Ul. It seems you are that wolf."

Speechless didn't even begin to cover it. Dee gaped at Baron, then at the wolf in the cage. So this was the prophecy that had had everyone walking on eggshells when she'd first arrived, the one everyone knew about, and yet no one would speak of. She was not just a wolf with a powerful and destructive gift, but the harbinger of the end of their species.

Her? Little Dee Carman who couldn't kill a spider and still cringed every time Faeydir ate a dead rabbit? "I don't want to hurt anyone-" she began, then stopped, seeing the cold glare from the Watch, and knowing that her protests would carry little weight. She had killed one of their own, after all, and the Den would not be at all forgiving if the situation were reversed, if a member of the Watch had killed someone from Il Trosa.

And then, in a sudden wave of clarity, she realised that this confrontation was the least of their current problems. "Are you handing me over to the Grey Watch?" she asked bluntly.

Baron snorted. "No."

"And are you going to put me down?"

"For killing a member of the Grey Watch? Again, no." The word was said with cold finality, his gaze cool and steady as he stared down Sempre-Ul.

The woman's eyes narrowed. "She will be the death of us all. Mark my words, Baron, this woman is a curse among you."

Baron pulled back his coat revealing the gun at his hip. "You trespass on my territory and threaten one of my pack. Trust me, Sempre, right now, Dee is the least of your concerns."

Sempre glanced at the gun, then at Andre, standing impassively to the side, then at John...

"You will regret this day," she told him coldly. "As will we all." She gathered her cloak around her, gave Dee one last, cold look, then the gathered women turned and climbed back into their van, dust tossed up in a cloud as the wheels spun, then gripped, the van hurtling off down the driveway.

The gathered Den members were silent. Dee felt their eyes on her, the full weight of their fear and apprehension finally making sense. She looked at each of them, her gaze falling on Andre last of all. Well. That put a whole new light on her Council 'assessment'.

"All right, you slack-arses," Baron announced suddenly. "We all have better things to be doing. Simon, get back to Skip and the computers. Find me some info on that lab. Raniesha, you should be building bombs. John, Silas, get the weapons ready. Caleb, in Tank's absence, you're 2IC. I'll see you in the library in ten minutes. Move it, people!"

The group scattered and moments later, only five people were left at the gate. Baron and Caroline, Mark and Dee, and Andre, as silent and impassive as always.

Dee turned to Baron, a tight knot in her gut. "Did you know what I am?"

Baron was silent for a moment. "Yes. And no." He sighed, and headed slowly for the house, Dee falling in beside him. "Since you arrived and we realised your wolf was a separate being from you, there have been rumours. Concerns. People know of the prophecy and were understandably cautious."

"Then why didn't you say anything?"

Another pause. This wasn't important, Dee reminded herself. They had a war to start, a wolf to rescue, and then there was the lab. If Tank had been taken to the same place she had – a likely scenario, given the Noturatii's desire to learn to create shifters – then he was probably being tortured right now, along with any new 'test subject' they tried to convert.

"Because I'm not prone to jumping at shadows and believing stories that were made up by people who still believed that the earth was flat," Baron said finally.

"What?" That made no sense.

"I don't believe the stories of Faeydir-Ul. As far as I can tell, they were made up by shifters generations after our species came into existence, as a way of trying to make sense of a gift that they couldn't understand." He frowned. "And I was perfectly comfortable with that neat little explanation until you showed up and your wolf insisted that she existed before she was merged with you." Well, what do you know? Baron actually sounded perplexed, pulled for once out of his own solid view of the world. "And then for some reason, shifters also needed a bogey man, a tale to scare small children with at night, so Fenrae-Ul was invented, the end of days for our kind, so you'd best be careful who you convert and keep an eye on anyone who seems a little odd, or they might just end your species."

"And yet here I am," Dee pointed out. "Able to separate human from wolf. The embodiment of your prophecy."

Baron shrugged. "But that's the thing with prophecies. You can predict just about anything, and if you wait long enough, it's almost certain to come true. And in the meantime, it creates a terrific lot of worries that you can hold over people and threaten them with on occasion." They had reached the house.

"What about you?" she demanded of Caroline, when the group stopped at the bottom of the stairs.

"I believe in assessing each wolf on their own merits," Caroline said bluntly. "It's true, you have some unusual gifts. But what your intentions are, how you mean to use those gifts, remains to be seen."

"And you?" Dee went on, turning to Andre. "You're here to see if I should be put down, aren't you?"

"Since Baron first told the Council about you, they've been understandably curious," Andre said, taking no offence at the sudden interrogation. "What I'm here to do is assess the situation, measure your abilities and report back with my findings. I'm in no position to judge you, one way or the other. Your fate is for the Council to decide." Well, that was nicely vague.

"I understand your concerns," Baron interrupted. "And they will be taken seriously and addressed properly at a point in the future. But right now, we have other problems to deal with. Skip is currently working on the theory that Tank has been taken to the same lab you were kept in. And I realise your escape from there was rather traumatic, but I was hoping you might remember something that would help us find it. Either you or Faeydir must remember how you escaped, maybe a landmark you saw, or a street name? Anything that can help us pinpoint its location."

"Oh gosh. I can try…" she began, and then another, much more alarming thought occurred to her. Mark would know where it was. But he couldn't tell Baron himself without exposing his secret. But maybe if she could get a few minutes alone with him, she could ask him, and then maybe pretend to 'remember' when she spoke with Baron?

Where the hell was Mark? she wondered suddenly. He'd been with her at the gate, had walked back to the house along with Caroline and Andre, but now he'd mysteriously vanished.

"Come into the library," Baron was saying, as Dee scrambled for an excuse to disappear for a few minutes. "I need to know everything you remember about the lab, the location, the layout, any security systems you might have noticed."

Where the hell was Mark?? "Okay," Dee said, meekly following him up the steps. "I don't think I remember much, but I'll give it a go…"

# CHAPTER THIRTY-FIVE

Mark sat at the table in the library, feeling Caleb's curious eyes on him as the pair of them waited for Baron.

The hard drive Mark had stolen from the server in the Noturatii lab sat on the table in front of him, along with a thick file detailing the lab's location, its security systems, its layout, information he'd bought, stolen and hacked in the months leading up to his ill-planned solo attack on the lab.

He'd lain awake for hours last night, contemplating his course of action. He could have given the drive to Dee, asked her to give it to Baron, but the obvious question then was if she'd stolen it herself, why had she waited so long to hand it in?

He could have simply told her the location of the lab, gotten her to lead Baron back there, claiming to remember the way, but that would do nothing for them as far as getting past the security system – which, by Mark's reckoning, would have been significantly upgraded since his last visit.

He could, of course, do nothing, keep his mouth shut and pretend ignorance, but to do so would be to send his pack mates – not to mention Dee herself – into a trap that could well get them all killed.

Or he could pray for a miracle, hoping that Skip would somehow come up with the information they needed all by herself. She'd been working on hacking the Noturatii database all night, a steady diet of coffee and chocolate keeping her and Simon going, but Mark knew that she'd been trying to hack that same database for the past three years with little to show for it. It was optimistic to the most ridiculous degree to think she'd suddenly find the answer now.

The door opened and Baron, Caroline, Andre and Dee walked in, all looking surprised to see him there.

"Mark?" Baron glanced at the hard drive on the table, then at the file, then back at Mark. "Something I can help you with?"

Mark knew the exact moment that Dee figured out what he was doing, and the look on her face was going to haunt him for a long time. "I have something to show you," he said. "About the Noturatii lab." He detailed the information calmly, the story of his break in, his reasons for going there in the first place – there was little point in leaving anything out since Baron would just prise the details out of him anyway – watching as their faces grew grim, then surprised, then finally shell-shocked as they realised the value of what he was handing over. "So if Skip can access these files," he said finally, pushing the small device across the desk towards Baron, "then she should be able to find enough information to hack their database. And then we get the layout of the building, security systems, guard patrols, the works."

Baron was silent for a long time, staring at the drive, an unreadable expression on his face. Then he picked it up, handed it to Caleb and said, "Get this upstairs to Skip."

Caleb left in a hurry, leaving a room full of angry, astonished faces. Baron turned to Dee. "Am I to assume that you knew about this?"

"Parts of it," Dee admitted. "I knew Mark had helped me escape. Not at first, mind you. I didn't really remember anything at first, and it took me a while to get Faeydir to explain what had happened. And yeah, I probably should have told you," she added, with a hint of insubordination, "but you'll excuse me for feeling a sense of loyalty towards the man who saved my life."

Andre raised an eyebrow at that, and Mark felt cold as he realised it was more than just him who would be in trouble here. With Andre here to assess her suitability as a wolf, he'd probably just cost Dee a good part of the good will that Andre had seemed to be feeling towards her last night.

Baron's expression was grim. "What you've just confessed to are the actions of a traitor," he said flatly. "And while we're going to have to deal with that as the entirely serious matter that it is…" He glanced at Caroline, then at Andre. "Right now, we need to get Tank back. So I vote we shelve Mark's piss-arsed stupidity for another day."

"Agreed." Caroline said immediately.

"I'm sure the Council would agree with you," Andre said. "Depending on your time frame for an assault, I could have reinforcements sent in-"

"I appreciate the offer," Baron told him, "but with all respect for Tank, he's too much of a liability to let this go on for even a day. He knows too much about Il Trosa, and if they break him, we won't have to worry about Fenrae-Ul ending our species. The Noturatii will do it for her."

Baron stared at the information on the screen in front of him. He was loathe to admit it, but the hard drive Mark had stolen was going to be the key to their success. Since his break-in, the Noturatii had upgraded their security, of course, but with the information on the drive, Skip had been able to hack their server and discover a wealth of detail on their new systems and security measures. The battle would be fierce, and he acknowledged with a heavy heart that they were likely to lose good shifters in the process.

But this wasn't just about Tank. Even if it had been, he'd still have risked his life, might have called for volunteers to storm the lab with him – knowing that almost the entire Den would have put their hand up in an instant.

But given the experiments the Noturatii were conducting in that hell-hole, this wasn't just about one man. It was about the survival of their entire species. If the Noturatii were allowed to continue their research and discover more about shifter physiology, ways to create new shifters, and as a result, new ways to kill them, it could be the end for them all. So for that reason, he was willing to risk his entire Den. Each and every life beneath his roof could die tonight, at his command, twenty wolves who would stop running in one bold sweep of the brush.

But if they managed to shut down this monstrosity of a lab, it would be worth it. And what's more, he knew that everyone in the Den – damn, maybe even everyone in the whole of Il Trosa – would stand behind his decision one hundred percent. It was a humbling position to be in.

Every single shifter was gathered in the library, waiting for a battle plan, some of them glaring at Mark, others ignoring him. Some of them paced. Some stood. Some had grown tired and now sat on the floor – they'd all been up late last night, and it looked like tonight wasn't going to offer them much sleep either. But despite the risks of going in with some of his Den not at their peak, there was little to be gained from waiting. Aside from the obvious risks in leaving Tank in the Noturatii's hands, he strongly suspected that no one would sleep tonight, regardless. There was no rest to be had until this battle was fought and won – or lost, as was the cold possibility.

He turned away from the screen and looked up to address the gathered shifters. "Good work, Skip. It's going to be a tough battle, but we've got enough information to give us a fighting chance. So here's what we're going to do…"


Dee stood before the long bookcase in the library, apprehensive about what was about to be revealed. She'd long wondered where the Den kept its supply of weapons, Silas having taught her to use a number of different guns in the past few months, the supply of ammunition seemingly endless, but whenever she'd asked questions on the subject, the answer had been the same – a curt 'It's a secret' that had put the subject firmly to rest.

Now though, she watched as Baron tapped a code into the key pad hidden behind the thick volumes on the top shelf, and then stood back in awe as the entire wall swung open.

On the other side there was a wide room, guns, knives, swords all hanging in line along the walls, rows of ammunition stacked neatly, and on the back wall, several dozen Kevlar vests.

"All right, everybody. Suit up," Baron said, striding to the back of the room and handing out the vests. "Guns all round. Knives, if you know how to use them. Andre, choose whatever you like."

"Thank you," the assassin said, but shook his head. "I came well prepared. I have my own supply."

"Raniesha, you've got those explosives ready?"

"Four dozen charges," she shot back, strapping on her vest. "I'll take half of them, and you can share the rest between you."

"Two pistols," Silas said to Dee, handing her the guns and a holster. "You prepared to pull that trigger?"

Dee fought to find her voice for a second, momentarily overwhelmed by the memories of pain and torture she'd endured in that place. "Absolutely," she said, returning his stare unwaveringly.

"Glad to hear it."

"George? You got that food ready to go?"

"Already in the vans," the aging man replied, strapping on a vest along with the rest of them. Too old and not particularly skilled in battle, George was one of the shifters assigned to driving the vans. But it had been impressed upon them that just because they weren't going into the lab itself, that didn't mean they couldn't get caught in the crossfire. On Baron's instructions, George had prepared a huge pile of sandwiches, snacks, water bottles and raw steaks – it was a five hour drive each way, and going in hungry wasn't going to help anyone.

But the biggest surprise of the weapons supply was still to come. Once everyone had their weapons and vests on, Baron cast a critical eye over the crowd, then announced, "Okay, folks, suit up."

Dee's first thought was that they already had, Kevlar vests and combat boots, everyone clad in black leather or dark clothing… but then half a dozen people shifted, and it was only then that Dee realised what else was hanging on the back wall. Below the rows of vests, there were more suits hanging up, and she'd assumed they were spares, or perhaps different styles for different battle situations. Now, she realised they were… holy hell, they were Kevlar vests built specifically for wolves. Not only that, she saw, as she watched Baron strap one of them onto Caroline's wolf, they had rows of spikes along the flanks, down each leg, thick metal plates over the spine. They were wolven suits of armour!

It was both an obvious necessity and a completely unexpected idea, but it made perfect sense. Wolves could be killed by bullets just as surely as humans could.

"Is Faeydir going to be okay wearing one of these?" Mark asked, appearing beside her with a suit in hand.

Rather more than just okay, Dee thought sardonically, as Faeydir eagerly shifted, tail wagging, barely able to stand still from the excitement as Mark did up the straps. A real battle, against a hated foe, and her wolf was chomping at the bit to get out there and start kicking arse. Once she was suited up, she shifted back, then grimaced at the sharp jolt she felt from the effort.

"Easy," Mark said as he saw her flinch. "The more equipment you're carrying, the harder it gets to shift. It'll be a little rougher than usual, but it's worth the effort."

Dee nodded, then helped Mark into his own suit. Aside from physical protection from bullets, the spikes would also make it much more difficult for anyone to grab the wolves, the spikes forming rows of miniature daggers that would lacerate anyone's hands. She made a mental note to keep her distance from her comrades when in wolf form, and made sure Faeydir understood that as well.

Finally they were both finished, and Mark shifted back. He gave her a hard, almost desperate stare. "I'll be okay," she said before he could say a word. He hugged her tightly, a quick, fierce embrace, and then it was time to go.

"May those who run, run fast and true," Baron said, everyone suited up and armed to the teeth.

"And may those who fall find glory in the House of Sirius," the Den replied in unison.

"Ladies and gentlemen," Baron said, with a humourless grin. "The dogs are about to go to war."

# CHAPTER THIRTY-SIX

The rows of warehouses were ominous, and Dee gritted her teeth, pushing the instinctive fear down. Terrible things had happened the last time she was here, and a strong sense of foreboding was not helping her focus.

*Are you okay with this?* she asked Faeydir. Her response took a moment to translate. She showed Dee an image of the picture on her bedroom wall, the pack of wolves running through the snow, accompanied by a sense of satisfaction so strong in made Dee stumble. *So we're part of the pack now, right?* An image of dead scientists lying bleeding on the floor, accompanied by a spark of glee. Well, at least her wolf was on board with this crazy plan.

They weren't bothering to be discrete. The Den's four white vans had pulled up with all the subtlety of an action movie, tyres screeching, engines roaring.

They piled out of the vans, Baron and Caleb at the front of the column, then John, Silas, who was ignoring his not insignificant injuries, Caroline, who preferred knives to firearms, and Andre, who looked as calm as if he was taking a stroll along the beach. Dee, Mark, Skip, Raniesha and a handful of others trailed behind, while those not so talented at fighting – Alistair, George and Heron, to name a few, waited with the vans, ready to make a quick getaway. Assuming, of course, that any of them came out alive.

Baron quickly shot both security cameras mounted on the outside of the building. The sudden loss of feed would doubtlessly alert the Noturatii to their presence, but it could still buy them precious seconds as the security guards rallied to repel an attack that they were unable to assess, their electronic eyes blinded to the Den's numbers and strategy.

They reached the door, and Baron paused only a moment before they started raising hell. "Weapons out. Shoot anything that moves. If Tank isn't retrievable, put him down. It's better that way, both for him, and us. Kwan?" he snapped, and the Korean man darted forward. "Do your thing."

231

When they'd been planning this assault, Dee had assumed that Skip would be in charge of breaking through the security locks – surely she had a dozen devices that could fake fingerprints or iris scans. But the actual plan was both a lot simpler, and a lot more surprising. Caroline wasn't the only shifter in the Den with unusual abilities, she'd learned. Kwan also had a mysterious talent – the ability to manipulate electrical currents, and when he'd first joined the Den, he'd cause no shortage of mischief, unexpectedly turning off all the lights in the manor, or making the television change channels by itself. It had taken Baron months to figure out who was doing it, and how, but as well as just causing mischief, the talent had some far more serious uses.

Kwan stared at the security panel, one hand running lightly over the metal case that secured it to the wall. Skip had found out the type of device they were using, and after a quick look at the design, Kwan had assured them that he could open the lock. He closed his eyes in concentration now, fingers moving slowly, like a musician coaxing notes from a violin, and then the red light on the panel flashed to green, and the lock on the door clicked open.

Wow. That was handy.

Inside there was another door, this one with a guard, and Caleb had put a bullet in his skull before he'd even realised what was happening, his body hitting the floor with a thud.

Baron silently gestured for Skip and Silas to head off to the right – Skip's task was to erase any and all video footage of their arrival or activities, and Silas was her bodyguard – a task he seemed to relish as he carried a gun in each hand, with another one on each hip, and enough grenades to take down a small building.

The moment the pair was gone, Baron nodded to Mark, who took point down the long staircase towards the labs. They had all studied the layout of the building, of course, but Mark was the only one who had been inside before, who knew the layout in three dimensions, rather than via two dimensional lines on a screen.

Three guards tried to intercept them, the first too stunned to do anything but gasp before he was dead, the other two putting up token resistance, which Andre quickly quashed. He was lowering the last guard to the floor, a knife in his lung, before Dee had even registered that he'd moved, and she allowed herself a split second to be impressed by the Council's training. No wonder they inspired unquestioning loyalty from the rest of Il Trosa.

But that was when their progress was suddenly halted.


Li Khuli was roaming the corridors when the alarm went off. She'd been expecting it ever since they'd brought the shifter in, and she felt a surge of glee now that the moment had finally arrived.

She lived for moments like this. Ever since she'd been abducted as a child, off the streets and away from the gang who alternately protected and abused her, she'd been in training to fight, to kill, to torture.

She'd become good at it, her first kill a simple kitten, then an adult cat, then dogs of various sizes, before her trainers had set her loose on one of the other trainees. It was meant to be a simple training exercise, a test to see who was the fastest and strongest, her instructions to break the girl's arms and then let her go.

But she hadn't. After breaking first one arm, and then the other, she'd seen the look of cold defeat in the girl's eyes, had hated her for her weakness, and she'd felt more powerful than ever before in her short life. So she'd grabbed the girl's head and twisted, feeling the raw pleasure of her neck cracking, and then watched in fascination as the girl collapsed, eyes blank, skin pale.

Her trainers, far from angry with her for disobeying their orders, had praised her, congratulated her, and led her off to be paraded in front of the other Khuli children, an example of the true nature and purpose of their training.

It had been almost as exhilarating as feeling those fragile bones crack beneath her hands.

She'd killed many people throughout her life. Business men, politicians, police officers and detractors from the Noturatii. But there was nothing she liked better than killing a shifter.

It wasn't because she harboured any particular views about their inherent evil. It had been impressed upon her from an early age that they were abominations, dangerous, evil, terrorists and traitors to the human race. But in her own mind, none of that mattered. No, the reason she loved to kill shifters was that they were harder to kill. Injure one form, and they would take on the other, and the fight could begin again. Take away their weapons and they would fight with fists and boots and teeth. They were tough bastards, and the last one she had killed – an assassin like herself – had taken no less than three hours to die, limbs broken, chunks of flesh removed, one foot cut off completely, but still he'd fought her, employing throwing knives, bullets from a tiny, concealed pistol, even a grenade. But she'd survived, and the shifter hadn't, dying finally with his body contorted in agony as she'd slowly removed his internal organs, wondering which one would be the one to make him bleed out.

And now she smiled as the building-wide alarm went off. A quick check via her ear piece and she knew the situation – the exterior cameras had gone off line, and security was rushing to meet the enemy in the upper levels.

She switched channels to the one used exclusively for her five assassins and gave them their instructions.

And then she headed for the basement, the lowest level where the experiments were carried out.

Jacob had given her orders. Thought he knew her plan of attack. He expected her to meet the shifters in the hallways and pick them off, cutting off their invasion before it had really begun.

But Li Khuli had other plans. She didn't just want to kill them. She wanted to make them suffer. Let them see the progress the Noturatii had made towards their demise, and then feel their own life being choked slowly out of them.

So the labs were where she would make her stand. Assuming any of the dogs managed to make it down that far.

A small, quiet, strangely peaceful part of her really hoped they did.


Baron was feeling strangely calm as he took cover in a doorway and popped off round after round from his semi-automatic. The guards were thick in the halls, surging out of every doorway like ants from a disturbed nest, but he felt no fear of them.

They were well trained, organised, but the narrow fighting space hampered their attempts to kill the shifters, and his own team were expert marksmen, every shot made to count. Head shots, mainly, as the guards wore bullet proof vests, just as the Den did.

"Cover!" Raniesha yelled at one point, tossing a grenade down the hall, and the explosion was deafening, a blast of heat surging back at them as every member of the team dove for cover. The lights went out as the ceiling was ripped apart, electricity in this section of the building disabled, and they waited for long, painstaking seconds as the smoke cleared. Sprinklers burst into action, drenching them and the fire that had broken out, but they ignored it. They had a mission to fulfil, a species to protect, a friend to liberate-

Baron twisted to the side, rolling and swearing as a heavy body dropped down on top of him. A knife missed his chest and lacerated his arm instead, but he had no time to assess the damage as his attacker regained his feet and launched a second assault.

A bullet to the head stopped him in his tracks, the body hitting the floor before Baron even registered that he'd pulled the trigger.

He didn't have any time to gloat, though, or even to check the cut on his arm, as he saw another four of the black-clad men filling the hallway, fighting in close quarters with his best warriors. Andre, Caroline and John were front and centre, and it took only a split second to assess the situation.

Assassins. The Council wasn't the only faction in this war to employ specialised fighters, and from the way these men moved, they had been trained by experts. One of them had relieved Caroline of her gun, and they were now fighting hand-to-hand. Andre was being kept busy by a second, while John had shifted and was tearing chunks out of the other two. Damn, but he was good in a fight.

Baron raised his gun, but quickly lowered it again. Bullets were a no-go – there was a high risk that he'd end up shooting Caroline or Andre instead. The rest of the shifters had held their ground a short distance back along the corridor, no doubt recognising this fight as beyond their capabilities, and Baron found himself wishing to have either Tank or Silas at his side.

Caroline went down for a moment, and Baron moved to go to her aide, before realising that she had just kneecapped the assassin and finished him off with a knife to his neck. That left a gap in the fight, and Baron used the split second opportunity to shoot one more assassin in the head, leaving John to rip the throat out of the remaining man.

That left just Andre, who unfortunately found himself in a more open section of the hallway. Which meant less cover and more space for the assassin to move.

Andre was holding his own though, seeming to almost play with the man as he sidestepped and ducked and wove. The assassin was too cocky, Baron thought, as he watched the fight. Too confident in his own skills and probably not having realised who he was up against.

A loud crack signalled the end of the fight. Andre broke the man's elbow, flipped him around and slit his throat.

A quick check of the hallway – all clear – and then he turned to Baron and straightened his trench coat.

"Shall we?" he asked, as if inviting the alpha to join him for dinner. And Baron grinned.

"We shall."


Huddled against the wall in terror, Dee fought to keep herself from shaking. Baron had done his best to prepare her for this, and then there had been another pep-talk from Mark in the van on the way here, but in her naivety, she'd expected something more like a scene from an action movie – lots of cover, their enemy being lousy shots, nice gaps in the battle to gather her wits.

This was a blood bath. The shifters were expert marksmen, but so were the guards. Nate had already been shot, withdrawing to join Kwan and Aaron at the entrance – their job was to secure the exit and make sure there were no obstructions to a hasty get-away. There were dozens of guards dead, their bodies coating the hallways red, and the mess that the grenade had left… Movies never showed you the full extent of body parts littered about, nor conveyed the smell of burnt flesh and running blood.

So far, Dee hadn't managed to get off a single shot herself, easing along the hallway in the middle of the column of shifters. Baron had explained the tactics – until they were on the laboratory level, he and his best fighters would stay at the front, carving a path through the mayhem. Mark was near the front as well, guiding them all down into the bowels of the building, while Dee hung back, waiting for her own opportunity to act, and dreading it at the same time.

Finally, though, the five assassins who had unexpectedly rained down on them were dead and they were off again, the quick, shuffling run-then-duck as they made slow progress towards their goal.

Down stairs, along hallways, through doors and down more stairs. Dee didn't remember it being this far down, from her panicked flight all those months ago, but Faeydir kept nodding, anticipating the next turn, the next doorway even before Mark had given the direction.

Once past the initial surge of guards, the hallways were surprisingly empty. Administration staff seemed to have fled further into the building, while the major security presence here was already dead.

And then they came to a flight of stairs, narrow, white, a biohazard sign on the door above the landing, and Mark came to a halt.

Faeydir's emotions were a mess of contradictions, fear, anticipation, glee at being able to end so many lives committed to evil, as well as a strange sense of sorrow. *We're going to make it out alive,* Dee reassured her hastily. *You will see the snow and the sky again. I promise.*

Any trace of distraction vanished, and Faeydir focused on the stairs ahead. Another flash of those wolves, running through the snow…

"When we get to the bottom of the stairs, the cages are to the left," Mark said, letting Baron take the lead, and easing backwards to join Dee, to take on his next assignment. "Directly ahead is a science lab where they keep all their records and chemicals, and the experimentation rooms are to the right. Security will be tight. And if they've just captured a new test subject, I'd expect every scientist in the building to be somewhere on this floor."

"You all know what you have to do," Baron said grimly.

And then there was no more time for thinking, as Baron led the charge down the stairs, and the Noturatii's laboratories swarmed to life.

# CHAPTER THIRTY-SEVEN

Phil sat in the lab, trying to concentrate on his computer as the sirens continued to blare outside the room he was working in. More than half an hour had passed since the first alarm went off, security guards scattering, Li Khuli's terrifying assassins heading for the upper levels, and somehow Phil had expected it to all be over by now. They'd hired the most fearsome weapon the Noturatii had to offer, and Li Khuli should have been up there, in the thick of it, wiping out this branch of the shifters once and for all.

Why were the sirens still sounding?

He took a deep breath and returned his attention to the screen, the results of their experiments to create a new shifter. Blood pressure charts, neural activity, read outs of static electricity, heart rate, pupil dilation – nothing had gone unattended in their latest test subjects, and he was determined to crack the mystery-

"O'Brian," Jacob snapped, marching into the room suddenly. "What have you got?"

Phil all but jumped out of his seat. Jacob scared the pants off him at the best of times. "Sir! I wasn't expecting you back so soon."

"So you've been sitting around doing nothing?"

"No sir! Of course not, sir."

"So? What have you got?"

Phil fumbled for his glasses, and then for his notes. "Well sir," he said, hands shaking as he tried to read the figures. "Unfortunately, sir, the first test subject was not successful. She died almost immediately after we infused the shifter blood into her. We followed the instructions precisely," he rushed on, seeing Jacob's glare. "The initial experiments suggested that the convert had to be of the opposite gender to the shifter, so the capture squad picked up three women. We followed the notes, the strength of the electric fields, the ratios of human to shifter blood, the temperatures and pressures. Everything that was recorded by Andrews."

"And it failed."

"But then we experimented on the second girl," Phil said, trying to sound enthusiastic. And probably failing.

"And?"

"She's still alive, but she seems to be having some adverse reactions to the infusion. Her heart rate is elevated, her electrolytes are out of balance. Linda's with her now, keeping her stable." The resident doctor had insisted on the best medical equipment money could buy, and Phil was grateful for it now. If the girl died, at least Jacob couldn't blame them for not being diligent enough.

"And the third girl?"

"Her results were... inconclusive."

"Inconclusive how?" Jacob demanded, sounding more impatient.

Phil tried hard to stop stuttering and just get on with the report. Jacob was hardly going to be impressed with this bumbling idiot routine. But the sirens kept wailing in the background, keeping his nerves on edge. Were the alarms getting louder? "The, uh... her initial reaction was promising. Elevated heart rate, increased neural activity, muscle convulsions – all the same signs Andrews reported in his successful test case. Except now she's..."

"She's what?"

"She doesn't seem to be able to shift."

Jacob's eyebrows rose in an expression of utter disdain. "Oh? Do explain."

"We're running more tests, sir. Blood samples, subjecting her to electric shocks, we're monitoring her neural activity. We will find answers, I assure you, but it will take time."

Jacob snatched the papers out of his hand and gave them a cursory once-over. "Has Melissa reviewed these results?"

Phil fought not to bristle. Ever since that meddling woman had been placed on his team, it had been clear she was a favourite of Jacob's. Despite his own greater experience and technical knowledge. "Yes sir. She's currently with the shifter, trying to coax some more information out of him. Damn waste of time if you ask me-"

"I didn't ask you."

"No, sir."

A booming explosion suddenly rocked the lab, and Phil actually fell off his stool as the noise sounded far, far closer than was safe.

"What the fuck is going on out there?" Jacob asked no one in particular. He pulled out a gun, headed to the door and cracked it open. Then quickly closed it again. "Where the fuck is that Khuli woman?"

"I haven't seen her since the shifter was brought in-"

"Shut down these computers," Jacob snapped at the entire room. "Secure the samples. Lock everything of value in the safe. We can't lose this again."

Something large thudded into the door. "I want this lab secure!" Jacob barked, then hastily made his way to the back of the room. "Upload everything you've got to headquarters."

What? But he'd already started shutting his computer down...

"And do not open that door for any reason," Jacob finished, opening a cover to a key pad on the far wall. He tapped in a code and Phil's eyes opened wide as a panel in the wall split open, revealing a secret passageway. How the hell had he not known that was there?

"Protect this data," Jacob ordered as he stepped inside the passageway. "We are closer to winning this war now than we ever have been!" A dozen scientists leapt up from their seats, computers and test tubes abandoned, and dashed for the passageway. But Jacob jabbed a control panel on the far side of the door, and the panel slid closed, the exit sealed up before their eyes.

Son of a bitch! He was running away, leaving the rest of them to face the carnage. The scientists pounded on the door, desperate for a way out.

"Bloody hell," Phil muttered, reaching under his desk to retrieve the hand gun he kept beneath it. The lock to the hallway door groaned, and he snapped his laptop closed, tucking it under his arm, then took cover behind a filing cabinet.

The lock shattered as two bullets were fired rapidly into the mechanism. The door burst open, revealing three men. Three dangerous, armed and angry men. The one at the front of the group was terrifying, tall and broad shouldered with golden eyes and a flaring trench coat, but it was the man beside him that turned Phil cold with terror. A young man, little more than a boy, but the look on his face was one of pure malevolence.

Shifters.

And suddenly, Phil knew that every story, every fairy tale he had ever been told about them was true. Ruthless, vicious, merciless... and at once he remembered that threat from the shifter in the cage. The promise that his days were numbered.

Fuck me, he thought, as he raised his gun with surprisingly steady hands. Perhaps the shifter had been right after all.


As per her instructions at the briefing in the library, Dee broke off from the rest of the group and followed Mark and Raniesha along the hall to the experimentation rooms. If the Noturatii had a new shifter captive, they would have wasted no time in kidnapping more 'test subjects' to convert. And depending on the state of said subjects, their job was to either rescue them, or put them out of their misery, and then blow the lab to smithereens.

Getting to their destination was a long, slow slog, guards filling the hallways, gun fire blocking their passage until Andre had waded into the thick of things and taken out a dozen soldiers with precise shots, every single bullet finding its mark, and one of them taking out two guards at the same time.

Raniesha was no slob with her own gun, though, cutting a path through the wave of security, and Mark was not far behind, engaging one in a brief hand to hand scuffle before slitting his throat, then shooting him in the head.

Scientists and office workers scattered, screaming, trying to flee, and while she had a gun in her hand, Dee found herself not quite able to shoot it. Taking life was abhorrent to her, no matter how evil these people were, and she ducked and weaved down the hall, taking shelter behind furniture and a fridge... a fridge? Really?... while Mark and Raniesha did the dirty work.

The door to the experiment room was locked, but true to form, Raniesha pulled out a wad of explosive tape, set a charge and yelled for Dee to duck. She did, barely making it behind a filing cabinet before an explosion ripped the door off its hinges, the heavy metal slab thudding to the floor with a loud clang.

More guards inside, more guns, and Dee didn't even have time to glance around the room before the fight was on again. She found herself raising her gun, pulling the trigger once, causing a dark-haired guard to buckle then collapse, and then suddenly Dee was no longer a woman with a gun in her hand, but a wolf, teeth bared, hackles up, Faeydir launching herself into the fray, the wolf clearly harbouring none of Dee's doubts about killing. She tore out throats, broke bones with powerful jaws, toppling men who paled in terror at the sight of her, no matter how battle hardened they might have been.

A sharp pain in her shoulder made Dee flinch, but Faeydir ignored what was most likely a bullet hitting her Kevlar vest, too busy as she turned her attention to a small woman in a lab coat, desperately trying to hold her ground beside another woman, strapped to the table. Faeydir leapt for her, missed as the woman moved with surprising speed and tried to flee the room. But she didn't get far. Faeydir grabbed her leg, biting down hard, then went for her throat once she hit the ground. A moment later, the woman was dead, Faeydir discarding the body with a sense of pride as she sought out new prey.

Finally, the room was clear, though gun shots and yells still sounded from down the hall, and suddenly Dee was back, lurching unsteadily on her feet as her wolf retreated. Their orders had been clear – the shifters had been split into three teams, each team with an objective, and firm instructions to focus solely on that, trusting that the other teams would take care of matters in other areas of the building, so Dee set about assessing the room while Mark and Raniesha guarded the door.

Three women were strapped to metal tables – they seemed to have expanded their operation since Dee was last here, as she clearly remembered being the only one in the room during her captivity – and she looked around, a cry of dismay escaping her as she examined the first woman and found that she was dead.

The second woman was a mess, screaming hysterically, her words incomprehensible, though she had an IV line taped into her arm and a series of surgical cuts over her body. A wealth of medical equipment was attached to her, a heart monitor, a blood pressure cuff, ECG electrodes.

Shifter? Or human? Dee checked in with Faeydir, who scented the woman carefully and answered Dee's question by presenting her with an image of a rabid wolf, crazed and slobbering. A rogue, then. Fuck. But maybe they could still help her, Dee thought frantically, working to unlock the cuffs around the woman's wrists and ankles. "We're here to help you," she yelled over the woman's screams. "Please, if you'll just calm down-"

The instant her hands were free, the woman grabbed the gun at Dee's side, shoved the muzzle into her own mouth and pulled the trigger. Blood splattered the far wall as her body slumped over, then slid gracelessly off the table.

Dee sorely wished she had time to throw up as she forced herself to retrieve the gun, sliding it back into its holster with shaking hands. She took a deep breath to steady herself, and then wished she hadn't, the scent of blood thick in the room.

Numbly, she went to the third woman, and a cursory glance suggested she was dead as well, until Dee saw a flutter over her ribs and realised she was breathing. Her eyes were open, but she lay still as a corpse, her skin pale, her eyes vacant.

"Hello?" Dee waved a hand in front of her face. "Can you hear me?"

The woman blinked, eyes sliding sideways to meet Dee's. "It's in my head," she whispered, horror struck, face turning even paler. "It speaks to me."

*Shifter?* Dee asked Faeydir. And then she all but burst into tears as Faeydir again brought up the image of the wolves in the snow, and then very deliberately inserted a new wolf into the picture. So this one wasn't crazy. Yet.

Not wanting to repeat her previous mistake, Dee stepped closer and carefully took the woman's hand. She was freezing, her fingers clammy. "We're here to help you. Do you understand me? We've come to get you out of here."

Faint comprehension dawned in the woman's eyes. "You're police?"

Dee figured she could just run with the easiest explanation for now, and nodded. "That's right. We're police, and these people are terrorists, and we've come to stop them."

"Oh thank you, God. Thank you. Oh God, get me out of here."

"I'm going to unlock the cuffs. You're going to come with us, and no one is going to hurt you."

"It's in my head," the woman repeated, on the verge of hysteria. "It's in my head."

"I know," Dee told her, remembering her own fear when Faeydir had first made herself known. "I know. And we can help you with that."

Hope flittered onto the woman's face. "You can help?"

"Absolutely." Actually, Dee had no idea if that was true. Baron had said that converts who couldn't accept the wolf went mad. But then again, she herself had beaten the odds, hadn't she? "What's your name?"

"Gabrielle."

Dee activated the controls to unlock the cuffs, then helped the woman – Gabrielle – sit upright. "Are you okay? Can you walk?"

"I think so." She was unsteady on her feet, but willing enough to stagger along with Dee, her arm around her shoulders.

"Let's get out of here, guys," she said to Mark and Raniesha, who both regarded the dazed woman with carefully blank expressions. "She's one of us," Dee said shortly. "So let's get ghost, shall we?"


Left to the cages, Mark had said, and Baron ploughed his way through a dozen or more security guards, fists and elbows employed to carve a path just as often as bullets. He grabbed one dazed guard and spun him around, using the man's gun to shoot another guard behind him, then slammed his elbow into the throat of a guard coming up on his right, crushing his wind pipe before shooting him in the head.

He, Caleb and Caroline were tasked with getting Tank free – or putting him down – and he glanced back down the hallway to see how the other teams were faring. Andre, John and Simon had just busted into the main laboratory and were no doubt causing terror and mayhem in there, while Dee, Mark and Raniesha had disappeared into the experiment room at the far end of the hall. Caroline shot two more guards who popped out of a room to their left, while Caleb fired at one who had noticed them retreating, from further down the hallway.

Around a corner, along another hall, then through a door to the right, and holy fuck, Baron thought. It was Fort Knox for creepy science wannabes. Steel bars, electronic locks, motion sensors, cameras, alarms and a whole bunch of other things he didn't recognise. He hoped that Skip and

Silas had the cameras off line by now, or there was going to be some real interesting video footage for the Noturatii to analyse later on.

The first row of cages was empty, so he kept going, gun drawn, walking on silent feet as he flattened himself against a wall and peered around the corner to the next row...

Bingo. A small huddle of soldiers and one scientist stood outside one of the cages, ignoring the sirens blaring down the hall, and he supposed they must have a naïve sort of faith in their security team if they were content to just sit around here and chat while all hell broke loose elsewhere.

He held up his hand to Caroline and Caleb behind him, four fingers, indicating the number of opponents they would have. He gestured for Caroline to take the far right guard, Caleb to take the one on the left, and he would take the middle one. The scientist was less of a threat and could be taken out after the main defences were taken care of. He held up three fingers, then two, one...

Caroline swung out from behind the row of cages, gun drawn, taking a split second to locate and target her enemy. And in that split second, Baron realised they had walked straight into a trap. Fuck! It wasn't a huge surprise to think the Noturatii would have set up a few extra defences along the way, and they'd planned this assault on the assumption that not every security measure would be detailed on their database, but fuck...

A thick row of bars sprang up out of the floor behind them, no doubt triggered by a pressure sensor Caroline had just stepped on. Another panel sprang up in front of the group of Noturatii workers, Caroline's perfectly aimed bullet colliding with the barrier... and going no further. Bullet proof. Fuck.

The guards had spun around immediately, guns drawn, wary eyes on the three intruders, but the scientist stayed where she was, a triumphant smile sliding onto her face as she continued to stare at whatever was in the cage. Presumably Tank, but Baron couldn't be sure from this angle.

"Well, well, well. What have we here?" She turned to face them, looking them up and down like a cat eyeing a trapped mouse. "Three shifters. So good of you to visit."

Baron said nothing, and knew that neither of his companions would either. There was no point baiting the tiger, and anything they said was likely to give away information that the Noturatii were better off without.

"What? No angry accusations? No threats? Your fellow pet has been full of them." She jerked her thumb at the cage, and Baron eased sideways to try and get a better look inside. That was Tank, all right. Bleeding, unsteady on his feet – he'd probably been drugged. But he was at least able to stand, and that meant that hopefully they'd be able to extract him, rather than put him down.

"Nothing to say? Pity. Oh well. How about you tidy yourselves into the cage, then?" The woman tapped a few buttons on a control panel attached to her wrist, and the cage door adjacent to Caleb opened with a clang. Baron merely sighed, and gave the woman a 'you've got to be kidding' look.

"No? That's fine. How about we give you a little motivation, then?" She nodded to one of the guards, who opened the door to Tank's cage – God knows what they'd dosed him up with if they weren't afraid to let him out – and tugged the man out to stand in the middle of the hallway. He stepped behind him and put the muzzle of his gun to Tank's temple. "Into the cage," the woman commanded. "Or your friend dies."

Interesting. Baron retreated just a fraction, allowing his wolf senses to come to the fore... and immediately knew that the woman was lying. Tank was far more valuable to them alive than dead – they couldn't keep testing new converts without a live shifter, and whoever ran this hell hole would not be happy about losing their only captive.

Of course, he didn't consider himself and his team to be captives, bars and barriers aside.

"How about we work on a different kind of deal," he said, watching the woman's reactions closely. "You let him go, and we won't kill you all."

# CHAPTER THIRTY-EIGHT

John surveyed the room as he followed Andre into the lab, and felt his blood boil. Scientists. White lab coats. Computers and needles and instruments of torture all around him.

A dozen or more unarmed scientists stood gaping at him like sheep for the slaughter. Andre was already in action, taking down the closest ones, one who threw himself at them with reckless abandon, quickly killed with a bullet to the head, and another, who tried to run through the door to freedom – a doomed plan that saw him choking on his own blood a moment later.

John took his time in focusing on the other men and women in the room. Even members of his own Den were scared of him at times, and he turned the full force of that predatory air on these devils. He grinned and shifted, slowly, so they could get a good look at him, anticipate what was going to happen next. In his armour, he was fearsome, and John knew it. In addition to the regulation Kevlar vest and body spikes, he had also crafted a helmet of sorts for himself, short spikes over the brow of his head, wicked blades that curved back from his ears to his neck, and when he bared his teeth and growled...

One of the men fainted, and John rolled his eyes. For fuck's sake, this was supposed to be a challenge! The Noturatii, their worst enemy, and they were wetting themselves like schoolgirls. One man grabbed a knife, held it in a shaking fist before him. "Stay back, you demon. Or I'll kill you!"

Finally, a little backbone in one of them. John growled, paced forward, dodged the clumsy blow aimed his way, and was on the man in an instant, long, sharp teeth ripping through the flesh of his neck like it was a tender steak.

And then pandemonium broke out. The scientists scattered, some racing for the door, to be cut down by Simon and Andre, some hid behind cabinets or under desks... Really? When a *wolf* is after you? And some fled to a panel in the far wall, thumping their fists on it, desperately punching numbers into some sort of control panel.

One of them, though, seemed a more lucid sort. He held a small pistol in his hand and fired without hesitation. The bullet hit John in the chest, and he grunted, paused a moment as pain ripped through him. But he'd been through enough torture to know how to deal with pain, to know how to turn it back on itself and channel it out again as raw fury. He went for the man, only to pull himself up in disappointment as he turned tail and ran. But instead of clumsy efforts to hide, this one still had his wits about him. He headed straight for a small room at the back of the lab, dashed inside, and slammed the door. John grabbed the handle with his teeth and yanked, then, when that yielded no results, shifted again, and tried to open it as a human.

No luck.

But no matter. They would deal with the man sooner or later. In the meantime, there were a dozen more people waiting to die.


Andre was torn between relief and disappointment as he surveyed the room. Intellectuals. Nerds. Not a warrior among them. It would make his job easy, but also prod the gnawing guilt he habitually felt at killing those so helpless.

No matter. He had a job to do, and he would do it without hesitation-

He pulled himself up short as a small, lithe woman dropped down out of the ceiling, landing gracefully a few metres in front of him. She was short, slight of build, with dark skin and hair cut short against her scalp, and he felt his entire body go on alert.

Killing the guards had been easy. Killing the assassin had been a good work out, the first real challenge he'd faced in years, and it had been invigorating to meet an opponent of worth for once. Not that that had helped the assassin, now dead lying on the floor with his blood painting the tiles beneath him. But the woman who stood before him now...

By Sirius himself. Andre's blood turned cold as he recognised the tattoo on the woman's cheek. A Satva Khuli. The Noturatii's version of himself. And, as he understood it, their training was more brutal, more thorough even than his own. He'd been lucky to survive some of his trials. What the hell had this woman survived to reach the rank she held now?

The Khuli seemed to recognise in himself the same thing he'd recognised in her – a ruthless killer who would stop at absolutely nothing to reach his goal.

Andre slowly put his weapons away, sheathed his knife, holstered his gun. Neither would help him now, and he needed both hands free to deal with whatever it was she was going to throw at him. The room around him faded away, the sounds of John ripping out throats, of Simon popping off rounds of bullets at guards who fought to break into the room. The Khuli was the only threat now, the only real barrier between himself and his goal.

And he sent a brief prayer to Sirius to receive him with honour into the afterlife.


John was in his element. He leapt from one body to the next, teeth put to good use, the taste of hard-earned blood in his mouth, adrenaline pumping in his veins as years, decades of hate and anger ripped free and set his blood on fire. These monsters were going to die. He leapt and bit and tore and growled, feeling blood running into his fur, dripping from his face, feeling flesh between his teeth and if he'd been in human form, he might just have cried at the beauty of it all. One scientist stabbed him with a scalpel blade, a tiny, pathetic sort of knife that would have made John laugh if his mouth wasn't full of human flesh.

Another tried to hit him with a metal post. Missed. Slipped in the blood on the ground and died with a gurgling scream as John ripped his throat out. He was dimly aware of screams in the room, of bodies moving around, but he focused solely on his next target, and then the next, a deep wound carved into the Noturatii, as deep as the wounds they had carved into himself.

Finally, the last body fell, a hard crack as the woman's head hit the floor, possibly splintering bone, and John shifted back to human form, scanning the room for-

He froze, backed away slowly into a corner. Not from fear, but simply in an effort to stay out of the way. Fuck it all, what the hell was Andre fighting? And how had he missed her arrival?

The woman was almost supernatural, as strong as Andre, despite her smaller size. As quick as lightning, ruthless, determined – the perfect counterpart to Andre's formidable skills. And from the looks of it, the Council warrior was barely holding his own.

John all but held his breath, not willing to make the slightest move that might distract the man from his task. He would have willingly fought alongside Andre, of course, but any attempt to break into the battle now would be as likely to kill him as to help him. The woman was surreal.

He watched, eyes fixed on the pair as they grappled, throwing out kicks and punches that rarely hit their target. Andre succeeded in knocking the woman to the floor at one point, only to leap out the way as she struck out with her legs, each shoe tipped with pointed steel blades that could maim him enough to throw the balance of the fight.

Andre was no slouch in the fighting department, though. And he put

every resource available to him to use. In one moment, he was throwing a punch at the woman. Then he'd shift, a split second blur as powerful teeth snapped at her limbs, then he'd be back in human form, spinning behind her, catapulting himself off furniture, over a desk, behind a chair, then back into wolf form so fast John barely caught the shift, landing a bite to her leg, catching a kick to his jaw, then back in human form, a gun in his hand, no time to pull the trigger before she deflected the muzzle and tried to put him in an arm lock.

Fuck, this one was going to be close.

Andre ignored the burning in his lungs as he fought the Khuli. She was more beast than human, instincts honed to razor sharp, lightning reflexes. One moment her hand was empty, then there was a knife in it, a blow meant to disembowel him managing instead to only graze him, then the knife was gone and a pistol took its place, deflected by a timely strike from Andre, and then her hands were empty again, those vicious spikes on her shoes spinning his way. She was relentless – as was he. There was no pause in the battle, no respite to reassess their opponent, to take stock of the room, the available cover or objects that could be makeshift weapons. There was only the fight, the woman, the invigorating, captivating, sickening dance on the razor sharp edge of life and death.

And if he lost, he knew, she was going to kill every single member of their Den. And so defeat, in this most solemn of games, was simply not an option.

A stab at her midsection missed. An elbow to her face merely grazed her cheek. A jump to put distance between them gave her more room to strike faster and harder at him, and he caught the foot aimed at his face, anticipating her violent twist, releasing her before she broke his wrist, but too soon to throw her off balance, as he had hoped.

The Khuli were legendary, even amongst the Council's assassins. Battles between them and the Khuli were rare, but the outcome was never assured, a solid 50-50 tie hanging over them all in the tallies of who had killed more of whom.

A tie that Andre was determined to break.

And while the Council had invested heavily in the best training it could find, martial arts experts from around the world, deadly games between its own assassins to hone their skills, they had also pursued more clandestine routes of securing victory. There was no misguided sense of honour in their ranks, no rules about taking it easy on a female opponent, no shame at using the most underhanded tactics to weigh the outcome of the fight. Victory was the only important outcome.

And they had refined their weapons with that singular purpose in mind.

He was getting the hang of the fight now, learning her style, anticipating her next move. Not that it gave him much of an advantage, the Khuli learning his own moves almost as quickly as he learned hers.

But they were both landing more blows now, small scratches, tiny cuts that would go little way towards killing their opponent.

Andre let loose a burst of static electricity, let his form blur as if to execute a shift, a signal she had learned to anticipate by now, and he saw her weight shift to the left, a subtle movement aimed at avoiding his next attack.

He never completed the shift. Surged back into his human form in the blink of an eye and lashed out with the tiny wooden spike that sat hidden inside his glove. Buried the tip in her arm, barely an inch deep, no more than half a millimetre thick.

And with that one successful strike, the battle was over.

Not for him, of course, as she struck back at him, limbs flying in a dance that could prove just as lethal as it ever had, but for her…

The fight went on for another minute or so, a knife grazing his abdomen, a fist missing his face by scant millimetres.

But then, as the seconds ticked by…

The Khuli paused. Stopped. Pulled back, the first break in the fight since it had begun long minutes earlier. A stray glance at the puncture wound in her arm that would have provided Andre with the perfect opening in the battle. If it had been necessary.

She stared up at him with a look of pure disbelief. And then she collapsed on the floor, her body convulsing as the poison took over.

Breathing hard, Andre took out his gun, pointed the muzzle at her head, and pulled the trigger. And the Khuli lay still.

Andre glanced around, seeing Simon still stationed by the door, surveying the bodies of fallen guards outside. John stood beside the wall, his face expressionless.

"There's a scientist in the store room," he said, his voice seeming loud in the suddenly quiet room, and Andre holstered his gun.

"Let's get him out, then," he said, fighting back the nausea, the triumph, the warring sides of victory and defeat that always haunted him when he took another life.

John watched as Andre pulled yet another weapon from his arsenal. This one was a… crossbow? "A little archaic, isn't that?" John wasn't fancy in his choice of weapons. Teeth, or guns, depending on which form he was in. Quick, simple, effective. Trust a Council stooge to be all fancy about it.

"You might want to step back," Andre said, and John did, because okay, the guy might be a poncy show off, but he was a straight up killer at the same time. The way he'd shot that ninja-assassin-girl in the head...

Andre shot the arrow cleanly at the door. It stuck, a light flashed on the tip, and then an explosion ripped through the door like it was made of tissue paper. A man inside screamed, then the clatter of glass breaking and things falling off shelves came at them from through the smoke.

Impatient for more blood, John strode forward, grabbed the man by his collar and yanked him out of the room. He held a laptop in one hand, and John felt a stab of glee as he wondered what secrets Skip would coax from the little machine later. And then he realised a split second too late that the man also held a glass bottle in his other hand. A flick of his wrist, and the bottle shattered on the floor at John's feet, splattering him with a chemical. And from the sudden searing pain that shot up his leg, he knew he'd just been doused in acid.

# CHAPTER THIRTY-NINE

Outside the cage where they'd been holding their captive, Miller stood tensely, eyes fixed on the shifters trapped in the hallway, gun drawn, though it wouldn't do much good just at the moment. The barrier was bullet proof, and he took the time to wonder whether it was because the Noturatii wanted to protect its members, or to prevent them from shooting valuable specimens.

The man leading the new arrivals was huge, as big as the man they held captive, and Miller kept his focus on him. He'd be fearsome in a fight. Though the woman looked just as capable and more pissed off. Hmm. Best not to underestimate her. Blood was splattered over them, and he wondered how many guards they'd taken down to reach this point. And where the hell this legendary Khuli was. After she'd been over the lab with a fine tooth comb, their defences were supposed to be impenetrable.

The third man had only one eye, and he wondered why a fighter with such a liability had been brought along... until the man suddenly shifted into a huge grey wolf, who seemed to grow larger by the second as his hackles came up and his head went down, teeth bared in open threat. The wolf, surprisingly, had both eyes – eyes that fixed themselves on Miller with lethal intent.

Miller was awed by the sight. The wolf wore armour in a deep red colour, full body coverage and yet the design was such that it wouldn't impair his movement in the slightest. Their recent captive had refused to shift, no matter what 'incentives' – namely, torture – they'd offered him. But watching one shift of its own accord? It was beautiful. Graceful. Smooth and seamless in a way Miller had never imagined it could be.

"No deal," Melissa said beside him, in response to the man's suggestion that they just let each other walk away. "Besides, I think you're rather at a disadvantage to be bargaining with us."

The man smiled – *smiled* – a look filled with genuine humour and no small threat of death. "Don't say I didn't give you the choice."

Footsteps from further down the hallway… oh fuck, there were more of them? The guards should have killed them all! Miller gripped his gun tighter, a dozen escape routes for the guards and Melissa mapped out in his head. They could always capture another shifter, but Melissa was a key component in these trials, her and Phil the brains behind an operation that seemed to get more complicated with every new discovery. Without those two, they'd lose ten years of hard research and progress.

Three more shifters arrived at the end of the hallway, two humans and one wolf, and the huge man seemed not at all surprised by their arrival. No, that wasn't a shifter, he realised. That was Phil! The head scientist, stripped of his lab coat and glasses, and looking more than a little dazed, had a gun held to his back and looked utterly terrified.

But as he watched, the shifters took stock of the situation, the captive with the gun to his head, the bars…

"Control panel's in the ceiling. Just above you," the leader said to a tall man wearing a trench coat, the one with a gun to Phil's back, and how the fuck did they know where it was? Then Trench-Coat pulled out a crossbow, and before Miller could blink, the ceiling was on fire, smoke pouring out of the hatch, flames crawling along the ceiling. Trench-Coat went for the bars trapping the others in, shoving the metal back into the floor, while warrior-girl went for the barrier. Gloved fingers couldn't get a grip on the glass, but another explosion popped off inside the ceiling hatch, fresh smoke pouring through the gap and the wall protecting them all from sudden death retracted, leaving three guards and a headstrong scientist facing off against five angry shifters.

Negotiate, Miller thought desperately, scrambling for a deal that would get all of them – or most of them, at least - out of here alive.

But Trench-Coat was way ahead of him. "How about we all stay calm. We've got something you want," he said, shoving Phil in the back and making him stumble. "And you've got something we want. So how about we arrange a nice little trade, and we all get to walk away alive."

Melissa glanced at their captive, who remained impassive, despite the showy entrance of his fellow shifters. "How do we know you won't just shoot us once we let him go?"

Certainly a valid question. But just then, another man swung around the corner, with dark hair and a cold, steely expression on his face, though he looked younger than the others. But then he pulled up short as his gaze landed on Melissa. And that hard face turned pale.

"Sarah?" The word came out jaggedly, a husky cry of disbelief, and Miller realised that Melissa looked as startled as the young man did.

What the hell? But as Miller tried to catch up with whatever it was that was going on, he noticed that the other shifters seemed just as surprised as he was by the young man's sudden question.


After helping Dee and Raniesha get Gabrielle up the stairs, Mark had checked in with Kwan and Aaron, guarding the door, and learned that there had yet to be any sign of Baron and his team. And despite his orders to do his job and get out, Mark had grabbed Dee and kissed her hard on the mouth, and then bolted back inside the building. He had led them all here, after all, and as his life was likely forfeit at the end of this parade, he'd just as soon go down fighting. If Baron had gotten into trouble – which was more than likely, given the defences of this place – then an extra pair of hands – and teeth – wouldn't go astray. He'd run back down the stairs, navigating the place like he'd lived here for years, followed the hallway along to the cages, expecting to find them all locked in a fight, perhaps wounded, maybe pinned down and unable to escape, or worst case, possibly already dead. He'd braced himself for all manner of horrors and chaos when he turned the final corner, seeing smoke filling the hallway, flames licking along the ceiling.

But then he'd caught sight of…

Nothing could have prepared him for this. Sarah! His sister! The one he'd been looking for when he came to the lab in the first place, the one he'd given up for dead. She'd been captured after all! She was surrounded by guards, their guns drawn, Tank standing patiently as they threatened to shoot him, and his gut lurched to think that perhaps she'd been kept here all these months, ready to be the next test subject in the Noturatii's sick experiments.

"That's not my name," Sarah snapped at him, and Mark's heart sank at his mistake. Perhaps she'd given them a false name, tried to protect her identity? Not that it would matter now. They were going to kill them all, free her, so there would be no one left to threaten her.

"We can help you," he tried again, taking a step forward, dimly aware of the stares of disbelief from Baron and the other shifters. "We can get you out of here-"

"What the fuck do you think I am?" The cold, hard statement was delivered with all the hate she could muster, and it was then that Mark finally felt himself pulled up hard, felt reality snap back into place.

And saw the gun in Sarah's hand.

"You've joined the Noturatii." Even as he said it, he didn't really believe it.

"Well, bravo," she said coldly. "Of course I joined the fucking Noturatii. After I found out what they'd done to you. What you'd become." She looked him up and down, an expression of pure disgust on her face. "And the fact that you chose this? God, how could you do that? How could you not see what you are?"

"Not to break up the party or anything," Baron suddenly snapped, still holding his gun steadily aimed at the guards, "but what the fuck is going on?"

"This is my sister," Mark said, not bothering to disguise the truth as anything other than what it was. "The one I came here looking for when I found Dee."

"*That* is your sister? One of the eggheads behind the Noturatii? Oh, good work." He muttered something under his breath, and Mark decided he was better off not knowing what it was. To think, he'd come here to rescue her, and all the while she was...

"Why did you join?" It was a tiny detail in the big picture, an irrelevant side track to a life or death situation. But he had to know, and this was likely the only chance he would get to ask.

"I saw a photo of you. On the internet. When you were supposed to be dead."

"How did you find it?"

"Why does it matter?" she asked impatiently, then cursed. "Oh, what the hell. It was attached to an article I was studying about leukaemia, when I was in my final year at university. Only in the photo, you were in your mid twenties, when you'd supposedly died when you were seventeen. So I did a little digging, and that led me here."

Mark let out a sardonic laugh. "You 'found' a photograph? Believe me, Sarah, *no one* finds out about the shifters or the Noturatii without one side or the other telling them. You didn't 'find' the Noturatii. They planted that photo for you to see. They assessed your reaction to the news, and then they recruited you. Nice to see where your morals led you. To kidnapping innocent people and torturing women-"

"Melissa!" one of the guards snapped suddenly, a tall, black man with a military air about him. And Mark realised that Tank was getting impatient with all the chit chat and had started casing the hallway for cover, had started taking covert glances at his captors to assess their weaknesses, and Military Guy had noticed the change in his mood. He was good. Still their enemy, but well trained and alert, and Mark could almost regret having to kill him. He'd be a worthy ally if he was on their side.

"No deal," Sarah — no, Melissa snapped, no doubt reverting to a previous conversation with Baron and his team. "We're not giving up the captive."

Now what? Mark thought blackly. They could have a shoot out, but more than one of them was going to end up dead, and having come so far to find Tank alive, only to lose him now...

Andre made a small, contemplative sound, and fitted another arrow into his crossbow. And, without any warning, fired it at the wall beside Melissa's head.

The arrow embedded itself in the plaster, a small, flashing light on the head, as the guards snapped back to attention, guns trained on them, their own guns pointed at the guards. "Well, let's think about this," Andre said calmly. "I detonate that charge, and you're all dead anyway. And don't think I won't take out one of our own to see you out of the picture. I would rather he walk the next world than spend his life as your sorry prisoner, and I'm fairly sure he'd agree with me."

Tank met Andre's eyes and gave a small nod. A ghost of a smile crossed his lips, and Mark had to wonder what the hell they'd done to him in the past twenty-four hours to make him ready to pass into the Hall of Sirius without so much as a word of protest. Tank was a fighter... but Andre wasn't done yet.

"So here's the deal. You give us your captive, and we give you your scientist, who, I'm led to believe, is the brains of this operation."

The scientist in front of Andre whimpered. But the look on Melissa's face was far more interesting. She glanced at the other man and a look of near-glee crossed her face, quickly quashed and replaced with a neutral contemplation that didn't fool Mark for a second. A little professional rivalry, then? She was willing to sacrifice a member of her own team, not for a strategic advantage, but for a personal one.

God, he really knew nothing about his sister at all.

"Deal," the military guy said, before Melissa could reply, and she gaped at him, aghast that he would dare commit to such a horrendous offer.

"At least one of you has some sense," Baron muttered to Mark's right, but Melissa wasn't done being difficult. Perhaps she thought herself heroic. Or maybe she was just too stubborn for her own good. He remembered that about her – even as a young girl, she'd had the backbone to stand up for what she wanted, the persistence to see her schemes through. And Mark felt a wave of longing for the girl she had been. And a swell of sorrow for the woman she had become.

"Same question I asked you before," Melissa demanded, shooting a glare at the guard. "How do we know you won't just shoot us once we release him?"

Andre fingered the detonator for the arrow. "Let me put it this way," he said. "What choice have you got?"


Miller fought for calm as he watched Melissa argue with the shifters. She was a scientist, not a soldier, armed with a single small pistol against wolves, semi-automatics and explosives, and she wanted to play hardball? She was going to get them all killed if she wasn't careful. Miller stole another glance at the arrow in the wall. He'd already seen the destruction one of those charges could wield, and he didn't like their chances if Trench-Coat decided to press the button.

"Enough!" he snapped at the woman, then shoved her behind himself when she glared at him again. The chit could get as mad as she liked later, but for now, he was taking charge. "You bring Phil out to the front," he instructed, stepping in to take their prisoner from the guard watching him. He pressed his gun to the back of the man's neck and twisted his arm behind his back to keep a hold on him. If he tried anything funny, the other guards would take him out.

The leader of the shifters brought Phil forward, holding him in a similar manner, gun to his head, and they met in the middle of the hallway. "Both of us step back," the leader instructed, and Miller obediently took two steps back, keeping his gun up, half his attention on the warrior-woman down the hall, who was looking a little trigger happy for his liking.

At the leader's command, Phil stepped forward, skirting around the captive shifter, who watched him go past like a fox watching a hen. Then the captive stepped over to his leader, who never took his eyes off Miller.

These guys were good, Miller had to admit. Not prone to distractions, no weaknesses in their defence, advanced weapons. It reinforced his idea that there were two groups of shifters in England, and that they were dealing here with the more modern, more tech-savvy of the two. It was an odd feeling to respect his sworn enemy so much, but it was impossible not to feel a certain admiration for a small group that had managed to infiltrate this lab – and blow half of it up, if the earlier explosions had been anything to go by.

When Phil reached him, Miller retreated with the man back the way he'd come, while the shifters did the same.

"So now you walk away?" Miller asked, once they'd retreated to the corner. The explosive arrow was still flashing away in the wall, and he had to wonder just how good their word was going to be.

"Give me your gun," the former captive said, and the leader did so without hesitation. Miller honestly had no idea what the man was going to do. Would he honour the deal struck by his comrades, or–

Melissa screamed, an ear-piercing shriek as the captive raised the gun and shot Phil in the head. He hit the ground with a thud, blood spraying over the guards behind him, and Miller took up a defensive position in front of Melissa. If they wanted to take out their other scientist, they'd have to get through him.

"He had it coming," the captive said. And Miller remembered that cold threat uttered in the cell – the captive had promised that Phil was going to die, and he wondered for a moment just who else was on the man's hit list.

The shifter locked eyes with Miller, and for just a moment, he felt his world tilt. Was he about to die? If so, he had a thousand sudden regrets… and the odd thought that he was grateful that his death should come at the hands of such a worthy foe.

"One day, you and I are going to settle our differences," the captive said, eyes never wavering from Miller's. "But it's going to be in a fair fight. No guns. No wolves. No backup. Just you and me, and then we find out what you're really made of. Let's go," he said, turning to the other shifters. They began a coordinated withdrawal, backing away, weapons drawn, until the last one had rounded the corner. And Melissa watched them go, her face stricken, as if someone had just kidnapped her only child.

# CHAPTER FORTY

"Go," Baron ordered sharply, as the last of the team rounded the corner away from the guards. "Up the stairs. Then blow whatever charges are left." Including the one next to the prison cells. And if the guards hadn't moved by then, too bad.

"NO!" A high pitched shriek followed them around the corner, and the sounds of a scuffle, shoes squealing on the linoleum floor...

"Go!" Baron shouted. Andre and Caroline grabbed Tank and half-led, half-dragged him up the stairs. Caleb shifted back into human form and drew his gun, John remaining in wolf form as they both headed up the stairs, acting as rear guard for their newly recovered member. And then that woman scientist, Melissa, skidded around the corner, eyes wide and frantic, and for a split second Baron had the thought that she'd come after Mark. Seeing her brother again after so many years, however much she denied family ties, was bound to be unsettling, and perhaps she wanted to...

Shoot them. A bullet flew past Baron's head, clipping his ear and making him duck and swear, while thanking the stars that she didn't have better aim, and then a second gun shot from his left made his ears ring, a high pitched scream piercing the air...

And holy fucking hell, Mark had just shot her. Melissa sat on the floor, hands pressed to an ugly wound in her leg, trying to stem the flow of blood as Mark stood beside him, gun raised, looking for all the world like he wanted to have another go at her.

The military guard skidded around the corner, throwing himself in front of the woman, gun drawn, a stricken look on his face. "Leave," he pleaded, torn between helping the woman and keeping his gun trained on them. He stuck with the gun. "Please, just leave."

"Let's go," Baron ordered Mark, then yanked him away when he remained frozen in place. Up the stairs, along the hallways, past dead guards and bloody puddles. He hoped everyone else was out, knew he'd need a full accounting of the team before they left. No one was being left behind.

"Andre! Hit it," he barked, as he and Mark caught up with him and Caroline, Tank staggering along robotically. Andre paused only a moment to hit the detonator in his pocket, and an explosion ripped through the lower levels, shaking the building.

"Up! Out!" Baron ordered, taking up the rear guard. But thankfully there was no more resistance, all the guards already dead or fatally wounded.

Up at the final hallway, Silas and Skip joined them. Silas was bleeding – Baron couldn't tell if it was from his old wound, or a new one, but it didn't seem to slow him down as he raced along the hallway to freedom, keeping Skip safely tucked behind himself.

Finally they reached the entrance, Kwan and Aaron still keeping guard, both to protect the drivers, and to secure their exit route.

"You're the last," Kwan informed him as Baron dashed out the door. "Full head count, twenty shifters and one newbie. Dee said she's a convert from the lab. Nate and Cohen were both shot, but they're alive. It's not fatal."

Baron filed the information away for later. Questions about the new girl would have to wait until Tank had been taken care of and the rest of the Den was safe. He trusted Dee and Raniesha's judgement enough to know they wouldn't have brought her with them if it wasn't in all of their best interests.


Out into the night, shifters scattered left, right and centre. Mark broke off from Baron and Andre as they helped Tank into a van, making a beeline for the one where Dee was waiting. Silas and Skip ran for another, Silas sparing a brief nod to Heron, who was hanging out of the driver's seat of another vehicle, and Heron nodded back, relief all over her face as she watched Skip leap into the back, before she swung back into the van and got herself strapped in.

"Caroline! This way!" Dee yelled from inside her own van, and Mark arrived at the doorway to see her and Raniesha pinning a wolf to the floor, a deep, bloody wound on Dee's arm evidence of a vicious bite. Caroline switched direction and ran for the van, as the remaining shifters piled into the rest of them. The last door slammed shut, then burning rubber and squealing tyres signalled their exit from this killing ground.

Alistair was at the wheel, Mark noted briefly, navigating midnight traffic with ease as he took corners at breakneck speeds, hightailing it out of London. The other vans broke off, each taking a different route back to the estate, making any pursuit more difficult, while Caroline turned her attention to the wolf writhing on the floor.

"New recruit," Dee gasped, throwing all of her slight weight onto the wolf's neck. "Gone a bit mad in the chaos."

Caroline didn't waste any time, just pounced on the wolf and zapped her, the electricity shocking everyone in the van as the wolf was forced to turn human again. The girl convulsed once, opened her eyes, and let out a blood-curdling scream.

"Sedative!" Caroline ordered, and Mark dove for the emergency medical kit under the seat. He drew up a dose of sedative and tossed it to Caroline, who plunged the syringe into the girl's leg, emptying it with one quick thrust.

Another scream left the girl as she struggled, arms flailing, legs thrashing, and Mark leapt onto her, helping Raniesha hold her down. The third scream was weaker, a keening wail that tailed off quickly, and then the girl fell limply against the floor.

But the emergency was by no means over. Mark grabbed a tube of antiseptic, gauze and a bandage from the med kit and squeezed behind Caroline to get to Dee. He didn't bother being delicate about it – the wound was bleeding profusely – and he simply squeezed a thick dollop of cream onto the gauze, pressed it to her wound and set about wrapping the bandage around. "Keep pressure on it," he told her when he'd finished, and she nodded, lips pressed into a thin line as she hauled herself onto one of the seats.

Raniesha and Caroline were trying to hold the girl still, not because she was struggling any more, but as a consequence of Alistair's crazy driving. Mark grabbed a blanket from the rear of the van and set it under the girl's head, then pinned a knee to her shoulder, relieving Caroline of the task while gripping the side of a seat to steady himself. Caroline set about checking the girl over – she didn't seem to be injured, thankfully, and as soon as they were out of the warehouse district and heading towards the motorway, Alistair calmed down a little. No point getting the attention of every traffic cop in London, after all. And if the Noturatii were following them? A slower pace would allow Alistair to pick out any suspicious tag-alongs in the rear-view mirror. Making the girl as comfortable as possible, Mark settled into a seat beside Dee.

"You okay?" It was a silly question – she was likely terrified, adrenaline pumping, and she had a nasty wolf bite on her arm, but like all things in this crazy life, it was all relative.

"Faeydir's going nuts. Ranting about the girl, and revelling in having killed some of the bad guys, and it's like having a two year old on a sugar high stuck in my head. Did we get Tank?" It was a tremulous question disguised with a lot of bravado, and Mark was grateful that he was able to give her an honest answer.

"We got him out. He's alive, injured, but he should pull through."

"Oh, thank God." Dee visibly sagged against the seat, while Raniesha looked relieved at the news. "See, Faeydir? We got Tank back- Oh shut the fuck up!" She lowered her head into her hands, and Mark automatically reached out and rubbed her back. He had no idea how she coped with having another living creature in her head all the time, and it was no surprise that Faeydir was feeling rather high strung at the moment. The strain of it, after everything else that had happened tonight, would be enough to send anyone over the edge.

"Hang in there," he murmured to her, massaging her shoulders gently. "The worst of it's over. We're headed for home. Just hang in there."


A few kilometres west of Mark, Baron was fighting not to curse. He, Andre and Tank had made it into the van without incident, with John in wolf form leaping inside just as the door swung closed, but it was clear that Tank was in a bad way. Aside from the drugs, he was bleeding from a dozen wounds, so Baron gently coaxed his shirt off, and gritted his teeth to hold back the string of curses he sorely longed to utter. He'd seen enough wounds in his life to know what torture looked like.

"John, get me the med kit." The boy was still in wolf form, lurking near the back of the van so as to avoid injuring anyone with his armour.

The van swung round a corner, sending everyone inside crashing into the wall or the seats, and Baron did swear this time. "Heron! You drive like a ten year old in a go-kart, you mad bitch!"

"You want me to pull over so the car tailing us can catch up?"

"What the fuck?"

"We're being tailed. Don't worry. I'll lose them."

He swore to himself again, clinging onto the edge of the seat and rubbing his head where he'd cracked it against the door.

John was still lurking behind the seats, his armour having carved a nice new groove along the car's interior, and he swore again at the boy's stupidity. Surely he could see this wasn't the time or place to be in wolf form?

"John! Med kit!"

"John can't shift," Andre said quietly, from where he was shining a light in Tank's eyes and assessing his reflexes. "He was injured."

That got Baron's attention. It was hardly surprising that some of the Den had been hurt, but if John was flat out refusing to shift? Generally that meant that the injury he'd sustained as a human was life-threatening. Baron felt his heart lurch in his chest. "What happened?"

"Mad scientist threw acid over him. He's going to need a cold shower to wash it off, and I'd strongly suggest you get him under the water *before* he shifts. Either way, he's going to have some nasty burns."

"Fuck…" He looked over at John, locking eyes with ones that were almost as familiar as his own, and the wolf just stared back at him stoically.

"We'll get you fixed up at the house." It was a completely unnecessary statement – of course they would. What the hell else were they going to do? But he needed to say it, to let John know he hadn't been forgotten. Crazy boy was unpredictable that way, sometimes wanting to be left alone, other times throwing tantrums if he was ignored.

Baron quickly released him from his armour, then reached for the med kit himself, taking out antiseptic, wound dressings, a bottle of local anaesthetic.

"Hold on!" Heron yelled from the driver's seat, and they all did – all except Tank, but Andre anticipated his lack of response, and held him steady as the tyres squealed and the van fishtailed as it flew around a corner. The engine revved, throwing them all backwards as the vehicle shot forward, then around another corner.

"I think we've lost them. But I'm going to take the long way home, just in case."

"Home," Tank said suddenly, blinking at Andre with a frown, then turning to see Baron leaning against the seat beside him.

"We're going home, buddy," Baron told him, putting a gentle hand on his shoulder. "Hang in there. We're taking you home."

# CHAPTER FORTY-ONE

The van Mark was travelling in was the first one back to the estate. The manor was dark – they'd left before nightfall, and no one was left inside to turn on the lights. It was both heartening, and eerie – heartening because the entire Den had pulled together to rescue one of their own, and succeeded, with a few injuries, but no fatalities. And eerie because for as long as he'd lived here, Mark couldn't remember a single night when he'd seen the place looking so deserted. This was home, the only one he'd had in a very long time, and he felt a lump in his throat as the reality of the day hit him. He was a traitor to Il Trosa, and might very well be put down because of it.

Gabrielle was still out cold, and Alistair stopped the van directly in front of the manor. "Help me get her out," Caroline barked, throwing open the door, and the three women gently manoeuvred the girl out the door, Caroline taking her in her arms to carry her into the house. "Alistair, tell Baron we're plus one the second he gets back. This one's going to be messy." Alistair nodded once, then eased the van down the driveway to the garage.

Dee, Raniesha and Mark all followed Caroline through the house and down into the cage room, turning on lights as they went, which made the house seem more welcoming, but no less empty. Caroline placed Gabrielle on a cot in one of the cages. "Raniesha, you stay with her. I need to head up and debrief whoever arrives back. And Dee, go get your wound treated properly, then get some sleep. Mark?"

Mark nodded, expecting the inevitable.

"Into the cage," Caroline said shortly, pointing to the one beside Gabrielle's.

Mark didn't argue. In Baron's absence, Caroline was in charge, and as things stood, he was a criminal. Jail time was entirely appropriate. "Could someone bring me a change of clothes?" he asked, heading into the cell and shutting the door behind himself. His current set were splattered with blood, and besides being uncomfortable as hell, he didn't think Gabrielle would appreciate the sight when she woke up. He didn't even bother suggesting that he go get them himself, before being locked in the cage. The answer would have been no.

"I'll send some down," Caroline said, her voice gentling just a touch. Then she gave him a long look... and strode away. Dee gave him a hopeful, worried gaze, and fell in behind Caroline.

The chaos just wasn't going to stop, Baron thought, as Heron pulled the van up in front of the manor. They were the last ones back, the other three vans already parked in the garage, and before he and Andre even had Tank out of the van, there was a line up waiting to talk to him. Caroline was front and centre, but she took one look at Tank and apparently decided to make her report quick. "We've got a new shifter in the basement," she said shortly. "A girl we took from the lab. She's contained for now, but she'll need attention sooner rather than later." With that simple declaration, she stalked away, leaving him to manhandle Tank across the driveway.

Skip was next. "Radio silence from the Noturatii," she reported. "Two vans were tailed, but lost their pursuers, the lab blew up in a big, pretty bonfire once we were out and so far there's no reaction from any international division. There will be, but it looks like it's going to take a day or two for them to regroup. So yay, we kicked arse." With a girlish bounce, she dashed off back into the house, probably to go back to monitoring her computer feeds.

Caleb was the last one, with an injury report. Clearly, he was taking his position as 2IC seriously until Tank was back in the game. "Plenty of injuries, five serious, but none fatal. Nate's going to be out of action for a while. George is treating the injured in the kitchen. I've put a list on your desk. Is there anything you need?"

"Hold the fucking door," Baron ordered, guiding Tank to stagger up the stairs into the house, Andre supporting him on his other side. "And put some blankets on the sitting room couch. Tank's not going to make it up the stairs tonight."

"On it, boss." Caleb dashed away, while Baron steered Tank in a slow shuffle across the foyer.

Half an hour later, Andre sat in an armchair, watching Tank sleep. The assault on the Noturatii lab had been tense, fraught with potential disaster, and he'd been impressed with the depth of Baron's planning. And even more impressed with the smoothness with which the entire operation had been carried out. Injuries had been inevitable, and casualties very likely, but they'd come out the other end with no one killed. Which made Andre's job of reporting the entire incident to the Council far more pleasant than if he'd had to report a failed assault or a list of fatalities. The entire Den had been a credit to their species, intensive training and strict discipline coming together to deal a significant blow to their enemies.

And now, Tank was resting, his injuries treated, his mind soothed by Andre's peculiar talent for hypnosis, and Caleb was watching over him with all the attentiveness of a mother hen.

Caleb glanced at Andre. "You want to go take a shower?" he asked. Both of them were still splattered with blood – a minor inconvenience, given the stakes of the battle, but a change of clothes would be nice, none the less. And the brief respite would give Andre the chance to check in with the Council, not just to report on the battle, but to give them the unfortunate news on Mark's betrayal and update them on Dee's status as Fenrae-Ul. They were not going to be pleased about that one.

"Call me if you need anything," Andre said in a tone that would brook no dissent, before he let himself out of the room, heading for his quarters.

At the top of the stairs, he passed George's room – silence from inside as he was presumably asleep – then Silas's room, hearing faint swearing from beyond the door. The man was probably having his wound treated again, though Andre doubted the foul language was the result of pain. Silas was too stoic for that. More likely he was pissed off at whatever fuss was being had over him and trying to shoo his nurse out of the room.

Baron and John had headed upstairs a while ago, after Tank had been settled on the couch, so that Baron could treat John's acid burns, and he passed their door next.

And stopped, as he heard yelling from inside. Before coming here, he'd been briefed that Baron and John were in a sexual relationship, and he'd taken the information at face value, thinking nothing more of it. Now, though, he caught a few choice words through the door, and stopped to wonder just what the nature of their relationship was-

The door burst open and John leapt out into the hallway, naked aside from the bandages on his arms, an angry red burn on his right leg stretching from ankle to groin, and a look of panic on his face.

"You keep your hands off me, you mother fucking dog shit!"

Baron appeared in the doorway, looking tired and fed up. "Go back inside, John."

"You stay away from me!"

Andre looked from one to the other. Baron spared him a brief glance, while John seemed totally oblivious to his presence. "John," Baron said, as if talking to a child throwing a tantrum. "I need to treat your burn. Your leg is injured. Go back inside."

"Uh…" Should he intervene? And if so, what the hell was he supposed to do? Baron was right, John needed the wound treated, but the younger man was reacting like Baron had just tried to rape him. "John?"

John's eyes swung round, seeing Andre standing there. He swung back to Baron with bared teeth. "Oh, so you're going to get your lackeys to hold me down again? You sick fuck!"

Andre opened his mouth to protest the accusation – just what the hell was going on here? But without warning, Caroline appeared at his elbow. "Could I see you in your room?" she asked brusquely, and when Andre didn't move, she actually reached out and grabbed his wrist to pull him along. It took all of Andre's will power to not retaliate, perhaps twisting her arm behind her back and pinning her to a wall, or perhaps kicking her legs from under her and toppling her to the floor. No one had dared touch him in so forceful a manner in years, and he stopped dead in his tracks, his greater weight and strength pulling Caroline up short.

"John?" he tried again. "You okay?"

"Leave them alone," Caroline said abruptly. "And I need to see you in your room. Now."

Okay, so Andre might be out of the loop here, but he wasn't an idiot. Clearly there was more going on than met the eye, and if Caroline was on board with it as well as Baron… He could at least spare her the time to explain. Ignoring John and Baron's ongoing argument, he followed Caroline down the hall to his own room.

Once inside, he turned to Caroline with folded arms, not at all happy about lacking what was apparently important information. He'd expected a swift explanation, Caroline not the type to waste time with idle chit chat, but once the door was closed, she seemed suddenly lost for words.

"Well?"

She chewed on her lip, apparently thinking things over. "What have you been told about John?"

Before coming here, Andre had been given a dossier on each of the Den's members, details of their background, their conversion, any known physical or psychological issues they might have. But John's file had been all but empty. And the lack of detail was more telling than a thousand idle platitudes could ever have been.

"Nothing. His information is all on a need-to-know basis. And apparently, I don't qualify."

Caroline looked momentarily surprised by the news. "Ah." And now she was obviously reconsidering telling him whatever it was she had been going to say. "Look, they're complicated-"

"If Baron is abusing a member of his Den-"

"John can get a little out of control. Baron keeps him in line. The alternative was putting John down, and we agreed a while ago that that wasn't the best option. It was a decision with the full support of the Council."

A serious issue, then, and one they hadn't bothered briefing him on. But then again, he hadn't come here to deal with Baron and John. He'd been sent to assess Dee, nothing more.

"It's not comfortable for the rest of us, but it's important that you leave them to themselves."

Andre waited a moment for more information, then realised it wasn't coming. "I will have to report this to the Council," he said. And was a touch more annoyed when Caroline merely shrugged.

"As you see fit. But I doubt they'll have anything more to say about it than I already have."


Melissa sat in the Noturatii's medical bay, in their headquarters in east London. Though larger than the laboratory complex that had been destroyed earlier, this base was far less well equipped for scientific endeavours, and Melissa was distraught over all the equipment that had been lost, the data that had been destroyed. Some of it, of course, had been uploaded to the Noturatii's central database, but their most recent experiments on the test subjects had been lost. Months of work down the drain because of those damnable creatures.

Melissa flinched as the doctor placed another careful stitch in her leg. After a hefty dose of local anaesthetic, removing the bullet had gone fairly smoothly, but the amount of blood all over the place had left her pale and trembling – not from blood loss, but from a strange kind of terror over her own injuries. She'd never been shot before...

Melissa fixed her eyes on the far wall and tried to ignore what was happening to her leg. The focus of this base, likely her new post, was a split between recruitment, fundraising and media control, the administrative backbone of the Noturatii's British presence, with another base on the south coast dedicated to training new recruits and security personnel, and a third in Liverpool, which served largely as a weapons development and storage facility.

After she'd been shot, Miller had hauled her arse out of the hallway and down through the emergency escape tunnels. Not many of the staff had escaped, most of the scientists killed in the lab, ninety percent of the security staff cut down by the shifters and a handful more killed in the explosion that had totalled the complex just minutes after Miller had gotten her to safety. The bastards had detonated their explosives after they'd gotten clear of the place and anyone left inside...

They'd met up with Jacob here, the wily leader having vanished like a ghost in the middle of the fighting, and Melissa had mixed feelings about how quickly he'd abandoned ship. From a purely pragmatic perspective, he'd made the right choice. Jacob was a vital part of their operation, and without him, they'd be floundering for weeks until the International Division could send a replacement. With the breakthroughs they'd made in the lab, such a delay was inexcusable.

So she was trying to ignore the feelings of hurt and betrayal that kept playing through her mind. Which were really more a consequence of his cool greeting when they'd arrived here at Headquarters than due to the fact that he'd cut and run in the first place. A sardonically raised eyebrow had been sent her way, along with a curt "Well, I suppose that's better than nothing," before she'd been sent to the medical bay, while Miller had received a much warmer welcome. A grin. A warm-toned "I knew I'd hired you for a reason" as his gaze had lingered on the blood stains on Miller's clothes and then, when Miller had declared himself fit for duty, he'd been hustled off for a debrief, Melissa forgotten about immediately.

Melissa winced as the doctor tied off the last stitch and began dressing the wound. True, she hadn't come here for cuddles and warm, fuzzy feelings, but she'd expected a little more concern from her boss when she'd spent the last few months working herself to the bone to try and understand the experiments on the shifters and how to make the next breakthrough for their cause.

The door opened with a thud and Jacob stuck his head in. "Still here?" He glanced at the wound on her leg. "It won't kill you. Come on, into the office." And with that, he was gone.

The doctor finished his work and gave her a nod, his persona as cool and disinterested as any of the staff here, and Melissa hopped gingerly to the floor. The wound still stung, but the anaesthetic was still working for the most part, so she ignored the pair of crutches the doctor thrust at her and headed for Jacob's new office.

Inside, the man was at his desk, already typing furiously at his computer. "Well," he said when he saw her, and then pressed his lips tight together, a sure sign that he was in the foulest of moods. And it was no wonder, Melissa reminded herself, counselling herself not to feel put out. He'd had his entire lab destroyed, lost dozens of his staff, and she was upset that he wasn't pleased to see her? Grow up, she told herself sharply.

"Phil's dead," Jacob said bluntly. "Which is a serious setback, given how much he knew about the conversion process." Melissa wanted to remind him that she'd worked alongside Phil for the entire operation and knew almost as much as he did. But she held her tongue. Besides, with Phil out of the way, they would be needing a new Head of Science, and she was the most experienced person left from the Conversion Project- "So I'm sending for a new research team from the USA," Jacob said, stunning her. "Doctor

Evans will be leading the team. She's got over twenty years experience in the Noturatii and two degrees from Princeton. I expect you to make her welcome."

Melissa nearly choked on her own tongue at the news. A new boss. From America. Poker face, she reminded herself, knowing how much Jacob hated theatrics. At least he'd hired a woman, though. The men in the lab had always treated her as a bit of a tag-along, rather than a real partner.

"Yes, sir," she agreed, since there was no other real option. "How soon until a new facility will be set up?"

"That's the spirit," Jacob said sarcastically. "Get right back in the saddle. I'll send you a report with the full details."

He turned back to his computer, as clear a dismissal as she was going to get, and Melissa let herself out of the room.

She hesitated a moment, not sure what to do next, and then headed for the offices in the eastern wing. Hopefully she'd be able to find a computer to use and she could review the data they'd managed to save on the latest experiments. New research team aside, seeing the shifters up close and personal, seeing the *thing* her brother had become, had only strengthened her resolve. The shifters were a blight on humanity and needed to be wiped off the face of the planet.

And she was going to be the one to do it.

# CHAPTER FORTY-TWO

It was a little after 7am when Mark woke up. Raniesha had disappeared, and Caroline sat in her place, gaze fixed on Gabrielle. The girl was coming around slowly, small movements and the odd moan alerting Caroline to her progress.

Baron had come down around 4am, looking exhausted but determined to fulfil his duties before hitting the sack. Though there hadn't been much to do at the time. Mark's future was still pending, with Andre in discussions with the Council on the best course of action, and Gabrielle couldn't be dealt with until she woke up, so he'd soon gone back upstairs, leaving Mark to a fitful sleep.

Caroline noticed Mark stirring and gave him a nod, but her attention was mostly taken up with the girl. Gabrielle moaned again, flailed one arm and coughed, and that was enough for Caroline. She pulled out her phone and had Baron on the line in an instant. "She's coming around," was all she said before hanging up, and not two minutes later, heavy thuds could be heard on the stairs.

Baron came through the door but didn't come any further, no doubt not wanting to scare the girl. They'd not been nearly so considerate of Dee when she'd arrived, Mark thought with just a touch of resentment. But to be fair, he reminded himself, this time around they knew a lot more about the girl's circumstances, and would have to add some serious concessions knowing that she was likely terrified.

Gabrielle sat up suddenly, eyes wide, a sound that was half scream, half whimper coming from her throat. She looked down at herself, startled to find her arms and legs free, and patted herself all over, checking for wounds, or perhaps for unexpected alterations to her body, given where she had been recently.

And then she noticed the room, and the two people with her, and her fear came back full force. "Why am I in jail? I didn't do anything! You've got the wrong person. I was kidnapped! I'm not a terrorist-"

"Whoa, easy, *easy!*" Caroline urged her, coming to stand at the bars. "You're not in jail. This is a private medical facility. We've simply put you in an isolation ward because we're not quite sure what's happened to you yet."

Anyone thinking clearly would see through the lie in an instant – isolation wards had glass barriers and air filters and teams of medical staff standing by, not iron bars and leather-clad security guards. But Gabrielle was not processing reality terribly well right now, and she seemed to swallow the story easily enough. She glanced sideways at Mark. "What about him? Why's he in a cage?"

"It's not a cage," Caroline said, a blatant lie designed only to help her keep control of the situation. "And he's in isolation because he was injured."

Gabrielle looked Mark over. "You don't look injured."

Mark thought fast. He could hardly tell her he was awaiting trial as a traitor, not when Caroline was trying to convince her that this wasn't a jail. "I was exposed to a toxic chemical," he lied, tossing out the first plausible explanation he could come up with. "They're waiting to see if I have a reaction to it."

That was good enough for the girl, and she turned back to Caroline. "Who's he?" she demanded, catching sight of Baron, lurking in the corner.

"He runs this facility. He just came down to see how you're feeling. Do you remember what happened?" A good way to stem the flow of questions was to ask some of her own, and the trick worked, Gabrielle coming to a screeching halt as her thoughts suddenly turned inward.

"I was kidnapped. They tortured me in a lab. Were they terrorists?"

"Yes. And do you remember who we are?"

"A girl said you were the police. You rescued me. But why don't you have uniforms? Police have uniforms."

"We're a special operations unit. We do a lot of undercover work, so uniforms don't really feature in our line of work. Listen, we're going to help you, but the things the people in the lab were doing were quite complicated, so we're going to need to monitor you for a couple of days. You can't go home just yet-"

"There's a... a *thing* in my head." If Gabrielle had been scared before, she was petrified now, white as a sheet as the wolf no doubt started to make its presence known.

"It's quite possible that you're still hallucinating," Caroline told her gently, and Mark had to wonder just what the hell was going on. She was behaving as if Gabrielle had a disease that could be cured, that her going home was a real possibility, and Mark had never known the Den to lie to its new recruits quite so blatantly, a dangerous practice as it set up all kinds of false expectations that would most likely end up with the new wolf being put down. "The terrorists gave you some odd medications that could mess up the way you're thinking."

"I think Andre should take a look at her, now she's awake," Baron put in, then added, for Gabrielle's benefit, "He's one of our medical specialists. He'll be able to work out what drugs you were given and what the effect on your mind has been."

Gabrielle nodded timidly. "Okay."

"Are you hungry?"

Gabrielle looked surprised, though more at herself than with Baron. "Yes. Very hungry, actually."

"I'll have some food brought down." Baron disappeared out the door again, leaving Caroline and Mark to hold back the tide of questions.


It was mid morning when Dee woke up, her dreams of the lab so vivid that she was actually startled to find herself in her own bed. The bite wound on her arm was throbbing, despite having been cleaned properly and dressed before she went to bed, and she wandered into the bathroom, finding a packet of painkillers, and quickly downed two tablets.

Faeydir was awake and agitated, hungry, concerned about the new shifter in the basement, wondering what was going to happen to Mark. She didn't entirely agree that he was a traitor, particularly when her own rescue had been the result of his actions, but she did agree that loyalty and secrecy were important to Il Trosa, so Dee was relieved to find that she had a basic understanding that Mark was in a lot of trouble.

They couldn't go down into the basement, Dee reminded her – they had to wait until Baron or Caroline invited them down, but she did suggest that Faeydir go get herself some breakfast. It would be a relief to be out of human form for a while, at least until the pills kicked in, and Faeydir seemed happy with the arrangement.

Downstairs, the entire Den was in a sombre mood, either concerned about Tank's recovery, Mark's fate, or Gabrielle's problematic conversion, and there was little conversation in the kitchen, despite more than half the Den having gathered there, waiting for news.

And when it finally came, some two hours later, none of it was good.

Baron opened the door and led a frowning Caroline and a pensive Andre into the room. "Tank's recovering slowly, but it's going to be a while until he's back to full speed," he announced without preamble. "Mark's future is still a work in progress. And Gabrielle... sorry folks, but it's not looking good." There was a round of muttering, complaints and disappointment filling the room in a low grumble, and then Baron turned to Dee. "Dee? Could we see you in the library?"

Dee's eyebrow rose in surprise, and then fell in consternation. She'd known about Mark's betrayal, she reasoned as she stood up, and it was likely that there would be repercussions for her about having kept it a secret. But when she sat down at the library's long table, the topic of conversation was far from what she'd expected.

"Gabrielle's not doing well," Baron began. "She's currently under the impression that she's hallucinating the wolf, and Andre's spent a couple of hours trying to assess whether she's capable of merging with it." He glanced over at Andre, who picked up the explanation.

"All indications are that she's not going to accept the conversion," he said grimly. "She's terrified, convinced she's going mad, and the wolf is already getting antsy about her human. She shifted once, completely unintentionally, and the wolf was aggressive and couldn't be reasoned with. If she stays in this state much longer, she'll end up going rogue."

Dee stared at the table, remembering the image Faeydir had shown her of a new wolf in the pack, a new friend and companion, and she felt a wave of sorrow at the news. "I'm sorry," she said, not knowing what else to say. "Do you want me to talk to her?" Her own conversion had been trying, to say the least, and perhaps they thought that if she shared her own experiences-

"I'm afraid that's not going to help," Andre said softly. "I'm sure you'd be more than willing to try," he added, at her disappointed expression, "but I've seen enough rogues to know when it's a hopeless case."

"Then what do you want me to do?" They wouldn't have called her in here just to break the news gently. But short of talking to the girl, Dee wasn't sure what she could do to help.

Thick silence filled the room, and Dee had a vivid recollection of the time when Baron and Caroline had asked her to let them find out her bloodline. Something horrible was coming, and Dee braced herself-

"We'd like you to try and remove the wolf from her. The way you did with the woman from the Grey Watch."

Dee felt Faeydir go still, and knew that her wolf had grasped the implications of the request immediately, though Dee's own thoughts were struggling to catch up. "You want me to what?"

"You are the Destroyer," Andre explained, as gently as possible, and Dee had to remind herself not to take offence at the name. "You're capable of separating human from wolf – the only one with that kind of ability. Now, under normal circumstances, we'd have no choice but to put Gabrielle down. There's never been another option before. But with you here…"

"If it was successful," Baron said, "there's a chance Gabrielle could recover. Go back to her normal life."

"But the wolf would die," Dee said, heartbroken at the knowledge.

Faeydir, too, was grieved by the prospect, though she hadn't yet either agreed to or refused the plan.

"That's true," Baron said, the idea clearly weighing heavily on him. "It's not something I like to ask – and certainly not a decision taken lightly. But the alternative is to kill them both. This is simply the lesser of two evils."

Dee sat in silence, weighing up the alternatives. The very limited alternatives. "But what about what she knows? She saw me shift in the lab. She's been inside our Den, met some of our members. That doesn't strike me as the kind of security risk you'd be willing to take."

"That part of the decision is not Baron's to make," Andre spoke up again. "I've spoken with the Council. This is certainly an odd situation – as I said, we've never had another option before, so this is new territory for all of us. But Gabrielle never chose to become a shifter. She was kidnapped and it was forced upon her. She knows next to nothing about Il Trosa or the shifters, she doesn't even know that the Noturatii exist. As far as she's concerned, she was taken captive by a common, garden variety terrorist group, and she currently believes that they were testing chemical weapons on her, which have made her hallucinate. Though she saw you shift, she doesn't believe for a moment that it actually happened.

"There are risks involved, of course, and we'll have to monitor her when – if – she goes home, to make sure there are no long term repercussions from this, but none of us like the idea of killing an innocent girl just because the Noturatii are practicing a new form of hideousness."

Dee let all the implications of the request sink in. "I'll have to ask Faeydir," she said finally, knowing that without the wolf's cooperation, she'd have no chance of successfully separating the girl from the wolf anyway. Hell, she didn't even know how she'd done it the first time.

"Then do so," Baron said, the three of them sitting and waiting patiently for her. So she closed her eyes and sent the query to Faeydir, an image of Gabrielle, healthy and well, and a dead wolf on the ground. It wasn't a request or a demand, a deliberate lack of obligation in the mental question. Rather it was simply a query about what Faeydir thought of the idea.

An image came back, not unexpectedly, of a live and healthy wolf with a dead girl beside it. And in the same vein as Dee's question, it was devoid of demand. Just a suggestion, a query to better understand the situation.

"I assume that letting the wolf live and Gabrielle die isn't an option?" she asked. "Faeydir would like to know."

The three senior shifters looked at each other warily. "I don't think so," Baron said, after a moment. "Gabrielle has a life, a family. Friends. And as unfortunate as it is for a wolf to die, it comes with far fewer complications. Not the least of which is how the hell do we look after a purebred wolf smack in the middle of civilisation."

"Maybe that's something you should think about for the future," Dee blurted out. "Because this is bound to come up again, but next time it might be a convert who's had years of training and knows all our secrets. And then maybe you won't want to deal with the complications of having a human running around who could betray you all to the Noturatii, so in that case, maybe letting the wolf live might be a better option." Faeydir was all on board with the hypothetical situation, fair play, she thought, to let a wolf live then, if one was killed now.

"I'll talk to the Council," Andre said immediately. "It shouldn't be too hard to set up a sanctuary somewhere. Russia, maybe, or Romania. Somewhere with a sparser human population and where wild wolves live already. Something that wouldn't catch too much attention from the public."

She was starting to like Andre, Dee realised, as his suggestion came out sincerely and thoughtfully, and she believed that he had every intention of seeing the issue through.

"And so what does Faeydir think of the current situation?" Baron prompted her, and Dee fell silent again, her thoughts turned inward. Long minutes later, after a heartfelt conversation with her wolf, she lifted her head. "Faeydir agrees to kill the wolf," she said, her voice catching with the knowledge of what she was about to do.

"Then let's get this done," Baron said, standing up. "The sooner Gabrielle is well and off this property, the better for all of us."

# CHAPTER FORTY-THREE

Dee trod the steps down into the basement with trepidation. When she had done this before, it had been a spur of the moment thing, a battle for survival against a vicious and angry foe.

Now, though, she was about to kill a creature that was confused, lost and innocent. It was a gut-wrenching contrast, and Dee had to fight back a wave of nausea as she opened the door.

The first thing she saw when she entered the cage room wasn't Gabrielle. Nor was it Caleb and Heron, sitting outside her cage, trying to keep her calm. Rather, the first thing that grabbed her attention and hung on with a force that pushed the air from her lungs, was Mark.

He was sitting on his bed, calm and serious, no doubt fully aware of what was wrong with Gabrielle, though whether he'd have been told what Dee was about to do was another matter. He came to the bars, relief and hope and sorrow all warring on his face.

Dee went over quickly, ignoring the glares from Caroline and Baron, and took his hand, giving it a quick squeeze. "I have to see to Gabrielle first," she said, by way of apology.

"Gabrielle?" Mark looked predictably confused. So they hadn't told him. But then realisation struck, and he looked both horror stricken and relieved at the same time. "You're going to..." He glanced at the girl, knowing he couldn't say more, not openly. "I mean, Fenrae is..."

"Yeah."

"Fuck..." That one, softly breathed word said it all.

Forcing herself away from Mark's cage, Dee turned to Gabrielle. The girl had clearly taken a turn for the worse. She was sitting on the floor, leaning against the bars and rocking herself, Heron sitting beside her, just outside the bars, trying to keep her calm. "It's in my head," Gabrielle repeated like a mantra. "I can't get it out, and it's crazy. Noise. Sounds and pictures and… god, it's like my body is trying to crawl out of my skin." She scratched at her arms reflexively, and Dee could see there were already raw gouges on her arms where she'd been clawing at herself. It was distressing to see how much the girl suffered, and confronting to imagine that Dee herself might have ended up in a similar state, had fate turned out just a little differently for her.

"Gabrielle," she said, approaching the bars and crouching down to talk to the girl. "My name's Caitlin. I'm here to help." No sense giving her her real name, but giving her some sort of name to call Dee by would help Gabrielle see her as a real person, one here to help, rather than just another stranger sent to poke and prod her.

"It's in my head," Gabrielle told her pleadingly. "They said I was hallucinating, but I can feel it." She looked down at her arms, and then suddenly they were paws, a shift coming over her fast and jarring. The wolf seemed just as distressed as the girl, letting out a yelp, then a series of pained whines.

"Dee? Do your thing," Caroline ordered, and it was only months of practice at reading her moods that allowed Dee to realise that she was just as stressed as everyone else in this, her grief and concern manifesting as anger, as most of her emotions did.

Dee nodded and let Faeydir come to the fore, not completing the shift, but holding just on the edge of it, skin tingling, body tight and uncomfortable. Faeydir reached out and felt the two halves of the girl easily, human and wolf, and began to pull, separating the two-

"Stop!" Dee shouted, jerking back from the cage, startling the wolf and everyone else in the room. "You can't do it like that." Just as had happened with the wolf from the Grey Watch, Gabrielle's wolf was gaining strength, while the human side of her was fading. And the problem became obvious after a moment's consideration. She waved Caroline over, holding a murmured conversation so that Gabrielle couldn't hear her – if she could even understand them, now that she was in wolf form. "If we're going to kill the wolf, then she has to be in human form," she informed Caroline. "Otherwise it'll work the opposite way."

Gabrielle, in wolf form, was pacing now, snarling, unhappy with the cage, unhappy with the people staring at her.

"All right," Caroline said, reaching for the key and opening the lock. "But this is going to get ugly." The wolf wheeled around and lunged for her, though the door was still closed, teeth snapping through the bars. "Tank, I'm going to need you to hold her down," Caroline said automatically, before glancing back at Caleb, and swearing. "Fuck. Sorry. Caleb." It was yet another disturbance to the Den, Tank the go-to-guy for just about any crisis, and his absence was once again felt keenly. "Caleb. Can you hold her down?"

Caleb nodded, rising to stand beside Caroline, while Baron and Andre took up flanking positions, just in case she managed to escape from the cage.

Caroline counted down silently with her fingers, three, two, one, and then in a coordinated rush, she flung the door open, Caleb darted through and tackled the wolf – she was small, but strong, and got her teeth into his arm despite his considerable skills, and then Caroline was on them both, electricity sparking across the cage as she zapped Gabrielle.

Caleb swore fluently, but didn't let go, and Dee imaged he must feel like he'd just been kicked by a horse, having experienced Caroline's talents herself on more than one occasion. Gabrielle convulsed and shifted, her body lying prone on the floor, a faint moan coming from her lips.

"Get back," Dee ordered, already reaching for Faeydir, feeling for the two halves that needed to be separated. Caroline and Caleb dashed for the door, neither one wanting to be caught up in Faeydir's potent magic, and with a gut-wrenching twist, Dee yanked at the fabric of the creature's soul and felt the wolf half dislodge, stutter... and fade. Tears pricked her eyes, Faeydir retreating fully, as if wanting to hide from the horrific act.

Gabrielle lay still on the floor, her hand twitching faintly. "It's done," she told Caroline, and the alpha went forward again, put a hand on Gabrielle's back and shocked her... to no effect.

Caroline breathed out a sigh. "It's gone." She turned to Andre. "She's all yours now."

"I'll take her upstairs," Andre said, coming forward to pick the girl up. "Waking up in a cage will just scare her all over again." He picked her up carefully, supporting her lolling neck against his shoulder, and headed up the stairs.

"What happens now?" Dee asked, watching Andre go, trying to stop herself from shaking.

Baron was watching her carefully. "Andre will reassess her, see if she's fit to be released, and plant a few mild hypnotic suggestions that will help her get over the trauma and reinforce the idea that she shouldn't talk about this too freely. Something along the lines that a covert police unit took down a covert terrorist cell and talking about the details could harm national security. And possibly earn her jail time."

Dee snorted. "So lies, half truths and manipulation. Just another day in the office, right?"

Baron looked mildly amused, a concession that said he knew her complaint wasn't serious, but none the less, he replied to her concerns. "She gets to live. And to go free, albeit with some trauma under her belt. A few lies as a price for freedom? That sounds like a fair exchange to me, don't you think?"

"Faeydir's considering pissing on your shoes right at the moment," she informed him grimly. "Not saying anything will come of it, but you might want to watch where you step for the next few days."

Baron let out a laugh, a brief moment to relieve the tension before he had to go and face up to the rest of the Den about what they had just done. "I'll keep that in mind."

Caleb and Heron followed Baron out of the room, leaving Dee alone with Caroline, and she was acutely aware of Mark, still watching from inside his own cage.

Dee glanced at him, then back at Caroline. "Can I…?"

"You two can have a chat," Caroline said. Dee waited, and then realised that Caroline wasn't going anywhere. She sighed, but made no protest. For all that she would love to be able to talk to him privately, she knew the Den wasn't about to take the risk that they would try to plot an escape together. She went over to the cage bars and wasn't surprised when Mark reached through and took her in a fierce hug. The bars between them were hard and uncomfortable, but Dee wouldn't have pulled away for all the world.

"Are you okay?" she asked, not bothering to keep her voice down. Caroline's hearing was excellent, and for all her harsh persona, Dee was confident that nothing said here would go beyond these walls. Caroline, like the rest of the Den, was very good at keeping secrets.

"I love you," Mark replied, kissing her as well as he could with the bars in the way. "And God, I'm so sorry you just had to do that." It was just like him, to be concerned about her when his own life was the one in danger.

"It was for the best," Dee said, trying to convince herself of that very thing. "Like Baron said, Gabrielle gets another chance at life. I'm fine. Really. But what about you?" she insisted.

The look on Mark's face all but broke her heart. "I have no regrets," he said in a whisper. "I love this Den. I love Il Trosa. But finding you was the best thing that's happened to me since the day I was converted." He bent down and looked her square in the eye. "No matter what happens, I have no regrets."

Dee felt hot tears sliding down her cheeks. "I don't want you to die."

Mark had no reply to that. Instead, he stroked her cheek with trembling hands. "You are strong," he told her firmly. "You and Faeydir, you both have a long life ahead of you-"

"Not without you!"

He tugged her forward and kissed her forehead, then gave her a stern, grim look. "You have the power to destroy this Den. Find it within yourself to love them. No matter what happens to me."

Dee felt her blood run cold. When she'd discovered that she was Fenrae-Ul, she'd sworn that she'd never destroy the shifters, never let herself get twisted to the point where revenge was the only option. And she clung on to that promise now. Even if Mark died, she told herself firmly, taking her sorrow out on Il Trosa was a betrayal of his memory, his wishes. Even so, the temptation to lash out would no doubt be strong. And she had no idea how Faeydir would react if she lost Mark. The wolf loved him just as much as Dee herself did.

"Dee?" Caroline snapped from her post a few feet away. "Time to go."

"I love you," she whispered through the bars, stealing one last kiss. And then she forced herself to turn and walk out the door, her heart pounding, her legs shaking, and at the doorway, she turned back, took a long look at Mark. And wondered if it would be the last time she ever saw him.

Andre sat in front of the computer in his bedroom, a secure, encrypted connection set up to Il Trosa's headquarters in Italy. Four Council members looked back at him from the screen, and, he knew, another eight sat alongside them, waiting apprehensively for his latest report. He was certain that none of them were going to like what he had to say.

"It's confirmed," he said, cutting to the chase without even saying good morning. "She is Fenrae-Ul."

"She managed to separate the wolf?" Amedea asked, an Italian woman in her forties.

"She has. Caroline confirmed that the wolf no longer exists in the convert."

Thick silence followed as the Council members weighed up the heavy news. Though some of them had been sceptical when first presented with the possibility of Fenrae-Ul's reincarnation, cold, hard evidence of Dee's abilities was cause for concern for even the most pragmatic of them.

"Well, that makes things more complicated," Feng said finally, an Asian man who had served on the Council for more than ten years. "Particularly when we still have to decide Mark's fate."

"Mark's situation is complicated," another Councillor said. "His actions were treasonous, but he did show a marked about-face at the end. Based on what you've said, I have little reason to believe his loyalties are still divided."

"Whether his loyalties are divided now or not is hardly the question," another woman interrupted. "His actions were a betrayal against Il Trosa, regardless of the fact that he shot his own sister in the end. He could have put his Den, and our entire species, at significant risk."

"Before we get embedded too far in this particular argument," another voice said, and everyone fell silent as Eleanor, the most senior member of the Council spoke up, "I believe we have a more complex issue that we need to consider. Andre, you mentioned that Fenrae-Ul has a significant romantic attachment to Mark. Correct?"

"Yes, Ma'am."

"And let's leave aside for the moment the fact that Dee herself could be considered to have committed treason by failing to report Mark's actions to the Den. In the natural course of things, I would consider Mark's life to be forfeit. Whatever his motivations or intentions, he broke his vow to Il Trosa. But to move against him in any significant way now would risk angering the one person who could be considered a more potent threat to Il Trosa than even the Noturatii." Eleanor looked at the Councillors around her. "Would you seriously consider taking that risk?"

Silence. And then… "I think such a move would be unwise," Feng said. "Indeed."

"But Mark's actions cannot go unpunished," another woman said, the youngest member of the Council, a woman in her early forties by the name of Elise. "To do so would risk a revolt right across Europe."

"I'm not suggesting we do nothing," Eleanor clarified. "I'm merely suggesting we might need to take a more tactful approach to the situation than we might otherwise consider."

"But what punishment other than death would be considered satisfactory given his crimes?" Feng asked.

Eleanor looked thoughtful, a wealth of wisdom and knowledge shining out from her wrinkled face. "Here's what I suggest we do…"

# CHAPTER FORTY-FOUR

Two days later, Faeydir lay in the grass, her head on Tank's leg, both of them enjoying the sun for as long as it lasted. Tank had been keeping to himself, aside from Baron and Caroline's regular visits to his room, but this morning he'd ventured out in wolf form – no doubt to avoid any awkward conversations – and gone to lie under the trees on the lawn. Dee had been inclined to leave him alone, not feeling like she had the right to trespass on his time and space, but Faeydir had had other ideas. After insistently requesting a shift, she'd slunk outside, going to lie in the grass a short distance from the white wolf. And when he hadn't moved or offered any protest, she'd spent the next hour gradually sliding closer, until they'd been nose to nose. She'd licked his muzzle tentatively and received a half-hearted lick in return. They'd spent the rest of the afternoon laying in the grass, peaceful and silent, while Dee watched on and wondered where her stubborn, mischievous, argumentative wolf had learned such diplomacy.

Gabrielle had been returned home, a tense exercise that Alistair had planned down to the finest detail, and that had been executed with precision by Baron and Caroline. They'd had to call in a few favours from their contacts in the police force, mostly to lend some credence to Gabrielle's belief that the shifters were, in fact, police, but aside from a few sideways glances, there had been no further consequences from the detectives.

Footsteps on the grass got Faeydir's attention, and she lifted her head to see Caroline standing a few feet away. "We'd like to see you in the library," she said, and Faeydir got up with a parting nuzzle to Tank's leg, obediently following the woman inside. They shifted on the stairs, so that it was Dee who sat down at the table, and when she saw Andre sitting there as well, she immediately assumed that a conclusion had finally been reached about Mark's future, the Council having been taking their sweet time over actually making a decision. And if she was getting a private audience about it, the news could hardly be good.

But once again, Andre's first words surprised her. "I've finished my assessment of your suitability for life in Il Trosa," he announced, and Dee sat up straighter, having completely forgotten that that was why he'd been sent here in the first place. She waited in silence, surprised at how much she wanted to stay. It wasn't just that the alternative was a fast and painless death. It was that she had genuinely come to love these people – Mark's fate aside – and she'd grown to accept this life, to respect and admire her wolf, and the thought that she might be found wanting was gut wrenchingly disappointing.

"So…" Andre said, apparently choosing his words carefully. "It's true. You are the destroyer."

Oh, that didn't sound good. Dee bit her lip, wondering if she should protest her innocence. Okay, so she could separate wolf from human, but that didn't mean she was going to set out to end their species.

"I've spoken to the Council at length about your particular manifestations. As far as prophecies go, the Council is not prone to jumping at shadows. But none the less, your talents are both unique and dangerous. I personally don't have much experience as far as prophecies go, but in all the books, it seems that people inadvertently make a prophecy come true by their very act of trying to avoid it. Imagine this," he went on, at her surprised look. "We decide to put you down, but in the attempt you somehow escape – the usual case with ancient prophecies is that nothing would quite go according to plan. So you run away, and we send assassins after you, but you manage to kill them with your unique abilities, and suddenly we have a war on our hands, which, if it got out of control, could lead to the destruction of our species, exactly as we're trying to avoid. Stupid. Completely stupid.

"So we're going to take the opposite route – we let you stay, accept you as a member of our family. No harm, no foul, no need to start a war. But," he went on, "I would strongly recommend that you agree to extra training for your talents. This ability to separate shifters from their other half is powerful, and your wolf, being as independent as she is, makes it unpredictable. The Council would like you to come to Italy for a time. Not right away," he added, and Dee realised she must have looked quite startled at the idea. "Perhaps next year. For a month. Maybe two. Not just for our curiosity, but for your peace of mind."

Dee felt strangely relieved at the suggestion. While being forced to go to Italy under lock and key would have been a scary idea, an open invitation for training was a far more welcome plan. It would be nice to get a better handle on her new abilities, and to understand her wolf better. And if it was only a temporary measure, with her free to return to her Den afterwards, she was willing to consider it. "I'll keep it in mind," she told him. "But for right now, I still feel like I'm on a learning curve just with the regular goings on around here. And Faeydir likes it here. I think she wants to spend a little time just enjoying the scenery before we head into more intensive training."

Andre smiled. "Fair enough. Now, onto the other matter at hand." He went to the door, opening it to reveal Caleb and Mark on the other side. With a nod to Caleb, he let Mark into the room, then closed the door, shutting Caleb out.

Oh boy. Dee glanced at Caroline, who appeared her usual pissed-off self, and then at Baron, whose face was carefully neutral. No clues as to the outcome there.

"I've already filled Baron and Caroline in on the Council's decision. I haven't told Mark yet, but considering your relationship with him, he's agreed for you to be here for this discussion."

Dee looked up at Mark, who gave her a tight smile and a nod, as he took the seat next to her.

"It goes without saying," Andre began, "that your actions were an act of betrayal against Il Trosa. You swore to forsake your natural family, and by merely researching them, never mind planning a one man assault on a Noturatii lab, you put not just your Den, but your entire species at risk. The fact that your knowledge of the lab assisted greatly with Tank's rescue and led directly to Dee joining Il Trosa are happy, but not entirely relevant circumstances. The Council views both situations as coincidence, rather than having any redemptive value on your part."

Mark sat quietly, no doubt having resigned himself to the very worst outcome, and Dee wanted to yell and scream at him, to protest, to insist that he at least attempt to defend himself. But Andre wasn't done yet.

"The one thing that weighs in your favour is something that happened during the raid on the lab." He fixed Mark with a look of utter bafflement. "You shot your own sister."

"I have no sister," Mark answered immediately. "When I found out that Sarah had completed a biology degree at university, I couldn't have been prouder. But she's using that knowledge to work for the Noturatii, to bring about the extinction of the wolf shifters. She may not like what I am, she may hate me, as her brother, for lying to her, but that's between me and her. But when she comes after my people?" Mark shook his head. "If we ever have the misfortune to meet again, I wouldn't hesitate to kill her."

Andre stared at Mark intently, no doubt weighing the truth of his words. "I'm glad we've reached an understanding about that." He paused, the silence heavy. "The Council has decided not to put you down," he announced finally. "But that is not to say your crimes are simply to be forgiven. Your punishment will be as follows: You will be demoted to the rank of omega. You will hold the lowest rank in this Den for a full year, after which time you may resume challenging the other wolves for status, but you may only do so in order of rank. No skipping fights to climb the ranks quicker. You will be permanently excluded from any kind of service to the Council and you are disqualified from ever holding the rank of alpha. Until further notice, whenever you leave this estate, you will do so under escort. You will not be permitted to own a laptop or use a computer unless you are monitored at the time. And you will be branded with a traitor's mark on your left cheek, forever bearing the shame of this betrayal. Do you understand the conditions of this sentence?"

"I understand and accept them," Mark replied without hesitation. And while Dee was aware that these were significant consequences to his actions, all she really heard was that Mark was not to be put down. Her relief was profound, making her heart thud in her chest. Until the last part of the punishment hit home.

"Wait... branded? What do you mean, branded?"

Andre held up his hand, displaying the symbol of the Council on his palm. "Branded. The same way I was. With fire."

Dee looked to Mark in alarm. "No, you can't! That's barbaric!"

"It is the way of our people," Baron informed her flatly. "When is the branding to be done?" he asked Andre.

"Immediately."

Mark remained unmoved by the announcement, while Dee felt her heart speed up again, this time in panic. "No! You can't! It's not right!"

"Dee?" Caroline interrupted, fixing her with a firm glare. "Mark has received a great mercy in not being killed for his treason. All things considered, this is a very light sentence. There are far worse things the Council could have decided, death being only one of them."

And didn't that just sum it all up. She looked at Mark pleadingly, asking for a reason, a protest, an explanation, *anything* that would make this better. But he gave her the opposite of what she wanted, not a protest, but bland acceptance of the punishment. "Caroline's right. If this is the price of freedom, of life, then I wholeheartedly accept it."

What could she say to that? He got to live. He got to stay. "All right," she said weakly. "If that's the way it has to be, then let's get it done."

# CHAPTER FORTY-FIVE

Three days later, Dee lay in bed with Mark, both of them naked. The brand on his face was still raw and red, but he didn't complain about it, though it must hurt like hell. The brand was in the shape of a lopsided V, an upside down reflection of the brand on Andre's hand.

She reached up and stroked his face, his uninjured cheek, and he gave her a wry smile.

"It's fine," he said, not for the first time. "I deserved it."

"Don't say that," she protested, though she was slowly coming to understand the strict honour code among the wolves, and knew that feelings ran deep about his betrayal of Il Trosa. While there were those who supported him, there were far more people here who felt his actions were a gross breach of trust, and when the time came for him to climb the ranks again, it would be against serious opposition.

Tongues were wagging throughout the Den about Dee's determination to continue her relationship with Mark, her relatively high rank seen as a serious barrier to a relationship with an omega wolf, but she had simply ignored the gossip. Further to Mark's demotion, Dee had been forbidden from assisting him in any way in his new role as the lowest ranking wolf, a ban that included everything from bringing him better quality food to letting him sleep in her room. He'd been moved to the bedroom just above the stairs, a small, noisy room that echoed every time another member of the Den walked past, but Mark had taken on each and every restriction with calm acceptance.

So now they were in Mark's room, his smaller bed making it a bit of a squeeze for both of them to lie comfortably. But that was just an excuse for her to snuggle closer, Dee reasoned, noting the way their legs were entwined, their hips touching, Mark's arm resting across her waist.

"It was worth it," Mark insisted, touching the edge of his wound.

"Even though your sister turned against you?"

"Even then." He leaned over and kissed her. "If I hadn't gone to the lab in the first place, I'd never have met you."

Dee couldn't help smiling. It was a touching and heartfelt sentiment, even though Faeydir protested that it wasn't entirely true. If Mark hadn't been there, she had been perfectly capable of killing the scientists herself, she told Dee stubbornly. And even back then, she'd known they had to head north. There was a good chance they would have met up with the Den one way or another, regardless of Mark's involvement.

*Whose side are you on?* she asked the wolf in annoyance, and Faeydir replied with a swift image of Mark's face, a warm, tender jolt of feeling accompanying the image.

"Faeydir's giving you a hard time?" Mark asked, making Dee realise she'd drifted off for a moment, and she smiled bashfully.

"No. She's just agreeing with me that you coming to get me was a good thing." She touched his cheek again. "Despite the price paid."

Mark smiled, and then the expression deepened, overtones of a more sensual interest colouring his face. "A very good thing," he agreed, leaning over to kiss her again. "What about you? Do you like living here? I know you didn't really get much choice in the matter, but do you have any regrets?"

Dee thought about that, taking the question seriously despite the urge to simply dismiss it. "Yes. And no. I miss my family. This isn't a life I would ever have chosen for myself. But all things considered, I'd say I did pretty well out of it. I have a new family. You. Skip. Tank. I have so much to learn, and I just love knowing that there's more to life than we usually see. A whole underworld of magic and conspiracy and a private war going on. It's incredible the shifters and the Noturatii have managed to keep the whole thing a secret for so long."

"And there's a certain irony in that," Mark said. "Il Trosa keeps it a secret for fear that society will condemn us and slaughter us all. The Noturatii keep it a secret for fear that society will embrace us and there'll be a population boom. If either of us ever figure out which way the tide will go, the war is effectively over. One way or another."

"But isn't there a risk that one day someone will get sick of the secrecy and just out you to the general public?"

"It's possible. But that's one of the reasons we're so careful about who we recruit. We've been doing this for six hundred years, and we're pretty good at it by now."

"And detractors are hunted down and killed, right?" Dee's expression turned quizzical. "All of them? No one has ever escaped? You're certain there's no small, secret shifter pack living in some remote place, keeping their heads down, living their own lives?"

"That's why the Council started training assassins. Since the 1750s, no rogue shifter has ever escaped execution. If there are hidden cells, they would have to have formed before that, and endured in secrecy ever since. Again, it's possible, but very unlikely."

"Hm."

"Why?" Mark asked, as Dee reached out to stroke his arm, then across his chest, then lower. "Are you thinking of cutting and running?"

"What? No. It's just…" She ran her hand over his hip, noting the way his muscles twitched. "You can't be the first wolf to have been punished for conflicting loyalties. I was just thinking that other people must have been in situations like yours and looked for a way out."

Mark took her hand and moved it to the right a little, drawing a pleased smirk from Dee. "I've got plenty of reasons to stay," he said, lifting his hips a little.

"That you do." Dee's hand tightened its grip, effectively cutting off the conversation. A moment later, Mark rolled her over, keeping his groin within reach of her hand, and began his own exploration. Starting at her face, her eyelids, her nose, her lips, then down over her throat in a sensual trail that made her skin tingle. He followed the path of his hand with his lips, down over her collar bone, then paused at her breasts, lips and tongue making her sigh in pleasure before his hand slipped down further still, teasing her stomach and thighs before setting up a delicious rhythm between her legs. The movement of Dee's hand faltered, drawing a husky chuckle from Mark.

"I'd walk through hell a thousand times just to have you here with me," he told her, sliding over to cover her body with his own. "I'd kill a thousand of the Noturatii. I'd destroy a hundred labs. And I'd get my arse kicked by Baron as many times as necessary if he so much as looks sideways at you."

Dee laughed at that one, the sound husky and distracted as she spread her legs further, wanting, needing to feel his satisfying weight on top of her, and then wanting to feel something more. "Faeydir might object to that," she said. "She's quite the ferocious warrior and resents the idea that she'd need protection.

"Damn belligerent she-wolf," Mark grumbled, teasing Dee's flesh for a moment longer. Most likely just to make her squirm again, Dee thought happily.

And then, as Mark finally filled her body with his own, another image flashed into her mind, one that brought a very different kind of pleasure.

"Faeydir wants puppies," Dee gasped as Mark set up a slow, lazy rhythm, her hips rolling in time with his thrusts. That made Mark pause, though he didn't seem put out by the idea.

"Does she now?" He punctuated the statement by kissing her, long and slow, his clever fingers reaching down to urge Dee along. And the move was so effective that all rational thought was put on hold for a while, slow kisses and intimate caresses culminating when Dee grabbed onto Mark's backside and hung on tight as she rode the waves of her climax, Mark letting out a groan a moment later, his body thrusting hard into hers until he sighed and went lax above her.

Dee stroked his shoulders, blissfully relaxed and not inclined to move. Until Faeydir gave her a nudge, wanting an answer to her impromptu question.

"Can people be converted as children?" she asked softly, not sure if Mark was falling asleep or not. But he lifted his head and slid over to the side, giving her more space. "Or can wolf puppies be converted into shifters? As far as I've seen, it always happens the other way around, with a human first, but that's not to say it couldn't be possible." It surprised Dee how much she liked the idea of children – because she was assuming at this point that they would be shifter children, the human side hers to nurture and teach, and the wolf side Faeydir's. Because Faeydir had been quite clear in her request. She didn't want 'children', she wanted 'puppies'. The two were hardly the same thing, from a wolf's perspective.

"Firstly, yes, it's possible to convert human children," Mark said, stroking her arm, "but we tend not to. Becoming a shifter should be a choice, not something to be inflicted on people. Then again," he said, speculatively, "no child raised by Il Trosa has ever refused to become a shifter when they came of age. Some of them actually asked for it a lot earlier than that. That would be a question to put to the Council, but probably not until I'm past my year's probation," he added, reminding Dee that two parents were required to raise children, according to Council regulations. "As for converting wolves? No. It's been tried – it was once thought to be an easy solution to our declining population, but the new human side experiences... problems. When a wolf is created as a fully functioning adult, they have an innate ability to do certain things. To hunt, to track, to socialise with other wolves. And yes, we've often wondered how they come upon such knowledge, with no clear answers, but the simple result is that it works. Creating a new, adult human has a whole pile of other problems, because most of what we need to function in society isn't based on instinct, or on simple, needs-based skills, like hunting for food. An newly born adult might be able to speak, but which language? They can eat, but don't have the slightest idea about how to cook food. They lack all but the most basic social niceties, since a lot of our culture is based on customs with lots of tradition but no inherent logic. Training a human adult to function in society is a nightmare, and after a few attempts that went badly, the Council banned the conversion of wolves into shifters."

"So if Faeydir wants puppies, we'd have to convince the Council to let us convert children?"

Mark looked over and frowned at the glum expression on her face. "It's not that far out of the realm of possibility," he assured her, leaning in to kiss her. "It's been done before. But what about you? You're serious about children?"

Despite having just made love, despite having had her entire body kissed and caressed by his, that one question felt suddenly raw, like a part of her she'd never shown anyone before had just been exposed. Because what she was asking for, if her answer was yes, was not a fling, not a boyfriend, not a 'let's see where this goes' relationship, but commitment. And that scared Dee, perhaps even more than it might be scaring Mark. And she turned the thought over in her mind, not just the idea of having children, but of having them *with Mark*. Albeit via adoption, since having them naturally wasn't a possibility.

"Yes," she said finally, her voice small, very aware of the deep frown on her face. How was he going to react-?

"Awesome." He kissed her again, deep and passionate, until she was gasping for breath. And when he pulled back, he was grinning. "Like I said, we might not get clearance for adoption for a while. But we can put in an application, at least. Get Baron and Caroline used to the idea."

Dee was laughing, the sheer joy of the idea making her giddy. "Perfect," she said, sending the answer to Faeydir, a clear 'maybe', with overtones of Council approval and pictures of wolf puppies shifting into human children. Faeydir snorted in disbelief, astonished that humans could have anything of value to teach their young ones, when they had such a poor sense of smell, when their teeth were barely useful for anything. But underneath her disdain was a warm undercurrent of hope, and Dee resolved to do everything in her power to see that Faeydir got her chance at motherhood.

It was a complicated life, all things considered, with plenty of hurdles left to cross and the constant danger, from the Noturatii, the Grey Watch, and her own very unique fate hovering over her. But here, now, with Mark lying beside her, with Tank recovering in the sitting room downstairs, with Baron and Caroline yelling at each other in the foyer and the 'thud-thud-thud' of Silas stomping along the hall... Dee wouldn't have traded it for the world.

# EPILOGUE

Miller waited in the café, a public place in Manchester that was none the less quiet and out of the way, waiting for a meeting he wasn't sure was ever going to happen.

The message had been cryptic, but the Noturatii were more than used to dealing with that, and Jacob maintained the stance that any and all leads should be followed up on. Even the weirdos who were so high they didn't know reality from hallucination might occasionally have a real lead, an avenue for attacking the shifters that other, more grounded folks might have overlooked, and Miller had developed the professional patience to accept the fact that 90% of his 'assignments' might end up being a complete waste of time. That was the way of it when fighting a six hundred year old clandestine war.

Just then the door opened, admitting a slight girl dressed in a grey robe. She looked around nervously before seeing him. And by the way she tensed, she was certainly not used to these covert sorts of meetings.

The girl didn't come over straight away, instead going to the counter to order a coffee, waiting while the barista served it to her in a take-away cup, then she came and sat down at his table, glancing around. Nope, no stealth skills there. Her jittery behaviour all but screamed 'illegal meeting', and Miller preferred to keep his operations a little more on the subtle side than this girl was behaving.

"You got my message?"

Obviously, or he wouldn't have been here. "I did. Thank you for contacting us."

Silence, as the girl stared out the window, fiddling with the foam on her cappuccino. "How can we help you?" Miller asked finally.

"I need you to do something for me," the girl said, not looking at him, and Miller had enough experience reading people to realise that she was feeling guilty as hell about something. Interesting. "And in return, I'll give you some information." She glanced up at him, fear and anger warring in her eyes. "I need you to... kill someone." The last two words were said in a whisper, determination replacing fear. "There's a girl. She's dangerous."

"Hold on a second," Miller interrupted her. He'd seen a lot of crazy in the last few years, but never faced a request quite so blunt as this one. "What makes you think we'd kill someone for you?" Thank God the café was deserted. This was *not* the location he'd have chosen for this kind of conversation. "We're not a bunch of thugs for hire. We're a covert government agency fighting terrorism-"

"I know exactly who you are," the girl snapped. And Miller instantly shut up. Not because of her tone, but because if she knew who he was, who the Noturatii were, then she damn well knew that the existence of the shifters was a fact. And that made this meeting a whole lot more interesting.

"There's a girl. Who's not a girl," the girl said. "You know what I'm saying?"

Meaning a girl who was a wolf. Miller nodded.

The girl slid a folded sheet of paper across the table. "That's a map. I don't know her exact location, but I've highlighted the most likely areas. She's in her early thirties, maybe. Brown hair. Five foot three. And I think you've met her before. At least, your organisation has, if not you personally."

Dee Carman. Their convert-turned-escapee. She fit that description perfectly.

"I want her dead."

"Why?" Despite his years of training, Miller was having a hard time keeping his face neutral. Fuck, this was the lead they'd been waiting for.

"Like I said. She's dangerous. That's all you need to know."

Miller fingered the paper, but resisted the urge to open it. "Consider it done." It wasn't likely the Noturatii would actually kill her, of course. Not at first. She held too much information, held the key to their failed science experiments. She was far too valuable to simply be killed. But this slip of a girl didn't need to know that.

"Don't try to contact me again," the girl said, then stood up. "I've given you information, now you keep your end of the bargain. And do whatever you like with whatever else you find there."

Miller watched the girl walk away and finally gave in to the urge to look at the map she'd given him. It was of the Lakes District, various areas coloured in in clumsy green highlighter. And the full weight of this revelation hit him hard enough that it distracted him from even the idea of following her, seeing where she was going.

A second pack. Confirmation, in black and green, of something he had suspected for months. Dee wasn't in the north-east of England, not a part of the pack that lurked in the forests and gullies. No, she was in the north-west. Along with that mob of animals that had torn up their lab.

The map still left a lot of area to cover, but it narrowed down the pack's location considerably, when mere moments ago the only solid direction they'd had was 'north'.

Miller pulled out his phone and dialled Jacob's number. The phone rang once, then the Noturatii leader answered. "You're not going to believe this…" Miller said.


Genna slipped away from the café, feeling at once guilty, terrified and triumphant. The woman, Dee Carman, was a menace to their species. The Destroyer, sent to wipe them all out. The Grey Watch had spoken of almost nothing else since her visit to their camp, when she'd ripped the human right out of one of their shifters. Then there had been that disastrous visit to Il Trosa's estate – a trip Genna herself had not been permitted to go on – which had achieved nothing and resulted in Sempre being in a foul mood for days.

And then they had discovered that, despite a rather frantic attempt to re-convert the wolf, the woman that Rintur had been could not be brought back.

Contacting the Noturatii had been a desperate move, but Genna held no regrets about that part of the plan. Ensuring her own get-away, when she would likely be tailed by Noturatii operatives, had been a far more nerve-wracking prospect, as had getting away from the Watch for a day without her absence being noticed. But the Noturatii?

Ironically, they were the shifter's best hope for maintaining their species. They'd survived the war with the Noturatii for hundreds of years, and the day would come, sooner or later, when society would once again embrace the mystical elements, much as they had during the reign of the ancient Greeks and Romans, when shifters had lived openly, revered as gods, temples erected in their honour.

But that would never happen if this Destroyer got to them first.

Her map, scant on detail though it was, would lead the Noturatii straight to Il Trosa's doorstep. And very soon, a big part of this war would be over. One way or another.

# ABOUT THE AUTHOR

Laura Taylor has been writing since she was a teenager, spending long hours lost in imaginary adventures as new worlds and characters spring to life. The House of Sirius is her first published work, a series of seven novels following the wolf shape shifters and their war with the Noturatii.

Laura lives on the Central Coast of NSW, Australia and has a passion for nature, animals, hiking, and of course, reading.

https://www.facebook.com/LauraTaylorBooks
laurataylorauthor@hotmail.com
http://laurataylorbooks.weebly.com/